O N E
AMONG US

D1520821

PAIGE DEARTH

ISBN 10: 1502492253

ISBN 13: 978-1502492258

Library of Congress Control Number: 2014911458

CreateSpace Independent Publishing Platform

North Charleston, South Carolina

SOME DIRT ON THE AUTHOR:

Born and raised in Plymouth Meeting, a small town west of Philadelphia, Paige Dearth was a victim of child rape and spent her early years yearning desperately for a better life. Living through the fear and isolation that marked her youth, she found a way of coping with the trauma: she developed the ability to dream up stories grounded in reality that would provide her with a creative outlet when she finally embarked on a series of novels. Paige's debut novel, *Believe Like A Child*, is the darkest version of the life she imagines she would have been doomed to lead had fate not intervened just in the nick of time. Her second novel, *When Smiles Fade*, is a tale of endurance, perseverance, and the courage of one young girl to fight back against injustice. Both novels are compelling proof of the fine balance this author is capable of achieving between what lives on in her imagination and the evil that lurks in the real world. Paige is currently working on her fourth novel.

CONNECT WITH PAIGE:

Visit her website at www.paigedearth.com and sign up for the Quarterly Paige newsletter.

Friend Paige on Facebook at www.facebook.com/paigedearth.

Follow Paige on Twitter @paigedearth.

For my daughter, who holds in her heart all that matters most to me.
Love,
Mom

***

Written for Natalie

Acknowledgments

Love and gratitude to my husband for his tireless efforts to help me find my way.

My sincere thanks to all of you who read and share my stories. Through you, a way will be found.

To my buddy, Barb, at www.disantoart.com: the future holds great things...including picnic baskets.

Much appreciation to Alex, who spent many hours breathing life into my new website. Check her out at: www.pumpkinhour.com.

Happy 80th birthday, Aunt Barbara...your continuous support and love is priceless.

Big E: I'll love you 'til the end!

HOPE MATTERS

The young woman trolls streets littered with trash and seedy people, scanning for a buyer. You watch intently as she bends down to talk to a man who pulled his car up to the curb where she's waiting. You wonder how she got there and how she can do what she does. Suddenly, she notices you watching her. All she wants is to be like you because she's long since forgotten who she is.

She barely resembles a real person. She's convinced that there is no way out and that she faces a bleak future. She can't imagine anyone wanting to help her, and she's too confused and ashamed to help herself. She is, after all, a prostitute. Just look beyond the skimpy, tattered clothes and worn-out, high-heeled shoes, and you'll recognize a person no different than you are. She was taken from her family and forced to sell her body.

Now do you view her differently? You know you should help her because underneath all the makeup and shabby clothing, there is an unwilling participant who is just looking for someone to give her a small sign of hope.

Do something, because hope matters.

~Paige Dearth

The First Twelve Hours of Captivity

Eleven-year-old Maggie threw up when the man behind the camera demanded that she remove her jeans. "What the fuck," Vic, the photographer, mumbled as he walked over and pushed her down on the bed in the makeshift studio. Then he ripped her jeans off with so much force that it felt as though a layer of her skin came off with the denim. Vic threw a towel at her. "Now wipe up that slop and take your fucking shirt off," he ordered.

Maggie was sobbing; she was stricken with an overwhelming sensation she'd never felt before, a feeling that she was going to die. She had no control over her emotions as she tried not to piss off the man with the camera any more than she already had. She removed her T-shirt slowly. "Good," Vic huffed. "Now lie down on the bed and take your underwear off."

Maggie shook her head. "I don't want to do that. Please don't make me do that, mister." Her small voice quivered.

"That's it," Vic screamed. "John William, get the fuck over here and handle this. I don't have all day for one kid. We have a fuckin' business to run, here."

John William thudded over to the bed where Maggie sat huddled, trying to cover her body, and he backhanded her across the face. Blood dribbled down her split lip and into her mouth, its coppery taste threatening to excite her gag reflex again. Before she could regain her senses, he pulled her panties off. Maggie pulled her knees up to her chin and wrapped her arms tightly around her legs as she sat naked on the bed with the two strange men watching her.

She was alone and terrified. All of her senses were heightened by the evil surrounding her. She didn't know what they were going to do to her. Her parents had warned that no one should ever touch her private parts. But here, in this crumbling cement room, she had no choice. Maggie had an overwhelming feeling that the two men were going to do things to her that they shouldn't, and this intensified the vulnerable feeling that gnawed at her gut, jeopardizing her ability to follow their instructions.

Vic looked at Maggie, his face devoid of any kindness. "I'm going to tell you this one time and one time only. I want you to spread your legs apart so I can take some pictures. Just drop your knees to your sides. Do you understand?"

Maggie nodded, not wanting to be hit again. Once Vic was back behind the camera, he looked over at her. "OK, spread your legs like I told you to."

Maggie dropped her knees to the sides, and he began to snap pictures. "Now, I want you to reach down and touch yourself."

Maggie froze, not knowing what to do. John William stepped in, grabbed her hand, and placed it roughly between her legs. "That's it. Put your fingers inside," Vic coaxed her.

Inside where? Maggie wondered, feeling filthy and ruined. Not knowing what she was supposed to do, she remained motionless. Vic strode over briskly, grabbed her hand, and shoved her fingers inside of her. Fear mixed with adrenaline coursed through her body—she thought they had broken her. She had no idea there was a hole between her legs before that moment. They had just started sex education at school, but nothing could have prepared her for the horrible acts she would be expected to perform to her body.

Vic turned to John William. "The next time you bring a new kid in here, make sure they're ready for me. You understand?" he demanded.

John William nodded and glared heartlessly at Maggie. The look was so demonic that it was almost blinding. She shrank away from him, and a deeper level of fear ran uncontrollably through her body, seizing her muscles, paralyzing her.

After Vic took several more pictures, he told her to put on her clothes and leave. As Maggie quickly dressed, she wondered if they had gotten what they wanted and would take her back to the mall now. She was certain that her mother was still at the mall, searching for her. Maggie decided that when the two men let her go home, she would never tell anyone about the pictures they'd taken. Maggie feared that she would be in trouble if her parents found out what she had done.

However, ten minutes later, John William pulled Maggie into her cell and pushed her toward a cot. When he reached the doorway, he turned. "You have a lot to learn. I suggest you pay attention and do what we tell you to do. I'm going to cut you a break since it's your first night, but if you ever embarrass me like that again, I'll bash your brains in."

Maggie's hope of going home quickly vanished as his words bounced inside her head. *Since it's your first night.* She instantly understood that they weren't finished with her yet. Her heart beat faster as she tried desperately to hang on to the hope that they would let her go.

He raised his voice. "You are to obey everything that you are told to do! If you weren't worth so much money, I'd fuck the shit out of you right now."

Maggie was shaking. She didn't know exactly what he was talking about, but she knew enough to understand that John William wanted to do bad things to her, dirty things. She clung to the cold block wall of the cell, unable to wrap her mind around what was happening to her.

"Take off all of your clothes," John William instructed.

Maggie did as she was told quickly this time.

He looked at her with lust. "Now bring me your clothes."

She quickly scooped them up and carried them to him. John William grabbed them from her arms.

"For causing such a scene tonight, you can sleep naked. So you can get used to it, you little whore," John William taunted.

After John William left her and locked the heavy door behind him, Maggie sat on the dirty cot. She wept from the very depth of her soul. The unrelenting fear was suffocating and inescapable. This had been the hardest day of her young life. She had only been missing for twelve hours, but it felt like a year to eleven-year-old Maggie.

She cried herself to sleep that night, thinking of her family, and when she woke the next day, her nightmare continued.

One Day Prior: The Capture

Maggie was only thirty feet from the line of people at the pizza counter in the food court inside the Plymouth Meeting Mall. As she walked by the large glass doors that opened to the parking lot, she saw two teenage girls standing just outside the entrance. They were talking to a man with a puppy. She watched as the girls took turns holding the dog. Then, as they passed Maggie on their way into the mall, she heard them talking about how adorable the puppy was. "Wasn't that man nice?" one of the girls said. "I wish my dad felt that way about dogs and would let me get a puppy."

Maggie looked out the glass doors at the man holding the puppy; he turned the dog in her direction and lifted a paw, as if to wave at Maggie. She stood glued to the glass door, smiling at the tiny pile of fur in the man's arms. She opened the glass door just a couple of inches. "He's so cute. What's his name?" Maggie asked.

"I just got him today, and I haven't named him yet. I'm taking ideas, though. What do you think I should call him?" John William asked sweetly.

"I don't know," Maggie said shyly, not able to take her eyes off the fluffy mound of fur.

"Would you like to hold him?" John William offered.

"I would, but I really shouldn't. I can't leave the mall," she explained.

"You're not leaving the mall. I'm standing five feet away from the door. What's the difference whether you're standing five feet inside or outside of the door? Besides, I'm not allowed to bring him inside," John William said.

Just then, the puppy gave a small bark at Maggie.

"See, he likes you. I think he wants you to hold him," John William told her.

Maggie looked around and then over her shoulder across the food court at McDonald's. She saw her mother and brother in a long line waiting to place their order. Deciding they'd be quite a while, she agreed.

"OK, but just for a minute. If my mom finds out I went outside, she'll ground me for sure," Maggie explained.

She stood next to John William, and he handed her the puppy. It immediately started to lick her face.

"See, he loves you already. What's your name?" he asked.

"Maggie. He's the cutest puppy ever." She kissed the top of the dog's head and handed him back to John William. "I have to go back in. Thanks for letting me hold him," she said.

John William took the puppy from her and set him on the ground. To his delight, the dog did exactly what he'd hoped. It ran off toward the parking lot.

"Oh my God," John William exclaimed, pretending to be worried. "He's gonna get killed by a car. Please help me catch him!" he yelled to Maggie as he ran in the direction of the dog.

Without thinking it through, Maggie darted off to help rescue the puppy. She was running behind John William when he turned. "You run down that lane, and I'll meet you at the far end. That way, he can't get away," he rasped.

Maggie ran between two cars and down the lane to the very end, where she stood behind a red van. When John William met her, he was carrying the puppy. "Thanks for your help. He could have been killed," he said and handed the puppy to her.

She took him into her arms again. "Pup, you could've been killed. You have to be more careful," she cooed.

"This is my van," John William told her as he opened the back door.

Maggie looked inside and saw a small dog crate.

"Why don't you put him in the crate for me, and I'll get his bowl from the front seat. I want to give him some water. He must be thirsty from all that running around," he said with a smile.

Maggie watched as John William started toward the front of his van. Only then did she climb in to put the puppy in the crate, but before she made it that far, she was wrapped in an overpowering embrace. She panicked; the desire to flee surged through her body.

John William shoved her toward the crate, and she quickly scurried to find her footing. He was right next to her when he yanked a rag doused in chloroform from a small bucket on the floor of the van. He grabbed her around the waist and put the rag over her mouth and nose. She was unconscious in seconds.

When Maggie woke up, she was lying in the back of the van, hogtied and gagged. Her head was pounding and the motion of the van churned the nausea that swirled in her belly. As her vision began to clear, she saw a young boy lying next to her, bound and gagged in the same way. The boy was much younger than she was—five or six, she guessed. He lay lifelessly, and she hoped he wasn't dead.

Maggie started to weep. She thought about how stupid she was to follow the man outside. Her mother had warned specifically about adults using pets to lure children in so they could steal them.

Then she thought about her mother. *Why had she insisted that she was old enough to get pizza by herself?* Her mom had said no at first, but Maggie had begged, "Come on, Mom. I'm not a baby. I'm eleven years old. I can walk to the other side of the food court by myself."

Lorraine, Maggie's mother, wanted to show her daughter that she trusted her and finally agreed. When Maggie headed to the pizza line, her mother took her younger brother, Keith, to McDonald's for a happy meal.

Maggie wanted the other kids at the food court to think she was cool. The fifth-grade girls from her class, who always left Maggie out, were celebrating a birthday with a pizza party at the food court. She wanted to show them that she had independence and was too good to join their stupid little group.

Still, in the back of the van with a man she didn't know, she tried to keep herself calm. The little boy lying next to her finally woke up. He looked at her pleadingly, but there was nothing she could do to help. She tried to keep her eyes from revealing her own fear, but it was a wasted effort.

Suddenly, the van came to a stop, and the back doors opened. John William reached in and clamped his large hand on one of Maggie's ankles. Then he reached down with a knife and cut the thick rope that kept her legs and arms tied together. He pulled her out of the van and into a field, putting one of her arms behind her back. She felt the handcuffs fasten on her right wrist and then her left. The cold steel of the cuff cut into her flesh, and she looked at John William for mercy.

Ignoring her, John William did the same to the small boy, who was crying and squirming in an attempt to escape. John William slapped the boy, and after the child fell to the ground, he put his dirty white sneaker on the child's back while he handcuffed him.

Maggie looked around frantically for someone who could help them. Since it was dark outside, she knew they had been in the van for a long time. John William took each of them by the arm and dragged them down a dirt path with high grass on either side. Maggie could see a stark, stone building ahead. The building was as frightening as the man who had taken her from the mall. It stood like an abandoned castle against the moonlit night sky.

Maggie's New Home

J ohn William led the children through a heavy steel door and down a hall with jail cells on either side. It was obvious that no one else was there. "Where are we?" Maggie squeaked through the gag that was tied at the back of her head.

"Silence," John William demanded.

Her mind raced as they walked through the decrepit prison. *Oh my God, how will I find my way home?* After he took them through a block of cells, he stopped to grab a flashlight from a stool next to a small steel door. John William pulled the two children along, down two long flights of rusted metal stairs, deeper into the bowels of the building.

Finally, they were walking down a dark, narrow hall. The flashlight threw off a spooky yellow haze, and Maggie knew that her abductor had delivered them to hell. On either side of them were tiny cells. Mounds of dirt poured into the hallway from some of the cells, where the building's foundation had given way to the force of the earth pressing in from the outside.

Unlike the cells two floors above them, these cells had solid steel doors with small, rectangular openings in the middle. John William stopped midway down the hall and took them both into one of the cells. He made the little boy lie down on the cot. Then he removed his gag and handcuffs. "Don't you move," he ordered.

Shutting the door behind them, he led Maggie to the cell directly across the hall. After her gag and handcuffs were removed, he abruptly left. Maggie began to pray that whatever was happening to them would end quickly. That someone would come and rescue them.

Maggie heard the small child whimpering. Then she heard John William ask the child, "Why were you such a bad little boy?"

"I not bad," the child insisted.

Maggie heard the first couple of slaps and the child begging John William to stop. "You will not be disobedient to me."

Maggie heard the sound of whipping as John William's belt flew across the boy's back. The boy screamed as each lash landed, and then suddenly, he went silent. Maggie paced in her small dark cell. She willed the child to make a sound so she would know he was still alive. Then the door to her cell was unlocked and John William stood before her like a giant. He stared down at her with an icy expression. "Why were you such a bad little girl?"

Maggie's survival instincts kicked in. Having heard what John William had just done to the boy, she whimpered, "Because I was jealous of the other girls in the mall. I'm sorry. I won't do it again."

John William paused and sized her up. "Good girl. Now are you willing to accept your punishment?"

"Yes," she muttered, beginning to cry. "But I swear I'll be a good girl."

For the first time, John William smiled. His crooked, yellow-brownish teeth were twisted and looked sinister. "OK then."

He sat on her cot and told her to come over to him. She stood next to him shaking, her arms crossed over her chest. He pulled her down across his lap and spanked her with his open hand. After three hard whacks on the ass, he forced her to her feet again. "Tonight, you go to bed without dinner."

"OK," Maggie responded, humiliated from the spanking. Maggie had learned her first lesson: whatever happened, she always had to agree with John William if she wanted to live to see her family again.

Who's There?

———————————— ▬ ————————————

After Maggie heard John William's footsteps fade away, she called out across the small hall, "Little boy? Are you OK?" When there was no response, she called out a little louder, "Little boy? Can you hear me?"

Maggie jumped when she heard a girl's voice from the cell to her left. "Shut up before we all get punished, you idiot!" the angry voice rattled.

Maggie was shocked into silence at the realization that someone else was down there with them. She was relieved to know they weren't alone. Then her fear soared as she wondered how long the girl had been there. "Don't be mean," she heard an older girl say in a calm voice. "They just got here."

"Who's there?" Maggie asked in a trembling voice.

It was the older girl who spoke. "There are several of us here. My name is Cali. I'm the oldest. I'm in the cell to your right. Shana is on the other side of you, and Max is next to the little boy who came in with you."

"Why are we here?" Maggie asked with desperation. "I just want to go home."

"We all want to get out of here, sweetheart. You need to settle down. Now, what's your name?" Cali asked in a soothing voice, trying to calm her.

"Maggie. That guy took me from the mall," she said sadly.

Cali gathered herself together. "The guy's name is John William. That's what we have to call him. We were all taken from different places. Everyone is gonna to be fine. You have to stay calm, though, and just do what he says. OK?"

"But what's he going to do to me?" Maggie asked.

Cali wanted to prepare the girl, although she knew that nothing could prepare someone for the horrors that they lived. "John William will come back tonight and take you upstairs to have some pictures taken. Maggie, the pictures will make you feel very uncomfortable, but try to remember that if you don't listen, they'll hurt you, OK?"

"Uh-huh," Maggie muttered, fearful of what was to come. Then she felt around in the dark until she found the cot with the dusty, worn mattress. She climbed onto it and rolled into a fetal position. She lay awake for several hours, praying that her mom and dad would come to rescue her.

Only when she fell asleep that night did she escape her suffocating fear. It was hours later when the sound of a cell door being unlocked awakened her. She scrambled to her feet to look out the small opening in her door. She quivered as she watched John William pull Shana across the front of her cell. Shana was crying, but went along with him without much resistance. She heard Cali tell her, "It's OK, Shana. You'll be all right. Just do whatever they want you to."

When the hall went black again, Maggie spoke. "Cali, what's going to happen to Shana? Who are *they*?"

Cali thought before she spoke. If she wanted the girl to live, she'd have to tell her what was happening, "How old are you, Maggie?"

"I'm eleven," Maggie muttered.

"Maggie, these people want to do things with you that only grown-ups should do with each other. Do you know what sex is?" Cali asked, wishing she could hold the scared girl.

Maggie's head started to spin. The only thing she knew about sex was that it was something that old people did. She knew it involved getting naked. She had seen a show on cable TV in which a couple was lying in a bed, and they looked like they didn't have any clothes on. Her father had walked into the room and shut off the television when he saw what she was watching.

"I don't know exactly what it is. I know that people take their clothes off and get in bed together," she responded, her stomach clamping down into a tight knot.

"Yes, Maggie. They get naked in bed together. When they come for you tonight, just do what they ask. Tomorrow, I'll explain things to you, OK?" Cali said, dreading the conversation she would have with her in the morning.

Maggie's First Full Day

In the morning, she stayed perfectly still on her cot. From within the dark and damp walls of the prison cell, she had no sense of time; she didn't know whether it was night or day. Her thoughts wandered to the day prior—the day she'd made the biggest mistake of her life.

Maggie was still lost in morbid thoughts of the pictures they'd taken of her just hours before. A light went on in her cell, and she bolted upright on her cot. She looked up at the round, globe fixture on the ceiling that was protected by a steel cage. It cast a dim light over the tiny cell. She looked around. The cell was barren except for the cot and a toilet. The toilet looked like a large, white tree stump with a hole in the center. She walked to the toilet and squatted over the hole. She peed quickly; afraid something gruesome would come out of the black hole in the center and suck her down into it.

Then the cell door opened, and John William stood staring down at her. In the dim light, she was finally able to get a good look at him. Her eyes slowly wandered to his neck and lingered on his Adam's apple, which protruded from his throat as if a hard-boiled egg was caught there. He had a very long, narrow face, and his black eyes sat too closely together. Limp, shoulder-length, greasy, blond hair hung around his skull like yarn, making him look as crazy as he was. He was over six feet tall, and his shoulders seemed permanently hunched. His long arms stopped just above his knees, and his hands were as big as Frisbees. He appeared to be dim-witted and creepy—the type of man who gave grown women the heebie-jeebies. Maggie realized that she'd been so focused on the puppy that she hadn't really looked at John William, the most horrid man she'd ever seen.

John William threw Maggie's clothes at her. "Get dressed fast. It's time for breakfast," he stated.

John William watched as the beautiful Maggie studied him. He saw the look of revulsion that he had grown accustomed to seeing on the faces of girls and women, including his own mother.

Maggie's expression brought back memories of his childhood. John William's parents never allowed him to play with the neighborhood children, repeatedly telling him, "The other kids hate you. They make fun of you because you look like a goon. You are the ugliest person who ever lived. You get your nasty looks from your grandfather."

When John William was nine, his parents punished him for misbehaving by forcing him to remove all of his clothes and tying him to a metal chair that they kept in a small closet under the stairs in their home. They would leave him there for hours.

Because of the verbal and physical abuse his parents subjected him to, John William was deeply depressed at a young age. He was an outcast among his peers and, by middle school, he was a love-starved, confused boy who was the focus of his peers' ridicule.

At school, children teased him mercilessly, but he never dared to fight back, fearing that his parents would tie him to the chair in the closet. As the years passed, he grew increasingly resentful toward his parents and the other kids at his school, especially the girls.

After being widely rejected by the various cliques in high school, John William began spending his free time alone in seedy areas of Philadelphia, where he learned that people who were feared got respect. When John William met a lunatic who convinced him to kidnap a nineteen-year-old girl, he got a taste of power, and for the first time in his life, he felt like he fit in. The children he kidnapped needed him for basic survival, and that purpose in life was validating. He had finally found a way to get the respect that he deserved.

In the narrow hallway between the cells, also illuminated by dim overhead light, Maggie looked around at the children who had gathered. They all appeared to be like robots. They were despondent, as if someone had stolen their souls. The dark circles under their bloodshot eyes revealed that pain and despair were the overarching themes among them. Maggie wondered how they all got there, and she hoped it wouldn't be long before they could all go home.

Maggie waited with anticipation as John William opened the cell of the young boy who had been brought there with her. The child staggered into the hallway, saw Maggie, and threw his arms around her legs. She bent and picked him up, holding him tightly as he put his head on her shoulder and began to cry softly.

"Let's go," John William instructed.

The group walked down the hall in silence to another steel door, which John William opened. Inside was a long room containing a large metal picnic table and benches. Each child took a seat. Cali motioned for Maggie to sit next to her, and Maggie slid in beside her, still holding the small boy tightly.

"Now listen," Cali whispered. "It's important that you pay attention to what he tells you to do. After we're done eating, he will take us to the showers upstairs. We all shower together so it's no big deal."

Maggie looked over at the teenage boy, Max. He nodded to acknowledge her. She looked back at Cali, her eyes filling with tears.

"Look, Maggie, none of us care that we see each other naked, OK? We are all in the same boat here, and the more you resist what they want from you, the worse you'll make it for all of us. You'll get used to it, I promise."

"But I don't want to get used to it. I can't stay here. I want to go home," Maggie said, stating the obvious. She concentrated on her breathing, not wanting the other kids to think she was a baby. "How old are you guys?" she finally managed to ask.

Cali answered for all of them, "Max is fifteen, Shana is twelve, and I'm seventeen."

Then Maggie asked the question that had been stuck in her throat since they spoke from their cells the night before. "How long have all of you been here?"

"Too fuckin' long!" Shana blurted.

Max gave Shana a scalding look. "Five years," Max offered.

Shana looked Maggie over. "Three years."

Finally, Cali spoke. "I was thirteen when they brought me here."

As Maggie did the math in her head, a small gurgling sound escaped her lips. Cali quickly put her arm around her. "You have to be quiet. John William gets really mad when any of us cry."

"Yeah, he'll let you cry when you're with the clients upstairs. He says they like to see us scared. But when we're down here, he gets really pissed. So if you're gonna cry, do it without making any noise," Shana offered.

Maggie looked down at the small boy in her lap. "What's your name?" she asked with as much courage as possible.

The blond, blue-eyed child looked up at her. "Seth."

"Seth, my name is Maggie."

"Aggie!" the young boy managed with a big grin.

"Do you know how old you are, Seth?"

Seth held up four chubby fingers.

"Wow, four years old. You're a big boy."

Just then, John William came back into the room. He motioned for Cali to come over to where he was standing. Maggie watched as he slid his hand over her breast. He turned and took the padlock off the large cupboard standing against the far wall. Cali quickly pulled plates and spoons from inside and rushed back to the table, where she gave the children one of each.

Cali raced back to where John William was standing and stood before him. The other children watched as John William put his hand on her ass, pulled her to him forcefully, and kissed her with an open mouth. Shana and Max had both lowered their heads, but Maggie watched, unable to rip her eyes away. She was mortified at what he was doing to her. It was easy to see that Cali was scared of him, and as he groped the teenager, he looked over at Maggie, licked his lips, and pointed at her.

Maggie peed herself as fright rocked her to the core. John William looked at her wet pants and started to laugh. He loved the power and control he had over the little rodents. It made him feel important. "You're pathetic, girl!" he said, pushing Cali to the side.

He walked over to Maggie, pulled Seth from her arms, and pounded him down on the bench next to her. "Stand up and take those pissed jeans off," he said angrily.

Maggie hesitated for a moment. John William grabbed her arm and picked her up off the bench. "Do it!"

Maggie quickly took her jeans off. He smiled. "Underwear too."

Maggie stood naked from the waist down with all of the other children watching her. "Now, I want you to clean this mess up. You'll have to stay like that until your clothes dry. Look everyone, look at the baby who pissed her pants," John William chanted.

The other kids looked on, just as they were told to do. They had all been there. They all knew what she was going through. They had surrendered themselves completely in order to survive. It was humiliating, but it was necessary.

After Maggie cleaned up the urine with her jeans, she sat down on the bench. The cold metal against her skin made her squirm. The others watched her as John William and Cali left the room. Max wished he could do something to protect all of them. He was small and thin for fifteen, no match for John William. He leaned toward the center of the table so Maggie could hear him whisper. "Look, Maggie. It'll be all right. You can't let that rotten motherfucker get to you. He's going to try to wear you down. All he wants is for you to be afraid of him. It makes him feel dominant. But remember that he's just a big asshole. You need to make him think you're afraid of him. That way, he won't bust your shoes as much. If he thinks you ain't scared, he'll fuck with you until he knows you are scared. You get it?"

Maggie nodded. She didn't have to pretend to be afraid of John William; she was petrified of him already. She looked at Cali, her eyes pleading. "I don't wanna be here. I wanna go home. Maybe if we all stick together, we can find a way out of here."

"None of us want to be here, Maggie. Maybe you're right. Maybe someday we'll find a way out," Max lied in an attempt to comfort her.

At that moment, Cali and John William came back carrying a large pot of oatmeal. Cali served the oatmeal, and John William gave each of them a small glass of water. "Eat up," he told the children. "Then it's time for showers."

The children ate their breakfast in silence. Maggie was too hungry to realize that the lumpy, lukewarm oatmeal was tasteless. As she mindlessly ate the slop in front of her, Maggie prayed that her parents would come that day and put an end to her nightmare.

The shower room was completely open, providing no privacy. Moldy shower heads on one wall spit out small streams of water. Maggie followed the older kids, keeping her eyes glued to the floor. She helped Seth get undressed and washed his hair for him. The others were like soldiers. To them, it was just a way of life. They had been doing it for so long that it didn't matter anymore. They seemed not to notice that their circumstances were hopeless.

After the children showered, John William took them back to their cells. This time, he left all of their doors open. It was now Cali's job to talk to each of them and get them ready for their clients. Shana and Max knew what to expect, but when it came to satisfying the clients, each of them still needed some coaxing. She wanted them back in one piece, and she had assured John William that Maggie would be ready.

Cali walked into Maggie's cell, where she was lying on her cot with Seth. "Hey, Maggie, I want to talk to you about tonight."

"Why? What's tonight?" Maggie asked, already dreading the answer.

"They're going to bring us all upstairs, and people are going to look at us. The thing is, we'll all be naked. There's nothing to worry about, though. No one is going to hurt you. The clients just look at us."

Maggie felt like she had swallowed a golf ball as terror moved from her stomach into her chest and settled in her throat. She knew there was nothing she could do to fight back. She threw herself into Cali's arms and started to cry. Her chest heaved as she pleaded with the teenager to tell John William that she couldn't do what he wanted her to do. Cali stroked Maggie's hair. "That isn't an option, baby. This is what you have to do if you don't want them to beat you and do awful things to you."

"What about Seth?" Maggie asked, hoping she could stay in her cell and babysit him while the others went upstairs.

"Seth will stay down here while we are upstairs," Cali told her matter-of-factly.

"But he's, he's just a baby," Maggie argued.

"I'm not a baby," Seth grunted. "I go to the bafroom in the potty."

Maggie and Cali ignored his protests.

"Just be ready, Maggie. Please. It will be easier for you if you're ready to do whatever they want. We'll all be together. That has to mean something, right?" Cali asked, trying to make the best out of a dreadful situation.

Maggie nodded and lay down on the cot, pulling Seth snugly against her body. She thought about her mother and father. They were probably going crazy looking for her. She was sure her little brother, Keith, missed her. He was the same age as Seth and always wanted Maggie to play with him. The two of them loved spending time together.

Thinking about Keith made her feel better. She wondered who would read to him until she got home. Then Maggie leaned into Seth's ear and whispered, "The two of us are going to be OK. Don't worry. I'll find a way to get us out of here. We just have to be brave."

If only Maggie felt brave.

Later that evening, all of the children except Seth were taken upstairs to a darkened room. There was a four-poster bed in the middle of the room. The bed looked ominous with black sheets and large, overstuffed, dreary-gray pillows. John William led the children to a corner and told them to undress. After Maggie removed her clothes, she stood nervously, wanting nothing more than to vanish. Another man in a leather mask and tight black underwear walked into the room. He ordered all of them to stand in front of the bed. Like little androids, they lined up, oldest to youngest. The man in the leather mask walked over to the door and opened it.

Twelve people—eight men and four women—entered the room. They stood and stared at the children, a few of them smiling as if they were looking at their Thanksgiving dinner.

Suddenly, music began to play. At a nod from the creepy masked man, Cali and Max moved around to the side of the bed and got on top. They began to kiss while Maggie and Shana stood at the side of the bed and watched. Maggie's eyes bulged out of their sockets when she saw how Max was touching Cali. He was putting his hands on her boobs and rubbing between her legs. Then Cali pushed Max down on the bed and put his penis into her mouth. Maggie was repulsed at the sight of what Cali was doing to Max.

After several minutes, Cali and Max stopped what they were doing. Getting off the bed, they led Maggie and Shana to the foot of the bed, where they stood in a line again. The strangers walked by them, looking them over, getting a better look at their faces. Each of them paused to take in the beauty that Maggie had to offer, and a few of them leaned in to sniff her hair. After the strangers left the room, the kids dressed, and John William led them back to their cells.

Chapter One

Maggie spent the next twenty-four hours alone in her cell, which was part of the break-in period. This was when the abductors used isolation, fear, humiliation, and physical punishment to make their victims submissive. Alone with nothing but her own thoughts, Maggie contemplated what was to come next. *How could she get away? Would her parents ever find her? What else would John William make her do?* Remorse crushed in on her as she recalled the events at the mall that led to her capture. As the hours of loneliness wore on, she tried to remember happy times with her family, but her mind always drifted back to her new reality.

The next night, John William took the children upstairs one at a time. Maggie sat on the edge of her cot. Hours passed as she waited for John William to come and get her. When she heard the door of her cell unlock, she had to fight back the scream of terror that was lodged in her chest.

John William took Maggie to a different room this time. When she stepped inside, there was a single bed shoved against the wall. She was told to sit on the bed. A few minutes later, a tall man walked into the room. He wore pleated, brown pants; a white, button-down shirt; and suspenders. He walked over to the side of the bed and smiled down at Maggie. "Hi, sweetie. Daddy's home. Now, be a good little girl and take your clothes off. Do it nice and slow, the way Daddy likes it."

Maggie's limbs when limp, but she remembered what Cali had told her about getting beaten. Tears dribbled down her cheeks as she removed all of her clothes very slowly. He had her lie on the bed while he stood and looked at her for a while. Then he asked, "Were you a good girl today?"

Maggie nodded at him vigorously.

"I asked, were you a good girl today. When Daddy asks you a question, he expects to hear an answer," he said, becoming odder by the moment.

"Yes, I was a good girl today." Maggie's voice cracked.

"Well, Mommy said you were very naughty. She said that you kicked the neighbor's dog and, as much as I hate to do it, you know that Daddy has to punish you for it. Right?"

Maggie pleaded, "Please don't punish me. I swear I won't be bad again. Please."

"It's too late for that, sweetheart. If you do something bad, then there have to be consequences. Now, go ahead and lie on your belly."

Maggie turned over on the small bed, putting her head to the side so she could watch the odd man. Her jaw went limp, and her muscles tensed as the man took all of his clothes off. He picked up his belt.

"OK, now this is going to hurt me more than it hurts you," the man said calmly, as he slashed the belt across her bare ass. He whipped the belt across her flesh two more times before he told her to turn onto her back again.

The man stood over Maggie naked, with an erect penis. Her head was buzzing, and her own heartbeat hammered against her eardrums. She didn't know what would happen next and feared that he was about to kill her. She began yelling, "No!" over and over again.

Less than a minute later, John William came into the room. He strode over to the bed and bent down close to her ear.

"Listen, you little bitch. This guy ain't just anybody. He owns that virgin pussy of yours and has every right to have it. Now stop yelling before I crack your fucking head open."

After John William left the room, the man approached the bed again. "Now, where were we?" he asked with a sickeningly sweet smile. "Oh yes, you were about to show me how sorry you were for being a bad girl today."

Then the man slid on top of Maggie and began to kiss her. Maggie wiggled under his weight as she struggled to breathe. The man seemed not to notice as he stuck his large tongue into her small mouth. She was confused and petrified. Maggie was utterly helpless to fight back. After an extended period of touching and kissing her, the man entered her swiftly. She felt as though he had rammed a burning stick between her legs. Maggie's shrill scream shattered the silence of the room, and this made the man even more eager to proceed. Then, after about a minute, Maggie faded into a state of shock. The darkness, which she had feared just the night before, swaddled her and provided an escape from her misery.

Maggie lay motionless as the stranger took her virginity in a dirty, depressing room on the second floor of an abandoned prison.

Chapter Two

—————————◼—————————

Atwenty-minute drive from where Maggie was forcefully losing her virginity, her parents, Rob and Lorraine Clarke stood in their living room, talking with the police. In the first moments when Lorraine couldn't find Maggie at the mall, she felt as if her heart had come to a screeching halt. She had fought for every breath. Her body ice cold, she frantically hunted through the food court like a wild animal. Shoppers looked on as Lorraine's self-control vanished and she became increasingly hysterical. Her guttural sobs made everyone around her feel the throbbing sorrow wedged in her heart. Feeling Lorraine's anguish and deep loss, shoppers pulled their own children closer to them, silently thankful that they weren't suffering such heartbreak.

Even after the police and Rob arrived, Lorraine felt frozen in time. She wanted to turn the clock back to undo the decision she'd made about Maggie. Lorraine yearned for the past so she could make the right decision and go with her daughter to buy a slice of pizza.

As each event unfolded—the arrival of the police, the crowd of onlookers gathering, and then Rob's arrival—Lorraine held to the belief that Maggie would reappear and they could go on with their lives. But after hours passed without any sign of Maggie, thoughts of her daughter being molested and murdered played through Lorraine's mind. Rob tried to soothe her, but there was nothing he could say to keep the dark thoughts from seeping into her mind or his own, sending the couple further into the murky stickiness of their reality.

Lorraine had become frenzied and refused to leave the mall without Maggie. She lingered until the mall closed. She had to be certain that Maggie wasn't just lost in the sea of people. The police practically had to force her to go home. She agreed only after they promised to patrol the parking lot throughout the night.

Lorraine blamed herself for all that was happening to them. She never should have allowed Maggie to go off alone. She knew better than to let the children out of her sight. Even in the first hours of pure chaos, Lorraine believed that her husband would hate her as much as she hated herself for the life-altering decision she'd made.

Lorraine wanted the police to find her daughter immediately, and after many hours of telling her story to them, she grew tired. She had explained it at least a dozen times while standing in the food court, but they kept coming back to her with the same question: *why did Maggie go off by herself?* Lorraine explained through anguished sobs that her daughter had begged to be allowed to buy a slice of pizza by herself, and Lorraine had finally given in. One single moment of poor judgment would cause a lifetime of regret.

Now Lorraine sat on her sofa remembering every detail of her daughter. She could see the silky, jet-black hair and the soulful, ocean-blue eyes. Maggie had been a precious gift from the moment she was born. Her sweet demeanor and later, her insatiable appetite for learning, made her the teacher's pet as each new school year rolled around. Of course, Lorraine loved the attention Maggie received from her teachers, but it made it difficult for Maggie to make friends. The other girls in Maggie's class thought she was a geek and envied all of the attention she received from the teachers.

Maggie had a sharp sense of humor and would often verbally spar with her father while Lorraine was cooking dinner. Maggie teased her father about being an old man, even though he was only forty. She mocked the clothes he wore and often told him that he smelled bad, although he never did. Rob would pretend to be offended, and they would banter back and forth, laughing until their stomachs ached.

Lorraine and Rob were a down-to-earth, well-liked couple. The two had met during college and were married in their early twenties. A few years after they married, they bought a two-story home on a half-acre lot in Conshohocken, Pennsylvania. Lorraine was an eighth-grade teacher, and Rob was a computer analyst at a large engineering firm. They waited until they were in their late twenties before they had Maggie, and they'd planned to have just one child. To their surprise, seven years later, Lorraine became pregnant with Keith.

Of the two, Maggie was the rock star. As a toddler, adults would stop and listen to what she had to say. She was charming and charismatic, which made her easy to engage. As she got older, Maggie's love of reading accelerated her ability to be clever with words. She was her parent's pride and joy. They loved Keith just as much as they loved their daughter, but being the firstborn, she secretly held a special place in their hearts.

Before Maggie was stolen, Lorraine and Rob would lie in bed at night and talk about their children. They agreed that Maggie would be something very special when she grew up. Rob was confident that she would become a doctor and find the cure for cancer. Since kindergarten, they'd told Maggie that she could be anything she wanted to because she was capable of learning. This encouragement gave Maggie the motivation to go above and beyond in everything she decided to do. She was a very special child.

But now, with Maggie missing, Lorraine and Rob sat silently on the sofa together. Each of them prayed she would be returned to them soon. They had no idea what had become of their little girl. As the minutes of waiting turned into hours, their agony grew to higher levels. The emptiness engulfed them, making them feel as though they were completely hollow inside—rightly so, because while they didn't know it at the time, their daughter had been forced into human sex trafficking.

Chapter Three

———————————————◼———————————————

Myles Cabello, the "owner" of Maggie and the sex-trafficking cartel, left her lying on the bed. He had raped her three times that evening before getting dressed. He was in a hurry to catch a plane back to his hometown in New York, where his wife and three kids waited. As Myles left the bedroom, he told John William, "Don't let anything happen to that one. I'll be back to visit her. I don't want to find one mark on her. You understand?"

Myles reviewed photos of all the new children who were brought into his concealed locations in the Northeast corridor. When he saw the pictures of Maggie, her beautiful, innocent eyes had caused a stir in his groin. He'd made a special trip to Pennsylvania to be the first to have the lovely child.

After John William returned Maggie to her cell that night, Cali went to her, carrying a bowl of warm water and an old T-shirt. She bathed the young girl as best she could in an attempt to remove all the reminders of Myles from her small body. The teen could see bruises that indicated that Maggie had been badly hurt. She told John William that Maggie would need a glass of whiskey to ease some of her pain so she could recover. Cali managed to get Maggie to drink most of the whiskey, and a short time later, the child slipped into sleep.

The next day, Seth ran into Maggie's cell while she was still sleeping and threw himself across her body. As she woke slowly, memories of where she was and what Myles had done to her flooded back. Cali and Max walked into her cell just as the reality of what happened sank in. The teenagers sat on the edge of the cot. Maggie immediately wailed, "Cali, a man did horrible things to me last night. I think that he did something really bad to my insides. He hurt me so much."

Cali's throat filled with bitter bile, and she looked to Max for support as she began to console the child. "I know, Maggie. I know what he did to you. The first time always hurts the most. It'll get better," she said, trying to reassure her.

"No, it won't get better! I'm never letting anyone do that to me again!" Maggie shouted.

Seth stared at Maggie with a confused expression, wondering why she was so upset. Maggie stood to use the toilet, but her small, thin legs gave out. Max jumped up to help his little friend over to the toilet.

"Maggie, we are all in this rattrap together," Max said. "When you are with these scum-sucking pigs, you are alone in your own sadness, and nobody is there to care, but when we are together, you aren't alone anymore. Get it in your head that we look after each other even though no one else seems to give a fuck about us. When it gets as bad as it did last night, you have to believe that someday, things will get better, and until that day comes, all us kids are family."

Maggie wanted to hold onto Max and never let him go, but she was too weak even to respond. She wanted him to grow big, hard muscles so that he could beat up John William and get them all out of there.

Having lost all modesty, Maggie sat on the toilet to pee. She groaned when her urine passed through her like liquid fire.

She had just finished when John William walked into the cell. "Let's go. Breakfast."

Maggie looked over at the man who had stolen her from a life she adored, and anger welled up inside of her, giving her a small boost of energy. John William had made her leave the loving family she'd known and put her into this new life, one of fear and pain.

Maggie scowled at him. "I'm not hungry."

"I don't give a shit if you're hungry or not," John William said without compassion. "Get your ass out here. Everyone eats when I say they eat."

Maggie's newfound courage quickly dissolved when John William took a few steps toward her. She stood from the toilet and obediently followed Cali and Max into the hallway. Seth tagged along behind, his small hand firmly holding onto hers.

At breakfast, Shana watched Maggie closely. Finally, after John William had left them to eat, she said, "So who were you with last night? Huh? You were with Myles, right?"

Maggie looked up from her flavorless oatmeal. "Who's Myles?"

"Myles owns us, you pea brain. He usually comes for me. But you've ruined all of that. I hate you!" Shana spat.

"Shana, stop it!" Cali cut in. "She didn't do anything. She can't help it that Myles wanted her. I'm sure this doesn't change anything for you. He'll keep you safe, just like he always has."

Shana looked over at Maggie again. "Yeah, well, Cali better be right. Otherwise, I'll kill you."

Maggie looked to Max, who quickly shifted his gaze back to the bowl in front of him. Then he swallowed hard and spoke. "Shana, you've been here long enough to know how this works. It's not like they gave her a fucking choice. Lighten up on her and try to remember back to your first time with Myles. Just because he protects you doesn't make it any easier."

"Whatever, Max. Fuck you, too! All I know is that Myles better come back for me, or I'm gonna fuck her up," Shana argued, her bark way bigger than her bite.

What is Shana talking about? Maggie wondered. She didn't do anything, and she never met anyone named Myles. She would ask Cali after breakfast. The last thing she wanted was for one of the kids not to like her. Worse yet, what if Shana really beat her up or even killed her? She didn't want to die in this terrifying place. She wanted to go home to her family. Besides, being left out at school was one thing, but here, not being accepted would push her deeper into hell.

Chapter Four

———————————————■———————————————

"Who's Myles?" Maggie asked Cali as soon as they were alone.

"Myles is the big boss. He runs all of the places where they keep the kids," she answered.

"What do you mean *all* of the places?" Maggie wanted to know.

"Well, just like here, there are lots of different places where they kidnap kids and sell them for sex. Sometimes they move us around. I've been to three other states since they took me. But don't worry; if Myles likes you, they will keep you here," Cali explained, trying not to alarm her.

"Is that why Shana is mad at me? Is she afraid they will move her somewhere else?"

Cali considered how to answer without worrying Maggie. "That's part of it. The other part is that if Myles likes you, he'll come back to see you. Before you came here, he came to see Shana. I know you don't understand all of this, but some of the clients can be mean. Sometimes they do things to us that hurt more than Myles hurt you last night."

Maggie hung her head, unable to believe something could hurt more than what Myles had done to her. "So, are you saying that someone is going to hurt Shana?"

"It's possible. Now that he wants you, it means that John William can give her to anybody. It's the way things work. But you have to remember that you didn't do anything to make it happen. Shana is just scared now. Myles has kept her safe for the past year," Cali explained.

Maggie let the new information sink in before she asked her next question. "Does that mean that only Myles will have sex with me?"

"No, baby. It just means that they won't let you be with anyone who does things that are extra mean," Cali explained, feeling the younger girl's fear.

"Extra mean how? Like, what do they do?" Maggie persisted.

Cali let out a loud sigh. It made her sick to have to explain these horrible things to the younger kids. But when she was taken as a young teen, one of the older boys that the cartel was trafficking at the time sat her down and explained everything to her. Knowing the truth didn't make it easier on the kids, but it did take some of the mystery out of what would happen to them. It gave them a little advantage with some of the clients so they could manipulate which acts they would be required to perform. It also let the kids know that they weren't alone in their intolerable situations.

"Well, some of the clients like to get rough. They hit and bite you. But…"

The prolonged pause made Maggie's anxiety soar.

"Sometimes they do really bad stuff, like burn you or put things inside of you that they shouldn't," Cali finally said.

The information bounced around in Maggie's head, making her woozy. "So, then, until my parents come for me, it's good that Myles likes me?"

"Yes, Maggie, it is. But don't forget that Myles is the person who started all of this shit. So, he's still a dangerous man, and you can't trust him. Just do what he wants you to, and you'll be OK," Cali advised.

"Aggie, why are you scared?" Seth asked, instinctively knowing that something was wrong with her.

Maggie scooped Seth up into her arms. "I'm just worried about how we're going to get home. That's all. But guess what? I'm going to stay with you until you can go home to your mommy and daddy," she assured him.

"But I want my mommy now. I'm scared too," he whimpered.

"I know you are, and that's why whenever John William lets us, I'll be right here with you," she told him, kissing his forehead.

Then she looked at Cali. "We're gonna get out of here. We have to. Right, Cali?"

"Sure, baby. We'll get out of here. Just remember that until that happens, we need to take care of each other. That's all we got. Can you remember that for me?" Cali asked.

"Yeah, I'll remember. Oh, Cali, John William calls me a little whore. What's that?" Maggie asked, not having been exposed to such names.

"Maggie, John William is a jerk. Don't pay any attention to what he calls you. He's the worst kind of person alive. We all have to listen to him because we're here. Someday, all of the horrible things he's done and said will come back on him. Just ignore him when he calls you names," she instructed.

When Cali went back to her cell, Maggie sat and replayed their conversation. She was thinking that if she was really sweet to Myles, he might let her go home. Then her thoughts drifted to Shana, who was upset that Maggie was Myles's favorite now. It was just like school, where the kids hated her because all the teachers loved her. She pulled Seth closer to her and vowed to do everything she could to keep the two of them safe. She didn't know then the price she'd have to pay to keep them safe.

Chapter Five

In the following two weeks, Maggie had three visits from Myles. He continued to play the "daddy" who had to punish her for being naughty. In her third week of captivity, Myles came to see her again. She was taken up to the room where they always met, and when he walked in, he sat next to her on the bed.

"From now on, I want you to be my little whore, and I'll be your master. What that means is that I'm going to teach you to do different things that I like. In return, I'll do things that make you feel good too. You understand?" he asked. But he didn't wait for an answer.

That night, Myles taught Maggie how to give him a blow job. When he had finished, she spit out his cum, and he slapped her hard across the face.

"There you go being naughty again. When a man cums in your mouth, the only decent thing to do is swallow it. Do you understand?" he said sternly.

"Yes," she replied, no longer feeling like a human being.

"Good, my little whore. Now, show your master some loving..."

When Myles was done having sex with Maggie, she pulled the sheet up to her chin.

"Master, if I'm a really good girl, will you let me go home?" she asked hopefully.

"Ha! You are home. I suggest you get that idea out of your head real quick or it'll make your time here much harder," he explained as he lit a cigarette. After a couple of drags on his smoke, he threw it to the floor and let it burn. "Now, go on and get dressed."

Myles dressed. Before leaving, he looked back at the beautiful young child. "I'll be busy the next few weeks and won't be able to come and see you," he said.

A feeling of pure ecstasy shot though Maggie's body. She was delighted at the thought of being left alone for a couple of weeks. Not having to be subjected to unwanted sex was a great relief. Myles grabbed the doorknob and turned back one more time.

"While I'm away, I have some very special clients that want to visit you. Now, you remember the things that I taught you and be certain to make all of your clients very happy."

As he closed the door behind him, a single tear fell from Maggie's chin. She was far more educated about sex than she'd been when she arrived. She now knew some of the things that would be expected of her. Maggie was coming to accept that she would have to do things she hated in order to survive.

Then her first real client taught her things that would change the person that she was to become.

Chapter Six

———————■———————

Three days later, John William entered Maggie's cell carrying a dress.

"You have a client tonight. He's paying a lot of money, and you need to look good. I'm gonna take you to the shower so that you can clean up."

Maggie grabbed Seth's hand, and they followed John William into the hallway. Cali stood at her cell door and reached for Seth. He was going to stay with her while Maggie took a shower.

Seth yelled, "I want to go with Aggie." But he stopped whining abruptly when John William turned and scowled at him.

"I'll be right back," Maggie said soothingly.

Then Maggie looked up at Cali, who could see that the girl was troubled, and it struck her that Maggie had never been alone with John William outside of the cellblock—and she'd never been in the shower without the other kids.

"Um, John William," Cali started slowly, "would you like me to come with you so I can fix her hair and put her makeup on?"

John William pretended to consider it; he loved mind-fucking the kids. "Nah, don't worry. I'll take good care of her. When she comes back, you can fix her up."

Maggie followed John William into the shower room, where he told her to strip. She quickly obeyed and started for the closest shower.

"Hold on there a minute. Come over here and let me take a closer look at you," John William said in a creepy tone.

Maggie's legs were shaking as she walked over and stood before him. He spun her around so that he could take in every inch of her. Then he reached down and rubbed his large hand between her legs. "Make sure you wash that stink bucket real good. You got a real meat

41

lover coming in tonight," he said, tormenting her, as he pushed her toward the shower.

Relieved that he didn't do anything else to her, Maggie ran under the closest shower head. John William watched as she scrubbed her whole body and finally washed her hair. When Maggie was finished, she walked over to the hook where her towel was hanging. John William was standing next to it, and as she grew closer, he gave her a wicked grin.

"Someday, I'll tap that ass, girl. I'm working myself up to it. But you can be certain that I'll get a piece of that," John William said, cupping her ass with his oversized, hideous, apelike hands.

Maggie shrank away from the horrific, foul man. John William was ugly inside and out, and she knew that she'd hate every filthy, vile inch of him for the rest of her life.

Late that night, when her cell door opened, Maggie stood and quietly walked with John William. Her long black hair fell softly around her tiny shoulders and her magnificent ocean blue eyes popped with the black mascara that Cali had applied for her.

When she entered the client's room, soft music played, and candles burned on the nightstands on either side of the bed. She quickly settled herself on the edge of the mattress. She sat alone, listening to the music, until the door opened, and a man in his mid-thirties entered the room. He was short and lean. He wore a neatly trimmed beard and mustache. His black suit was meticulously pressed, and he walked toward her with grace. "Hello, I'm Dr. Barnes. I'm here to teach you about the human body," he announced.

Dr. Barnes, who wasn't a real doctor but rather, a self-proclaimed home-remedy expert, loved nothing more than to flaunt his knowledge. Medicine and the human body had been his obsessions since he was a teenager. He spent hours at the library reading medical journals and books on self-healing.

Maggie sat perfectly still. She didn't utter a word and despised the feeling that Dr. Barnes gave her. Then he walked over and asked her to stand. He unzipped her dress and let it fall to the floor. Maggie stood in her underwear, and he examined her skin as if expecting to find something wrong. When he was satisfied that she was healthy, he told her to remove the rest of her clothes.

For the remainder of their time together, he explained the differences between the male and female body parts, using both of their bodies as teaching aids. He boasted about the number of books he'd read. "They know me by name at the library. I get the utmost respect when I go there."

Two hours later, when he was finished having sex with her, he left her lying on the bed.

When he was ready to leave, Maggie spoke. "Dr. Barnes?"

"Yes?" he answered, turning back to her.

"If you ever come back here again, will you bring me some books to read? I love to read, and there aren't any books for us here," she explained timidly.

Dr. Barnes smiled. "Of course, my darling. How about if I bring you a new book each time I come to visit? Would that make you happy?"

"Yes," Maggie answered.

Then she thought: *what would make her really happy would be if they all died*. But for now, she'd take the books. That night, she remembered what her parents had taught her: learning as much as possible would make her capable of doing anything. Obtaining knowledge would be her new goal. Besides, someday when she went back to her family, she wanted them to be proud of her for *something*.

Chapter Seven

Over the next several months, Maggie was sold only to high-paying clients. Myles still came to see her at least once a week, and he was on his high horse about "teaching her things." All of the things that Myles taught her were dehumanizing. She quickly realized that it was all just a sick game, and she was a pawn.

Dr. Barnes also visited her regularly and kept his promise to bring books to her. When he gave Maggie the first book, John William took it away. The next time he bought Maggie for the evening, Dr. Barnes asked if she had finished reading the first book. Maggie explained that she wasn't allowed to keep it.

Dr. Barnes was infuriated and called Myles. "I'm bringing Maggie books to make her smarter and more desirable to me and to your other clients. There's no bigger turn-on than a chick with fucking brains in her head. If you want me to keep coming back week after week and paying you all this money, then you better tell that fucking imbecile, John William, to let her read the books I bring to her."

From then on, Maggie was allowed to keep all of the books that Dr. Barnes brought for her. Some of the books were young adult novels, and others were educational. She especially loved the books that taught her something. Each week, after Dr. Barnes was finished having sex with Maggie, they would sit on the bed and talk about what she had learned from reading. Her ability to retain information was remarkable. With each book she finished, Maggie felt like she was becoming more powerful.

Life at the prison was unbearable for all of the children. None of them were actually living; rather, they existed as toys for the wicked. Unlike the others, Maggie now had something to distract her when she was alone.

45

Over time, Shana withdrew. She was being trafficked to the cartel's most sicko clients. She got all of the clients who were into sadism and derived their sexual gratification from the pain and cruelty that they subjected her to. She became more reclusive, and nothing the others tried to do to nurture her worked.

Myles protected Maggie, but the others all had to endure an occasional thumping by malicious clients. But because of Shana's youth and beauty, the demented seemed to be lining up to get time with her. Shana still blamed Maggie for stealing Myles from her. Secretly, John William had planted that idea in her head. He told Shana that Maggie had deliberately set out to make her suffer. He said that Maggie had "come on" to Myles to keep her sorry ass safe.

"I was there, and I saw it," John William said. "She was flirting with him. She kept telling him that she was so much prettier than you, which we all know is true. Maggie is the reason that you're getting your filthy little ass whooped. Don't forget that, you raunchy dirt ball."

John William thrived on his supremacy over the defenseless kids, and the more psychological turmoil he caused, the greater his domination.

Shana was livid to learn that Maggie had set out to harm her intentionally. She never considered that John William was lying, and she couldn't feel anything but hatred for the other girl. She wished that Maggie would die and took every opportunity to express her loathing. One afternoon, Shana stormed into Maggie's cell.

"So, you think you're hot shit, huh? Well, you're not," Shana yelled and punched Maggie squarely in the nose. Then she bent down to where Maggie lay on the dirt floor. "You're going to tell Myles that you hate him and don't want to see him anymore. You understand me? You should have to be with these fucking freaks, not *me*!" Shana fumed.

Maggie looked up at her with blood dripping from her nose and cried, "I didn't do anything to you, Shana. Why are you always so mean? Why don't you just leave me alone?"

Shana yelled back, "You heard what I just said. If you don't tell Myles that you hate him, I swear to God I will fuckin' kill you. You're such an idiot. You're always talking about going home and getting out of here. Well, here's a wake-up call: you're never leaving! They don't let us go! They keep us and use us up until we die. This is your life now, you bitch!"

Cali heard the commotion and rushed into Maggie's cell. "What the hell is going on? Oh my God, what did you do to her, Shana?" she asked when she saw blood streaming from Maggie's nose.

"That's just a taste of what I'll do to her if she doesn't get Myles to take me back," Shana shot back at Cali.

"What are you talking about, Shana?" Cali asked, shocked.

"She stole him from me, and now I'm stuck with all these crazy-ass pricks that get their rocks off by hurting me. It's all her fault, and I hate her! I hope she dies," Shana bawled.

"Stop it! You're just making things worse, Shana," Cali said.

"I'll stop it when you stop letting her think that someday she's going home. You know that none of us are getting out of here alive. But you never tell her that. You just keep leading her on so she thinks everything will be OK. Well it *ain't* gonna be OK," she screamed, directing her words at Maggie.

That night, having overheard the girls screaming, John William purposely sold Shana to the lowest bidder to stir the shit pot a little more. Shana was given to an ex-con, with the words "Born To Raise Hell" tattooed on his forearm. When he entered the room, his contemptuous demeanor instantly terrified Shana. The man's bloated body and ash-white, pockmarked face repulsed her. He approached Shana, placed a dog collar around her neck, and dragged her around the room by the leash as she struggled to keep up with him and avoid choking to death. His treatment of her quickly deteriorated and, that night, two floors above where the children sat quietly in their cells, Shana was brutally raped and tortured. Each time she yelled in pain, he picked up his pocketknife and cut her tongue.

When John William brought Shana back in the middle of the night, he woke Cali and told her to tend to the girl. Cali started to shake when she saw Shana's condition. Maggie heard Cali telling John William in a panicked voice that she didn't know what to do for her. The bruises would heal, but there was so much blood coming from Shana's mouth that Cali feared she was bleeding to death.

Chapter Eight

———————————■———————————

"John William," Maggie yelled from the opening in her door, "let me out so I can help Shana."

"Shut the hell up and go to sleep, you little whore," John William yelled back to her.

Then, after several moments, he considered that if Myles found out that he had let the lowest bidder take Shana just to prolong the fighting between the kids, Myles might kill him. John William reluctantly went over to Maggie's cell and opened the door, not because he was letting the bitch tell him what to do, but to cover his tracks with Myles.

Maggie rushed into Shana's cell. She gasped when she saw the bruises on Shana's arms and legs. Shana looked as if someone had tossed her into a clothes dryer with large rocks. Gathering herself, she pushed forward to where Shana lay on her cot.

"She's bleeding from her mouth," Cali said in low voice.

"OK, Shana. Open your mouth. I need to take a look at what's wrong," Maggie urged.

When she did, her tongue was swollen to twice its normal size. Maggie turned to John William and said, "I need you to get a bowl of *clean* water and a couple towels."

John William left the three girls in the cell and locked the door behind him. He returned a few minutes later with the items that Maggie requested. She soaked one of the small towels in water and gingerly began to clean Shana's tongue. But as she wiped, the cuts kept bleeding. Maggie was able to see many slashes on Shana's tongue.

"OK, John William, you have to bring me a small glass, baking soda, and salt—right now!" Maggie ordered.

John William's angry eyes bored into Maggie.

"I'm sorry, John William. *Please*, can you bring me the stuff I need?" she managed.

When he returned with the three items, the first thing Maggie did was mix a palm full of salt into the glass of water. She looked at Cali and then over at Shana, who was only partly coherent. "Shana, I'm going to hold the glass so that you can take this salt water into your mouth. I don't want you to swallow it. Just hold it in there for as long as you can and then spit it out."

Shana gave her a slight nod.

Maggie moved closer. "It might burn. I don't know. But it's going to help."

Maggie helped Shana take in small amounts of the salt water until the glass was empty. Then she made a thin paste of baking soda and water. "OK, Shana. I need you to open your mouth wide and stick out your tongue as far as you can."

Maggie scooped the thin, white paste out of the glass with her small finger and covered Shana's tongue with it. Then she stood and turned to Cali. "That's all we can do for now. We need to make her gargle with salt water and put this paste on her tongue every hour or two."

Then Maggie looked at John William. "We need to sleep in here with Shana to put this paste on her tongue. It's really swollen, and I'm scared something bad will happen to her when she's sleeping."

John William left the cell without saying another word and locked the door behind him.

Cali watched Maggie for a minute. "How did you know what to do, Mags?" she asked, using the pet name that she came up with the week before.

"I read it in one of the books that Dr. Barnes gave me. It's all about home remedies. The salt water will help so the cuts don't get infected and the baking-soda paste is supposed to help make it feel better and heal faster," Maggie explained.

"Wow. That's some crazy shit, Mags. You did real good tonight. I didn't know what to do to help her. I'm proud of you, baby," Cali said, running her hand down Maggie's arm.

"Cali? I feel like it's my fault that this happened to her. It looks like whoever she was with was really mean to her. Is there anything we can do to help her?" Maggie asked naively and with true concern.

"I'm not sure there's anything we *can* do right now, but I bet we can figure something out," Cali assured her.

Cali wanted to give Maggie hope that they would find a way to fight back. Cali knew deep in her heart that the odds of getting out or taking control were slim to none. But she wasn't willing to dampen Maggie's spirit or her belief that one day they would all be set free. She was pretty certain that day would never come for herself or for the others, but she had a feeling that Maggie's fate would be different. She just hoped it was for the better.

Chapter Nine

———————————————◼———————————————

Several months later, when the children were led to the room where clients looked them over so they could take their picks of the litter, an exotic woman named Sabrina was among the perverted freaks. She had been living with one of the cartel's regulars for over a year. Her boyfriend, Bernie, was a kinky bastard, and kids really turned him on. After Bernie and Sabrina had dated for a couple of weeks, they decided to move in together. Shortly after they started living together, he broached the subject of kiddy porn with her. Over time, she became more open to the conversation, but she remained standoffish.

Sabrina had no family, and since Bernie was a successful business owner who paid people to run his business for him, the two spent every minute of every day together. Bernie liked the fact that he was the only person who ever talked to Sabrina, and she seemed content with being cut off from the rest of the world. When he first told her about the group of children available to them, she was hesitant. Then, she began asking questions. How many were there? How old were they? Where were they kept? How much did they cost?

None of her questions were ever answered. Bernie explained that she couldn't know any of the details because that was the deal he'd made with the cartel that owned the children.

"You and I can go there so that you can see them. I'll let you pick whichever one you like. It'll be so fucking good, believe me," Bernie assured her.

Finally, Sabrina agreed to indulge Bernie's obsession with children, although she warned him that she didn't know what to expect or how she would react to it.

Bernie blindfolded Sabrina and drove to the abandoned prison. It was protocol to bring in newcomers that way until the cartel was certain the person could be trusted. Once inside the room, Bernie removed Sabrina's blindfold, and she watched as the children removed their clothes for the audience.

Sabrina's heart raced as she stared at the innocent little human beings standing before them. When Sabrina's eyes met Maggie's, the woman was mesmerized. It was as if she could feel Maggie's pain. Typically, clients never made eye contact, but an unspoken connection was made between the grown woman and the young child.

Sabrina leaned into Bernie. "That one," she whispered, pointing at Maggie. "I want that one."

Bernie turned to her and smiled. "You have very good taste, my dear. She is the most expensive of them all. She's also the youngest. I've had her before, and she is just delicious."

Sabrina gave him a dim smile. "OK. Can we go now?" she asked.

"No, darlin', the show isn't over yet. Just a few more minutes and we can go and purchase our goods," Bernie said with excitement.

Like soldiers, the children formed a line at the foot of the bed. The clients walked by them, and when Bernie got to Maggie, he put his mouth next to her ear. "My girlfriend has picked you. You are a very lucky little girl."

"Thank you, sir," Maggie responded, as she had been taught to say when she was given a compliment.

Maggie had lost all sense of ownership of her body. She nurtured her mind and turned her body over to the men who owned it. She didn't fight it any longer. She had learned over time that fighting didn't serve her well. Fighting them meant punishment, and her desire was to make it as easy on herself as possible. After all, she didn't want to end up like Shana, being sold to the cruelest of the cruel.

Thirty minutes later, Maggie was alone with the couple. Bernie took his clothes off and instructed his girlfriend and Maggie to do the same. He led Sabrina over to the bed and had her sit on the edge. Bernie instructed Maggie to stand in front of him. "OK, Maggie, I want you to give your uncle a blow job. Do it real slow so your aunt can see everything."

Maggie slowly got down on her knees, but before she could begin to give Bernie what he wanted, Sabrina stopped her. "Hold on now, Bernie. I thought little Maggie could just watch us. I mean, it would be a total turn-on to me to know that she's peeking. You know, pretend like we're her mom and dad and she is spying on us. Doesn't that sound good?"

Maggie waited with anticipation as Bernie thought about it. She'd never simply "watched" before.

"Yeah, I like that," Bernie stated. "But while we're getting it on, I want you to sit on the chair over there and play with yourself."

Maggie rushed over to the chair and sat down. As the two adults engaged in sex, she stayed on the chair and did exactly what Bernie wanted her to do. The child was numb to all of it. Bernie kept his eyes glued to Maggie while he pursued his girlfriend. Every so often, Maggie would catch Sabrina looking at her not with lust, but with raw sadness.

When it was all over, the three of them dressed while Bernie talked about what a great evening it had been. Sabrina grabbed her purse and dug through it until she found what she was looking for. "Here," she said to Maggie, "do you like candy? I thought you might like it."

It had been a long time since Maggie had a piece of candy. John William fed them oatmeal for breakfast, peanut butter sandwiches for lunch, and boiled hot dogs with instant mashed potatoes for dinner. It was the same food day in and day out; it never varied.

Maggie looked at the candy bar with longing as her mouth watered. "We're not allowed to have treats like this. John William would never let me keep it. Thank you, anyway," she said with regret.

"Well, then John William doesn't have to know. Right, Bernie? We'll just sit here while you eat it," Sabrina said, sitting on the small chair in the corner.

Maggie took the candy bar from her and pulled the paper off as though it was Christmas morning. She bit into the candy and chewed as quickly as she could, as if someone would steal it from her. She gobbled the bar down in under a minute and looked at Sabrina.

"Thank you. That was so delicious," Maggie said.

Bernie had watched the young girl and his girlfriend while all of this transpired. He didn't care for the sentiment between Sabrina and the kid. In his mind, these kids were little sluts; he had never viewed them as human, and the exchange with Sabrina had ruined the image of Maggie in his mind's eye. He preferred Maggie to remain a "thing" and not a person. That was part of the lure.

"All right, enough of this shit," Bernie stated. "Let's get the hell out of here."

On their drive home, with Sabrina blindfolded again, Bernie lectured her about the candy bar incident.

"What's wrong with giving the little girl a candy bar?" Sabrina wanted to know.

"That's not the point, Sabrina. This is about sex; it ain't about kids and being nice to them. She's not your fucking daughter, OK? We go there for one thing. Once you start that sappy shit, you kill the whole mood. If you're going to do that shit, then I'll go by myself the next time," Bernie stated.

"OK, Bernie, OK. I won't do it again. I promise. I want to go back with you, honey. I had so much fun tonight," she sang sweetly.

For the rest of the ride, Sabrina thought about nothing but the beautiful little girl they had left to be consumed by demons.

Chapter Ten

The next day, after showers, Maggie went to talk with Cali, who was sitting in Max's cell with him.

"Hi, guys. I wanted to tell you about that couple last night. The weirdest thing happened. After they…you know, well, the lady reaches into her purse and gives me a Nestle Crunch bar. Oh my God, it was so good! I forgot how much I love candy."

The two teens listened with a bit of envy. The kids never got any food other than what John William provided. Cali and Max remembered how wonderful it was to eat chocolate. They rarely allowed themselves to think about the amazing things that were no longer a part of their lives, but now they clung to this opportunity to live through Maggie.

"Was it as good as I remember it being?" Max asked.

Maggie nodded and smiled mischievously.

"Oh man, did you let it melt in your mouth so that it coated your tongue? I used to love doing that," Cali stated.

"No, I gobbled it down as fast as I could. I was afraid the woman was playing a joke on me and would take it back. Or John William would come in, and I would be in trouble for eating it," Maggie said, feeling gluttonous.

Maggie had thought it would be a good story to share with her friends, but when she saw the nostalgia on their faces, it made her sad to have reminded them of something they'd lost. It was the small things that each had taken for granted before their captures that they missed most—a hug from a loved one, toilets that flushed, or taking a shower in private.

Max noticed the sudden change in Maggie's demeanor. "Come here, Maggie," he said, giving her a squeeze. "We think it's great that you got to have a treat. You know how it works. We don't think about these things that much. But when one of us gets any bit of pleasure, I think it's important that we share it with each other. Fuck, there's nothing wrong with that. It beats thinking about being a prisoner all the time, right?"

"Sure. Sorry if I made you feel bad, though. If she comes to see me again and brings more candy, I'll try to save some and sneak it back to you guys," Maggie offered.

"No!" Cali snapped. "You won't sneak anything back. Maggie, if John William ever caught you doing that, there's no telling what he'd do to you. He looks for reasons to punish us. Promise us that you'll never try to do that."

Frightened by Cali's reaction and the thought of John William punishing her, Maggie agreed.

A short while later, Maggie left to talk to Shana and Seth. They were sitting in Seth's cell, and Shana was telling him a story about when she was a little girl and her parents took her on vacation to Disney World. Seth listened intently as she described having breakfast with Mickey Mouse. They looked up at Maggie as she walked in.

"What do you want?" Shana asked, annoyed that Maggie had interrupted her moment of sweet remembrance.

Maggie wanted so much for Shana to like her. "I just wanted to see what you guys were doing. You know, I went to Disney World, too. When I was eight years old, my parents—"

"Guess what?" Shana interjected, cutting Maggie off.

"What?" Maggie asked, hoping they were making a connection.

"I don't give a shit what you did when you were eight years old. It doesn't change the fact that you stole Myles from me, and I still hate you. I'll always hate you. So why don't you take your bony little ass out of here and find someone else to bother," Shana barked, turning back to Seth.

Maggie was stunned. She looked on for a few moments more, willing herself not to cry, and then she quietly turned and left them. Back in her own cell, she sat on the dirt floor next to her cot. She desperately wanted Shana to like her. Maggie had believed that by helping her when she had been beat up that Shana would suddenly like her. She never asked for Myles's attention and hadn't done anything to hurt Shana intentionally.

Maggie despised her own existence and the little whore she'd been reduced to just as much as Shana did.

Chapter Eleven

Maggie had been missing for just under a year. Lorraine sat at her kitchen table, nursing a third cup of coffee. From the moment her daughter disappeared, she did not let a day go by without doing something to try to find her. However, Lorraine's relentless pursuit of Maggie left her son and husband feeling neglected. The tragedy had put an insufferable strain on the whole family.

Rob had made it a point to spend more time with Keith since his daughter disappeared. He did it because Lorraine was unable to concentrate on anything other than her deep, unrelenting, nagging loss. But Lorraine thought the reason Rob smothered Keith was because he no longer trusted her to watch over their son. She didn't blame him. She would feel the same about Rob if the tables were turned.

Immediately following Maggie's disappearance, the media swarmed the house day and night. Search parties sprang up out of nowhere. Volunteers came in from New York, New Jersey, Maryland, and Washington, DC, to help look for Maggie. Then, over time, when there was not a single trace of evidence that Maggie was still alive, slowly but surely, people went back to living their own lives. Except for one person, that is: Detective Rae Harker, the lead investigator assigned to Maggie's case.

Rae Harker was a tall, black man, a touch under six feet tall. His lean body and bulging biceps made him look a lot meaner than he was. The detective had warm brown eyes, a slender face, and strong jawbones beneath his dark skin. When Harker smiled, which wasn't often, he gave off an air of ruggedness that Lorraine found comforting and oddly sensual, given the circumstances of their relationship.

Based on the length of time Maggie had been missing and the lack of a ransom demand, Detective Harker suspected that she was dead. He kept explaining to Rob and Lorraine that there was a high probability that Maggie had been murdered. Lorraine refused to believe that without seeing proof. She vowed never to stop looking for Maggie until she was found, dead or alive.

Shortly after the first month had passed and there were still no leads, Lorraine and Detective Harker began to meet regularly at the Clarkes' home. Lorraine was constantly harping on Rae not to give up the search for her daughter. Finally, the detective felt that he had to come clean with Lorraine.

"I won't ever give up my search for Maggie," Detective Harker vowed.

"Sure, you say that now. But then the next big case will come along, and you'll give up, just like everyone else," Lorraine said accusingly. "Why should I believe you?"

"You're right. There will be other cases that will require my attention." Harker hesitated, but then decided to give Lorraine the information she needed to understand his loyalty to Maggie.

"Three years ago, I took my eight-year-old daughter to the Eagleville Fair. She was at the top of the Ferris wheel when one of my junior detectives rushed up to me completely freaking out because a guy was holding a gun to a woman's head at the cotton-candy booth. I looked at my daughter at the top of the Ferris wheel, and we waved to each other. The ride had been stopping every thirty seconds to load more people into the empty seats. The young detective pulled on my arm. I looked up at my daughter again and knew it would be at least five more minutes before she was off the ride. So, I decided to leave her and go check out what was going on with the man who had the gun. By the time I got to the cotton-candy booth, another detective had detained the gunman, and the area was flooded with police officers. Satisfied that things were under control, I rushed back to the Ferris wheel. I stood and watched as people unloaded from the carriages. I watched a second time to make sure I hadn't missed the carriage my baby had been sitting in. I had been gone less than five minutes, and my daughter had disappeared." Detective Harker seemed to be caught in a depressing trance of reminiscence.

"Oh dear God, Rae, I didn't know," Lorraine said sadly. She was at a loss for words.

"You wouldn't have known, Lorraine. What I'm trying to say is that you and I are the same. We are the same person, Lorraine. We both made one bad decision that cost us everything. That's why your case is so important to me. I know how you feel. I understand the ongoing regret and self-blame. I get it," Harker asserted.

Lorraine lowered her head. "It's the worst feeling any human being can endure."

"Yes, it is. I became obsessed with finding my daughter, just like you," Harker stated.

"Did you find her?" Lorraine asked cautiously.

Detective Harker nodded. "We found her fourteen months after she was taken. The police found her body in a broken-down wooden shack in the middle of the woods one hundred miles from our home. When they discovered her body, my wife and I were relieved and devastated at the same time. We were relieved because she had been found and because she was no longer suffering. Yet we were devastated because the hope that we'd held onto for so long was gone. It was hard to move away from that place of hope. It left us with nothing to look forward to. And knowing she was dead meant that the pain would never subside. It is the most unnatural and unsettling feeling anyone can imagine. The unknown, the constant wondering and inability to stop your imagination from getting the best of you…it's enough to drive anyone insane."

For some reason, Harker felt that if he could return Maggie to her parents, he could redeem himself for failing his own child. But he didn't dare tell that to Lorraine.

Lorraine knew then that she and Harker would be friends for the rest of their lives. She trusted him more now than she had thought possible.

"Harker, did you have a feeling that your daughter was dead?"

Harker nodded. "So did my wife."

If truth were told, Lorraine wasn't certain if Maggie was dead or alive. That fact, in itself, made her feel inadequate. She wondered where her motherly intuition was. *Didn't she have any? Shouldn't she be able feel if Maggie was dead or alive?* Of course, she was a complete failure, Lorraine told herself. If she had any motherly instincts at all, she would never have let her kid go off by herself in the mall.

Chapter Twelve

Two weeks went by before Bernie and Sabrina came back to see Maggie again. Just like the first time, Maggie was instructed to sit on the chair naked and watch the adults engage in sex. When they were finished, the two adults got dressed.

"Maggie, let's get your clothes back on, and then we'll leave," Sabrina told her.

Maggie grabbed her T-shirt and slid it over her head. When she turned around, Sabrina was holding her underwear. "Come on. Let me help you," she told Maggie.

Maggie walked over to the bed where Sabrina was sitting. Putting her hand on Sabrina's shoulder, she put her right foot into her panties, and then her left. As Sabrina pulled the panties up for her, Maggie felt something poking her skin in the bottom of her underwear. She lifted her arm to reach back and find out what it was, but Sabrina quickly gave her a funny look that told Maggie not to do anything more. Bernie was still on the other side of the room buckling his belt.

"OK, Sabrina, it's time to go," Bernie said. Then he turned to Maggie. "We'll be back to see you again, and hopefully next time Aunt Sabrina will want you to join us instead of just sitting there playing with yourself. Wouldn't that be nice? Would you like that?"

"Sure," Maggie said without enthusiasm. "Whatever you and Aunt Sabrina want."

Maggie couldn't stop thinking about what was inside her panties. She hoped it wasn't something that would hurt her. By the look on Sabrina's face, she knew to wait until she was back in her cell. Maybe it was candy or a piece of gum, she thought hopefully.

After John William had locked all the kids in their cells that night, Maggie waited for over an hour before she reached into her panties and pulled out a small piece of paper. She slowly opened it and could see that something was written on it. In the dark of the cold, damp room, she squinted, straining her eyes to make out the message: *Flush all the notes down the toilet*.

Baffled by the message, Maggie went over to the toilet and looked down into the black abyss. The toilets in their cells didn't flush. Every few days, John William made Max open the metal flap with a stick and dump a bucket of water in each toilet to wash the waste down. Then he would let the flap close and dump another bucket of water in to fill it back up. Maggie sat down and peed. Then she took a small strip of newspaper they used as toilet paper and wrapped the note into it. She wiped herself and dropped it down the hole. Maggie didn't tell anyone about the note, not even Cali. She didn't know what the message meant, and she was afraid that Cali would be mad at her for bringing something from a client back to her cell.

The next night, all of the children except Shana were used by perverts and spit back into their cells. After John William locked Maggie's cell door, Cali called out to him. "John William, where's Shana? Is she OK?" she asked.

"Shut the fuck up and mind your own business," John William scolded. "She'll be back when she gets back. I don't answer to you, and if you ever question me again, I'll beat the shit out of you!"

"I'm sorry, John William," Cali immediately replied. "I didn't mean to upset you. I just wanted to know if you needed my help with anything. I mean, maybe you need me to talk to Shana and make sure she behaves," she babbled, trying to avoid a beating from John William.

"Well, when I need your help, I'll tell you to do something. Until that time, keep your mouth shut and stop interrogating me. You're my slave, and slaves don't get to ask questions or have an opinion. Understand?" he blurted. He stared at her, waiting for an answer.

"Yes, sir," Cali replied, wishing she could rip the metal door that separated them off its hinges and beat John William to death with it. Cali was a practical girl. She was raised to obey and respect adults, which is exactly what had landed her in sex trafficking.

When Cali was thirteen, she'd been walking home from school when a car pulled up next to her. The woman inside was hysterical. "My daughter was just in a car accident. I need to get to Beebe Medical

Center. They called and said she is probably going to die. I just have to get there. Do you know where it is?"

Cali, a compassionate girl, felt sorry for the woman, who looked to be the same age as her own mother.

"Yes, just turn right at the next light. Keep driving until you get to Savannah and make a left. Stay on Savannah, and you'll see Beebe on your right," Cali explained.

"Oh, please, honey," the woman begged, dabbing at her eyes with a tissue, "I can't remember all that. Just get in, and you can show me. Please, please, this may be my only chance to see my daughter before she dies."

Unfortunately, Cali got into the car with the woman, who turned around and drove in the opposite direction. On instinct, Cali reached for the door lever, but it had been removed. When she began to scream, the woman told her that a couple of men were sitting outside Cali's home, just waiting for a signal from her to kill Cali's mother. The woman drove her to an abandoned building nearby.

The woman shut off her car as Cali looked up at the old broken down building. Right before two men took Cali from the car, the woman leaned over and chastised Cali with a sneer. "You stupid girl. Didn't your mother ever tell you not to get into cars with strangers?"

Cali was forced into a van with other teens. She was taken to an isolated house, and since then, not a day had passed that she didn't regret her decision to get into the car with the stranger. She missed her family and home in Lewes, Delaware, as much now as she did when they took her four years ago.

Chapter Thirteen

———————■———————

Cali stayed up all night, waiting for John William to bring Shana back to her cell. Finally, at daybreak, she heard him trudging down the hall. She rushed over to her cell door and peered out the small window to see him dragging a lifeless Shana behind him.

As John William opened the cell doors, the children spilled out into the hallway. Cali didn't dare rush to Shana's cell. When John William opened Maggie's cell, he looked down at her with disgust. "I want you to go over to Shana's cell and fix her up. Something's wrong with the little wimp, and I expect you to figure it out and fix it."

Maggie scooted into Shana's cell. John William scraped his over-sized, sneakered feet on the floor as he followed her. Max and Cali exchanged worried looks. Shana was lying on her cot naked. Her hair was knotted, and her skin was raw, as if someone had rubbed sandpaper all over her body. Maggie's eyes were glued to Shana's feet. Both feet were covered in large, angry blisters.

"What did they do to her?" Maggie asked, feeling short of breath as icicles ran down her spine.

She looked at John William for an answer, but he continued to stare at Shana. "Just fix her. If she dies, it'll be your fault," he said coldly.

Maggie knelt down on the floor next to Shana. She looked at her raw flesh, afraid to touch her and scared that she might do something to hurt Shana more. Maggie could see that Shana had been burned. Based on what she had read, most of her body appeared to have first-degree burns. However, her feet were cherry red and blistered. Maggie fought back the fear that threatened to seize her own body and prevent her mind from functioning.

"We need to get her into the shower, fast!" Maggie said.

John William stepped into the hall where the other kids were huddled together, waiting to hear that Shana would be all right. "All of you back in your cells," he told the other kids.

After John William locked the last cell door, he went back and lifted Shana from her cot. He carried her to the shower and placed her on the broken floor tiles. Maggie ran to the nearest shower and turned on the cold water. Then she went back to Shana and gingerly dragged her under the water. She sat with Shana in her arms and let the cold water douse her entire body, but especially her feet, to bring down the temperature of her skin.

Almost thirty minutes later, Maggie's lips were turning blue and her teeth were chattering from the cold shower.

"We need to take Shana back to her cell. I'm going to need soap, water, and clean rags," Maggie delicately instructed.

Once back in the cell, John William left and returned with the items Maggie needed. She washed the blisters with soap and water and then she gently laid a clean cloth over the top of them. Maggie ran into her own cell and grabbed the pillow and wool blanket from her cot. She rolled them methodically and put them under Shana's feet to keep them elevated. There was nothing left for her to do but wait and pray that none of Shana's burns became infected.

Over the next twelve hours, Maggie stayed by Shana's side. Every couple of hours, Maggie would place cool water on a cloth and dab at the yellowish blisters on her feet. Shana, only half-conscious, moaned as the hours wore on. The blisters filled with fluid, and Maggie could only imagine how painful they were. Around dinnertime, John William stood at the doorway staring at Maggie.

"She's doing OK. She's in a lot of pain, John William. Is there anything you can give her to help?" Maggie almost begged.

John William's face showed no concern whatsoever. "Yeah, I'll get her something. Just make sure I'm not wasting my good drugs on this little tramp. You better be certain that she doesn't die. 'Cause if she ain't makin' money, then I ain't makin' money. You get me?"

"Yes," Maggie replied, almost offering to take on more clients for Shana.

When John William returned, he handed a small bag of pills to Maggie. "Give her one at a time."

"What are they?" Maggie asked.

"It's hillbilly heroin. Those little bastards will get her good and fucked up. Only give her one at a time. I don't need her overdosing on me. I've had enough drama out of that little bitch for one day. Just remember what I told you: if she fuckin' dies, it's your fault!"

In Maggie's desire to heal her "friend," she helped Shana swallow her first dose of OxyContin.

Chapter Fourteen

For the ten days that followed, young Maggie spent her nights satisfying clients and her days nursing Shana. Shana's feet were healing, and she was on a constant high from the hillbilly heroin. In her eagerness to numb herself to the pain caused by the burns, Shana quickly became addicted to the drug. Shana was callous with Maggie, reminding her at every opportunity that if Maggie hadn't stolen Myles from her, she never would have been burned.

Cali and Max were annoyed that Shana was so thankless to Maggie, who had slaved and watched over her. The two older teens sat on the floor next to Shana's cot. "You know, Shana," Cali said. "You could be nice to Maggie. She didn't do this to you. The kid has done nothing but help you. If you want to blame someone, blame all these fuckin' crazy pervs."

"I don't care what you say, Cali. I know what Maggie did. The minute she met Myles, she threw herself at him so that he would want her. You know it's true too!" Shana accused.

"Come on, Shana. Be real," Max chimed in. "She didn't even know Myles. He was the one who picked her, just like he picked you. Remember? We don't get to pick anything around here, and you know that. So knock off the shit, OK? It's just making it harder for all of us."

Shana shook her head but kept quiet.

"What happened, Shana? What did they do to you?" Cali finally asked.

Shana stared at the ceiling of her cell. Just thinking about the horrible things the man had done made her insides rattle. "It was a crazy older guy. He was into hurting me. At first, he was slapping me around the room. Then he took a brick out of his backpack. I thought he was going to bash my head in with it, but he just kept grating it all over my body. It fucking hurt like hell. He stopped and left the room for a while, but then he came back. He was carrying two plastic buckets, and I could see steam coming off the water. He started dancing and laughing when he saw how scared I was." She stopped and began to sob.

"Then he stuck your feet in the buckets of water?" Cali asked, unable to process the violence and cruelty that Shana had endured.

Shana nodded, but said nothing more.

"We have to get the fuck out of here," Max announced tearfully.

Cali looked at him, wishing it was possible but knowing there was little hope. She leaned over and pulled his head to her chest. She let Max cry until his last sob ended. She looked up at Shana, who was lying perfectly still on the cot, and wondered if any of them would make it out of there alive.

Maggie sat in her cell, reading a home-remedy book to Seth. He looked up at her with puppy dog eyes. "Aggie, I love you," he said with sweet innocence.

Seth adored Maggie; she was the person he turned to when he was scared. Seth and the others didn't know it, but it was his fifth birthday. Up until then, he'd been too innocent for sex trafficking, but now John William believed he was perfect for kiddy porn.

"I love you too, Seth," Maggie answered, feeling a tug at her heart for the small boy who she now felt belonged to her.

"Aggie? How comes you're crying in here at night sometimes?" Seth asked.

"Because I still miss my mom and dad a whole lot and I wish I could go home," she explained.

"But if you go home, are you going to leave me here?" the child asked with a pout.

"There's no way I'm leaving you here, Seth. You and me, we're family. We stick together, right?" Maggie stated.

"Yep. We stick together forever and ever. But when will we be able to go outside and play like you told me?" asked Seth, with the attention span of a gnat.

Maggie laughed at his abrupt shift to another topic. She pulled Seth closer to her and stroked his hair. "I don't know how or when, but I know something is going to change. I can feel it in my bones," she explained, more to herself than to Seth. "When we get out of here, we'll start our lives all over again. We can go to the park and sit on big blankets and eat ice cream. I bet our parents will be really good friends, and when we get old, we'll still be together every Christmas. We'll have a bond so strong that no one will be able to stand between us. I can see our kids growing up together. We'll never tell them about what happened to us in this rotten place, but we'll always know that we survived something horrible. I might even call my first son Seth. How does that sound?" Maggie finished, looking down at Seth.

Seth had fallen asleep in her arms, the rhythm of Maggie's sweet, soft voice allowing him to feel safe enough to let his eyes close. Even the five-year-old was keen to the evil that prowled throughout the prison.

That night, John William came for Seth. He took the young boy upstairs for the first time since he'd arrived in the godforsaken, abandoned building.

Seth was about to have his first photo shoot.

Chapter Fifteen

Maggie couldn't sit still while Seth was upstairs with John William. She worried about what they were doing to him. John William had only said, "They want him upstairs." He smiled as he watched her anxiety mount.

Two hours later, John William untied the child and carried him downstairs. As he was removing the tight knots from the nylon cord, John William obsessed on the thought of being tied up and confined. This fear had prompted anxiety attacks in John William since he was a child. Being tied to the chair under the stairs was far worse than the frequent beatings he received from his mother. *I'm in control now,* he reminded himself.

As John William put Seth into his cell, all of the other kids listened to the sounds of his tiny chest heaving in bitter sorrow.

"John William, please let me talk to Seth," Maggie begged from her cell.

"No. He's fine. Mind your own fucking business and go the hell to sleep. There are people coming to see you tonight," he told Maggie.

Maggie's stomach flip-flopped. Her worry for Seth still remained, but doing what clients wanted always made her edgy. Who and what would she face that night?

Later, Maggie sat on the edge of the bed, waiting for another client. Finally, she heard voices coming toward the room. She was relieved when she recognized Sabrina's laughter. Bernie entered the room first, followed by Sabrina.

"OK, let's change things up a little tonight, shall we?" Bernie stated.

"Well, um, like what?" Sabrina asked nervously.

"I was thinking that our stunning toy over here would participate," he said.

"Oh, Bernie, I don't know about that. I don't think I'm ready for Maggie to join us," Sabrina responded, batting her long eyelashes at him.

"Nah, not tonight, hon. Tonight, I get what I want for a change." Bernie turned to Maggie. "Take your clothes off." Then he looked at Sabrina. "You too."

Once Bernie had satisfied his deviant sexual desire, they all dressed. Sabrina slipped another note into Maggie's underwear. Alone that night in her cell, Maggie read the message: *Don't tell the others about me.*

Then, just like the first note had instructed, Maggie put the note in a small piece of newspaper and threw it into the toilet. For the first time in a little over a year, Maggie had a glimmer of hope that someone on the outside was going to rescue them.

Chapter Sixteen

———————————————— ▬ ————————————————

"Lorraine, how about if we take Keith to the park today? I think it would be good for all of us," Rob coaxed, sitting at the kitchen table with her.

"Nah. I have to look into some things, Rob. I read this article on missing children. It said to make a list of all the new, different, or unusual people that were around for a year prior to the kidnapping. I need to do research on all of the changes at the school and around our neighborhood. This could be the break we've been looking for. I just have too much to do," she explained.

"What kind of changes are you talking about?"

Lorraine perked up at his interest. "Well, they say you should find out if the school or anyone in the neighborhood did any remodeling or repairs. If they did, we get a list of contractors, take it to the police, and they'll be able to run some checks on all the people. The other thing I need to look at is all the home sales within an eight-block radius the year before Maggie was taken. Sometimes these maniacs go to open houses, like they're interested in buying a home, but they really just scope the neighborhood for kids."

Rob listened and couldn't argue with the logic behind what she said. Still, he couldn't help but ask, "How about if you tell Detective Harker, who you meet with every week, I might add, to do all of this stuff. Harker has more resources and easier access to this information than you do. I mean, Lorraine, that's his job. Besides, you know he'll do anything to help us find Maggie. I'm sure he would agree with me."

"I know, Rob. I also know that Harker is a good man and will never give up his search. But Maggie isn't the only case he's working on. No one is going to be as thorough as I am. I have to do these things myself. What if Harker gives it to some incompetent asshole who misses just one little piece of information? How would I ever be able to live with myself? I can barely live with myself now..." Lorraine's voice trailed off.

On several occasions, Rob tried to comfort his wife, but he, too, resented her for her poor judgment. He often told himself that if he had taken the kids to the mall that day, he would not have allowed his eleven-year-old to go off alone, not even for one minute. Other times, after he had a few drinks and couldn't hold back the unshakable bereavement that had cast a dull pain around his heart, Rob would sit in the basement alone and cry, unable to escape the hopelessness and feeling hatred toward Lorraine.

"OK, Lorraine. I'm not going to argue with you. But you can't forget that Keith is still here, and he needs us. If Maggie ever comes back to us, she needs to have a family to come back to," Rob said.

"If? What do you mean *if* she comes back to us? How can you give up so easily? I will keep looking until I find her. So go off to the park and do whatever it is that you do, OK, Rob? In the meantime, I'm going to look for our daughter," Lorraine growled, agitated by his apparent admission of defeat.

Rob left Lorraine sitting at the kitchen table, tears spilling down her cheeks as she wished that she could go back to the moment that she had made the worst decision of her life.

Chapter Seventeen

———————◼———————

In the weeks that followed, Maggie received two more notes from Sabrina. The first said, *I'm going to help you*. But it was the second note that filled Maggie with anticipation. It said, *I know who you are.*

Sabrina, whose real name was Abigail Loomis, was an FBI agent. She had been undercover for almost three years, working to break into the sex-trafficking cartel in the Northeast corridor. Her parents were told that Abigail had died in a car accident. The car had caught on fire, and the remains were charred beyond recognition. She had ruined her parents' lives to save the lives of innocent children.

Sabrina was immersed in her new life. She had no contact with the agency, except for the occasional anonymous note that she sent to the bureau, addressed to her commanding officer. The notes were always cryptic, just as she had been taught to write them. They gave little information. When she met and moved in with Bernie, the note read: *Living with one now*. There was never a return address, but the postmark always revealed the city in which she was living.

As Sabrina infiltrated the cartel and descended deeper into the sick world of pedophilia and human slavery, she wondered if she had the stomach to see it through until the end. Then she met Maggie. She had seen the girl's picture on a local television station when she had disappeared from the mall. The child's cobalt-blue eyes made her easy to identify. They were the most intense eyes she'd ever seen. When she saw the young girl standing in the room that first night, she knew she was Maggie Clarke, the eleven-year-old who had been kidnapped.

By chance, after several months of going to see Maggie with Bernie, Sabrina overhead two men chatting in a well-lit room while waiting to be taken to watch the children perform.

"Yeah, some guy told me last week that Al Capone served time here," she heard a wealthy looking, bald man tell his friend.

"Really? I wouldn't mind taking a look at the cell they kept him in," remarked the tall unattractive, unkempt fortysomething.

It was easy to figure out where they were after hearing that bit of information. Sabrina dragged Bernie to the library one day to take out a couple of books to read. While Bernie was skimming through years of *Sport Illustrated* swimsuit editions, Sabrina did some research on Al Capone. She found out that Capone had been incarcerated at a prison in Pennsylvania. Later that week, she wrote a note to her commanding officer. All it said was *Capone, PA Prison*.

Chapter Eighteen

Cali and Max noticed a change in Maggie. She seemed a little happier and more settled than the rest of them. While they were both relieved when any of the children showed signs of joy, Maggie's seemed to linger. They decided to find out what was going on with her. On a Saturday morning, after showers, Cali and Max went into Maggie's cell.

"Hey, Mags," Cali greeted. "What's going on?"

Maggie looked up from the new book that Dr. Barnes had given to her and smiled. "Nothing. Just reading this book that Dr. Barnes gave me. It's about a girl who gets her period," she said, showing them the cover of Judy Blume's book, *Are You There God? It's Me, Margaret*.

A smile crept onto Cali's face. She had read the same book right before she'd been kidnapped. While Cali reminisced, Max pursued the conversation. "So, you've been awfully upbeat lately. What's going on with you? One of your clients give you more candy?" he asked, trying to get her to open up.

"Nope. I wish," she stated simply, but her facial expression revealed there was something more.

"You look like you have a secret. We could all use a little sunshine, Maggie. Come on, what's got you so happy?" Max asked in a pleading voice.

Maggie loved the other kids, even Shana. But Max and Cali had been her rocks. They were always there for her and never let her down. Still, she remembered the note that instructed: *Don't tell the others about me.* Maggie felt a surge of guilt for holding out on her friends, the very people that she considered her family. She wanted to do what Sabrina had instructed, but she also wanted to share the news with the two people she trusted most.

Maggie's voice dropped to barely a whisper. "Did any of the clients ever say things and tell you not to tell anyone?"

The little hairs on the back of Cali's neck went stiff. "Like what kinds of things, Mags?" she asked gently.

"I don't know. Like things that make you feel good?" Maggie hedged.

"Well, once I had a guy who told me he was going to get me out of here and bring me home so that I could be his son," Max offered.

Cali chimed in, "Yeah, sure, there are always one or two people who promise to get you out. That just makes them feel more powerful. At first, you believe them and wait for them to make good on their promise. But months later, when you're still here, you know it was all bullshit. They get you all hyped up, and when nothing changes, you feel totally deflated. Did someone promise to get you out of here, Mags?"

"No, nothing like that." Maggie paused and filled her lungs with air as if she was getting ready to jump into a swimming pool. "That woman, Sabrina. She's been giving me notes. One of them said not to tell any of you guys about them."

Maggie looked at Max and Cali to see if they had a reaction. The looks on their faces told her that she had struck a nerve with them.

"It's nothing bad. It's just that her last note said, *I know who you are*," Maggie told them. "If Sabrina knows who I am, then maybe she'll send the police here, and we'll get to go home," she added, hoping the other two would agree.

Cali plopped on the cot next to Maggie. "Listen, Mags. First of all, it's really dangerous for you to bring notes back here. Where are they?"

"I wrapped them in newspaper and put them in the toilet," she admitted.

"OK, well, second, it would be really great if this Sabrina woman was for real, but I don't want you to get your hopes up. All these people know we've been taken from our families. They'll do and say whatever it takes to live out their own little fantasies," Cali explained.

"Yeah," Max added, "she might be turned on by making you think that she's gonna save you. It's always some fucked-up mind game with these pervs. I'm not saying it can't happen, but you gotta remember that none of these assholes wants to help us. If we get out of here, we could identify them, and they'd go to prison."

Maggie had never thought about any of the adults who had sex with kids going to prison. She accepted what Cali and Max were telling her—and even considered that there was a high likelihood that they were right. But she had a feeling about Sabrina. The other two weren't in the room with Sabrina. They didn't know that she was kind and looked at Maggie differently than any of the other clients had.

"But what if Sabrina is different? What if she's really going to help us?" Maggie protested.

"Then we will all be home soon," Cali assured her.

Max added, "Maggie, you sure are one special chick. I think you might just have enough hope for all of us. We just don't want you to be disappointed, OK? If nothing changes, we don't want you to be any sadder than you already are just being here. All right?"

"OK. But I still think that Sabrina is different. Just wait, you'll see," she told them with a child's optimism.

Max and Cali then changed the subject and started asking Maggie about some of the books she had read. She read almost three books a week now, and the older teens found her ability to retain information amazing.

While they were chatting excitedly, none of them knew that Shana had eavesdropped on their entire conversation.

Chapter Nineteen

The following week, after returning to her cell, Maggie pulled out the note that Sabrina had slipped into her panties that night. It read: *Help is coming.*

Maggie didn't throw the note down the toilet. Instead, she put the note in the toe of her worn sneaker and went with the group to breakfast. Once back in their cellblock, Maggie sought out Max and Cali. Removing her shoe, she pulled out the note and handed it to Cali.

"Fuck me," Cali breathed and handed the note to Max.

Max's adrenaline started to pump. They had both experienced empty promises, but Maggie's optimism had rubbed off on them over the past week.

"Christ! If this chick is for real, we're getting the fuck out of here soon. Oh my God, I could just piss my pants right now." Max's smile spread over his face. Even his eyes were smiling.

"So you believe me, right?" Maggie asked with excitement.

"I sure want to believe it, Maggie. I mean, I ain't gonna lie to you. I have my doubts. But I haven't felt this good in a long time. So even if it's all bullshit, at least I had the chance to feel this good again," Max said, looking to Cali for encouragement.

"You're right, Max," Cali announced. "Even if this turns out to be nothing, we deserve to enjoy this feeling of liberation for as long as we can."

Just then, they heard John William's heavy footsteps in the hallway. He stopped at Shana's cell. "Let's go, girl. We have someone that wants a little afternoon delight."

Shana froze. She was tired from the freak who had tied her hands and feet to the bedposts the night before as he repeatedly raped her. He had seemed unable to get enough of her. She was sore and mentally exhausted from the constant torment that her sick clients put her through. She had recently taken to giving John William blow jobs in the cafeteria in exchange for drugs. It was her goal to be high all the time so she didn't feel the pain and humiliation that accompanied her forced occupation.

After John William had shut and locked the door to the cellblock, Shana turned to him. "How about if I blow you for some dope?"

"Nah, that routine is getting old. What else you got?" he asked with authority.

Shana stammered, "I don't know, John William. I guess I could let you fuck me now, but the client might know."

"Hmmm, what else you got?" he asked, hoping she would offer something kinky, but knowing he could make her do whatever he wanted. He liked it when she pleaded with him for dope; it was an incredible high for him.

Shana thought hard about what she could offer him. She'd do anything to get drugs from him. She was a hardcore addict now. It got her through the sexual torture she had to endure.

"Well, I know a secret. Something about Maggie that I can tell you," Shana offered.

John William was surprisingly intrigued. "OK. First you blow me, and then you tell me the secret," he instructed.

When Shana was finished, she sat on the bathroom floor while John William pulled his pants up. "OK, so what's the secret you have for me?" he asked.

"Well, I overhead Maggie telling Cali and Max that there's a client who is giving her notes. One note said she knew who Maggie was, and the last note said that help was coming," Shana explained.

John William's posture turned rigid. He looked down at Shana with a pinched expression. "Oh really? That's good information. Where are these notes?"

Shana started to sweat, remembering they went down the toilet. "She put them in the toilet. But wait! Maggie was showing one to Cali and Max right before you came to get me today."

John William grabbed Shana under the arm and hoisted her to her feet. "Let's go. Your client is waiting."

"But…but…you promised me some hillbilly heroin," she begged.

The big buffoon reached into his pocket and took out two pills. He shoved them into her hand. "I need a little bit of water to take them."

His eyes narrowed into thin slits as he glared at her. "I don't care if you have to fucking chew them. There ain't no time for this shit. Take 'em or I'll take 'em back."

Shana threw the two pills into her mouth, crushing them with her teeth. The bitter taste tempted her to spit them out. But she kept chewing and swallowed them as fast as possible. She wanted them to take effect before her "afternoon delight" client.

Before John William sent her into one of the rooms on the main floor, he grabbed her shirt collar and put his nose to hers. "Where is Maggie keeping the note?"

Shana, feeling the initial effects of the magical drug, blurted, "She has the last one on her."

Chapter Twenty

John William stormed back to the cellblock. He strode into Max's cell, where they were all sitting. "You!" he said, pointing to Maggie. "Get naked, *now!*"

Maggie's skin started to tingle and a sudden dread hit her core. She quickly started to undress as the others watched. She stood naked and shaking before him. He was always in charge. He grabbed her shirt and pants one at a time and turned them inside out. Then he picked up her socks and inspected them. He had almost given up, thinking the little crack head, Shana, had lied to get drugs from him. He turned to leave and kicked Maggie's sneakers against the stone wall. He stopped suddenly and bent down to pick them up. He reached his fingers into the first sneaker, feeling around for what he was looking for. Nothing. He did the same with the other sneaker, and his large fingers skimmed over the note. He had felt the movement of the paper. Pulling the note out, his eyes bore into Maggie's.

"Well, what do we have here?" he asked in a demeaning tone.

"It's...it's just a note," Maggie answered. She unknowingly moved closer to Cali and Max, who were watching John William in horror.

"Let's see. It says, 'Help is coming.' Who gave this to you?" he hollered.

"I...I don't know," Maggie answered impulsively.

"Well, then I will just have to beat you until you remember," he stated.

He stepped forward and slapped Maggie across the face. Then he grabbed a handful of her hair and dragged her across the hall to her own cell. Still naked, she felt even more vulnerable. John William threw her on the floor and kicked her in the thigh. Maggie screamed, putting her hands over her face. "Please stop. Please, John William," she begged.

Cali rushed into the cell and stood before the monster. "She got the note from a woman named Sabrina. Please stop kicking her. She's just a little girl."

Satisfied that he had his answer, John William clamped his hand on Maggie's arm and pulled her up. He held on tightly as he dragged her along behind him. Max, Cali, and Seth looked on as they disappeared. The older teens were fearful they would never see Maggie again. Seth blubbered and held onto Max, who had picked him up during the beating they witnessed.

Upstairs, Maggie was forced to tell some of the higher-ranking cartel members everything that had happened. She told them the message on each of the notes. When she finished, she slumped in her chair, her fiery blue eyes devoid of any hope.

"Get her out of here," the top guy told John William.

Back in her cell, Maggie lay on her cot. Max and Cali tried to find out what happened upstairs, but she remained silent; her arms and hands were limp; her jaw hung loosely. Finally, she leaned up on one elbow. "I had to tell them everything. Our chance of getting out of here is gone, and it's all my fault," Maggie said bluntly.

"That's not true," Cali countered. "John William was looking for something when he came down here. Shana was the only one who was with him. She must've overheard us talking and told him about the notes."

Max nodded his head. "Look, Mags, you did what you had to do. They would've killed you if you didn't tell them everything."

Maggie curled up on the dirty cot. She thought about what she had just done. The odds were that they would never allow Sabrina to come and see her again. She liked Sabrina. Then she wondered if that spooky Bernie would come back to see her without Sabrina. She hoped not.

Little Maggie didn't know what any of this meant. But she would soon find out.

Chapter Twenty-One

That night, Bernie was called into a private meeting with two high-ranking cartel members. They explained what had transpired. They didn't need to explain the consequences.

The next morning, while walking her dog in Penn Treaty Park in Fishtown, a woman in her late thirties saw Sabrina's bare foot sticking out from under a large bush. She moved closer to get a better look, thinking her eyes had deceived her. That's when she saw Sabrina. She was naked and lying on her back. Her eyes were open; her pupils flat. Her throat had been cut so deeply that the woman could see her neck bone. Sabrina's head remained attached to her body only by the skin on the back of her neck. The woman started to scream and wave her hands wildly. Her dog was barking, unable to handle the sudden burst of emotion from his owner. Others flocked to the spot where the woman was screaming. Hands flew to mouths and throats as they took in the death that lay before them.

The forensic team studied Sabrina where she lay lifeless in the park. Sabrina's furrowed brows created long lines on her forehead. Her eyes bulged slightly, and her lips were locked in a tense pucker. Cuts and bruises on her inner thighs made the detectives certain that she'd been sexually assaulted even before the coroner had a chance to examine the body. Sabrina's grotesquely contorted facial features showed a combination of terror and pain. Based on all of the evidence they found on the body, the forensics team determined that she had been tortured for many hours before being killed.

Back at the prison, the cartel moved quickly. The five children were blindfolded, shackled, and loaded into a van. The van was driven at a high rate of speed for thirty minutes, and then parked. The back doors were opened, and several men roughly pulled the children out and escorted them into a farmhouse owned by the cartel in Skippack, Pennsylvania. There was a dilapidated barn several hundred yards from the equally broken-down house. There were no neighbors or other buildings for at least five miles.

The children were taken inside and led down to a basement twice the size of the house above it. The children looked around at the cinderblock walls and dirt floor. Soot from the old coal-burning furnace covered every surface like a thick layer of tar. In place of cells, each child was put into a large dog kennel. The kennels, constructed of chain link fencing with a door and a key lock, had been used for other children three years ago. Each contained a crib-size mattress. The only improvement to the children's living conditions was they could now see and speak to each other freely without the stone walls separating them. The downside was that they would share one open toilet in the corner of the basement.

When the children were left alone in the basement, Cali spoke first. "Shana! What did you do? What did you tell John William?"

Shana was feeling sick; she wanted more hillbilly heroin. "What does it matter? At least we got out of that nasty fucking place we've been living in. I don't know why the fuck you care where we are. It's all the same shit."

"What did you tell him, Shana? How the fuck could you do this to us?" Max asked.

"I told him about the notes that woman gave to Maggie. So what? It doesn't mean anything. Nothing happened to little Miss Wonderful over there," Shana stated, pointing to Maggie.

"We don't know what's going to happen to any of us now. That's the point, Shana. You put us all at risk. Why would you do something so stupid?" Max pressed.

"Because I wanted to get fuckin' high, OK? I need to get high so that I don't chew my own fuckin' arm off. You don't know what these pricks are doing to me. They hurt me, really, really bad! I just want this to end! I can't live like this anymore," Shana yelled.

Cali raised her voice. "We know it's hard, Shana. We all know you're going through really bad shit. But telling John William things that are none of his business won't help any of us. They could have killed Maggie for keeping secrets. You know that!"

"I wish they would kill her!" Shana responded. "Then maybe things would go back to normal."

"There is no normal for us," Max stated.

The three of them went silent, and the air grew thick with tension. "Shana, I know you hate me, and you think I did something to you on purpose. I really didn't do anything, I swear. And I don't blame you for telling John William what you heard. I know you're in a lot of pain, and the medicine helps you feel better. I just wish you didn't want me to die. All I want is to go back to my family. I'm not mad at you for what you did," Maggie said.

Shana stood and paced the kennel. She rubbed the back of her neck, trying to loosen her muscles to relieve the headache she'd had for hours. Now, in a sober moment, she regretted telling John William about the notes. She thought about the implications; maybe that woman was for real, and they would have been rescued. *Did she just blow it for all of them? What would John William and Myles do to that woman? What'll they do to Maggie?* Shana collapsed on the mattress and covered her face with her hands. She rubbed her temples but wouldn't make eye contact with anyone. She was too embarrassed to face the other kids. She may have blown their only ticket out of this nasty game.

With the children in their new location, only their long-term clientele, those who could be trusted, were told about the farmhouse. That night, the reconstruction of their business began. All of the children, including Seth, were taken upstairs. They were all to participate in a new feature film.

Chapter Twenty-Two

———————— ■ ————————

Detective Harker rang the Clarkes' doorbell. It was early in the morning, and Lorraine answered it with her hair and night-clothes in disarray.

"Harker. What are you doing here? Did you find Maggie?" Lorraine barked.

"No. But we think something significant happened. Can I come in?" Harker asked.

"Sure." Lorraine led him into the kitchen. She started a pot of coffee and then sat at the table across from Harker. "What happened?" she asked.

"The FBI contacted us. Early this morning, an agent was found dead at Penn Treaty Park. Apparently, the agent has been undercover for several years. Her mission was to find a way into the sex-trafficking ring," Harker explained.

"Wait, wait." Lorraine stood quickly, knocking over her chair. Her skin felt like it was burning. "Sex trafficking? You think my daughter is being sold for sex?"

Harker stood up next to Lorraine. He put his hand on her shoulder and looked directly into her eyes. "We don't know, Lorraine. But if she is, this agent infiltrated further than anyone in the bureau has before. The thing is, she was so deep undercover that she didn't talk to any-one at the FBI about what was going on. She sent very cryptic notes to her commander—almost a hundred notes over the last three years with only a few words on them. Her commander said they've pieced together most of the story. They knew she was living in Pennsylvania, and her last note, which he received after she died, vaguely mentioned a prison."

Lorraine felt her insides come to life. Her heart was pumping, and she was filled with an energy she hadn't had in a long time. She fidgeted as she considered the possibility that Maggie was forced into sex trafficking, a thought that made her knees weak. "So, what you're telling me is that you think Maggie could still be alive?"

"What I'm telling you is we still have nothing to indicate that Maggie is alive. However, we are waiting on further instructions from the FBI. Hopefully, they will provide us with useful leads. We may be able to find out where they are holding children. There's a chance that Maggie is being trafficked. I don't want to give you false hope about her being alive. I just want you to know there's a possibility," he stated.

My Maggie is still alive, she thought. *My baby is still alive*!

Lorraine sat at the kitchen table and put her hands around her mug. She took a long sip of the rich coffee. It had been a while since she'd actually tasted anything. That morning, the sugar and cream she mixed in her coffee filled her mouth. The flavors played over her taste buds, creating a sensation she hadn't felt in a long time…being alive. Her faith ignited and began a slow burn that warmed her heart.

Chapter Twenty-Three

All of the children were taken upstairs that night. The stairway from the basement was narrow and creaky. When they reached the main floor, the house was dark, and it was hard to take in their surroundings. They were led into a large living room. A bed had been set up in the middle with black lights overhead. Seth clung to Maggie's leg, his fingers burrowing into her thigh.

"It'll be OK, Seth," she whispered to him.

It wasn't long before the music started, and the children were told what to do as a group. Maggie held tightly to Seth's hand, and as Max pulled her onto the bed, she took Seth with her. The child was lying on his belly, and Maggie straddled him to keep his upper body out of view of the camera. She subtly reached her fingers into Seth's mouth and quickly shoved them as far down his throat as possible. Seth vomited all over the other children. John William came storming in on them. "Little fucking jerk off! What the hell is wrong with you?"

Seth looked uneasily at Maggie. She responded for him. "He's too young, John William. He's nervous and doesn't know what's going on or what's happening to him."

Seth sat on the bed holding Maggie around the waist as soaking tears fell from his eyes. To Maggie's relief, John William snatched Seth away from her and half carried, half dragged the small boy back down to the basement. She had spared Seth this time.

The next morning, the children were fed breakfast in their kennels. Then, two at a time, they were taken upstairs to shower. Maggie and Seth, the two youngest, went first. The steps from the basement were made of wood logs split in half, flat side up. They walked through the kitchen and into the enormous living room. Wooden beams ran the length of the ceiling. The plaster walls were cracked and chipped from years of settlement and neglect.

Two old chairs covered in red velvet sat where the bed had been the night before. Maggie noticed thin, lace curtains on the windows that overlooked the backyard. She strained to get a glimpse of the outdoors. She hadn't seen the sky or the sun since John William had stolen her. As she walked by the windows, the sun lit up the lace, and she could see there were things in the backyard...abandoned objects.

John William led them down a long corridor with rooms on either side. About midway down, he stopped and instructed Maggie and Seth to go inside. The windows of the bedroom were covered with fabric; no outside light entered the room. A king-size mattress was shoved up against the wall farthest from the door. To their right was a large fireplace; to the left, another door led into the bathroom, where a claw-foot tub sat on old and broken gray tiles.

"Let's go. Fill up the tub. You two bathe together. I ain't got time to take care of that little asshole," John William stated, gesturing toward Seth.

Maggie rushed to fill the tub with water. "Come on, Seth. Take your clothes off. We need to get a bath," she told him.

The small boy looked over at John William and took stiff, jerky steps away from the overgrown brute. The man scared the shit out of Seth.

"Come on, Seth," Maggie coaxed. "Let's get you undressed."

"Aggie, I don't want to take a baff," he told her, keeping his eyes glued on John William.

John William enjoyed watching Seth tremble with fear, "Get your filthy ass in that tub, or I'll give you something to be scared about," he roared.

Maggie used a bit of force on the boy to get him undressed. She lifted him up and placed him in the tub. She was starting to climb in with him when John William spoke again. "Come over here, you little whore," he ordered her.

Maggie walked over to him slowly, acutely aware that she still might be punished for her part in harboring the notes from Sabrina. Standing before him, she put one arm over her flat chest and covered her crotch with her hand. John William forced her hands to her sides and looked her over. "Myles is coming to pay you a visit tonight. I hope you get everything that you deserve. No one does stupid shit behind his back and gets away with it. You thought you were so clever, hiding your little notes, thinking that fucking bitch was going to save you. Well, now you see where it got you. Nowhere!"

Maggie's face dropped to the floor. Looking at John William was almost as painful as hearing his maddening voice. He droned on and on, berating them constantly. Maggie hated him. She stood perfectly still, holding her breath, until finally he slapped the side of her head as a gesture of dismissal. She turned and climbed into the bathtub with Seth.

Maggie washed the young boy quickly and then herself. John William's words played over in her mind: *I hope you get everything you deserve.* The anxiety of Myles's visit grated on her nerves. By the time she was returned to her kennel, her breath was short, and her throat was tight.

"Maggie? What's wrong?" Cali asked, as she watched her friend lose it.

"Myles is coming to see me tonight. John William said I'm in trouble. I'm scared, Cali. What if he kills me? Then I'll never go home again," she whined, not able to express the depth of her worry with words.

"Good!" Shana yelled. "I hope he beats the shit out of you. Then you'll get a taste of what you did to me."

"Stop it, Shana!" Cali barked. Then she looked back at Maggie. "Mags, everything will be OK. You're gonna have to play dumb. Just tell Myles you didn't know what to do with the notes. Tell him the woman forced you to take them and threatened to tell lies about you. Do whatever you have to do to curb his anger. OK, Mags? Do you hear what I'm saying?" Cali persisted.

But Maggie was lost in her own sick thoughts. She started to shake and broke into a cold sweat. There was nothing for any of them to do but sit and wait for Myles to arrive and dish out Maggie's punishment.

Chapter Twenty-Four

When Maggie reached the top of the ladder, it opened into the attic. She gasped at her surroundings. The wooden rafters were exposed. The walls were the original wooden sheathing of the house. They were water stained where rain had leaked through the battered roof. A small lamp on a desk at the other end of the attic cast an eerie glow, throwing shadows across the room. The dust-covered floor creaked as Maggie walked toward Myles.

Several men stood around the desk where Myles was sitting. He peered over at her, his black mood penetrating her entire being. She could hear the sound of her heart in her ears—boom, boom, boom. Her legs went limp, and she fell to the floor. She didn't want to live, yet the thought of death made her more afraid.

"Take a bow, Maggie. You've managed to put our entire operation in jeopardy," Myles said. He stood and moved around the desk. "You think you're pretty smart, don't you?"

Maggie shook her head, unable to utter a word. It was as if her tongue was glued to the roof of her mouth. She looked up at Myles, her eyes begging for mercy. Myles was wearing a white wife-beater; his tanned arms and shoulders looked as if they were chiseled from stone. His muscles were tense, and his jaw was taut.

"Please, I'm so sorry," Maggie pleaded in a quiet voice.

"Sorry isn't enough, Maggie. What you've done can't be excused. When you do bad things, you'll always be punished. That's what you're about to learn. You're nothing but a rotten kid, and from now on, you'll be treated just like all the others."

Myles's bitter, seething voice had the impact he had intended.

Thoughts of Shana flashed through Maggie's mind. Shana had sustained ruthless brutality. Maggie shuffled across the floor on her hands and knees in a feeble attempt to get away from Myles. But there was nowhere to run.

"That's right, go on and slither into the corner, you little fucking snake. There's nothing that's going to protect you," Myles said, confirming her mounting fear.

Myles turned on his heel and addressed the other men in the room. "Let's go," he told them. "John William, you know what I expect you to do."

The men followed Myles down the ladder and left Maggie alone in the attic with John William. He approached and towered over her. His breath came out in bull-like puffs. His hands dangled at his sides as if they were dead weight. He leaned into Maggie, his demonic eyes alive with craziness. He purposely unbuckled his belt and slid it out of each pant loop slowly to give her the full effect. Then he lifted the belt and brought it down hard on her. The slap of leather stung her skin. The buckle ripped holes in her cheap, thin T-shirt. Maggie curled into a ball and covered her head with her hands. But it was no use. Nothing would prevent the punishment that awaited her.

Three days later, John William delivered her back to the kennel. Cali and Max stood as he roughly carried her in and practically threw her on the thin mattress. She was naked. Her body was covered in bruises, welts, and angry red marks that looked like circles of blood. Maggie never opened her eyes, and the others, with the exception of Shana, hoped that she wasn't dead or near death.

"John William, please let me help her," Cali begged.

"You can't even help yourself, bitch. Be quiet or you'll be next," John William barked. Then he locked Maggie's kennel and trudged up the stairs, shutting off the light before slamming the door. In the blackness of their homemade dungeon, Cali tried to get Maggie to speak.

"Mags? Are you OK? Mags? Can you hear me? Come on, baby, answer me. Let me know you're alive. Sweetie, give us a sign. Tell us about one of the books you've read. Come on, Mags, *please*," Cali begged. Then she sat against the chain link fence of her own kennel, unable to stop the flood of tears. Feeling helpless and frustrated, Cali allowed herself to let the heavy sobs control her. Cali ached to hold Maggie and willed her to be alive.

Eventually, even Shana began to worry whether Maggie would be OK. After all, Maggie *had* healed her many times, and she never *really* wanted her to die. On the other side of the room, Max was consumed with consternation. He tried to be strong for all of them and fill them with an optimism he didn't feel.

"She's going to be fine," he said. "As soon as John William comes back, we'll ask him to let us help her. Maggie is strong. She's a survivor."

But no one believed him any more than he believed himself.

Chapter Twenty-Five

Cali had just fallen asleep when she heard a small groan escape from Maggie. Her senses sprang to life. "Mags? Mags? Are you awake? Mags, talk to me."

But there was no response; maybe she'd dreamed it, Cali thought.

Just then, Seth, who had slept through all the commotion, called out, "Aggie? I'm scared. I had a dream about a monster that was gonna eat me."

Seth's voice broke through, and Maggie's mind began to swim back to the surface from the deep place it was hiding. "Seth," she whispered. "I'm right here. It was only a dream."

"Mags? Oh my God! Mags, you're alive!" Cali squealed.

Then the others heard Maggie as she dry heaved. She hadn't eaten anything in days, and she was dehydrated. On the second day of isolation, Maggie had squirted a small amount of urine into her hand and had drunk it. That was the extent of her intake in the three days they kept her from the others.

Maggie made animal like noises as her stomach rose and fell in violent spasms. "Try to crawl toward my voice, Maggie," Cali instructed. "Come over to me. Let me help you."

Maggie's fingernails dug into the dirt floor as she pulled herself toward Cali's voice. Cali stretched out against the chain link fence, slid her hand through, and began to stroke Maggie's face. As she drifted back to sleep, Cali stayed awake, never taking her hand off Maggie.

In the morning, when John William went to the basement to awaken the children, Cali begged him to let her help Maggie eat. "She's going to die, John William."

Myles had instructed John William to make sure that Maggie lived. But he acted as if he had to consider Cali's request. "What are you gonna do for me?" he asked dryly.

"Anything you want! Just let me go in with her," Cali pleaded.

John William took Cali by the arm, unlocked Maggie's kennel, and pushed Cali forward. He came back a few minutes later and threw down two bowls of oatmeal and two glasses of water. Cali rushed over and grabbed the water. She put Maggie's head in her lap and got her to swallow small amounts of water. Then slowly, with the patience of a saint, she fed Maggie the oatmeal.

It took several days for Maggie to regain her strength. Seeing the improvement, Max and Cali set out to understand what had happened to her.

"Maggie, what did Myles do to you? You know, they kept you away from us for about three days," Max offered from his kennel.

"I can't remember everything, Max. I know they took me up to the attic. I remember some of the stuff they did. There were a lot of men; all of them had sex with me. It wouldn't end. Most of them hit me and..." Maggie's voice trailed off at the memory.

"And what, Mags?" Cali pressed.

"And they brought me out to a barn in the middle of the night. First, they put chains on my hands and hung me by my wrists. After a long time, I couldn't stand the pain anymore. I thought the chains were going to cut my hands off my arms. After a while, they hung me from my feet. They jabbed me with lit cigars. That's where the burns are from," Maggie explained, pointing to her hips and lower abdomen.

"When I woke up, I wasn't in the barn anymore," Maggie continued. "I was in a small cage. I could barely move because it was so tiny." Maggie began to shake. "After that, every time they had to pee, they would do it into the cage I was in. They said I was their toilet. The last thing I remember is them throwing a whole bunch of snakes in the cage with me. I couldn't get them off me. I was freaking out. All the men were laughing at me. Some of the snakes bit me...and then I woke up here," Maggie said. She sat on the dirt floor, grabbed fists full of hair on either side of her head, and rocked back and forth.

Cali grabbed Maggie and held her tightly.

"I'll n-n-never do a-a-anything to try to g-g-g-get away a-a-again," Maggie stuttered.

Cali looked at Max across the room. Then, she turned and looked over at Shana, who was lying in a fetal position on the dirt floor of her kennel, scared that what had happened to Maggie would happen to her next.

Chapter Twenty-Six

While Myles still saw Maggie regularly, he also opened her up to more clientele. He didn't trust the girl any longer, and as a result, her days of being sold only to his high-paying perverts were over. On the main floor of the house, the original homeowners had built a study with floor-to-ceiling bookshelves. The cartel converted the study into a waiting room for clients. For entertainment, they had erected a pole in the middle of the floor.

When John William informed the three girls that they would dance and strip for the waiting clients, Maggie pursed her lips, and her eyes bulged as if she was about to go into a full-blown seizure. Shana, on the other hand, no longer cared what she had to do. She was constantly high. Shana took pills from John William and any of the clients who offered them to her. Drugs weren't a problem, in the eyes of the cartel, if it meant the kids would be more desirable. That's exactly what drugs did for Shana. She was willing to perform sexual acts without the slightest trace of resistance. She gave herself over to them completely.

"Cali, I can't dance," Maggie confided, when John William left them alone in the basement. "What am I supposed to do?" She was always on edge now, fearing they would severely punish her again.

"Well, I'm going to teach you how, so don't worry about it. Besides, Maggie, you can do anything. Never forget that," Cali assured her.

Cali had loved gymnastics as a young girl. Before she was kidnapped, she'd dreamed of going to the Olympics and winning a gold medal. Those skills would come in handy now in her fucked-up life.

While Maggie had recovered physically from the trauma of her punishment, she had lost her sense of independence and confidence. Cali wanted Maggie to regain her spirit, and she was determined to teach her how to dance. She would have done anything to help Maggie.

She knew that the young girl was special. Cali didn't know why or how, but she was certain that Maggie's life would have meaning.

Maggie was processing the new information. "If I can dance, does that mean I won't be sold for sex anymore?"

"No, baby. It means that you'll be able to dance for the clients while they are waiting their turns. I'll teach you how to dance and strip," Cali explained.

"Strip? I have to strip?" Maggie whined. She already hated what she was doing with strange men.

"Really, Mags? What's the difference? You have to strip when you're alone with these assholes. It just means there'll be more guys watching you, that's all. Hopefully, the guys that are willing to sit around and watch won't be as crazy as the assholes that blow in here, fuck us, and leave," Cali said, trying to present the "bright" side.

"OK. I guess so, Cali. What do you think, Max?" she asked, knowing he was listening to their conversation.

"I think it might make things easier for you. Like Cali said, the guys who are willing to sit around and wait could be less violent," Max told her.

"I hate this," Maggie declared, but she was resigned to doing what was expected of her. "But you swear you'll show me everything you know? I don't want to piss Myles off. I never want them to punish me again."

That same afternoon, John William took the three girls up to the second floor. They all stood around the pole, looking at it as if aliens had just plunked it down in the middle of the floor. John William turned on the music. "Let's go. I want to see what you got."

Cali quickly stepped up and began dancing with one hand on the pole. She used some of the moves from the gymnastics routine she had memorized for competitions in middle school. Then she put her left hand on the pole above her head and placed her right hand at waist height. In one swift movement, she swung her legs up, clamped the pole with her knees, and let her head hang.

Maggie watched in awe as Cali manipulated her body in different ways. Cali was fluid and graceful. It all looked so easy. Cali's feet were back on the floor, and she began to shimmy up the pole as if she were a monkey. As soon as her feet hit the floor a second time, John William stopped the music. "You are supposed to strip, you brainless tramp!"

When John William turned the music back on, Cali began to strip, and when the song finished, he seemed somewhat satisfied with her performance. Then Cali walked over and put her hand on Maggie's shoulder.

Maggie flinched at her touch. She couldn't imagine doing all the things that Cali had just done. Not without looking like a complete fool.

Cali leaned in closer to Maggie. "Come on, Mags. It'll be fine. I'm gonna show you everything."

Chapter Twenty-Seven

Maggie awkwardly held onto the stripper pole and danced at the same time. She was embarrassed and doing everything in her power not to break down and cry. When she looked over at John William, his eyes narrowed and glittered with malicious amusement. Seeing this, she straightened her back and closed her eyes to hear the rhythm of the music. She allowed her hips to sway; she bent her knees and elegantly waved her arms, as if they were wings. Maggie hated John William, and deep inside she suspected that he knew that she was far smarter and wiser than he would ever be.

Cali instructed Maggie on how to work the pole. She talked her through all the movements until the music stopped. The two girls looked at each other when it was over, both feeling victorious and sharing the exhilaration of achieving something in the face of John William's skepticism.

Witnessing their excitement, John William said, "That sucked, Maggie. You dance like you have a stick shoved up your ass. You better learn to dance, little girl, or I'll tell Myles you can't do it. Then you'll be completely useless to him, and who knows what he'll do to you."

At the thought of making Myles angry, Maggie's blood starting pulsing faster through her body, and she felt like she was going to faint. She stared at the wall in front of her and remembered what she'd read in one of the meditation books that Dr. Barnes had brought for her. *Block everything out and concentrate on breathing evenly. Empty your mind and don't think about anything but your breath. Inhale, exhale.* Within a couple of minutes, Maggie was able to slow her own heart rate and suppress her anxiety.

Maggie scooped up her clothes and dressed quickly. She stood back against the wall as Shana walked up to the pole and began to dance.

Before she grabbed the pole, she lifted her shirt with her thumbs, exposing her belly as she danced, and then finally removed it. She unbuttoned her jeans and slid them over her flat hips, exposing the tiny panties she was wearing, and then leaned back against the pole and started sliding down as she spread her legs apart.

John William began to feel a sexual stirring. Shana was blitzed out of her mind, which contributed to her sleazy performance. She was sitting on the floor, leaning against the pole, with her legs spread wide. One hand was in her panties, and she rubbed her own breast with the other. She masturbated until she came. John William, hormones raging through his gargantuan, beastlike body, walked over to Shana and undid his pants. Cali and Maggie had no choice but to stand on the sidelines and watch him fulfill his sick lust for Shana. His movements were jerky as he rammed himself between her legs. He gritted his twisted, yellow-brown teeth, and his fleshy eyelids fluttered until he twitched and convulsed as if he was having a full-blown seizure. It was the most repulsive scene the two girls had ever witnessed.

John William stood as Shana slowly got dressed, still groggy from the dope and the orgasm she'd given herself. She smiled at Cali and Maggie as she staggered over to them. "Who needs a fucking pole when I got a hole," she chanted in a sickening voice.

"Stop it!" Cali threatened, her teeth clenched.

"Why? Why should I stop? If you can't beat 'em, you might as well join 'em. I'm tired of getting my ass kicked all the time. At least I know how to fucking please a man," she said, raising her voice.

"Just because they are treating you like a whore, doesn't mean you have to act like one," Cali threw back at her.

"Whatever, Cali. I really don't give a shit what you think. All you ever worry about is little Miss Wonderful here," she said, and gave Maggie a sternum poke.

Instinctively, Maggie took a step backward and covered her chest. Her eyes dropped to the floor. She didn't want to fight with Shana, who was clearly stoned. Maggie felt sorry for her. They were all unhappy with their circumstances, but inside, Shana was a simmering pot of oil just waiting to boil over.

"Let's go, maggots, back to your kennels," John William ridiculed.

That day marked a significant passage for Maggie. She had finished her first lesson in pole dancing and stripping. She didn't know it then, but those lessons would someday save her life.

Chapter Twenty-Eight

—————————————◼—————————————

"Did you find her?" Lorraine snapped, as she flung open the door after seeing Detective Harker through the peephole. "Lorraine, I have something that I want to show you," Rae Harker explained.

Harker reached into his pocket and removed a small plastic bag. Inside was a white, flat stud earring with a purple and green daisy painted on the surface. He handed the small bag to Lorraine.

She looked at the bag closely. She focused on what was inside, allowing her eyes to adjust and take in the small object. A slow smile came to her lips as the realization of what she was seeing sank into her whole, physical being. Then her stomach squeezed into a tight knot, and her heart felt heavy. She didn't know what he was going to say once she revealed what she knew.

Lorraine looked up at Detective Harker with a perplexed look. "This earring belongs to Maggie. Where did you find it? She's dead, right? You're here to tell us she's dead," she accused.

Harker knew the earring belonged to Maggie. He had seen the earrings a million times as he gazed at the picture of Maggie that was propped up on his desk.

"No, Lorraine," Harker said sternly, grabbing her arm to steady her. "We didn't find her, and we don't know that she is dead. The FBI sent local police to all of the abandoned prisons in the state to see if we could find anything. We checked out an abandoned prison close to here. It looks as though people were living in some of the cells. In one of those cells, our team found this earring."

"An abandoned prison?" Lorraine asked in disbelief. "What are you saying, Harker?"

"I'm saying that if our theory is accurate, Maggie could have been one of the people who was living there. Remember that woman from the FBI I told you about? The one we found murdered?" Harker asked.

Lorraine nodded.

"Well, we think the cartel realized that she was an undercover agent. They probably killed her and moved their captives somewhere new," Harker explained.

Lorraine moved over to the sofa and plopped down on it. She ran her hand through her hair several times, thinking about what she just heard. "How…how many other cells were lived in?" she finally managed.

"It looks like five of them," Harker said.

A gurgling sound escaped from Lorraine's throat. "She isn't alone. That means she's not alone. I have gone to the brink of madness thinking about her with some maniac all by herself. But now I know she isn't alone. There are others with her?" she asked desperately.

"Lorraine, all this earring tells us is that there's a strong possibility that Maggie was kept there. We still don't know *if* she's alive and *if* we will ever find her. We'll keep searching, I promise you that. But I want you to understand that none of this means shit until we actually find her. OK?" Harker asked with heartfelt concern.

Lorraine nodded and let her head rest on the back of the sofa. It finally registered with Lorraine that her beautiful, intelligent daughter was being sold for sex. Her child was a sex slave. Images of Maggie being fearful and alone played in her mind's eye until she couldn't stand it a moment longer.

Then Lorraine shut her eyes and had a long, sorrow-filled cry.

Chapter Twenty-Nine

Over the next several weeks, Cali, Shana, and Maggie took turns dancing for the clients. Cali was a superstar, although most of their clients wished she were younger. Shana was sloppy, but her overtly sexual moves kept her afloat. It was Maggie who drew the most attention. She was learning new moves from Cali. She was beginning to take control of her body as she got lost in the music. Her stunning beauty made up for her inexperience at dancing and her lack of athletic ability on the pole. Despite her awkwardness, it wasn't long though before Maggie became the featured dancer.

In his late teens, Max was beginning to show signs of becoming a man. His body had filled out, and he was sprouting facial hair. Both he and Cali were "outgrowing" their desirability to clients. Because of this, Max was often sold to men who liked to dominate. Max began to grow intolerant of being trafficked. His clients had become rougher with him, and it became more difficult for Max not to strike back.

It was a Friday night, and the house was packed. Men were littered throughout the main living area, all of them drinking and smoking heavily. The cartel had brought in six other kids for the weekend. It was the beginning of spring, and the cartel had circulated word of a special weekend to its clientele.

Max was bought at auction for a measly two hundred dollars. The man who bought him for the evening stood six feet tall. He had a thick head of matted, white hair. His brown eyes were barely visible under his drooping eyelids, and his left eye rolled off to the right while the other eye looked Max over with hunger. The blubber of his neck swallowed his chin, and rolls of skin flapped over the top of his collarbone like a turtleneck sweater made out of flesh. He hoisted his massive body from the chair and followed Max and John William into one of the bedrooms.

Max had been with some ruthless clients over the years. But this man, that the cartel called Marsh, had an insatiable appetite for young boys. Marsh was heartless. He was born without the ability to feel empathy or sympathy. He was the worst kind of predator. He never viewed any of the children as human beings; they were merely a way to satisfy his sexual needs.

"Let's go," Marsh ordered. "Take those clothes off, rodent."

Max had a really bad feeling about Marsh. His teenage hormones, which had lain dormant for the last couple of years, began to awaken. The fight-or-flight instinct was building inside him. His muscles began to tighten as he battled against his own desire to indulge in combat with Marsh.

Max forced himself to undress. His body stiffened as he looked at Marsh, who then ordered the teen to help him undress. When Max didn't do what he was told, Marsh took a few steps toward him and slapped him across the face.

"When I give you a command, I expect you to obey me, BOY!" Marsh yelled.

When Max still didn't move, Marsh reached into his coat pocket and took out a billy club. He placed the strap around his wrist and turned back to Max, who saw the club.

Marsh raised the club and landed a blow on Max's shoulder. The teen was knocked off balance and fell to the floor. Marsh dropped on top of him and began whacking him on the back with the club. Once Max was subdued, Marsh struggled out of his clothes, forced Max onto his knees, and made him lean over the bed. As he violently took Max, he hummed.

"Now, time for a little rest," Marsh said when he finished. "Then we go again. In fact, we're gonna go all night, my little bitch boy," he mocked.

Less than an hour later, Marsh stood over Max, who was still lying on the floor. He bent down, and Max opened his eyes to look at the swine who had already hurt him badly with the billy club.

"Come on, boy. Get up on your knees," Marsh instructed.

Max, intent on giving the man what he wanted so that he wouldn't beat him again, complied. When Marsh told Max to perform oral sex, the teen hesitated. Max didn't see the thick chain wrapped around Marsh's hand. When the heavy chain hit the side of Max's head, he was sure his skull was cracked open. Blood gushed from his hairline, and a steady stream ran down his arm.

Marsh swiftly wrapped the chain around Max's neck, blocking his airway. Believing he was going to die, Max landed the first punch in Marsh's stomach. It winded him, and he lost his grip on the chain.

Max pounced on him like a rabid animal. He punched Marsh until he was lying flat on the floor, then he stood and kicked him in the face several times. When that wasn't enough, he picked up the billy club and smashed it down on Marsh's head until he lost consciousness. Even then, Max kept pounding the club against Marsh's skull.

Max didn't realize he was screaming as he pummeled the depraved troll. Then the door to the room flew open. "What the fuck have you done?" John William shouted.

Max looked down at the pile of flesh on the floor in front of him. Marsh's face and skull were mutilated. There was blood everywhere. His thoughts were hazy from his fit of rage.

"He kept hitting me. He was choking me with that chain," Max muttered, coming back to his senses.

"Who the hell do you think you are? You're a servant!" John William ranted.

Two other men from the cartel appeared in the doorway.

"Get this little asshole out of here. We'll deal with him later," he stated, looking at Max.

The men took Max from the bedroom and locked him in another room across the hallway. John William turned his attention to Marsh. *Yuk*, he thought, *what a fucking slob*. He bent down and jammed two fingers into the fat around Marsh's neck. No pulse. "Shit!" he yelled.

John William closed the door behind him, leaving Marsh lying dead on the floor. He had to get rid of the body. Then he would deal with the boy.

Chapter Thirty

The two men took Max back down to the basement and shoved him inside his kennel. When Cali and Maggie returned, they found him walking in circles in his confined space.

"What's wrong, Max? What happened?" Cali asked once they were alone.

"Oh man. I fucked up really bad. I was with this asshole tonight. Man, he was brutal. He kept hitting me with a club, and then he started strangling me with a chain. I...I don't know what happened to me. I just fuckin' lost it and started beating the shit out of the guy," Max explained. "You know I'm gonna pay for this. Who knows what John William will do to me?"

"Jesus, Max," Maggie said. "Are you hurt? What happened to the man?"

"I don't know. Shit, I could've killed him for all I know. I just kept hitting him. I wanted him to die. I really did. When John William came into the room, the guy was lying on the floor. There was a lot of blood everywhere."

"I hope you did kill him," Cali said.

Max abruptly stopped walking in circles. "I hear ya, Cali. But it doesn't matter if he's dead or alive. I'm gonna be punished for this."

Cali and Maggie watched Max. He started mindlessly rubbing his own arms, as if to warm himself from the cold. He knew he would be facing the hardest time of his imprisonment. His mind betrayed him as he thought of the different ways they would torture him. Then, as if someone threw cold water on him, he realized that he had fought back for the first time. A small smile jumped onto his face.

"What the hell are you smiling about?" Cali asked.

"I was just thinking. I finally bit back. I mean, it felt so good. I *wanted* to bash that bastard's brains in. For once in my life, I took a stand. I know I'm gonna pay, but once the punishment is all over, I'll have tonight to hold on to. Maybe they'll get the message that we aren't going to keep taking this shit. We might just bust out of this shit hole. They need to worry about us. You guys hear me? They need to fuckin' worry about us!"

Max's false bravado was snuffed out an hour later when John William came down to the basement carrying a baseball bat. Maggie and Cali immediately stood up in their kennels. Even Shana managed to move over to the door of her small prison. Seth crouched in the corner of his own kennel, fearful that John William was coming for him. Max began talking incoherently when he noticed how dead John William's eyes were.

"I'm sorry, John William. I don't know what happened. One minute everything was fine, and the next, I just don't know what happened. It won't happen again. I'm sure it won't happen again..." Max said with remorse.

Without uttering a single word, John William unlocked the door to Max's kennel, strode over to the boy, and began hitting him with the bat. "You killed the fucking guy," he yelled, as he continued to hit him.

Max covered his head with hands, letting his forearms shield his face. But when John William broke the boy's right leg with the bat, Max fell to the floor and began to tremble. Irritated beyond belief, John William shoved the bat into Max's ribs in hopes of breaking a couple. The bat slipped, hitting Max under his left ribs instead. Intense pain burned through Max's side and shoulder. His piercing screams finally made John William retreat and leave the boy to think about what he had done to Marsh that evening.

Max stayed on the floor of his kennel, screaming in pain. The others could see that his leg was broken, but Maggie was more worried about the way Max was holding his left side. She hoped that what she thought might have happened to him, hadn't.

Chapter Thirty-One

Upstairs, John William remembered what Myles had told him to do to Max. "Break his fuckin' leg and put a hurting on the no-good son of a bitch. I want him to learn from this. Then, I want you to contact some of our outside pimps and see who we can sell him to. Now that he fought back, we ain't gonna be able to use him. He's more trouble than he's worth."

A short while later, John William appeared in the basement. He was carrying a box of medical supplies and two pieces of wood. "Maggie!" he snapped, opening her kennel. "Get your ass over there and bandage up that broken leg of his. Be quick about it, too."

Maggie practically ran from her kennel to Max's. She knelt down beside him.

"Max, I'm going to splint your leg. OK? It's going to hurt, but I have to do it," she explained.

Max only looked at her with confusion. All of the color had drained from his face. Maggie worked quickly to put the splint on his leg. She had no idea if she'd done it correctly or if it would help the bones to heal properly. By then, John William had retreated to the kitchen to eat with some of the other guys in the cartel.

"Max, it's me, Maggie. Do you recognize me?" Maggie asked him.

Instead of answering, Max fainted. When he came to, it was apparent that he was still confused.

"Tell me where you have pain, Max," Maggie stated more aggressively this time.

"My shoulder," Max managed. "And here." He pointed to the ribs on his left side.

"OK. How many fingers am I holding up?" Maggie persisted, holding up three fingers.

Max looked at her hand, but the fingers were so blurred he couldn't answer. Besides, he was in so much pain that he didn't care how well his eyes were working.

Maggie reached down and felt his belly. It was distended and hard as a rock. She suspected that it was filling with blood. She found a pulse on his wrist and counted the number of beats in what she estimated was a minute of time. She counted 160 beats.

"Cali? We have a problem," she said with concern.

"What, Mags? What's wrong with him?"

"I think John William ruptured his spleen. From everything I know, I think he's bleeding internally. If he doesn't go to the hospital, he'll die, Cali," Maggie cried.

"Is there anything you can do to help him? Come on, Mags. Think! What did your books tell you to do?" Cali asked, panicked.

"There's nothing I can do, Cali. He needs surgery by a real doctor. That's the only thing that can be done. But he doesn't have a lot of time," she added.

"How long? How long can he live?" Cali asked impatiently.

"I don't know. I just don't know," Maggie stated in anger.

Maggie lay on the floor of Max's cell, her body up against his. She put her arm around him and waited. There was nothing to do now but pray. John William came back a few hours later and found them. Maggie woke, feeling someone watching her.

"John William, Max needs to go to the hospital. I think you ruptured his spleen." Maggie pulled up Max's shirt, exposing his belly, which bulged with the blood that filled it. Suddenly, Max threw up, and blood splattered across the dirt floor of the kennel.

"He ain't going to no hospital. So you better think about all that shit you read and fix him up real fast," John William snarled at her.

"I can't! I can't fix him. Only a doctor can fix him. He's going to bleed to death," she pleaded.

John William opened Max's kennel. "Let's go! Back to your own place," he said menacingly.

"Please let me stay with him. Please, John William. Just tonight. I swear I'll do whatever you want. Please," Maggie begged.

"Anything? You'll do whatever I want, huh?" he sneered. "You'll do whatever I want just because I say so. You get that through your stupid little head." Then he paused, not to think, but to build her anxiety. "OK, you can stay with him tonight, but you owe me, and I always get paid." He chuckled as he heaved himself back up the stairs.

"Mags?" Cali called out. "What's going to happen to Max?"

"I don't know for sure, Cali. I don't even know if his spleen is ruptured," she responded in a defeated voice.

Then Maggie lay facing Max. She snuggled up to him as close as she could get. Putting her arm around him, she began to tell him a story. It was the *Adventures of Tom Sawyer* by Mark Twain, a story that Max had begged her to tell him repeatedly during their years of bondage. Max was hooked on Tom Sawyer's story and his ability to believe in his own daydreams and allow his imagination to become his reality.

Tears streamed down Maggie's cheeks as she told Max the classic tale. Every so often, when Maggie got to Max's favorite parts of the book, he would look up at her and smile. When she finished telling him the story, she silently held him in her arms.

"Tell me the story about my dad, Maggie, please," Max asked softly.

Chapter Thirty-Two

"Do you remember when you were nine years old and your dad took you hunting for the first time? The two of you drove a couple of hours to your cabin in the middle of Pennsylvania. On your way, there was a blizzard as you started to drive up the mountain. The two of you couldn't see past the hood of the car, the snow was falling so fast. Your dad was driving slower than you could walk because he couldn't see the road anymore, and to the right, there was a cliff that dropped to the bottom of the mountain. It took you hours to reach the top of the mountain. But you and your dad treated it like a great adventure, a matter of survival. When you finally got to the cabin, you made a fire in the fireplace and drank hot chocolate." Maggie paused to give him time to acknowledge the memory.

"I remember, Maggie. Keep going," Max managed.

"Well, the next morning after breakfast, your dad took you into the woods to hunt. You were lying on the ground behind a fallen tree, waiting for the deer to come out. It started to snow again, and you rolled onto your back and looked up into the sky past the huge trees. It was like you were transported to another world as you watched the snowflakes falling through the trees. You could hear the sounds of tree branches rattling and pine needles shifting as the wind shuffled them around. Man, Max, you were at total peace. You loved it there. You loved being one with nature."

Maggie stopped and brushed the hair back from Max's eyes. Her hand glided over his face and forehead in a gesture that reminded Max of his mother.

Max's eyes welled up. "Don't stop, Maggie. Finish the story," he urged.

Maggie tried hard to be brave for Max. But eventually, she let herself feel all the emotions that were pent up inside of her as she finished his story. "While you were looking up at the sky, your dad was high up in a tree nearby. Suddenly, you heard footsteps, and you were jolted back to reality. Your dad was standing over you, looking down with a puzzled look on his face. He said, 'Did you see the deer? He was standing fifteen feet from you, son. It was a clear shot.'

"Embarrassed and worried you had disappointed your dad, you told him you hadn't seen the deer because you were watching the snow fall from the sky. Then you held your breath, Max, just waiting for him to be mad that you weren't hunting the way he'd taught you to. Instead, your dad got down on his knees. Silently, he stretched out right next to you. He looked up into the sky for a while. You both did, watching the beauty unfold around you. The two of you listened to the odd sounds, and you could smell the pine trees and wood smoke from other cabins in the distance. Then your dad rolled onto his side and propped his head up in his hand.

"'Son,' he said, 'I've been coming out for many years—since I was your age—but I never noticed how alive I could feel until right now. Sometimes, we are so focused on what we want that we are blind to the things that make us happy. Like lying here with my son, watching the snowflakes fall. It's just incredible, and when I focus on what is right in front of me, nothing else matters. All my worries vanish. Thank you, Max. If you hadn't told me why you missed the deer, if you had lied, thinking I would be upset, I would never have been able to live this moment with you.'"

Maggie's voice trailed off.

Tears were streaming from Max's eyes and running down the sides of his face as the memory of his loving father played in his mind. His father was devoted to his mother and him. He was a good-natured man, and Max adored him.

Finally, Max opened his eyes, but his lids were heavy. "Thank you, Maggie," he said.

Maggie laid her head gingerly on his chest and put her arm around him. She heard the beating of his heart, and as the minutes wore on, his heartbeats grew weaker and slower. Before he lost all consciousness, Maggie propped herself up on one elbow and looked into his face.

"Max, I love you. You're the best big brother a girl could ever hope for. You're finally going to be happy, Max. You're going to be free," she croaked.

Max was too tired to open his eyes, but he squeezed her hand lightly. "I love you," he mouthed, his voice too weak to pass through his lips.

Putting her head back on Max's chest, Maggie closed her eyes and focused on the diminishing rhythm of the drum that played inside his chest, until his heart beat for the very last time.

Chapter Thirty-Three

M aggie was sobbing, her chest rising and falling so hard that she clutched at her ribs to steady them. The sounds that came from her made the others go silent.

After several long minutes, Shana spoke. "Is he dead, Maggie?"

"Yeah, Shana. He's gone," she bawled.

Shana was crying openly. "Do you think he was in a lot of pain?"

"No, Shana. He didn't know what was happening. He couldn't feel anything," Maggie lied, wanting to give the others some comfort.

"Cali?" Maggie called.

"Yeah, Mags?" Cali responded through chest-thumping sobs.

"Are you OK? He knew that we all loved him, and he loved all of us too," Maggie offered. They were all hurting. Each of them had lost a brother. All they had was each other, and now, one of them was gone.

"I know, Mags. I know," Cali confirmed, allowing herself to mourn openly.

"Aggie?" Seth called out from his kennel.

"Yeah, Seth?" she asked, wondering how he would be able to handle this loss.

"Is Max gonna come back?" he asked hopefully.

"No, Max died, honey. He's in heaven now, with God," Maggie explained.

"Are you going to die too?" Seth asked in a quivering voice, horrified at the thought of losing her too.

"No, Seth. I'm not going to die. I'm staying right here with you," she stated, wishing she had some control over keeping the promise she'd just made to him.

"Aggie, when I grow up, will I go hunting with my dad like Max did?" Seth asked, having felt like he was a part of the story Maggie told.

135

"I don't know, Seth. Maybe. Or, maybe you'll have different stories that make you feel good. Something that's all yours and that makes you feel special the way Max's story made him feel special," she explained, trying to sound optimistic despite her deep despair.

"OK, I like that too. Aggie, do you love me as much as you love Max?" Seth asked, feeling vulnerable and alone in his kennel.

"Of course I do, Seth. I love you even more," she added, hoping to relieve some of his anguish.

It wasn't long after Max died that John William's feet were banging down the wooden stairs. He stood at the door of Max's kennel and looked at Maggie, lying next to the boy with her arm and leg covering him. "Let's go. Time for you to go back to your own kennel, you filthy little animal," he grunted at Maggie.

Maggie jolted upright. "Max is *dead*!" she screamed. "You killed him, John William. You killed Max, and I hate your guts! I hope you die!"

If John William weren't so shocked to learn that Max had died, he would have beaten the hell out of her for the way she was yelling at him. Instead, he stood dumbfounded, wondering how the little wimp had died from a beating. Returning to his senses, he opened the locked door. "Come on. Back to your own space," he stated.

Once Maggie was back in her kennel, she rushed over to the side where Cali was sitting, and the two girls locked fingers through the chain link fence. They both leaned their heads against the fence, trying their best to have as much human contact as possible.

John William went back to Max's kennel, lifted Max's feet, and humped the dead teen across the dirt floor. He stopped, still hunched over, to give Cali and Maggie a sinister smile. He dragged Max over to the far corner of the basement. From under the wooden stairs, John William pulled out a shovel and began to dig Max's grave. When he was finished, he rolled Max's body into the hole. The corpse hit the bottom with a thud. John William slowly covered the body with dirt, threw down the shovel, and started toward the stairs. "We have clients coming soon. You bitches better get your shit together," he yelled.

That night, after Dr. Barnes was finished with her, Maggie looked him square in the face. "Dr. Barnes, I need some more books. I want more books on medical stuff. You know, how to fix people," she said carefully.

"Of course, of course. Oh, I just love it when little ones want to learn. I'll bring them to you next week," he sang.

Maggie was on a mission. She wanted to know as much about the human body as possible. "Oh, and one other thing," she asked the good doctor. "Can you bring me the book, *Harold and the Purple Crayon?*" Maggie wanted to help Seth use his imagination to begin to make his own wonderful memories.

Chapter Thirty-Four

Myles was very angry to hear that Max had died. John William explained that it was an accident that happened during the boy's punishment for killing Marsh. But an ominous feeling settled over Myles that this group of kids was jinxed. First, there was the bitch detective who had handed notes to Maggie and now there was Max's death. His instincts told him to cut his losses. There was too much at stake for him to worry about the four who remained.

"It's time to shake things up with this little group of misfits. I want you to reach out to our regulars. Get the ball rolling to sell these little shits off," Myles instructed John William.

"Are you sure about this?" John William prodded, not wanting to start all over again with a new group. He knew that if the kids he had taken were sold, then he would be back out on the street again, finding new ones. He liked the hunt and capture, but he cherished the power he wielded over his group more.

"Yeah, I'm fucking sure! What didn't you understand? Let me be clear. I want you to get some buyers in here, pronto. Call a couple of scabs from Camden, Philly, and Maryland. I want to be sure to find buyers for all of them. As for the little boy, I don't really care 'cause he ain't worth a pint of piss. Just get it *done*," Myles said.

On his way to the basement, John William thought about the guys he would call later that day.

"Listen," John William said when he reached the bottom of the stairs. "Things are gonna change around here. Cali, you're gonna get these rodents ready for some show time. We're filming tonight," he said, throwing a box of sexy lingerie into her kennel. Then he escorted Maggie and Shana into Cali's small prison.

"Why do we have to wear these?" Cali asked, suspicious of John William's intentions.

"Excuse me? Are you questioning what I'm telling you to do? Do you wanna end up like your little friend, Max, over there?" he sneered, looking over at the grave in the corner of the basement.

His tone gave Cali pause. "No, I was just wondering. OK, girls, let's see what's in the box," she said.

Cali put together outfits for each of them. They were all nervous. Any change in the normal routine made them anxious. After the girls were dressed, they stood in Cali's kennel looking at each other.

"You look disgusting," Shana told Maggie.

Maggie crossed her arms over her chest. She was already self-conscious about the outfit she was wearing and susceptible to ridicule. "I know I look disgusting," Maggie retorted. "I feel disgusting too. And so should you. We're just their little playthings, and being dressed like this makes it worse."

Maggie looked down at her body. She was wearing a corset, her undeveloped breasts lost in the cups of the top. The garter belt was too big and lay limply on her hips, making the attached stockings baggy on her long, thin legs. She glanced at Cali, who looked like a Victoria Secret model in her see-through baby-doll slip with a built-in push-up bra. Then she scanned Shana, who wore a mesh teddy. It looked like a one-piece bathing suit without all the material. The roundness of her full breasts poked out of the sides of the triangular cups. Maggie glanced at her legs, which bore the scars of days gone by in this life of punishment.

Shana snorted. "I told you two fools if you took some of the hillbilly heroin, you wouldn't feel so bad all the time. You're both idiots. It's easier to deal with this shit stoned. At least I can't remember half the shit that's happening. And another thing, *Maggie*, ain't nothing gonna change the fact that we're their little playthings, so give it rest. You're so fuckin' annoying with your goody-two-shoes routine."

Deep down, Shana felt all of the same things that Maggie did. She refused, however, to let anyone know. Her rough exterior was what kept her going. The drugs had numbed her mind and made her circumstances easier to accept. But she wanted to be free just as much as the others did.

A short time later, John William took the three girls upstairs. Each of them was filmed alone while the other two watched. Maggie was horrified when it was her turn. She had never been filmed by herself. With the other kids, she felt shielded from the camera in the mass of human flesh, but tonight she was there for everyone to see. She recited her lines as instructed. "Please pick me," she whispered. "I'll do whatever you want, and I'm worth every cent. Just choose me, and I'll show you."

Maggie's little plea to be picked would cause quite a stir among the local pimps who came to the house to view the film a week later.

Chapter Thirty-Five

———————————— ■ ————————————

Shana was sold first, since she was the least valuable. A pimp from Camden, New Jersey, bought her for one thousand dollars.

When the men arrived to pick her up, John William went into the basement and opened Shana's kennel. "Let's go, bitch. You've been bought," he barked.

"Ha! See," Shana said, turning to the other two girls. "I am the hottest one." Then she turned to John William. "You have any dope for me?" She leaned in. "It'll help me sleep when I get back down here."

"You're not coming back down here. You've been *sold*. As in, you're leaving with your new pimp to work the streets of Camden. Man, is your new boss gonna have a good time getting you under control. You were worthless to us at the auction. Your new boss, he ain't as nice as me...he ain't gonna let you *do* him for dope. You'll do him so that he doesn't kill you," John William said, tormenting her.

Shana looked terror-stricken. "Cali," she cried, "please don't let them take me. Please."

Shana turned back to John William and fell to her knees. She grabbed at his jeans. "Oh God. Please, John William. I don't want to go. I wanna stay with the others."

John William laughed. "Nobody cares what you want. You're a little crack ho, and this is where girls like you end up: in the shit hole of the earth." Then he put his large, slimy hand over her face and pushed her off him. She landed on her back on the dirt floor. She shuffled on her hands and knees as fast as possible to Cali's kennel.

Cali put her fingers through the chain link fence. "I'm so sorry, Shana. I'm so, so sorry," Cali told her.

"I don't wanna go. I wanna stay here with you guys," Shana cried.

"Shana," Maggie stated in a firm voice. "I don't want you to go."

Shana's face snarled angrily, and she burst into a fit of rage. "All of this happened after you came. Why did you have to come? It's your fault. Everything is your fault. It's your fault they hurt me, your fault that Max died, and your fault that I'm being sent away. I hate you, Maggie Clarke."

Maggie couldn't bear to think that these would be the last words they shared. "I know you hate me, Shana. But I don't hate you," she said in a quiet voice.

Shana turned back to Cali and kissed her on the lips through the fence. John William watched their sorrow-filled exchange with sheer delight. When he motioned for her to step out of her kennel, she ran over to Seth, "Come here, baby," Shana told him.

Seth moved to the fence and put his tiny hand over hers.

"You take good care of yourself, OK?" she said.

"OK, Shana. But where are you going?" the small boy asked.

"I'm going away, and we're probably never gonna see each other again. But remember that you're gonna be a really cool guy when you grow up. OK?" she muttered, not knowing what else to say to the child.

Having seen enough, John William grabbed Shana under the arm and pulled her toward the stairs. "Let's go. Time to become someone else's bitch."

As John William yanked Shana up the stairs behind him, Maggie and Cali huddled together at the fence that separated them. Cali broke the silence. "They're selling us off, Maggie. They're not going to keep us anymore. That's why they filmed us by ourselves. We need to wrap our minds around this."

Maggie began weeping. She hated her life as it was, but she had clung to the belief that someday she would go home to her family. The thought of continuing in this sick world without the other kids was unbearable. Maggie felt like she had the day John William took her from the mall. Then she looked across the basement and saw Seth, his eyes as wide as silver dollars, staring at her, waiting for her to make him feel safe, and she felt a gush of guilt. *If they were all separated, what would happen to Seth?* Worry about Seth's fate overpowered her fear of her own destiny.

Maggie did the only thing that she could think of: she sat on the dirt floor of her kennel and prayed that somehow they would all be OK and that Seth would stay with her.

Chapter Thirty-Six

Over the next week, men came to visit at all times of the day and night to check out Maggie and Cali. The routine was the same. The two girls dressed in lingerie, paraded upstairs, and stood in the middle of a room while men of all sizes and ages looked them over. In a week's time, at least eighteen men came to see them. Seth was always taken upstairs alone because when Maggie was there, he would whimper and cling to her, and selling a whiny kid to street pimps was nearly impossible.

Back in their kennels, Cali tried to keep Maggie's spirits high. "Look at it this way. If we're sold to pimps, then at least we'll get to be outside again. I mean, we'll be doing the same thing we are now, but at least we'll have a little more freedom."

"That doesn't change anything, Cali. We won't be together anymore. I thought when we got old enough, they would just let us go. I want to go home. I miss my mom and dad every day," Maggie said.

"I understand. But maybe if we're out on the streets, we'll find our way home. At least we won't be locked away where no one but these assholes see us. Right?" Cali argued.

"I don't know, Cali. I just don't have a good feeling about any of this. I'm so scared to be alone. And what will happen to Seth? He doesn't even know his last name or where he lived. How will he ever make it without us?" Maggie asked, wanting Cali to tell her that everything would work out for each of them.

Cali didn't have any answers. She wasn't streetwise. The only thing she knew about prostitution was what she'd learned during her captivity.

"Here's the thing, Mags. We don't have a choice. We have to make the best of what we got. This is all bad shit we're going through. None of us belongs here, and Max definitely didn't deserve to die here. I wonder how Shana is doing," she murmured.

"I know. I've been thinking about her a lot. Do you think she really hated me?" Maggie asked sadly.

"Nah, she was just as scared and frustrated as the rest of us. She knew in her heart that Myles did whatever he wanted. He protected her for a while, and when she lost that, she also lost her ability to cope with this bullshit," Cali explained.

"Maybe she was right. Maybe staying drugged up is the best thing," Maggie offered.

"Don't ever think that, Mags! The drugs are what got her sent to Camden. When I was waiting for a client the night before she was sold, I overheard John William telling one of the other goons that they had to sell her cheap because pimps don't like their 'property' already hooked on drugs. He said they like to get them hooked themselves," Cali said.

The girls lay quietly, waiting for Seth to be returned to the basement. When John William brought the boy downstairs, he put him in his cell and addressed Cali.

"Looks like your ratty ass will be leaving. You were gettin' too old, anyhow. Your new boss is gonna turn you out like a two-bit whore. You'll wish you were back here with me, girl," he rambled. "Get yourself together. They'll be back to get you tomorrow morning."

John William turned the basement light off as he went upstairs, leaving them in pitch darkness to face their demons. The contents of Cali's belly began to churn. She had known that this moment was coming, yet there was no way to prepare for it. She leaned against the chain link fence.

Maggie had started to breathe heavily when John William announced Cali's departure. There was a buzzing in her ears, as if she were listening to static through ear buds.

"Cali? What are we going to do? I don't want you to leave. What if I never see you again?" Maggie cried.

"Come on, Mags. It's gonna be all right. I want to tell you something. I want you to listen to me real close. Ever since I met you, I knew you were special. You're stronger than the rest of us. You know more things, and I need you to believe me about this. I always knew that you were the one among us that would make it out of here and find your way back. Do you hear what I'm saying?" Cali asked, serious as a heart attack.

"I hear you," Maggie answered mechanically.

"No! Mags, I need you to believe it. You're the one among us who *will* find her way back! You have to do it for all of us. To make things right. We've all lost so much, and when you break free, it won't be for nothing. You can tell our stories to others and make sure that our families remember us," she pleaded.

It was the conviction in Cali's voice that snapped Maggie out of her funk. "I believe you, Cali. I swear, I'll do whatever I can to find my way home again," she promised.

"Good. Another thing. When I get to wherever it is they're taking me, I'm gonna try to get a message to your parents. I don't know how, but if there's a way, I'll contact them…mine too. Your parents are Lorraine and Rob Clarke, and you lived in Conshohocken. What else?" Cali asked.

"My home phone number. If I tell you, can you remember it?" Maggie asked, excited that her parents would soon find out she was still alive.

Maggie recited the phone number, and Cali repeated it several times until it was fixed in her memory. A few minutes later, she repeated the phone number to Maggie again.

"Yep, that's it. Maybe you'll get home before I will," Maggie observed aloud.

"Not likely," a man's voice roared, and it was hot with anger.

Chapter Thirty-Seven

The lights flew on, and there stood John William. He had never left the basement. Myles was suspicious about Cali, sensing she would try to rescue the two kids who remained. Maggie's heart dropped in her chest, and her eyes darted around the basement like a wild animal as she wondered how much he'd heard.

John William walked briskly to Cali's kennel. "I heard every fucking word you said. We knew you'd be trouble. Well, sleep tight, girly, 'cause trouble awaits your ass in the morning," he vowed.

The two girls stayed awake all night, trying in vain to comfort each other. They knew the reprimand was going to be harsh, but neither could imagine the extent to which the cartel would go to punish her. John William entered the basement at dawn and heaved his heartless mass of flesh and bones across the basement. He took Cali and Maggie up to the room where they had stripped and danced.

Maggie and Cali clung to each other as they were led across the room. John William stopped and pulled a wire dog cage out from under a wooden table. The cage was forty-eight inches long and thirty inches wide. He bent down and opened the door of the crate. Looking at Cali, he said in an icy voice, "Get in."

Maggie was already crying, remembering how the men had pissed on her when she was forced into the same cage. Cali got onto her hands and knees and crawled into the cage. Then John William fastened three padlocks on the top, middle, and bottom of the wire door. He pulled on the door to be sure it wouldn't budge. Cali was hyperventilating inside the small space, which her body nearly filled.

"John William, please let her go. I swear, we were just talking. We're never going to try to run away. I swear," Maggie begged. At that moment, Maggie was willing to do anything to stop what was about to happen to them.

"I'll have sex with you," Maggie blurted.

John William swaggered close to Maggie. "You're damn straight you will. You can count on that."

"I'll do whatever you want. Please don't punish Cali. Please let her out of the cage," Maggie begged.

"Nah, I ain't gonna do that, and you're gonna have sex with me anyway. How do you like them apples?" he mocked.

Maggie heard footsteps approaching. It sounded like an army of people. She looked toward the doorway as Myles walked into the room.

"You two have deeply disappointed me," he said in a cold voice. "It's time for you to go your separate ways."

Myles pushed Maggie toward the cage. She dropped to all fours and twisted her fingers between the wires. Cali put her fingers over Maggie's, and the girls huddled together, only the wire standing between them. Neither of them spoke. No words could articulate what they felt. Fear gripped each of them so deeply that only death could release them from it.

Myles walked over to the girls. His facial features looked depraved. His anger was raw, and his demeanor was so incredibly coldhearted that no one would ever believe Myles had a wife and children whom he loved. "You," he said, addressing Maggie. "This is the second time you schemed to get away. In this business, we don't tolerate snitches or runaways. You see, if we did, it would jeopardize all that we've built. I've thought a lot about what I should do to punish you. Then it came to me. I can punish both of you at the same time. Kind of like a two-for-one." He laughed.

Then Myles stopped laughing and bent close to Maggie's face. "Such a shame. You had so much potential, and now you've gone and thrown it all away. Now it's time to pay the piper."

"Please don't separate us, Myles. Cali and I want to stay together. Maybe someone will want to buy both of us," Maggie begged.

Myles glared at her, his eyes clouded with pure contempt. "I can't sell the two of you together. That would ruin my reputation and my business. If I did that, it would only come back to haunt me."

Right before John William pried Maggie's fingers loose from the wire cage, Cali had a moment of unadulterated clarity. "Remember what I told you, Mags," she whispered. "You're the one among us."

Two of Myles's men picked up the dog cage and carried Cali toward the kitchen. Myles grabbed Maggie's arm and followed the procession. As they entered the kitchen, another man opened a door to the outside.

It was late November, and the wind whipped the cold air, making Maggie suck in her breath. There was no indication of a sun behind the thick, dark clouds. A light rain fell on them. Maggie, like Cali, was wearing only a T-shirt, and both girls instinctively hugged themselves against the cold.

Maggie took in everything around her. Their prison was three stories tall. Long balconies ran the length of the house on the second and third levels. Over the tall fence surrounding the property, the treetops looked as if they belonged in a supernatural-horror flick. The once-white house was pale gray from years of neglect. The windows were boarded up from the outside, which explained why there were only a few places inside where natural light penetrated. Weeds and bushes grew thick and thorny around the house, as if to keep people in, rather than out.

Maggie searched for the car that would take Cali to her new "home." Her desperation heightened as she realized that she might never see Cali again.

They walked on a crushed-stone path around a row of large bushes that surrounded an abandoned in-ground swimming pool. The kidney-shaped pool was filled to the brim with murky, brown rainwater, which, under the sunless sky, looked black. The wind blew leaves in menacing circles across the surface, sending small ripples of water to the edges.

For a fleeting moment, while moving through the backyard, Cali and Maggie's eyes met. "I love you," Cali yelled to her young friend.

"I love you too, Cali. Come and find me someday," Maggie called over the wind that whipped against her body.

Myles, still dragging Maggie along, stopped suddenly. John William stepped forward, wrapped his hefty arm around Maggie's waist, and hoisted her off the ground. Maggie watched as the two men strode to the edge of the pool and threw the crate, with Cali inside, into the water.

As the crate hit the water, the coldness jolted Cali's body. She felt as if tiny needles were being pushed through the surface of her skin. As she plunged toward the bottom of the pool, her eyes were open wide. The murky liquid blurred her vision. Within seconds, the cage hit bottom, and Cali's lungs began to fill with water. The oxygen in her bloodstream rapidly diminished as she battled to breathe. The cloudy water forced itself into her sinuses. Cali yanked on the door of the cage with all of her might, trying to break it free of the padlocks. This further depleted her energy and her store of oxygen.

A few minutes after Cali hit the water, she slipped out of consciousness and into the peacefulness of death.

Chapter Thirty-Eight

———————————————————————

"Nooo." Maggie screamed, digging her nails into John William's arm, a mistake she'd pay for later. "Pull her up. Please pull her up." Maggie pleaded, looking at Myles in terror. Maggie let out guttural sounds and lashed out, but she was no match for John William, who harnessed her securely in his beastly, hairy arms.

"Get her inside and ready for the next group. I've had enough of this useless drama," Myles told John William.

John William forcefully led Maggie back into the house. Before the door closed behind them, she glanced out to the yard. She imagined Cali under the water, struggling to get free from the cage. The images of Cali's death haunted her, and she slipped into a state of shock. She stood looking up at John William. She had nothing left to say to him. The burden of loss and grief was so powerful that she went limp and slumped to the floor.

John William showed no sign of remorse. He snatched a fistful of her long, black hair and walked toward the basement steps. Like a zombie, Maggie staggered to her feet and walked on, barely noticing the pain of her hair being yanked. In the basement, John William followed her into her kennel. He knew it would be only a few hours before an offer was made for Maggie.

Maggie walked over to her mattress and sat down. She put her head in her hands, and rocked like a small child. She wanted Cali to be alive. She wondered how she could go on without Cali. Her loss was too great for the young girl to bear alone.

A short time later, John William approached, his groin tingled. His ego soared as he recalled the scene outside and that bitch, Cali, plunging into the water. Maggie's deep sense of loss and the way she completely gave herself over to grief turned him on.

Kneeling next to her, John William pulled her T-shirt over her head and ripped off her panties. She did not resist as he effortlessly flipped her onto her belly and took what he wanted. When he was finished, he slapped her on the ass. "I told you all along I'd get it from you. It won't be long before you're out there on the streets, selling your scrawny little ass for twenty bucks to anyone who will have you."

When John William left the basement, Maggie dressed and moved to the front of her kennel. "Seth? Are you OK?"

"I'm scared. Where's Cali? Is she coming back, or did she go to see God like Max did?" he asked in a cracked voice.

"Yeah, Seth. Cali went to see God," she said.

Maggie was tired of fighting. She had been battling to keep a piece of herself since the day John William kidnapped her. Now all she wanted was an end to her suffering. She thought about all she'd lost since that day at the mall. It was too great a burden for her to bear alone. Now, only she and Seth remained, and there was no telling what the cartel would do to the two of them. The only comfort she had was that maybe, just maybe, Max and Cali were watching over them.

That evening, John William took Maggie upstairs to the room where the films were made. She was told to undress and sit on the bed. As she waited for what was to happen next, her thoughts wandered to her mother. It would Christmastime soon, and her mother loved all the excitement surrounding the holiday. She wondered if her mom had experienced a joyful Christmas since she'd been gone. She hoped her mother's life wasn't as grim as her own had become and clung to the idea that her mom hadn't given up hope of finding her.

The door opened, and John William brought four men into the room. She'd never seen them before, and she looked at them fearfully. They checked her over carefully. A man named Rock looked into her soulful blue eyes.

"Yeah, baby, you're a real looker, aren't you," he mumbled under his breath.

Maggie remained silent. She wasn't afraid any longer. Nothing could compare to the pain of losing Max and Cali.

Rock turned to John William. As if the other three men weren't in the room for the same reason he was, he said, "Let's go talk. I'm ready to make an offer."

John William grunted and looked at the others, who were still studying Maggie. They all nodded as they filed out of the bedroom. Up in the attic, in Myles's office, Maggie was sold to the highest bidder for ten thousand dollars. Rock had purchased himself an almost new, fourteen-year-old whore.

Before Rock left, Myles made another offer. "Listen, I got this boy. He's around seven. If you want him, I'll give him to you cheap."

Moments later, in the bright light of the kitchen, Rock looked at Seth. "Well, he's a little too young to turn out, but my old lady always wanted a little boy. She can have him for a while and play mom," he said, thinking aloud.

"I'll tell you what," Rock said. "I'll give ya five hundred bucks for him. He ain't no good to me this young. I'm gonna have to raise him for a couple of years. Gonna cost me money to feed him and keep him. You know what I'm sayin'. So five hundred's my final offer."

Myles looked at Rock as though he wanted to spit in his face. "Yeah, fine. Five hundred bucks. I need the little shit stain out of here. You come back with the cash tomorrow. *Early*."

"Sure, Myles. I'll be back in the morning," Rock promised.

Maggie wasn't within earshot during any of the negotiating. The only thing she knew was that the men were making offers. She stayed up most of the night worrying about Seth and what would happen to him if she left. It wasn't until morning that Maggie found out that Seth would be leaving with her.

Chapter Thirty-Nine

Ⅰt was just before dawn when the lights popped on in the basement, waking Seth and startling Maggie, who had been up all night worrying. John William opened Maggie's kennel, and she rushed over to Seth, who looked pathetic with his small arms extended through the chain link toward her. He was whimpering like a small puppy. She moved in as close as she could to comfort him.

"Get the hell out of the way, you whore. I need to open his kennel," John William said.

Together at last, Maggie hugged Seth close as they walked up the basement stairs for the last time. In the kitchen, standing next to Myles, was Rock. He was over six feet tall, and his arms were crossed over his massive chest in a threatening stance. Rock wore his hair long, combing it back with a greasy hair-care product. He had a full beard and a mustache. He was one of the most dangerous people in Kensington, where he lived and did all of his business. Rock was the biggest drug dealer and pimp in the area surrounding Center City, Philadelphia.

He got the nickname Rock when he was in his late teens and started pushing crack cocaine, or "cookie," on the streets. He looked every bit the picture of a man involved in a shady business. He patrolled Kensington Avenue regularly, keeping a close eye on his street dealers and whores, and was always on the lookout for young people to make money for him.

Rock was infamous for strong-arming people into doing what he wanted. Since he controlled most of the drug pushers and prostitutes in the area, he had any number of people at his beck and call. His reach was endless.

Maggie and Seth had fallen into the hands of one of the most ruthless men in Philadelphia. He showed no tolerance for disobedience and had high expectations for the people he considered his property. The fourteen-year-old and the seven-year-old stood before him, waiting to hear what would happen to them next.

"Let's go," Rock said to Maggie. "I wanna get you back to town so you can start makin' me some money." Then he glared at Seth. "You comin', too."

Seth squeezed Maggie's hand tighter as they followed Rock out to his car. The sky was clear that morning, and Maggie looked back toward the bushes where Cali lay dead in her cage at the bottom of the pool. Her eyes brimmed with tears as the great loss tugged at her heart.

"Listen, girl. Don't be doin' none of that cryin' shit, ya hear? I ain't got no time for that. Get the fuck in the car so I can get your sorry ass back to where you gonna be livin'," Rock demanded.

The kids slid into the backseat of a black sedan. The windows were heavily tinted, making it impossible for anyone to see into the car. Rock sped out of the driveway and eased onto a country road. Rap music was blaring. Seth was sitting so close to Maggie that if he got any closer, their hips would fuse together. Seth was seeing the outside world for the first time in his life that he could remember. His memories from before he was taken by John William were nonexistent, and now, with so much whizzing by the window, he was overstimulated and on the verge of panic.

After forty-five minutes, Rock turned off a highway and onto Kensington Avenue. They drove under a massive steel structure that ran the length of the street as far as they could see. Maggie would soon find out that the seemingly endless, prehistoric-looking steel centipede was the Market-Frankford Line of the subway that was elevated above the ground. Under the El, which the locals had nicknamed the structure, the streets were cluttered with prostitutes and drug addicts.

Maggie couldn't peel her eyes away from the young girls; many were just a little older than she was, and some looked younger. They wore skimpy outfits, and when they noticed Rock's car, fear stirred on their faces. They tried to appear to be working hard to find customers. Girls leaned into cars and talked with scruffy men who skulked on the sidewalks. Maggie didn't know that she was looking at her own future.

Rock drove to the edge of Kensington and parked in front of a large twin home. He turned to the backseat. "We're home. Your mama is waiting for ya inside. Don't ya go givin' her a hard time, either, or I swear I'll kick your ass."

Seth clung tighter to Maggie. Rock gave her a threatening glare.

"Come on, Seth. We need to do what..." Maggie stopped short, realizing that she didn't know the man's name.

As if he was able to read her mind, he said, "Rock. My name is Rock. That's what you call me."

"We need to do what Rock says," she coaxed.

Seth silently followed Maggie and Rock into the house. They stood just inside the front door. The living room to the left was massive and in need of fresh paint and new carpet. A black leather sofa and matching chair faced a television. Empty beer bottles and overflowing ashtrays covered black-lacquered end tables. Stale cigarette smoke hung in the air, and their nostrils filled with an acidy mixture of booze, smoke, and body odor. The dark, velvet drapes were shut tight, keeping out any natural light. To their right was a dining room that had been made into Rock's office. Six mismatched chairs surrounded a large table, on the middle of which sat a telephone and a handgun. Maggie cringed when she spotted the gun. She wondered if they would sleep in one of the bedrooms on the second floor, an option that gave her a tiny sliver of hope.

"Come on," Rock said.

They followed him down a narrow hallway that opened into a kitchen. Dirty dishes were strewn on the worn, red, Formica countertop. In one corner, a heavy, black woman sat at a patio table. She looked up from her coffee and jumped to her feet. "Oh baby, you really meant it. You brought me a son," she gushed, rushing over to Seth.

Seth pulled away from her, locking his arms around Maggie's waist. Rock's wife, Thelma, didn't take kindly to his reaction. "What the fuck, Rock? I thought you said you was bringin' me home a new son. He ain't acting like no son of mine," she barked.

Rock grabbed the back of Seth's neck and squeezed hard. "Go say hello to your momma, boy. This ain't the way ya wanna get started with her," he said, seething.

Rock loved Thelma. They had been together from the time they were fifteen. In fact, Thelma's father, Jackie, was the drug kingpin in Philadelphia until he was murdered. Jackie ran the black mafia and had taken Rock under his wing to be certain his daughter would have stability.

Jackie had set Rock up as a dealer in Kensington and had never allowed him to be a part of the mafia. By the time Rock and Thelma were twenty, they had expanded into prostitution. Thelma's father had set the couple up in business, and Rock's loyalty to her was unbreakable.

In the ten years since her father's murder, Thelma had slowly become a recluse. She was a heavy drug user, something she had promised her father she'd never be. Now she was a full-blown, drug-using agoraphobic and never left the house for anything. The walls of her home defined her world, a rather lonely one. She had tried for many years to get pregnant, and after she and Rock accepted that it would never happen, Rock began to bring young children home for her to raise until they were old enough to use as prostitutes or drug runners. It had been over two years since Thelma had a child.

Unfortunately for the children, brutal, murderous parents had raised Thelma. She lacked patience and compassion for children who didn't act exactly as she demanded.

"Come over here to me," Thelma said in serious tone.

Maggie moved toward Thelma with Seth at her side. "It's all right, Seth. This is our new mom," she reassured him, fighting back the creepy feeling she had in her gut.

"*Our* new mom?" Thelma shrieked. "Who the hell are you talking about, fool? I ain't a mamma of no whore. You lucky I lettin' you be in my house right now. You ain't livin' here, girl. The boy is, but you ain't, you filthy bitch," Thelma said heatedly.

But then, what will happen to me? Maggie's thoughts silently screamed inside her head.

Chapter Forty

Panicking, Maggie threw herself on Thelma's mercy. "Oh, please let me stay too. I can clean and take care of Seth for you. I'll do whatever you need. Just don't separate us," Maggie begged.

"Get this ho outta my house," Thelma told Rock, flailing her arms.

"Time to go," Rock stated.

Maggie grabbed Seth, and he clung to her. Rock marched over and pulled her off the small boy. Seth was hysterical and began to scream at the top of his lungs, "I wanna stay with Aggie!" Turning to Thelma, he spewed, "I hate you. I don't want to stay with you. I wanna go with Aggie."

Thelma slapped Seth across the face. "Well, I see you ain't got no manners. That'll be the first thing I gotta teach ya. Nobody yells at me, boy." Then she grabbed his arm and led him away from the kitchen.

As Rock forced Maggie toward the front door, she yelled, "Don't forget me, Seth. We'll be together again. I promise!"

The outburst made Rock livid. He planned to set things right once he got Maggie to the house where she would be staying. He silently strutted out to his car, Maggie in tow, and shoved her into the backseat. Ten minutes later, they pulled up in front of a broken-down row house on Kensington Avenue. Without uttering a word, he pulled Maggie from the backseat and climbed the cement steps to the front door.

Inside, the house was a flurry of activity. The scantily dressed young girls, with bare bellies and asses peeking out below their skirts and shorts, hardly noticed Maggie as Rock pushed her toward the living area at the back of the house. In that room, there were several men dressed in jeans and oversized T-shirts. Many of them wore thick chains around their necks and untied sneakers. The men watched as Rock brought Maggie into the room.

"We got us a new girl. This one has a mouth on her. She needs to be wrecked," Rock told them.

Wrecking a new girl was what pimps did to assimilate her into the world of prostitution.

A heavyset Latino man named Armando hoisted himself from a chair in the corner. "I got this one," he said simply.

Armando took Maggie upstairs to the master bedroom. Once inside, he made her get naked and stand in the middle of the room. As she stood there, not knowing what would happen to her, she began to sweat. A few minutes later, she started to cry. All the while, Armando sat on the edge of the bed, staring at her as if she were a feast he was about to devour. Twenty minutes later, Armando moved off the bed. He gave Maggie a massive shove, and she landed face down on the mattress.

She quickly flipped onto her back and faced her attacker. He came at her so fast she didn't have a chance to react. Before she knew it, he was inside of her. When she screamed, Armando hit her in the face. "Shut your dirty mouth. Nobody here cares what's happenin' to you."

"Please don't hurt me. I swear I'll be quiet," she pleaded.

Armando's laughter filled the room like the growl of a Harley motorcycle on a quiet summer night. It put her further on edge. "You bet you'll be quiet. Cause if ya don't, you're gonna make it a lot harder on yourself."

Armando stood and regarded Maggie carefully. "You sure are a good-looking bitch. Let me take a closer look-see at those eyes of yours." He inched closer to her face until his nose touched hers. The anger bubbling up inside her made Maggie's expressive blue eyes more intense.

Finally, she turned her head away from him. "Do whatever you're going to do to me. I don't really care anymore. Just get it over with already," she stated.

Armando put his hand around her neck and began to squeeze. She started clawing and scratching at him in an effort to make him stop. But Armando persisted, applying more pressure to her throat. As soon as he let go of her throat, he pulled her up by her hair and shoved her toward the bedroom closet. When he swung the door open, she noticed it was empty. On the closet floor was a small door with a deadbolt.

Armando unbolted the door in the floor and pulled it up. Then he stared down into the dark hole below.

Maggie watched, unable to comprehend what was happening to her.

Armando edged her closer to the hole. "You can get in easily, or I can throw you in there. Choice is yours," he stated.

Not knowing how deep the hole was, she sat down on the floor and put her feet in first. She tried to feel for the bottom, but her feet did not touch a solid surface. After several seconds, Armando lifted her from the sitting position and dropped her into the vertical box. Maggie's feet hit the bottom hard, and she thought she had broken her ankle. Looking up at Armando, she begged, "Just let me out. Please."

Armando slammed the small door in her face, and she heard him throw the deadbolt. Scrunched at the bottom of the lightless box, her limbs bent and tangled, she wondered if he would ever come back for her.

Several hours later, the lid of the box opened. Maggie stared up at Armando, and then he showed her the snake in his hands. Maggie began to scream wildly. Armando dropped the long snake into the box and slammed the lid closed.

After several minutes of screaming and a few bites on her legs, Maggie's animal instincts took over. She grabbed the snake in the darkness of the box and clamped her teeth down until the snake was in two pieces. Maggie couldn't have known that the snake wasn't poisonous.

When Armando checked on Maggie the next day, he was surprised to see that she had not only killed the snake, but had eaten most of it while she sat at the bottom of the dark, damp box.

Chapter Forty-One

Not a day had passed in the three years since Maggie had been missing that Lorraine Clarke didn't think or talk about her daughter. She wanted to believe Maggie was still alive; her guilt over leaving Maggie alone that one day never stopped consuming her.

The Clarkes had moved on with their lives, if there was such a thing after losing a child. They were doing the best they could to resemble a normal family. Lorraine and Rob's marriage had been put to the test. Each of them dealt with Maggie's disappearance differently. Rob wanted them to focus on Keith and being a family again. Lorraine wanted the same, but she was unwilling to let go of the ghost of her missing daughter. Because of this, Rob and Keith bore the burden of her unhappiness.

It was Halloween when Rob approached her. "Lorraine, I think we should consider selling this house and starting over somewhere new. We've come a long way, but you know as well as I do that we need to try something different to make our marriage work. There are just too many reminders of Maggie here. It makes Keith feel like an afterthought. So what do you say? Would you consider starting over somewhere new?"

Lorraine was appalled, a reaction Rob hadn't quite anticipated. "You're fucking kidding me, right? Are you actually suggesting that we leave this house so *when* Maggie tries to come home, she can't find us? My God, Rob! What the hell is wrong with you? How can you give up on our daughter so easily?"

"I haven't given up, Lorraine. I never will. But this life we're living, it's just not healthy for any of us. You've made a fucking career out of searching for Maggie. We can't go on like this. What about Keith? Huh? What about him and what's good for him?" Rob argued.

"There's nothing wrong with Keith. He's a well-adjusted little boy. I love him with all my heart, so don't you dare insinuate that I'm neglecting him," she yelled back.

Seeing that Lorraine wasn't capable of having a rational conversation, Rob decided to let the subject rest until another time. "Well, we aren't done talking about this, Lorraine. We have to do something before we lose everything. Losing Maggie was the worst thing that could have happened to us. We made it through that together. We might be holding onto this marriage by a string, but we are still here, the two of us, together, trying to get our lives back," Rob said. "I love you, Lorraine, but your inability to cope with this horrible loss is destroying our family."

Since their argument on Halloween, the couple had grown further apart. Lorraine was unwilling to consider leaving their home, and Rob was incapable of spending another year there with the spirit of his beloved daughter haunting him day in and day out.

A few days before Christmas, Detective Harker paid the Clarkes a visit. Lorraine threw open the door after she saw him through the peephole. "What is it? Did you find her?" Lorraine shot at him.

"Well, hello to you too, Lorraine. It's good to see you again," Harker said, trying to lighten the moment.

Lorraine glared at him. "Well? Did you?" she persisted.

"Can I come in, Lorraine?" Detective Harker asked.

Lorraine stood to the side while Rae Harker entered, and she followed him into the living room, where he sat down on the sofa. "First, we did not find Maggie," Harker started. "However, last night, the Camden police picked up a prostitute. She was high on coke and wouldn't stop talking. She told her cell mate she had been kidnapped and put into sex trafficking. She said there were other kids with her, and one of them was named Maggie."

Lorraine's hands flew up to her chest. "Where is this girl? What's her name? Can I speak with her?"

"Her street name is Shana. Her ID shows her as..." Harker pulled his notepad from his pocket. "Let's see...Emily Quinn. They ran the name. No record or prior arrests. The thing is, we don't know if that's her real name or not. These pimps have cornered the market on fake identities. The hookers never have real IDs, and they won't tell the police they were kidnapped or are being held against their will. Their pimps make sure they keep their mouths shut by threatening to kill them and their families," he explained.

Detective Harker paused for a moment, giving Lorraine time to absorb the information.

"Shana is back on the streets. Her pimp bailed her out. When the police asked her about what she told her cell mate, she denied all of it. Told them she was a runaway, and since she had ID that showed she was nineteen, they couldn't hold her," Harker explained.

Shimmying up to the edge of her seat, Lorraine pressed on. "What else did she say about Maggie? Did she say where we can find her?"

"No, she only said there were five of them," Harker said, "which is consistent with the five inhabitants we believe were held at the old prison. The girl said they were moved from the prison and kept in the basement of a house, and she was sold to a pimp in Camden. That's all I know, and I wanted to come here so you have the same information."

Just then, Rob and Keith walked through the front door. Seeing Detective Harker, Rob sent Keith up to his room and joined them in the living room.

"Detective Harker was just saying they picked up a streetwalker who said she was with Maggie," Lorraine said with an in-your-face attitude.

"Well, that's not exactly what I told you, Lorraine," Harker said. Then he repeated the information to Rob.

Lorraine was charged with a renewed sense of hope. After Detective Harker left, she found Rob in the kitchen. "See? I told you, Rob. We can't give up. Maggie's out there. She's alive, and someday she'll come home."

Rob sat silently for an uncomfortable amount of time. When he spoke, he was calm and deliberate. "Every time we get a piece of information—some of it bullshit, by the way—you open yourself up to being hurt all over again. This is the whole point of leaving this house, Lorraine. When we heal one little bit or take a tiny step forward, we get some piece of information that makes our hopes soar. And then, when it doesn't pan out, we go back to that dark place in our lives again. It undoes any good we were able to establish. It's a never-ending cycle. I wish Harker wouldn't come here unless they actually find Maggie. I feel like we're living in one of those movies where the character is running down a long hallway and, just when he's about to reach the door, the hallway grows longer."

Lorraine looked at him in disbelief. "We just got news that another girl was with Maggie a couple of months ago. It means our daughter is still alive!"

"It *means* that a cokehead hooker said she was with a girl named Maggie! That doesn't mean it was our daughter. You know what? I'm done with this conversation. Lorraine, it's time for us to move on. You need to decide if you're with us or not," he told her.

"Are you threatening to take Keith away from me? Is that what you're doing?" she demanded.

"No, Lorraine, I'm telling you that our son deserves a life where he's as important as his missing sister. I'm telling you that if I have to move on without you, then I will," he said firmly and left the room.

Lorraine slumped into the closest chair. What was happening to her family? How could God have done this to them?

Chapter Forty-Two

The next three weeks were hell for Maggie. She was kept in the vertical box in the closet for most of the time. Armando threw mice and bugs into the box with her after she killed the snake. It was like a game for him, and the more he tortured her, the more Maggie lost her sense of self. She was being reduced to an animal and a servant, which was all part of the wrecking period.

Armando only took Maggie out of the box for three things: to eat, to be brainwashed, and for sex. Bit by bit, he broke her down. Spending twenty-two hours a day in a cramped box was more horrifying than anything else she had endured.

"Come on, bitch. Give me your hands. Time to come out and play," Armando said after she'd been in the box for the first three days. He hoisted her out, and she crawled into the bedroom. Armando towered over her. "Fuck, girl! You stink. You need a damn shower before I can get within ten feet of your stank ass!"

Armando walked to the bedroom door and yelled, "Trinity! Get your fat, black ass up here, girl!"

Trinity, a longtime hooker, sauntered up to the second floor. She was only thirteen when Armando wrecked her for Rock. She had run away from an abusive mother, who was hooking her out to dirt bags in the neighborhood. After fleeing her home in Maryland, she found herself on Kensington Avenue, and Rock offered her a place to sleep. Trinity had become one of the most heartless prostitutes on the street. Now, when she wasn't hooking, she helped the men wreck the girls and punish them for disobedience.

"What cha need, Armando?" Trinity asked, reaching the bedroom.

"I need you to give this nasty bitch a shower. She fuckin' stinks, and I ain't havin' nothing that smells like that," he said. "You give me a shout when she's done, hear?"

"Yeah, I hear," she responded.

After Armando left the bedroom, Trinity looked at Maggie, who was sprawled out on the floor. She had shit and pissed all over herself in the three days she was held captive in the box.

"I don't know why I get stuck cleanin' these bitches up," Trinity said to herself. "Look at you," she said to a weak and unresponsive Maggie. "You done got yourself all shitted and pissed up. You fuckin' nasty, girl."

Trinity helped Maggie up off the floor. She took slow steps toward the bathroom. Trinity reached in and turned on the shower. "Come on, girl. Get yourself in there," Trinity ordered.

As the water splashed over Maggie's head, she began to feel alive again. Trinity stood with her arms crossed and the shower curtain open so she could watch her. "You need to wash that hair and clean that dirty puss and ass, girl. Ain't nobody gonna want to tap that thing. Man, you're gross."

"Can I have a glass of water, *please*," Maggie croaked.

Trinity eyed her up and down, and then she walked over to the bathroom sink. She grabbed an old cup from the back of the toilet and filled it with water. She handed it to Maggie, who was still in the shower. Maggie guzzled the water and looked to her for more. "Nah, 'nuff of that shit. I ain't your momma. Don't go lookin' at me with those sad eyes. I ain't no stranger to suffering, so ya ain't gettin' no sympathy from me."

Maggie finished showering and turned off the faucets. She slowly got out of the tub and took a dirty towel from the hook on the back of the bathroom door. After drying herself, she walked into the bedroom. "Are there any clothes for me?" Maggie asked Trinity.

"Ha! What you need with clothes? Nah, there ain't no clothes for you, white girl. All you need to do now is sit on the bed and wait for Armando."

Trinity studied Maggie closely. Minus the dark circles and pale skin that hadn't seen sunlight in years, she could see the young girl's beauty. Trinity put her hand on her chin and rubbed it as she thought about

Maggie on the streets. The girl would get a lot of business. The men liked young and beautiful hookers. Maggie was both of those things.

Trinity's glare made Maggie squirm. She wanted to know what she was thinking and find out what they were going to do with her. "What's going to happen to me?" Maggie finally asked.

"Lots a bad shit gonna happen to you if you don't do what you're told. I don't tolerate anyone breakin' the rules, and if you do, I'll *fuck you up* real bad. When ya break the rules, I gets in trouble too, so just do what you gotta do. It'll be a lot less painful," Trinity threatened.

Maggie said a little prayer that her pain would stop. But as they had for three years, her prayers went unanswered.

Chapter Forty-Three

Exhaustion had taken hold of Maggie. Her muscles felt heavy, and her senses were dulled—exactly the results Rock desired. With heavy eyelids, she stared at the wall, looking at nothing. Finally, she found the strength to speak. "Please help me. I don't want to hurt anymore," she mumbled.

"Ain't nobody that can help you, but you." There was a short pause, "She's cleaned up!" Trinity screamed.

The sound of the door being thrown open made Maggie jump. Armando approached her. "Here's the deal. You'll work for Rock, and you'll do everything that's expected of you. I don't wanna hear no whining or complainin', or you'll find yourself in a shitload of trouble," he said. "Stand up and show me what you got."

Maggie got off the bed and stood. She swayed back and forth, trying her best to keep her balance. She squinted in an effort to make eye contact with Armando. "How's Seth? Is he doing OK? Can I visit him?"

"You just ain't had enough, huh? You're not getting it. You don't get to ask for things, girl, you give things. Things that men want. You understand?" he pressed.

Maggie lost her footing and landed hard on the floor. Armando lifted her up and threw her on the bed. "Go get the others," he told Trinity coldly.

A few minutes later, there were several men in the bedroom. Each took his turn with her. When it was over, Armando hoisted her up by her shoulders. "Listen here. You Rock's bitch now. If anyone asks, you are eighteen years old. Even if the police ask, you're still eighteen years old."

"Nobody will believe me. I'm only fourteen," she managed to say.

"Damn girl, what ain't you getting?" Armando asked angrily. "Put this stupid ass back in the box," he instructed to one of the other men.

Maggie pleaded and begged for forgiveness as she was hauled over to the closet. She dropped into the bottom of the box like a brick. Quickly the door was closed, and the deadbolt was thrown. Disoriented and in pain, Maggie slumped against the rough wood. She began to hum the tune of "Itsy Bitsy Spider." She didn't know why, but it made her feel better. After that, her imprisonment went on for over two more weeks. She came out once a day for the three rituals. She was told over and again that she was eighteen years old, and if she ever told anyone who she really was, they would kill her and Seth.

"We know where your parents live, too," Armando lied. "Don't think we won't torture and kill them if you ever tell anyone who you are."

At the end of the third week, the small door opened, and Maggie started to cry. A bright flashlight was aimed at her face, and she recoiled from the painful beam of light. "How you doin', baby?" a man cooed. "Don't worry; I'm gonna help ya now."

Maggie was too distressed, and tired, to be relieved. She hoped that by "helping her," the man meant he would shoot her in the head.

"Come on, baby. Give me your hands," the man said softly.

With great effort, Maggie raised her hands into the air. The man pulled her out and gently laid her on the mattress. He bent and picked up a ratty blanket from the floor and covered her with it. Then he sat on the side of the bed and stroked her hair.

"Trinity," he said in a calm voice. "Bring me a glass of water for our Maggie."

He held the glass as Maggie took small sips of water. Maggie grimaced when she tried to open her eyes for the first time; the light was too painful to handle. Finally, with much effort, she opened her eyes. There, sitting next to her, was Rock.

She flinched.

Rock leaned closer to her. "No, baby, it's OK. Rock is here to take care of you now," he assured her.

Rock instructed Trinity to fill the bathtub with warm water. Then he gingerly carried Maggie into the bathroom and placed her in the tub. The heat of the water began to soften her stiffened muscles. Rock massaged her arms and legs. She let herself relax with his powerful, gentle hands rubbing away weeks of being cramped at the bottom of the box.

"Go make somethin' nice for Maggie to eat," he told Trinity.

As he rubbed Maggie's neck, he looked into her face. Her eyes smoldered with intensity. Rock was the first person in three weeks to show Maggie any compassion, and this tactic made her love him. Maggie felt her belly flutter as she watched him intently. She opened her arms, and he leaned over and hugged her close to him. "That's it, baby. Rock is here to take care of you now. Do you know how old you are?"

"I'm eighteen," she answered, wanting to please him.

"How did you get here?" he continued.

"I came here on my own. I love it here," she recited.

"Where do you live, baby?" he asked in a sultry voice.

"With my boyfriend," she said affectionately.

"Who is that, baby? Who is your boyfriend?" he sang.

"Armando is my boyfriend," she said with a pang of guilt, as if she was betraying Rock.

Rock saw that all-too-familiar look. "That's right, baby. But, me, I'm the one you really love," he said sweetly.

"Yes," Maggie agreed.

Rock was proud to have wrecked another girl, especially one as gorgeous as Maggie was. He was delighted to think of all the money she would make for him. But Rock wasn't aware of Maggie's ability to persevere through the most hideous circumstances.

Chapter Forty-Four

————————————————■————————————————

After Maggie had a few days of rest, Armando told her that she would start working the next night. "Trinity is gonna take ya out and get ya started. She's gonna teach ya how to lure men in and how much money you should get."

Maggie, no longer willing to argue, nodded. "Sure, Armando, whatever you want."

Armando smiled to himself. *Another bitch wrecked,* he thought. *This is just too easy.*

Maggie knew that everything happening to her under Armando and Rock's control was just as wrong as all the things John William and Myles had done to her. She also knew that Thelma had Seth at her home, and suspected that Armando would keep true to his word and kill the boy if she didn't do everything he told her to do. She had been having sex against her will since she was kidnapped. She hated every minute of it, but over time, she'd come to accept it as a way of life. It's just what she did, she told herself. It was not who she was.

That night, on Kensington Avenue under the train tracks of the El, Maggie realized that being a streetwalker wasn't easy. They stood in the cold in high heels and short skirts. They were forced to flirt and smile at all the scum-sucking maggots who happened to look their way. Maggie was intrigued by the prostitutes who fought over customers, and she gawked at the strung-out drug addicts who oozed onto the streets from small alleys with nothing on their minds but the next fix.

"OK, this guy walking toward us. He's a regular. I want ya to smile at him really pretty and ask if he wants to go on a date. Understand?" Trinity pressed.

As the man approached, Maggie plastered a fake smile on her face. "Hello, sir. Would you like to go on a date?"

"Ha! What's with the sir shit? Trin, who ya got here, Mary fucking Poppins?" the scuzzy man yapped. "Sure, honey, I'll go on a date wit' cha."

"What are ya lookin' for?" Trinity asked him.

"With this little hottie? How much for a regular?" he asked.

"We got a special tonight since she's new and all. Fifty bucks," Trinity said confidently. "Ya know that's a fuckin' steal, too. Just look at her."

The man rubbed his chin and took a long visual drink of Maggie. "Yeah, OK. But she better be good for that kind of money."

"Yeah, she'll be good," Trinity promised.

Trinity leaned into Maggie. "Take him back into the weeds in that open lot. Keep walking 'til you see a small path on your left. Follow the path and you'll see a mattress. Make sure he uses a condom; we don't need no pregnant bitches 'round here. Do him and get back here fast."

Walking through the tall weeds with the stranger, Maggie realized that this was the first time since John William had kidnapped her that she was roaming free. Little did she know that Armando was watching her every move after she left Trinity's side. They never let new girls go off on their own for the first couple of months, not until they could be trusted.

Once they reached the mattress, Maggie turned and looked at the man, waiting for instructions. "What the fuck are you looking at? Let's go; get undressed," he told her.

Maggie quickly undressed, shivering in the cold night air, and sat down on the edge of the mattress. "You're kiddin' me, right? What the fuck are you waiting for? Lay down on the damn mattress," he said, losing his patience with her inexperience.

He stood over her and quickly slipped on a condom. The cartel also required the men to wear condoms, but only to keep their property disease free.

"You're sure a beauty," the john panted, once he was on top of her.

When he finished, he stood quickly, took out fifty dollars, and threw it at her. By the time she got back out on Kensington Avenue, Trinity had another customer waiting for her. "Give me the money," Trinity stated. "Take this next guy back. He wants a blow job. Make sure you get twenty-five bucks when you're done."

Maggie's first night was horrid. She serviced someone every forty-five minutes. She'd done all the same things with men during her captivity, but here, in the open, she felt like a creepy-crawly bug in the night. When it was time to go back to the house, Armando came to walk with her.

"You did pretty good tonight," he said, taking the money from Trinity and counting it on the way back to the car. "Tomorrow, I wanna see ya do better. It costs a lot of money to keep ya happy. Ya already owe Rock ten thousand bucks for buying you out of that whorehouse you were livin' in," he explained.

"But no one told me I had to pay Rock back. I didn't even know how much money he had to pay," Maggie stated sheepishly. She had no idea how she would ever be able to repay ten thousand dollars. Then she spoke without thinking.

"Maybe my parents would pay Rock for me. I could call them and ask," she offered, with a glimmer of hope that she could speak to them again.

But as the words passed Maggie's lips, she realized it was the wrong thing to say.

Chapter Forty-Five

Armando remained silent for the remainder of the ride. Slamming the car into park, he bolted to the passenger door and flung it open. He reached in and yanked Maggie out by her arm. As they entered the house, the other hookers stopped and watched as Armando pushed Maggie up the stairs, berating her the entire way. They all knew she was going to get it from him.

Up in the bedroom, Armando took off his belt and started whipping Maggie. "What the fuck did I teach you, girl? Huh? How old are ya?" he screamed.

"Eighteen," she managed through sobs.

"Who do you live with?" he yelled.

"My boyfriend," she blubbered.

"Take your fucking clothes off," he said, seething.

Maggie practically ripped her clothes off. His anger made her anxiety skyrocket; she didn't want to go back into the box in the closet. "I'm sorry, Armando. I shouldn't have said what I did. I know that I'm staying here with you. Please don't hit me anymore," she whined.

"Get on the fuckin' bed," he roared.

He beat her with his belt until she passed out. Then he waited until she woke up and had sex with her to make certain she knew he was the boss.

The next night, she was on the streets again with Trinity when a teenage boy with bloodshot eyes, strung out on drugs, approached them. "Hey man, you got any money you can spare?" he asked.

"No! We ain't got no money for your sorry ass. Keep on walkin' before I knock the shit out of you," Trinity threatened.

As the boy walked away, Maggie stood staring at Trinity in wonder. "Who the hell are you eyeballin', girl?" Trinity demanded.

"No one," Maggie said, dropping her gaze to the ground.

"Listen," Trinity said. "You gotta learn to protect yourself out on the streets. People 'round here know I don't take shit from no one. I don't care who you are. You ain't gonna survive out here by bein' nice. So you need to learn to get tough, or these motherfuckers will eat you alive. You understand me?"

"Yeah, I understand. How long have you been a…doing this?" Maggie questioned.

"What? You were gonna call me a hooker? Well, that's what I am, and so are you. I've been out here for a lot of years. Been 'round long enough to know that there ain't no body gonna take care of you but you. Just like you, I had to learn how to survive out here. Ain't nobody gonna teach it to ya, either. Gotta learn it for yourself," Trinity said with pride.

Trinity's words of wisdom left Maggie feeling alone and unprepared to face life on the streets. Maggie had hoped that over time, Trinity would grow to like her, but there were no signs that Trinity felt anything but obligation to keep Maggie with her. It was her job.

Maggie decided to be more observant of how the other prostitutes acted. She listened to the things they said and watched them chase off men who wanted sex for nothing or tried to rob them. It appeared as though most of the girls had a sixth sense for the men who would cause them trouble. Maggie worried that she would never fully understand how to deal with the dangers of being on the street every day.

For the remainder of January, Trinity set up all of Maggie's tricks. Trinity had Maggie working continuously, giving regular sex as often as possible, in order to earn the maximum amount of money. Because of this, Armando and Rock were quite pleased with the work Trinity was doing, and this made her happy. She had always wanted to be in charge of the girls, and Maggie was her stepping-stone to becoming the boss on the streets. This title, given only by Rock, would bring special privileges and power.

Maggie, on the other hand, was exhausted. She felt weird cooing at men as they drove by. Her life was degrading. But she didn't know how to escape without getting herself and others killed. So Maggie did and said everything she was told. But inside, there was a slow burn, a desire for liberation. She longed to see her family again and fantasized about their reunion. She wanted to be returned to life as she knew it before John William had taken her from the mall.

Over time, Armando began to trust Maggie, allowing her to roam the house freely, as the other girls did. The house was a total shit hole, the armpit of the earth. Right inside the front door was a large, open room that was once a formal living room. The chandelier and sconces were long gone, but gaping holes in the plaster revealed where they once hung. Two floor lamps lit the gloomy room. Instead of furniture, there were old, worn-out mattresses where the girls partied and slept. A wide hall led to the main living area. This room had leather beanbags and recliners reserved for the men who ran the house. The girls were prohibited from sitting on them or even entering the room without being invited.

To the right of the front entrance was the kitchen. The cabinets and refrigerator were secured with chains and padlocks to keep the girls from eating whenever they wanted to. The girls were provided with one meal a day. One of Rock's men supervised a couple of the girls to put out food. The girls found their other meals on the streets by asking johns for a slice of pizza or occasionally buying a hot dog from a street vendor. Just off the kitchen was an old laundry room where Rock had installed a shower. All twelve girls used it; the upstairs bathrooms were off-limits.

When Maggie was in the house with the other prostitutes, she made it a point to keep to herself. She didn't like the other girls. They were hard and callous to each other. She understood their anger, and felt much the same, but she couldn't understand why they took it out on one another. As much as she wanted an ally, she didn't trust any of them. They were constantly fighting over men, cigarettes, and drugs. These arguments often turned into fistfights and hair pulling, which broke out at a moment's notice.

While the others fought, Maggie found a quiet corner in their living space and thought about Seth. She wondered if he was OK and if Thelma showed him any kindness. Rock visited the house where Maggie lived several times a week, and she was tempted to ask him about Seth, but she knew better. Rock and his men told the girls what they wanted them to know. She had learned that asking questions was a sign of insubordination.

By early February, Armando allowed Maggie to walk the streets alone. On her first night out, she wandered down Kensington Avenue, smiling at men and asking them if they needed a date. Men were attracted to her, and she had no problem earning her nightly quota. Because she was able to lure men in without much effort, she only offered hand jobs, and no one at the house was the wiser because she was able to do double the number of men to make up the difference in money. In a short time, Maggie became the most desired harlot on Kensington Avenue.

Then, on her travels up and down Kensington Avenue during her second week alone, Maggie noticed something that made her heart soar with hope. It was a sign at Kensington and Indiana Avenues; she followed the arrow and within minutes, she was standing in front of the McPherson Square Free Library.

This was the first time in a very long time that Maggie had something to look forward to. Her biggest problem was how to sneak away long enough to spend time at the library without being caught. She'd figure something out, she told herself. No matter what happened to her, it was worth the risk.

Chapter Forty-Six

It wasn't long before Trinity viewed Maggie as her strongest competition. Her temperament toward Maggie turned foul overnight. Rock had yet to make Trinity the boss on the streets, and Trinity's competitiveness spurred her to put Maggie down as often as possible.

"Listen, bitch! I showed you how to make money on these here sidewalks. You know damn right well who my regular customers are, and I expect you to back the fuck off my johns," Trinity told her. Several other hookers were watching, waiting for a fight.

"I'm sorry, Trinity. It's not my fault. I haven't even offered to go on dates with them. Your regulars have been asking me. If they're asking, I can't refuse. If Armando or Rock found out I turned a john down, you know what they'd do to me," Maggie explained, hoping for understanding.

"What Armando or Rock do to you ain't nothin' compared to what I'm gonna do to ya if you keep stealing my johns," Trinity spat. Then she shoved Maggie in the chest, knocking her to the ground, and spit on her as she strutted toward an approaching car in her "fuck me" pumps, swinging her round hips from side to side. She leaned into the open car window to show the man her voluptuous cleavage and smiled with all the teeth left in her rotted mouth. "Hey, baby, you wanna go on a date with Trinity?" she breathed.

"Is Trinity that girl over there?" the man asked, pointing at Maggie.

"No, motherfucker, I'm Trinity," she said in a shrill voice.

"Oh, well then, no. I want a date with that little vixen," he told her and pulled his car up to where Maggie was standing.

Maggie looked over at Trinity nervously.

The man looked her up and down. "How much?"

"I only give hand jobs. Fifteen bucks," Maggie told him.

"Only hand jobs? What the fuck is with that? I was looking for regular sex," he said, annoyed.

"Sorry, baby. Come back if you decide you want a hand job, OK?" Maggie offered.

The man put the car in drive and left. As soon as he was gone, Maggie began to walk in the direction opposite of where Trinity stood. She recognized that her "mentor" was in the kind of mood that would get her a hearty ass-kicking. Maggie was several blocks away, talking to another customer, when the same man came back around and spotted Trinity again. "Hey, you!" he yelled out the car window.

Trinity looked up from lighting a cigarette. Then she strolled toward his car as if she was in no hurry and completely disinterested. She bent down to look at the man. "Yeah, what cha want? I thought you wanted some of that white meat. Now you're back 'cause everyone knows dark meat is tastier than that nasty, dry, white meat," she chastised.

"Yeah, whatever. How much for regular sex?" he asked.

"Fifty bucks," she told him.

"Fifty bucks? Is your pussy made of gold or something?"

"What the fuck? You think you gonna get this shit for free?" she said with a dramatic wave of her hand across her chest and between her legs.

"OK, but I want it to last awhile for that much dough," he told her.

"Baby, ain't no man can last long with Trinity. You can move slow all you want. Ain't nothin' gonna stop you from blowing a load the minute you're between my sweet black legs," she said, trying to be seductive.

Trinity got into the man's car and they drove down Kensington Avenue. The john parked under the train tracks. Drug addicts and alcoholics stood around, stoking fires in large metal barrels. "OK, let's get in the backseat. It's too fucking cold outside," the man told her.

Six minutes later, they were finished. "I told ya, no one gonna last a long time wit' me," Trinity said, beaming in his direction. "Can you drive me back down to where we met, baby?"

"What do you think I am? Your fucking chauffeur? Get the hell outta my car, you crazy whore! You and that other whore, there's something wrong with both of ya!" he told Trinity.

"Ain't nothin' wrong wit' us. There's somethin' wrong wit' you!" Trinity argued. "I did exactly what ya wanted me to do, and I don't know what you're talkin' 'bout with the other girl. Ya left her ass and came crawlin' back to me," she announced victoriously.

"Ha! Is that what you think happened? Nah, that ain't it at all. That little white bitch only gives hand jobs. The only reason I came back for your skank ass is because I didn't want no hand job; I wanted sex. Now get the fuck outta my car," he hollered.

Without another word, Trinity got out of the car and slammed the door shut. *So that's what the bitch has been doing,* Trinity thought as she stomped her way back home. *The bitch is selling hand jobs for cheap and stealing all of my business. Just wait until Armando and Rock find out*! She reveled in the idea of Maggie getting what she deserved.

Chapter Forty-Seven

Trinity went back to the house immediately. She could barely contain her anger with Maggie and her excitement at being the one to deliver the news to Armando and Rock. She burst through the front door and, with intended drama, swaggered into the room where the men sat. Hearing her loud footsteps approaching, the men stopped talking. They looked over when Trinity stood in the doorway with her hands on her hips. She raised her eyebrows and pressed her lips tightly together, revealing her annoyance.

"What the fuck is wrong with you?" Armando asked, irritated by the interruption.

"Your bitch, Maggie, she's playin' all of us. A john I was wit' tonight told me that he wanted regular sex, and she told him she only gives hand jobs. Ain't no wonder why the ho is meetin' her quota and stealing customers from the rest of us," she fumed.

Armando watched Trinity closely, trying to gauge if this was a jealous rage or if she was speaking the truth. With that in mind, he tested her. "Well, I'll look into the matter. But I best not find out that you're lying to make yourself look good," he hedged.

"I ain't no mother fuckin' liar. I'm telling ya what the man told me. I think Maggie's the one who's lyin' to ya. She thinks she's better than all of us, including you and Rock. I suggest you go find out for yourself," she stated.

It was unacceptable for the girls to talk to the men in the house that way. Armando realized Trinity's outburst could only be fueled by truth. Still, he had to make sure Trinity didn't overstep her bounds. He stood, walked over to doorway, and grabbed a handful of her hair. "Don't you worry. I'll check it out. Let me be clear with you, though. Don't ya ever talk to me that way again." Then he shoved the side of her head into the doorjamb.

Once Trinity came to her senses, she left the house and went back out to the street. She began to gossip to the other prostitutes about Maggie. "Yeah, I told Armando exactly what that nasty slut is doin'. She's gonna be sorry...thinks she's better than the rest of us...thinks she pretty, too. Fuck that ho bag!"

The other hookers weren't any more inclined to feel sympathy for Maggie. She was a stunningly beautiful young girl, and they'd all smoldered with jealously watching the johns swarm to her like flies on shit. They hated her for that because it meant they all had to work harder to make their nightly quotas.

A few hours later, Rock stopped at the house to check with his men. Armando repeated the story Trinity had told him. "You get one of our guys she doesn't know out there to see what she's really doing. Get back to me, 'cause I wanna know right away," Rock instructed, boiling with rage at the possibility that Maggie was duping him.

A few hours later, a man approached Maggie on the street. "Hey, honey, you need a date?" Maggie asked enticingly.

"Yeah, how much for regular?" he asked, avoiding all niceties.

"I only do hand jobs. Fifteen bucks," she stated and batted her long eyelashes at him.

"Only do hand jobs? What kinda whore are you?" he pressed.

"Look, baby, that's what I do, OK? My man, he wants me to keep it simple," she replied.

"Well, your man is damn fool then. Just forget it. I ain't interested in no hand job," he told her and drove off.

Later that night, it began to snow heavily, and the wind whipped through the streets. Little white clouds shot out of Maggie's nose and mouth every time she exhaled into the bitterly cold air. There were practically no cars on the streets, and the foot traffic had nearly come to a halt. Just after two in the morning, with several inches of snow on the ground, Maggie climbed the broken-down steps of the row house that she secretly called the house of whores, slipping and sliding in boots with five-inch heels.

Once inside, the heat of the house hit her ice-cold bare legs and ass, which made her feel as if there were bugs crawling under the surface of her skin. She leaned over and scratched her legs, causing red blotches to appear. Quickly, she went over to the corner where she kept her clothes and put on an oversized hooded sweatshirt she had found in the trash on Kensington Avenue. It hung just below her thighs. Then she pulled on two mismatched socks and a pair of canvas sneakers. Pulling the thin cotton blanket over herself, she settled in to sleep. She was dreaming when the men lifted her from the mattress and stood her upright. Her eyes bolted open, and the first person she saw was Armando.

To her right, Rock leaned on the banister of the stairs. Armando stared at her for an uncomfortable amount of time. "Word on the street is that you're only givin' hand jobs. Is that true?" he asked.

"No! I don't know who told you that, but it's a lie. I swear," Maggie choked out, as she began to tremble.

"Oh, OK. So then my man, Jeremy, over here," Armando said, looking to his left as a man stepped into the room, "he's lyin' to me. That's what you're tellin' me, right?" he asked in a belittling tone.

Maggie looked at the man. She recognized him. He was the one she had told that same night that she only gave hand jobs. *Fuck, shit, balls,* Maggie thought. *I'm busted.*

She looked to Rock, who had been so nice to her, but he just held a steady gaze, showing no sign of pity. Tears spilled down her cheeks, and she struggled to put together a cohesive sentence as panic gripped her. "I'm sorry," she finally managed through uncontrollable sobs.

"Nah, you ain't really sorry," Armando told her. "But you gonna be."

Armando pushed her back down on the mattress. By now, all of the other prostitutes were huddled on the other mattresses, watching with anticipation. Trinity had a smile plastered across her face, waiting for Maggie to get what she deserved.

Armando towered over Maggie, looking like Blunderbore, the giant in "Jack and the Beanstalk." She thought he might trample her to death. She didn't know what he was going to do and wished one of the other girls would say or do something to help her. Instead, they sat by, entertained by the drama.

Armando finally spoke. "Jeremy, here. He works for Rock. We heard what you were doing and thought we'd check it out ourselves."

Maggie looked over at Trinity, who sat perched on a mattress victoriously. Then she turned back to Armando. "It was a mistake, Armando. I'm still new at this," she wailed, trying to play on sympathy that he didn't have for her.

Armando turned to Jeremy. "Go ahead, my brother. Take what's yours."

Jeremy dropped his jeans and was on top of Maggie in seconds. The other girls watched as she fought and flailed her arms and legs, trying to push Jeremy off. Then she felt the blade that Jeremy laid against her throat. "You best stop fightin' and make me feel wanted, or I'll slice you up like a watermelon," he threatened.

Maggie believed he would do just that, so she stopped fighting and pretended to participate. When he was finished, he climbed off of her and left the house. She quickly sat up on the mattress, traumatized and embarrassed that Jeremy had just taken advantage of her in front of so many people, especially the other prostitutes.

Rock approached her on the mattress. "Maggie, Maggie, Maggie," he chanted. "We can't tolerate liars in our little family. It costs a lot of money to keep you warm and dry, living in this house. Nobody takes advantage of my generosity. Ya see, that's what you did. Ya took advantage of me," he continued, bending down to rub her cheek gently.

At his soft touch, Maggie began to beg. "Please, Rock. I'm sorry. It'll never happen again. I swear."

Rock smiled into her terrorized face. "No, baby. I'm certain it won't happen again. Ya know, I haven't mentioned recently how happy Seth is. I mean, Thelma can be a little overbearing at times, but all in all, I think he's adjusted to his new momma pretty well. When he does act up, Thelma puts him in line. Now, if you were to do anything like this again or try to run, well then, that would really piss off me and Thelma, and we'd probably have to kill Seth just to get even with ya."

Just hearing Seth's name was comforting to Maggie. He was still alive; at least that was something. "I swear I won't do anything to piss you off again," she promised.

"No, I'm sure you won't," Rock said gently. "I have to go home. Armando's gonna deal with all of this now. So, just remember what I told you—that is, if you don't want to put Seth in harm's way."

As soon as Rock left the house, Armando commanded her to stand up. Still dressed in the clothes she had changed into, he told her follow him. They stood just inside the front door, and he slowly opened it.

The cold from outside rushed in on Maggie and Armando. They both stood watching the blizzard outside. The snow was heavy, and there was no visibility. Maggie couldn't even see the houses across the street. "Quite a snowstorm we're havin' tonight. See, like Rock just said, it costs a lot of money to keep you. Now that we know you weren't earnin' your keep, you're gonna have to stay outside tonight," he told her.

Maggie seized the doorknob. "But it's a blizzard out there. I'll *die* in the snow." She wept, gripped with fear.

"Yep, you just might. But I'm thinking you're a pretty clever girl. I mean, you managed to fool us for a pretty long time. So, now you'll have to figure this one out," he stated and pushed her toward the open door.

Maggie hobbled, her steps tentative, wondering if she'd get an even worse punishment if she were to stay in the house of whores. As Armando pushed her over the threshold, she clung to him. Fed up, he shoved her. She plummeted hard onto the cold steps and slid down the icy cement on her stomach.

By the time she landed on the bottom step, she was covered in snow. She sat up slowly, her eyes darting up and down the street. Where would she go?

Then she looked up at Armando, still standing in the doorway, her eyes pleading for mercy. He watched her for a moment, as if he might let her back into the house. Then he turned and shut the door behind him. The sound of the deadbolt being thrown was all she could hear in the silence of the cold, wet night.

Chapter Forty-Eight

Maggie slowly stood and grunted in pain from her scraped knees and chin. Her limbs trembled as she walked away from the house, looking for shelter. The stores were all closed. The wind and snow cut at her exposed skin like razor blades. Her oversized sweatshirt was wet. The streets were empty. Even the bums had found refuge. Snow had buried the trash. Everything was white.

Maggie shivered more violently as she took labored steps, one at a time. Her eyes were watering, and her lips began to turn blue. She started to trip over her own feet and became increasingly clumsy as the minutes passed. Maggie realized, as if in a dream, that hypothermia was setting in. She'd read about it in one of the books that Dr. Barnes had given to her, and in one fleeting moment of clarity, Maggie knew she had to get out of the snowstorm quickly.

She turned down an alleyway that led to open field. In the distance, she could see a high mound of snow, and she stumbled toward it. As if an angel had guided her movements, Maggie found herself next to an abandoned car. The tires were gone and the rear passenger door was missing. She hobbled around to the opening, and with quivering breaths, climbed into the car. Then she shimmied into the front seat. The temperature inside the car wasn't any warmer, but the broken-down vehicle gave her a safe haven from the wind and driving snow.

Maggie huddled, pulling her legs up under the large, wet sweatshirt. Her feet felt like two blocks of ice in the canvas sneakers, and her skin burned with pain instead of warmth. She could feel her body breaking down. Tears slid down her red, chapped cheeks. She curled up in a ball on the front seat, and with great relief, she thought, *just a little more time and I can leave this life.* She had reached her limit. She welcomed the hands of death to hold and comfort her.

Chapter Forty-Nine

Maggie was semiconscious when she felt herself being pulled from the car. She thought she was hallucinating, but someone was carrying her away from the car. She could feel her body wrapped in something warm and dry. She heard the snow crunch under the feet of whoever was carting her off. She tried to open her eyes, but her lids were heavy, and then everything went black as she slipped into unconsciousness.

When Maggie woke up an hour later, she was lying next to an Asian girl. They were both in their underwear. The stranger had her arms and legs draped over Maggie's, and their torsos were pressed together. The girl was looking at her with anticipation.

"Fucking A, you're alive. Thank God! I read that body heat is the best thing for someone who is freezing to death," the girl said, snuggling even closer.

Maggie gave the girl a small smile and fell back to sleep. For the next two hours, the girl massaged Maggie's limbs to increase her circulation. She kept Maggie covered in old towels and dirty clothes until she finally woke again.

When Maggie struggled to sit up on the edge of the mattress, the stranger rushed to her side to help. "How about a cup of hot tea?" she asked.

"I've never had hot tea, but I'd drink anything hot right now. Thank you," Maggie said gratefully.

The girl came back carrying two cups of steaming tea. She rested them on the empty wooden crate next to the bed. Then she opened her dresser drawer and pulled out a sweat suit and socks. "Here, you should put these on. They're dry. Your sweatshirt is still wet. I hung it in the bathroom. I took your shoes and socks off as soon as you got in here. I practically had to chisel the ice from your sneakers to get them off your feet," she explained.

Maggie took the clothes and began to dress. Her mind and muscles were fatigued as she struggled to put the dry sweatshirt over her head. The Asian girl jumped up. "Here, let me help you," she said with compassion. "My name is Juju. Lucky for you, I was looking out the window and saw you climbing into the car across the alley. I knew you'd die for sure if you stayed there. What's your name?" she asked.

"Maggie," she croaked. Her throat was dry and sore. She lifted the mug of tea and took a sip. As she felt the warm liquid coat her mouth and slide down her throat, she started to come back to life.

"How old are you?" Juju asked.

"I'm eighteen," she stated.

"Where do you live?" Juju asked, testing her.

"I live with my boyfriend," Maggie responded, as if she were a Stepford wife.

"Hmm. So, which one of those douche bags do you belong to? Arsen?" she asked.

Maggie shook her head.

"Diesel?" Juju offered.

Maggie shook her head again.

"It's Armando, isn't it?" Juju asked.

When Maggie hesitated, Juju knew she'd gotten it right. "Armando is a fucking dick. They all are. Rock is the biggest prick of them all. How did you get caught up with them?" Juju pressed.

"Rock bought me at an auction," Maggie stated, feeling like a piece of meat.

Feeling Maggie's self-loathing, Juju told Maggie her story. "Well, I work for Rock too. I'm one of his drug pushers. A couple of years ago, Rock was riding me hard to prostitute for him. I kept turning him down, and that was pissing him off something fierce. Then one day, I was in that convenience store down on Somerset. You know the one I'm talking about?"

"Yeah, I know it," Maggie said, intrigued.

"Well, I was in there, and I overheard these two goons saying they were gonna take Rock out at a party he was invited to. The party was a cover-up, just to get him there so they could kill him. Anyhow, I left that store in a New York minute and ran nonstop until I found Rock. I told him everything I heard," Juju explained.

"What happened?" Maggie asked.

"So, Rock went to the party, except he was ready for them. When they had Rock cornered, his men busted into the room and killed the guys. After that, Rock stopped bullying me about prostituting. I ain't got no family, and I needed money to live, so he gave me a job selling dope. Not too many girls sell; it's mostly guys. Rock's always pretty decent to me. I'm like one of the only people who ever saved his life. He told me he'd always watch out for me after that. Doesn't change the fact that he's an asshole. I see what he does to the girls that work for him," she finished.

"Wow, that's insane. So you know Armando?" Maggie asked nervously.

"Yeah, I know all of Rock's men. Armando is a total shithead. He'll do anything to make money. He ain't got no scruples. You know what I'm sayin'? Is he the one who put you out on the street tonight?" Juju inquired.

"Yeah, he found out I was only offering hand jobs to my johns," she confessed.

The two girls sat and stared at each other. Instantaneously, they burst into laughter. The whole idea was so absurd. Armando had put her out into a blinding blizzard because she was only giving hand jobs.

"How come Rock lets you live here on your own?" Maggie asked.

"'Cause I deal. If I was hooking, he'd make me live in one of his houses. He pays me to deal, so I can afford my own place, even if it is the ugliest place on earth. So how old are you really?" Juju wanted to know.

"Fourteen," Maggie said.

"Yeah? I'm fourteen too. I'll be fifteen in two months."

"I've been gone from home since I was eleven," Maggie confessed.

"Man, it sucks, don't it? I was twelve when my idiot mother ran off with some dude she met in a bar. Told me she'd be back in a couple of hours, and the bitch never came home. Eventually, I had to leave our apartment, and I slept at different friends' houses. Then when their parents got sick of me always being around, I hooked up with Rock. I've been living here ever since," she explained in one long breath.

Maggie let out a big yawn. "I'm sorry, Juju. I'm just so tired."

"No worries. It's time for some shut-eye," Juju said and crawled into the bed next to Maggie.

In the seconds that it took for Maggie to fall into a deep sleep, a feeling of happiness swept over her. Maybe she'd finally found a friend.

Chapter Fifty

Early the next morning, Juju gently woke Maggie. "Come on, Maggie. Get up. You need to get back to the house. You don't want Armando looking for you. That'll just piss him off more," she said.

Maggie rubbed the sleep out of her eyes, stood, and peered out the window. The sky was gray and twelve inches of snow covered every surface. With the city's filth temporarily hidden under a pure white blanket, Kensington looked like a beautiful place for the first time since she'd arrived.

"I don't want to go back there," Maggie said sadly.

"Yeah, I know you don't. But you have to. You don't want these dudes looking for you. No tellin' what they'd do if you tried to run off. I'll walk you back. You can keep the sweat suit. I have a pair of old rain boots you can have. They ain't warm, but at least your feet won't get wet," Juju offered.

When they reached the house, Maggie knocked on the front door. Trinity opened it slowly and scowled when she saw Juju standing next to Maggie. She turned and yelled, "Armando. Your stupid beotch is back."

Armando walked to the door and looked at the two girls. "What's going on, Juju?" he asked, clearly annoyed.

"Nothing. I was just walking Maggie back," she stated fearlessly.

"Oh yeah, why's that? You her fuckin' guardian angel now?" he asked.

"Might as well be. She would have fuckin' died in the cold half-naked last night if I didn't see her wandering around. Is Rock here?" Juju pressed.

"Nah, he ain't here. Why don't you take your nasty ass back to that rat hole of yours? You know better than to be stickin' your nose in other people's business. You might wind up hurt or dead or somethin'," he threatened.

"Ha! I sell more dope for Rock than anyone on the streets. You don't fuckin' scare me, Armando," Juju threw back.

Maggie couldn't believe the way Juju was talking to Armando. Surely, Rock would punish her new friend for being so disrespectful. But Juju didn't seem scared. For a fleeting moment, Maggie felt powerful through Juju. She wondered if Juju might be able to help her get out of her rotten situation. Maggie turned to Juju and gave her a long hug. "Thanks for everything," she whispered.

"No problem," Juju murmured back. "I'll see you around. You know where I live, so stop by, OK?"

Maggie nodded and followed Armando inside the house.

"So, you found yourself a new friend, huh?" Armando asked in a mocking manner.

"She helped me last night," Maggie said tentatively.

"Well, just because she knows Rock doesn't mean you're gonna get special treatment. Get some rest 'cause once the snow is cleared, you need to get back out there—you and these other good-for-nothing bimbo's," he said, gesturing at the hookers sleeping on every mattress in the room.

"I had a lot of sleep at Juju's last night. I'm not tired," she said, forgetting to whom she was talking.

"Oh yeah? Is that right? You had a little adventure out there last night? Maybe you should spend another night outside, since it was so good and all," Armando stated.

"No, I didn't mean it like that," Maggie explained, "I just meant that I'm not really tired. That's all, Armando," she said calmly.

"Yeah, well, I don't really give a shit if you're tired or not. Do what you want. But you better be ready to go out tonight and stay out for a while. You girls have completely fucked up our weekly earnings with this snow. You'll have to work double time to make up for it. No free rides around here," he said.

Except for you, Maggie thought. *Every day of your life is a free ride as long as we're out selling ourselves while you sit in here on your big blubber ass, sucking up everything you can get your hands on and treating us like a pack of numskulls, you big dick wad!*

"Sure, Armando, whatever you want," she responded.

Maggie sat on the floor, leaning up against the wall. She had a tiny bite of freedom the night before, and it tasted mighty good. She wanted to feast on freedom. Then her thoughts drifted to Seth and wondered if she could talk Rock into letting her see him.

Maggie liked Juju a lot, even though the night before seemed like a blur. Juju was so independent and strong. Maggie wanted to be just like her. The girl wasn't afraid of anything or anyone. In some ways, Juju reminded her of Cali. They both had that take-charge attitude, which comforted Maggie and made her feel as if someone was watching over her.

Maggie's thoughts were interrupted when Diesel, one of Rock's other goons, came into the room. "Let's go, you fucking cows. Get your shit together. It's time to get out there and make up for last night," he commanded.

Chapter Fifty-One

"It's over three years that Maggie's been gone, Lorraine," Rob stated.

"I know how long it's been. But she's out there, Rob. I just know it. I can feel it in my bones. At first, I couldn't feel anything, but now I know," she explained.

"I've been thinking that maybe it's time for you to go back to work. Don't you?" Rob said gently.

"Rob, if I go back to work, then who will continue the search for our daughter? You don't think Detective Harker can keep looking on his own, do you?" she asked calmly.

"I actually do think Harker can keep looking without you. This isn't just another case to him, Lorraine. He's emotionally invested, and you know it. While he continues to search, we'll keep praying. Can we agree we'll trust Harker and try to get more of our life back? Can you do that?" Rob was practically begging.

Lorraine watched Rob closely. The years hadn't been good to either of them. The prematurely gray hair and the lines around their eyes made them appear ten years older than their real ages. She knew the time had come to do something different. Maybe Rob was right, she thought. Rae Harker had a vested interest in finding Maggie. Maybe it was time for her to go back to work and to make life as normal as possible. She and Rob had managed to grow closer after Rob talked about leaving Lorraine and taking Keith with him. That was a wake-up call for Lorraine, and she didn't want to lose them just as she had lost her daughter.

"OK," Lorraine finally conceded. "I'll look for a job. But only part time, OK? If it goes all right, then I'll consider going back full time. How does that sound?" she asked, conflicted.

"That sounds like a great first step. If it's too much for you, we'll reconsider. But at least it's a start," Rob said soothingly.

Then he put his strong arms around her and pulled her close. She could hear the steady rhythm of his heartbeat, the sound that gave her comfort during her many sleepless nights since Maggie's disappearance. Once they'd gotten past the turmoil that threatened to destroy their marriage, they'd become more tolerant of each other. Counseling had helped to keep them grounded.

When Rob went upstairs to find Keith, who had a ball game, Lorraine poured herself a cup of coffee and picked up the telephone.

"Harker here," the voice on the other end said.

"Rae, it's Lorraine. Listen. I've decided to go back to work part time. I'm going to see how it goes and then maybe I'll go back full time," she told him.

"That's great news, Lorraine. I think it would be really good for you and your family."

"Yeah, I'm sure it will be. But you know what this means, right?" she asked, knowing him well enough to consider him a friend.

"Of course I know. It means that you're going to be even further up my ass to make sure I stay on Maggie's case and follow every possible lead, even if it means I have to go without eating for days," he joked.

Lorraine remembered the third week after Maggie's disappearance, when she was irrational and not thinking straight. She had screamed at Harker, telling him there was no time to rest—even if it meant he had to starve to death. "Eat while you're working! There isn't time for that shit right now!" were her exact words.

Lorraine laughed at the vivid memory. "Yeah, well, I meant what I said, and I still stand by it today," she said with a laugh. "All joking aside, Rae, I need to know you'll be just as persistent without me up your ass every minute of the day," she confessed.

"I give you my word. There is no one working on this case that wants her back more than I do. Well, except you and Rob, of course. Anyway, you know what I mean. Listen, find yourself a job you enjoy and try to make your life as normal as possible. It ain't easy. You know I speak from experience. But at some point, it becomes your new normal," Rae Harker assured her.

When Lorraine hung up the telephone, she called her old employer, the principal of the school where she'd taught eighth grade. The women had stayed in touch over the years. To Lorraine's delight, she was able to go back to work part-time as a teacher's assistant. There weren't any openings for a part-time eighth-grade teacher, but the principal said that two teachers who were well into their sixties planned to retire in the near future. When Lorraine hung up the phone, it dawned on her that Maggie would be in the ninth grade by now. With a stab of longing to hold her daughter in her arms, Lorraine went to find Rob and Keith to share her good news.

Chapter Fifty-Two

A s Maggie walked the streets the next night, stopping to bend and look into cars and purr out her cat call, she ran into Juju. "Hey!" Maggie yelled excitedly, waving from the other side of the road.

Juju was just finishing a deal and looked up to see Maggie. Juju smiled broadly, showing off her insanely sexy smile. "Maggie. Wait there. I'm coming over."

After selling to her last waiting customer, she trotted across the street. Juju grabbed Maggie around the waist and lifted her off the ground, twirling her around in a circle. Setting her back on her feet again, she looked into Maggie's magnificent eyes. "You doing OK? Did Armando give you any more trouble?"

"No," Maggie said gratefully. "He was fine after you left. I guess he was surprised to see that I actually managed to survive the night. So what are you doing?" she asked.

"Um, well, right now, I'm selling dope. It's what I do, remember?" Juju said, half joking.

"Yeah, I remember. I just wanted to know if you would be around later. I thought maybe we could hang out during the day tomorrow," Maggie offered, practically holding her breath as she waited for a response.

"Sure, we can hang out. Come by my place in the morning," she told Maggie.

Maggie sighed deeply. "Sounds great! I have to run. I gotta get my quota."

Juju looked at Maggie sadly, realizing that she easily could have been forced to sell herself.

Maggie didn't want any more trouble from Armando, and she had begun to offer regular sex to the johns. She insisted they wear condoms, even though some of the men offered extra money if they didn't have to use one. She hated every minute of it, but she knew that Seth's safety depended on her. She wouldn't do anything that would put him in harm's way.

It was just before eight the next morning when Maggie knocked on Juju's apartment door.

"Hey, girl!" Juju said excitedly. "Come on in. Do you want toast?"

"Sure."

Maggie studied Juju and was amazed by her good looks and physique. Juju had a heart-shaped face and flawless, warm-toned skin, complemented by greenish-blue eyes. Her dark-brown hair had a natural curl, and the shiny strands fell just below her shoulders. She had high cheekbones, the kind Maggie had seen on supermodels, and her upper and lower lips were equally plump. Her smile was vibrant. It lit up her face and invited kisses. While she was only five foot five, her body was lean, and her muscles rippled with every movement.

"I didn't realize how beautiful you are until now," Maggie stated, a little embarrassed that she had said the words aloud. Juju had Asian features, yet she looked like the all-American girl. "Are you Asian?" she asked.

Juju giggled. "My mother's Greek, and my father's Asian. My grandma on my mom's side used to tell me I was Grasian."

"Is Juju your real name?" Maggie wanted to know.

"Nah, my real name is Juliana June, but everyone always called me Juju. I don't remember anyone ever calling me Juliana. I think Juju fits me better anyway," she said with confidence.

"I agree. It's a great name," Maggie said. "I wish I had a cool name like that. Before I came to Kensington, my best friend, Cali, called me Mags. That's the closest I've ever come to having a nickname."

"Where's Cali now?"

"She died," Maggie told her, tears stinging her eyes. "They put her in a dog cage and drowned her in a pool."

Juju's eyes bugged out. "How do you know?"

"Because they made me stand there and watch while they killed her," she confessed, feeling like she'd failed Cali by not saving her life.

"Who made you watch?" Juju persisted, more than curious about Maggie's past.

"The people who sold us," Maggie admitted.

"Wait. Back up. You need to tell me everything," Juju said, hoping Maggie would share her story.

Chapter Fifty-Three

Maggie spent the morning telling Juju some of the things that had happened to her and the others over the last several years. When she was finished, she sat still. The two teens watched each other.

Finally, Juju spoke. "Holy fuck! So you're telling me that you were kidnapped when you were eleven, put into some freaky sex thing, Cali and Max were killed, and now you're here."

"Yeah, that's what happened. I worry about Seth. He's the one Rock took to his house to live with his wife, Thelma. Rock told me he'd kill Seth if I ever lied to them again. I wish I could see him so I would know for sure he's OK," Maggie said sadly.

"He's OK," Juju said tentatively. "I've seen him. A bunch of times."

"What? You've seen him? How?" Maggie asked.

"I go to Rock's house every two to three days to pick up my dope. He's a little blond-haired kid, right?" she asked.

Maggie nodded vigorously. "How is he? Is he doing OK?"

"The last time I saw him was a couple of days ago. He was very quiet. He was sitting on the sofa. Thelma said he was being punished for talking back to her, and he wasn't allowed to move or speak. I only know 'cause when I said hi to him and he didn't say anything, I asked her if something was wrong with him," Juju explained.

"What else? How did he look?" Maggie persisted.

"He looked...well, he looked like shit. He had a bruise on the side of his face and didn't make eye contact with me. I was gonna say something to Rock, but he don't like anyone getting into his business. I know they send him to school, though. I've seen him walking there a couple of times when I was in the neighborhood selling," she said.

"They let him go to school? Oh my God, I can go see him then," Maggie said joyfully.

"Yeah, they always let the kids Thelma raises go to school. Rock needs them to be smart enough so they can sell dope when they get older. Thelma doesn't want them when they get too old. She only likes to raise them—if you can call it that—when they're young," Juju said.

Then she added, "I can figure out what time he leaves the house, and we can meet him along the way to school. Would that work?"

"Yeah, that'd be good," Maggie said, and then she thought hard for a moment. "Are you sure you want to do that for me? I mean, if Rock ever found out, he might kill you."

"Rock is an idiot. He ain't gonna find out. He could care less about Seth. Just as long as that useless piece of shit, Thelma, is happy, he doesn't give two fucks about anything," Juju informed her.

Maggie sat back on the old folding chair with the cracked seat. She reveled in the thought of seeing Seth again. She'd missed him so much and wanted him to know that she loved him. She had worried over the months that he'd think she'd abandoned him. Now, with her new friend, she'd get to see him again.

"Hey, can I ask you something?" Juju said cautiously.

Maggie nodded.

"Do you ever think about calling your mom and dad?" Juju asked the question quickly.

"Yeah, like every day. But Rock and his guys know where my family lives. They told me they'd kill them if I ever try to contact them. Besides, I'm nothing like I was the last time they saw me. So much has changed, and I've done so many horrible things—they'd die if they knew everything I did. Believe me, I'd be a complete embarrassment to them," Maggie told her.

Juju was raised by screwed-up parents who were as irresponsible and stupid as they come. She could imagine how her mother would treat her if she were in Maggie's shoes—she would disown her, if for no other reason than not to have to be a mother anymore. Juju knew nothing about Maggie's parents, but based on her own experience, she believed that Lorraine and Rob Clarke would do the same to Maggie.

"Parents can really fuck you up. I'm probably lucky mine ditched me when I was still young before they screwed me up forever," Juju told her. "Let's make a plan to get you to see Seth. I'm gonna pick up more dope in the next couple of days at Rock's house. I'll see what time Seth leaves for school," she said.

Maggie was beaming. She was so happy to have someone she could talk to. "Thank you so much, Juju. I'll come back here in a couple of days," Maggie said.

"Hey, how about if we go down to Needle Park now? I can introduce you to some other people that I know. Most of them are drug dealers like me, but some of them are just addicts," Juju offered.

Maggie was a bit terrified at the thought of hanging out with dealers and addicts.

"Aren't you afraid to hang out with those kinds of people?" Maggie asked.

"I am those *kinds* of people, Maggie. There are some real assholes out there, but there are also a lot of decent kids that are doing it for the same reasons as you and me…it's all we know; it's how we survive. Don't get me wrong, I've had my problems with some real thugs. You learn who to trust and how to take care of yourself," Juju told her, as if it were the most normal thing in the world.

"Yeah, speaking of that, how exactly did you get me from the car all the way up to your apartment the other night?"

Juju flexed the muscles in her arms like Popeye. "I carried you up. You weigh like ninety pounds; you're so skinny. I just put you over my shoulder and carried you. I stopped to rest a couple of times, but that's it. I work out a lot, so I'm pretty strong. I had to learn how to defend myself on the streets. Being a girl and all, people think I'm an easier target. But I ain't. I know mixed martial arts—you know, kickboxing and grappling. I do a lot of training."

"Wow. So you know how to beat people up?" Maggie asked, not completely sure of what it all meant.

"I know how to defend myself. When people fuck with me, I give them an opportunity to walk away, but if they don't, I can handle it. Sensei, my teacher, has helped me a lot. He doesn't know what I do to make money—he would never approve—but he's taught me how and when to defend myself," she said humbly.

"I have to learn how to take care of myself on the streets too. That's what Trinity told me. She said there isn't anyone who's going to help me. I have to learn how to survive on my own," Maggie confided.

"Well, I know you're gonna be just fine. You're smart and beautiful. All that shit that happened to you just makes you stronger," Juju said, encouraging her.

A short while later, the two girls walked over to Needle Park. Even though the sign read McPherson Park, Maggie quickly understood why it was known by a different name. There were used syringes and small plastic bags scattered about. Empty beer and liquor bottles seemed to be growing from the earth, sprouting up through the snow. It was a depressing place, yet Maggie didn't feel threatened or unnerved by it. It was no worse than the prison or the farmhouse she'd once lived in. Plus, even though everyone was stoned, people seemed friendly.

Afterward, as Maggie walked back to the house to get ready for the evening, thoughts of Juju ran through her mind. She felt safe with her. She liked Juju a lot and wished that someday she could be just like her...strong, independent, and in control of her own life.

But Maggie's wishes wouldn't come true in the near future.

Chapter Fifty-Four

———————————————■———————————————

Several nights later, Juju spotted Maggie coming out of a vacant lot, followed by a tall young man who couldn't have been more than twenty.

"Maggie! What's up, girl?" Juju yelled.

Maggie smiled and waved. Then she turned to the man, who put money into the palm of her hand. She quickly walked toward Juju.

"OK, Seth has to be at school by eight fifteen in the morning," Juju said.

"Were you able to find out what time he leaves the house?" Maggie asked.

Juju smiled. "Sure did. He leaves around seven forty-five. Let's meet up at the Salvation Army store on East Alleghany Avenue. He's gotta walk by there to get to school."

"Perfect. Juju, I'm so excited. I can't wait," Maggie said with longing. "Juju, how did Rock get Seth into school? I mean, doesn't the principal ask questions?"

"Are you kiddin'? Rock runs this town. He's been payin' off the principal at that school for years. That way, the kids he brings to Thelma to ruin can go to school without a bunch of questions. Almost every person in that school is paid off by Rock. Once they get too old, Thelma doesn't want them no more, and then she gets a new kid to send there," Juju explained.

The next morning, just as planned, the two girls were standing in front of the Salvation Army store. In the distance, Maggie saw a young kid walking toward them, and adrenaline began to pump through her veins. As the child got closer, she noticed the long blond hair of a cute little girl. Her excitement faded until the child was only ten feet away. Then she recognized Seth.

"Seth?" Maggie proceeded with caution.

The child looked up, noticed who it was, and sprinted toward Maggie. Their arms were wide open as they came upon each other, and Maggie scooped him into the air in a loving embrace.

"Aggie! Oh, Aggie. Where have you been? Why didn't you come back for me?" the naïve seven-year-old asked.

"Oh, Seth, I wanted to come back for you. But they wouldn't let me. Then I found out that you go to school, so I came here to see you," Maggie explained, heartbroken.

"Can I come and live with you now?" Seth asked hopefully.

"Not yet, baby. Let me take a look at you," she said, holding the child at arm's length to scrutinize him.

Seth's hair hung well below his shoulders. His blue eyes were devoid of life and swallowed up by dark circles, an indication that he was suffering. He was pale and bone thin. Maggie's heart broke as she looked at him. She wanted more than ever to save him.

"How are they treating you?" Maggie asked, afraid of the answer.

"Thelma is mean to me," he cried. "She smacks me for nothing. She only leaves me alone when she's not taking her needles. And, Aggie, she doesn't let me do nothin'. She says I'm bad, and I don't even do anything bad. I hate her, Aggie."

"You're not bad, Seth. Thelma is wrong, OK?" she stated, at a loss for words.

Maggie turned to Juju. "This is our new friend, Juju."

"I see her come to the house," Seth said shyly, afraid she'd tell Thelma that he was bad because he talked to Maggie. "Is she gonna tell Thelma on me?" he asked in a whisper.

"No, Seth. Juju is our friend. She helped me find you. Remember Cali and Max?" she asked.

Seth nodded.

"Well, Juju is like them. We can trust her. But listen, when you see Juju come to the house, you have to pretend like you don't know her, OK? If not, then we'll all get in big trouble."

"OK, but when am I coming to live with you?" he asked again, wanting desperately for Maggie to stay with him and take him far away from Thelma.

"I'm working on it, Seth. You need to be patient. Do you know what that means?" Maggie asked, wanting to be certain he didn't blow their cover.

Seth shrugged.

"It means that you'll have to wait until we can get you out of there safely. If we make Thelma or Rock angry, they might hurt us. Do you understand?"

"Like John William hurt Max?" Seth asked.

"Yes, like that. Until then, I'm going to come here and meet you every day before school. I can walk you to school, and we can be together," Maggie explained.

Juju stepped forward and knelt to put herself at Seth's eye level. "Hey, little man," she said, "we're gonna be good friends. We're gonna be like the Three Musketeers, all for one and one for all."

Seth tilted his head. "Who are they?"

"They were three friends that never left each other. They stayed together all the time. They watched over each other and did everything together," Juju explained.

Seth visibly relaxed and smiled at Juju. "OK, we can be the three musky tears," he said with a smile.

Maggie felt warmth rush to her heart at Juju's words. She hugged Seth closer to her and as she held him, she mouthed, "Thank you" to Juju.

Maggie and Seth talked the rest of the way to his school. He told her how Thelma treated him, and that he wasn't able to talk to her unless she asked him questions. "Sometimes, she doesn't let me eat dinner 'cause she says I need to get tough. She told me I can't have everything I want, or I'll be a spoiled brat," he said solemnly. "But I'm real hungry when she does that and my tummy makes bubbly sounds when I try to go to sleep."

"Well, when we meet you in the mornings, I'll bring you something to eat," Maggie pledged.

As Seth left the girls to head into the school, he kept looking back over his shoulder to make sure Maggie and Juju were still there. He wanted to run away with them and go to a place where people were nice. He hated school. All the kids were mean to him. However, he did have one teacher who was nice to him, even though the rest of his teachers looked at him like a worthless piece of white trash. But now that Maggie was back, he had a tiny sliver of hope that he would get to leave his school and, better yet, get to leave Thelma and all her nastiness.

Chapter Fifty-Five

————————————■————————————

As the two girls walked back to the heart of Kensington, Maggie turned to Juju with a burning question. "Seth said Thelma has to take needles. Is she a drug addict?"

"Yeah, the bitch is a major junky. She'll shoot anything into her arms that she can melt down. I avoid her as much as possible when I'm in the house. She's as crazy as they come," Juju explained.

"Oh God, Juju. How am I ever going to help Seth? I can't even get myself out of my own mess," she said, defeated.

"Hey, what's with all the self-pity? Pull yourself together, or you'll never be able to help Seth. I don't know what the answer is right now, but I'll look out for him when I'm over Rock's house, and we'll see him every morning on his way to school. For now, that's what you got. It's better than what you had before, right?" Juju asked.

"Yeah, I guess," Maggie responded.

"You guess? Well, you need to do better than that. This is something. It's a start. We'll figure it out together," Juju said and put her arm over Maggie's shoulder.

Maggie was grateful that Juju had found her on that bitterly cold night. She didn't feel alone any longer, and now, Juju was helping her with Seth. She clung to the words Juju had just spoken: We'll figure it out together. Maggie realized that her friend was right...things were getting better.

As the months passed and summer drew nearer, Maggie began to worry more about Seth. Once school let out, she wouldn't have a way to see him. Thelma neglected and abused the poor little soul. He had told Maggie about all of the nights that he went to bed without dinner as he gobbled down jelly doughnuts like a savage on the mornings she met

223

him. He also cried about the slaps and punches Thelma rained upon him when she couldn't find "any of that white stuff for her needles."

Juju was Maggie's eyes inside Rock and Thelma's house. Maggie had come to learn that Seth was never allowed to go outside to play, so he had no friends. His easiest times were when Thelma was so high that she forgot he existed. On those nights, he could sneak into the kitchen after Rock left and make himself a mustard sandwich or fill a napkin with dry cereal. His worst times were when Thelma was waiting for more dope to be delivered. On those days, she would scream at him as soon as he got home from school. Seth's silence during her tirades infuriated her more, but when he found his voice to answer her irrational questions, he'd be batted around and told he was disrespectful. Over time, he'd learned that neither silence nor speaking saved him from her cruelty.

As the warmer weather approached and the days got longer, more undesirable people filled the streets of Kensington. This meant that Juju went to Rock's house more often to pick up drugs. One warm day in mid-June, two days after school let out, Juju was at Rock's house. As she moved through the house, she noticed that Seth wasn't anywhere in sight. She wondered if he was upstairs in one of the bedrooms and tried to find a reason to go up, but she didn't want to make Rock suspicious.

Juju's anxiety grew as the time drew closer for her to leave the house; she lingered, waiting for Seth to show up. As she walked down the front steps, she heard a commotion coming from the back of the house. Kids were screaming and laughing, but their laughter made the little hairs on her arms stand up. She slowly made her way to the back of the house like a ninja. Then she saw that five rowdy children had gathered. They were teasing and taunting someone, and as Juju turned the corner, there was Seth with a chain fastened around his ankle, just like a family pet.

Juju turned to the pack of kids, her teeth exposed like a rabid dog's. She seethed with anger. "If I ever catch you little motherfuckers teasing him again, I will rip your hearts out with my bare hands. Now, get the fuck outta here before I kill all of you!"

Juju got on her hands and knees and crawled over to Seth. "What happened?"

"Thelma said she wanted me to be outside since the weather is warm. But then when I got out here, she put this on my ankle. All the kids were watching, and then they started to laugh. Thelma told them they could look at me, but they can't play with me 'cause I'm an animal that doesn't have no manners," he said, sobbing.

"Well, Thelma's a no-good motherfucker who deserves—" Juju stopped herself in midsentence, remembering that she was talking to a very damaged seven-year-old boy. "Thelma is wrong, and she doesn't know anything about you. You are a sweet person, and she's just stupid. Nothing she says matters. You have to remember that. Maggie and me, we need you to be strong. Remember, all for one and one for all, buddy," she said, trying to give him hope.

Seth sat on the grass, his shoulders slouched, and his arms folded over his chest. He nodded without any enthusiasm. Juju looked into his lifeless eyes, and then she took in the dirty face and the hair so long and greasy that the kids said he looked like a girl. His clothes were a size too small, and his fingernails had dirt packed under them. He was a pathetic sight. Seth's tears ran through the grime on his face, leaving streaks of pink skin. Juju reached out and gave him a tight squeeze. "I have to run. Hang in there," she told him.

As Juju walked back to town, she was blazing with anger and fought the instinct to go into a violent rage on whomever she laid eyes. She wondered what it would take for Rock to give the boy up. She'd known Rock for a long time, and he wasn't one to do anything that would upset his beloved, belligerent, obnoxious beast of a wife, Thelma.

Seth's dull, flat, blue eyes were stuck in her mind, and the rumble of his belly rang in her ears. She walked faster as her desire to help him overpowered any discipline she had acquired over her anger. *There has to be a way to help him*, she thought.

A few blocks later, Juju saw Maggie leaning into a man's car. She waited on the sidewalk until Maggie approached. "I just saw Seth," she said, her eyes narrowing and her hands balled into tight fists.

Maggie's lungs froze in mid-breath, terror mounting about what Juju was going to tell her. "What's happened? Is he OK?"

"He is for now, but he ain't gonna be forever. We need to think of something soon. That crazy-ass, drug-sucking dunce, Thelma, is gonna fuck him up for the rest of his life," Juju said, her anger finally boiling over. She picked up an empty beer bottle and threw it against a building. The bottle shattered into a million pieces, making a loud noise that drew the attention of everyone within hearing distance.

"Bitch!" Armando screamed, pointing at Maggie. "Get your ass back to work!"

The two girls looked in his direction. "I gotta go," Maggie said. "I won't be any good to Seth if I get on Armando's bad side. I'll swing by your apartment in the morning."

"Yeah, in the morning," Juju mumbled, as she walked away.

Maggie turned back to Armando. "Sorry," she yelled and strutted toward a gray-haired man who was eyeing her with lust.

"Hey, baby," Maggie purred, "you need a date?"

Chapter Fifty-Six

T he next day, Rock pulled Juju into his living room. "Look, I know you've been hangin' out with Maggie. I ain't got no problem wit' that as long as the bitch continues to earn her quota. I want you to mind your business, though. Otherwise, ya ain't gonna be too happy," he said calmly.

"Yeah, Maggie's cool, Rock. We hang out, but she still sees to her work just like me. We ain't done anything to make you worry, and we ain't plannin' on doing nothin'," Juju answered coolly.

Juju saw movement in the hall and looked over to see Seth walking with Thelma into the kitchen. For a few seconds, she fought her instincts to run after them. Rock noticed the change in her.

"Why are you staring at them? They ain't none of your business. Like I said a minute ago, don't even think about causing any trouble," he stated and waited for a reply.

"Fuck, Rock. I said I wouldn't. Can we get my dope? I'm losing customers standing here talking to you about this shit," she said, acting frustrated.

Rock and Juju walked into the kitchen to get the heroin. He kept it in the freezer during the summer to keep it from melting. Juju stood beside him, watching him intently, knowing if he saw her look at Seth, who was sitting at the table, he'd be onto her. She followed Rock over to the kitchen table and sat across from Seth while he counted out bags. The boy looked at her, and she only dared to make eye contact once when Thelma pushed him off his chair and onto the floor because she heard his stomach growling.

Rock looked over at Thelma. "Come on, baby, why don't cha give the boy somethin' to eat?"

"When the boy can act like a human fucking being, that's when I'll let him eat," she yelled back.

Then Thelma stood, hurried Seth outside, and chained him to the railing of the back steps. Rock watched, and for a brief moment, Juju thought she saw empathy in his eyes. Then he went back to counting out bags. When he was finished, Juju scooped the small dime bags into her backpack and headed toward the front door. "The streets are packed. I'm probably gonna blow through these bags fast, so I'll be back later tonight or tomorrow," she said.

Once outside, Juju sneaked around to the back of the house. She crouched low and kept her body against the building so Thelma couldn't see her from the back window as she made her way over to Seth. "Here," she said, putting two cheese crackers in his palm. She pulled a bottle of water from her backpack. "Cup your hand," she whispered.

When Seth did this, she poured water into his hand slowly. He slurped it down as quickly as she was pouring it. "Eat the crackers and make sure to wipe your hands on the grass here," she said, pointing next to him. "You don't want bitch face to see that your hands are orange," she cautioned.

"Where's Aggie? Can you tell her to come and see me?" he asked in a frail voice.

"I'll tell her I saw you, but she won't be able to come here. Rock can't find out I talked to you. Remember that!" she told him.

"OK, but will you tell Aggie that I miss her?" he asked.

"Yeah, I'll tell her, buddy. Just hang on, OK? We're trying to figure something out. We're making a plan to get you away from here," she said, wanting to leave him with hope.

Seth watched Juju until she disappeared around the side of the house. Then he shoved a whole cracker in his mouth and gobbled it so quickly that he practically swallowed it whole. He sat chained to the railing and thought about going to live with Maggie. It was the only peace of mind he knew.

As the weeks passed, Juju went to Rock's every day. At the end of July, after a second trip to Rock's house in the same day to pick up dope, she began to panic. It had been five days since she'd last seen Seth, and she was worried that Thelma had killed him. She didn't tell

Maggie because she knew it would only make her crazy. Finally, Juju asked Rock, "So where's the kid? He ain't been around."

"What the fuck do you care?" Rock stated, confrontationally.

"I don't. I was just making conversation. He's usually around, or I see Thelma put him out back. I was curious, is all. Just forget it," Juju said, trying to seem disinterested.

"He's in the basement. His stupid white ass got sunburned out in the backyard. He looked like a tomato," he snickered. "Damn skin was peeling, and he kept crying. I gave him some lotion and put him down in the basement 'cause I figured Thelma would beat the shit out of him if he kept up that cryin' like a girl."

"Well, is he OK?" Juju asked nonchalantly, her heart bouncing against her ribs so hard she was sure Rock would see it beating through her T-shirt.

"How the hell do I know? I put him down there a couple of days ago. I left him with water and a bag of pretzels. Haven't seen him since," Rock said, as he casually went back to placing small amounts of heroin into tiny bags.

Juju hesitated, and after several minutes, built up enough nerve to ask her next question. "Can I go down and see the kid? I have an idea."

"Nah, you ain't seeing him. But tell me about that idea of yours," Rock said, annoyed.

Chapter Fifty-Seven

On Juju's way back to the apartment, after leaving Rock's house, she ran into Maggie.

"Hey, baby, you want a date?" Maggie asked a middle-aged, overweight slob.

"Nope, I got my own bitch at home. I don't need to catch none of your diseases," the man growled.

Juju heard what the man said to Maggie as she approached them. "Yeah, your bitch must be a real fuckin' saint to put up with you. You're a disgusting pig," Juju thrust back at him.

Maggie started to laugh. "One day, you're gonna get your ass beat, Juju. I've learned to ignore people like him. What's going on? Did you see Seth today?"

Juju shook her head. "Haven't seen him in five days. Thelma's high most of the time. Seems like all the time now. They've been keeping him down in the basement."

Maggie visibly cringed.

"Anyway, I had an idea and told Rock about it tonight. I'll let you know how it goes," Juju explained, smiling like a Cheshire cat.

"Are you going to tell me?" Maggie nudged her.

"Nope. Don't want to get your hopes up. I ain't got time to deal with your crybaby ass," she teased.

"My crybaby ass, huh? Come on, tell."

"Nah. If it works, you'll know soon enough," Juju said.

Chapter Fifty-Eight

In the clammy, dark basement at Rock's house, Seth was lying on the cement floor. His sunburn had faded since he'd been locked down there, but the blisters had popped, and his legs and arms were peppered with open wounds. Seth finished the food Rock had given him on the second day, and he was so hungry that his stomach was twisted in knots. He rubbed his belly and kept licking his fingers and dipping them into the empty pretzel bag, hoping to find a crumb. He was about to fall asleep again when the basement door was flung open, and the light from the upper floor blinded him. Seth looked up at Rock's large silhouette in the doorway at the top of the stairs. He was scared of Rock—even more scared than he was of John William.

"Get your ass up here, boy!" Rock commanded.

Seth began to climb the steps. "What did I do?" he asked tearfully.

"You didn't do nothin'. It's what you're gonna do," Rock stated with certainty.

Seth followed Rock into the living room. He had gone to the bathroom in his clothes while he was stuck in the basement, and the smell offended Rock. "You smell like shit, boy!"

Seth shrank away, afraid that Rock would hit him. "Come closer. I ain't gonna hurt you," Rock assured.

Seth stepped toward the sofa and spotted a discarded can of Coke on the floor. He eyed it with desire, thinking about the sugary liquid sliding down his dry throat. Rock followed his gaze.

"Go ahead. You can have it," he told Seth.

Seth moved toward the sofa. He wanted to run, but he was just too weak. He lifted the can and guzzled the warm, flat contents. After he drank every drop, he looked back at Rock.

"First things first. Let's go to the kitchen and get you a sandwich. Then you need to take a bath, 'cause I can't stand bein' in the same room with ya," Rock told him.

When Rock put the sandwich in front of Seth, he groaned. His limbs were quivering as he reached for the food he had longed for. When he was done eating, he sucked every finger. He wished he could have another, but knew better than to ask. Rock walked over to the sink and filled a glass with water. Seth drank the water without taking a breath.

"Ya never learnt no table manners, did ya?"

Seth shook his head. He didn't know what table manners were. The kids at school teased him that he ate like a pig, and he figured that Rock must be saying the same thing but in grown-up talk.

"Well, never mind that. Let's go upstairs and get you a bath. I need you to be really quiet. Thelma is sleeping off a four-day binge, and she might kill you if you wake her up," Rock warned.

In the bathroom, Seth stared at Rock. "Who the hell are you lookin' at, boy? Run the water and get your ass in the tub. I'll be back as soon as I can find something for ya to wear. Wash every inch, and be sure to scrub that dirt out from under your fingernails. Looks like you've been diggin' in your ass for gold," he criticized.

Seth blushed with embarrassment. He couldn't wait to get into the water and wash himself from head to toe. It had been almost two weeks since the last time he washed, and even then, Thelma only let him "sponge bathe" in the sink.

Rock came back into the bathroom about twenty minutes later. Seth was sitting in the tub surrounded by black water. "Ew, see now? That's just plain ol' nasty, boy. Get yourself outta there. Here, use this towel," he told him, grossed out by the filth Seth left in the tub.

"Come on," Rock said, leading him into a small bedroom across the hall.

On the bed was a semi clean pair of jeans and the T-shirt that Seth had been wearing when Rock took him and Maggie away from the house where Max and Cali had died.

"Get dressed and come downstairs." Rock turned back to him from the doorway. "Hurry up and be quiet," Rock instructed.

Seth finished dressing. He was trembling at the thought of Rock putting him outside again on the dog chain. The sunburn had been painful, and his skin was still raw. As he descended the steps, he thought, *Aggie, please help me. I don't want to be here alone anymore.*

Chapter Fifty-Nine

S eth crept into the kitchen, moving very slowly, fearful that something bad was going to happen. Rock was sitting at the table counting his bags of white powder and placing twenty small bags into a sandwich bag. He looked up from his mountain of snow. "At least you look half human now. You and me are gonna go out for a while. We're gonna drive around and drop off these bags to people I know. You're gonna help," he told Seth.

At the thought of leaving the house, Seth almost let out a yelp of excitement. Instead, a big grin washed over his face. "I like to help," Seth said, trying to get Rock to like him. "I used to help Aggie wash our clothes in the sink when we lived at the house with John William."

"Oh yeah, whoever the hell John William is. Well, that's good. All you have to do is follow my instructions," Rock said in a dismissive manner. "If you don't do exactly what I tell ya, then you'll stay here the rest of the summer. Ya got it?"

Seth nodded his head but didn't utter a word.

It was ten o'clock in the evening when Rock and Seth got into the car. They drove to different places, and Seth would shove the sandwich bag into his pocket and run to the person waiting. The person would give Seth a roll of money, and he would run back to the car and give it to Rock.

By twelve thirty, Seth was sound asleep in the front seat of Rock's car. Rock stopped at the house where Maggie lived on his way home to check in with his boys, leaving Seth in the car. As usual, there was an argument in full swing when he entered. Two of the hookers had gotten into a fistfight. One was accusing the other of stealing her cigarettes when she'd put them down on the curb earlier in the evening.

"What the fuck is this about?" Rock demanded.

"Bitches are fighting over a pack of cigarettes. Got into a damn fistfight, and the cops picked them up. Had to bail their rank asses out of jail," explained Diesel, the one who looked out for them.

Rock strode over to the two girls, who were sitting on a mattress, still arguing. He snatched up a handful of hair from each of them and banged their heads together. "Where ya whores think you are? Disney World? You stupid bitches cost me money tonight. What do ya think? I pull bail money outta my ass? Get your fuckin' asses up and get back out on that street. Don't come back until you made enough money to pay me back for your mother fuckin' bail," he yelled.

The girls quickly forgot about the cigarettes and hurried out the door. Rock turned to Diesel. "Looks to me like you can't handle your shit. These sluts don't run you; you run them. If you can't handle this job, I'll give your girls to one of the other men who can," he threatened.

"I'm handlin' my shit, Rock. I can't help it they fightin' over a pack of smokes," Diesel said.

Rock punched Diesel in the face, and he flew backward into the wall. By then, the other men were all watching. "That's right. You can't stop them from fightin' over a pack of smokes. But when you get their dirty asses out of jail, you put them back on the streets to work off the bail money, *after* you beat them. You don't let them sit on their lard asses in this house and continue to argue. You got me?"

Diesel nodded, rubbing his jaw where Rock's fist had landed. "Yeah, I got ya."

Rock sat down with his men and explained what he was doing with Seth. "The kid is gonna run drops for me to my pushers. That way, they ain't spendin' all that time coming to my house to get more dope. They can use that time selling," he told them.

It had been Juju's idea. While she recognized that it was a bad thing for Seth to be doing, she also knew it would get Seth out of the house and away from Thelma. She feared that the child would die in her care if something didn't change. The bright side was that Seth and Maggie would be in contact with each other on the streets.

The next morning, Maggie arrived at Juju's apartment at nine o'clock, the same time she arrived every day. She sat at the kitchen table while Juju made them instant coffee. "So, I heard some shit on the street last night," Juju announced.

"What now? Someone out killing prostitutes? That would be my luck," Maggie responded sarcastically.

"Nope. I heard there's a little blond-haired boy riding around with Rock to deliver dope to his pushers," Juju stated victoriously.

Maggie jumped out of her chair. "Seth is out on the streets? Oh my God! That's awesome," she blurted.

Then, in the next moment, Maggie paused. "He's helping to sell drugs?" she asked, scared for Seth.

"Yep. But he's selling to the sellers, Maggie. People like me. Besides, Rock's driving him to each spot. It's not like he's walking Kensington Avenue," she said. "It was my idea. Thelma left him outside for three days. He got bad sunburn. Rock said his skin was blistered and peeling off his body. Rock put him in the basement with a bottle of lotion for a couple days. Said he wouldn't stop crying, and he thought Thelma was going to hurt him more. So, I came up with this idea. I know it ain't what you want him to be doing, but it's better than being left outside or starved to death. Sometimes we gotta do shit that ain't what we want to do. You know that better than anyone," Juju rationalized.

Maggie understood, and she knew that Juju had good intentions. She gave her friend a hug. "You're right. I don't want him involved with selling drugs, but it is better than dying at the hands of that beast. Man, I hate that bitch. I hope Thelma burns in hell. There's a whole bunch of people I hope will burn in hell someday," Maggie stated vehemently.

Then Maggie realized that she would more than likely see Seth on the streets. She got excited at the very thought of holding him even for a brief moment. She had mothered Seth for almost half of his life. Unbeknownst to Maggie, Seth would turn eight in another month.

As if Juju could read her mind, she asked, "When will Seth be eight?"

Maggie shoved her hands into the pockets of her skintight jeans. "I don't know. He was too young when they took him. He didn't remember anything."

"Well, then we have to make up a birthday for him," Juju said, hoping to lighten her friend's mood.

"Yeah." Maggie perked up. "That would be cool. We'll pick a date. Then every year we'll celebrate it with him."

"OK, what date?" Juju asked, enjoying the game.

"We need something easy for him to remember. How about December 3? Get it? One, two, three?"

"Yeah, that's so cool. I love it," Juju told her.

Then Maggie had another thought. "Why don't we head down to Needle Park?"

"Really? Why do you want to go there? I thought you didn't want to hang with *those people*—people like me, let me remind you," she teased.

"Because I want to get to know as many pushers as I can, 'cause if they know Seth's with me, then maybe they'll watch out for him. If they like me, then they'll keep an eye out for him, right? Isn't that the way it works?" Maggie asked in a sassy tone.

A huge grin spread across Juju's face. "Yep, that's how drug dealers fly. See, you're learning. We ain't like you damn streetwalkers who will eat each other alive to fuck some smelly old man," she quipped.

Hearing Juju call her a streetwalker made Maggie feel as if a dozen butterflies had suddenly hatched in her belly. Maggie was a smart girl. While she'd known the truth all along, to hear it coming from her only friend suddenly made it very real. "Yeah, but I didn't pick my career; it sorta picked me," she responded sadly.

"Come on, Maggie. I was only messing with ya. You're much more than some low-down, dirty tramp. You're smart, and someday you're gonna be something great," Juju told her, convinced there were good things in store for her friend.

"Do you really think so?" Maggie asked, wishing Juju had magic powers and could see into the future.

"Of course I do. You'll see. First, we gotta help Seth. Then we'll work on what we're gonna do. You know, like what we're gonna be when we grow up," Juju said with optimism.

For the first time since arriving in Kensington, a spark ignited in Maggie—a tiny flame of hope that one day she could see her family again and help Seth to find his family. She had the feeling that something good was about to happen. She clung to that feeling as if her life depended on it.

In fact, it probably did.

Chapter Sixty

Over the next week, Rock and Seth nailed down the daily routine of delivering drugs. Rock saw his sales go up as a result and was pleased. Juju was happy on two levels: first, because Rock mentioned his increased sales to her; and second, because Seth was doing much better in his new situation.

Juju was one of Rock and Seth's regular stops. Rock parked on the street and told Seth to give the bag to the lady who would be waiting on the side of the house. When Seth rounded the corner, he saw Maggie waiting for him with Juju.

The boy ran to Maggie with open arms. Maggie lifted him into the air and quickly set him down. "You can't stay, Seth. You have to get back to the car fast. But I'll be here whenever you come by to bring something to Juju," she explained.

"Why can't I stay with you, Aggie?" he asked, his eyes filling with tears.

"Seth!" Maggie said sternly. "You can't cry. Rock will figure out you've seen me, and then we'll both be in big trouble. Come on now, you have to be brave and strong. Remember how brave Max was when John William would separate the girls from the boys? Remember how Max took care of you then?"

"Yes," he responded timidly.

"Well, that's exactly how you have to be right now," she stated. "Now go get back in the car and finish your work with Rock," Maggie told him, and gave him another quick hug.

Juju rubbed the top of his head. "See ya later, little man," she said with a big smile.

The two girls watched as Seth ran around the front of the building to Rock's car. As he slid into the passenger seat, Rock asked, "What took you so long?"

"I tripped when I was running over to the girl. I'm OK, though," Seth lied.

"Good. Next time, be more careful," Rock instructed.

Day after day, Seth delivered drugs to Rock's pushers. Doing this, he was able to see Maggie almost every other day. There was never time for talking; it was always a quick hug, a peck on the cheek, an "I love you," and off he would run. But it was a vast improvement over the life he'd had since school let out for the summer.

This new job for Seth helped to ease his troubles at home to a certain extent. Thelma still denied him of any kind of love or encouragement. Many nights, he slept out in the backyard, chained to the railing. He still had to endure her short temper and stinging slaps to the head, arms, and legs. But the one thing she could no longer deny him was food. Rock insisted that she feed him.

"The boy needs to be fed so he can run this shit, Thelma. So make sure he eats. And another thing: he needs to take a bath every day. Ain't nobody wantin' dope delivered by some foul-smelling kid," Rock demanded.

Thelma didn't like Rock telling her what to do. But he so rarely took a stand on her parenting that she honored his request and made sure Seth was fed and clean. Out of all of Thelma's cruelty, the verbal abuse was hardest for Seth to process. Bruises on the skin faded, but bruises on the heart and mind left scars that took a lot longer to heal.

Chapter Sixty-One

O n September 28, Maggie's fifteenth birthday, she finally faced her past head on. She started the day with her normal routine. She left the house of whores, stopped at Juju's for breakfast, and then walked to the library when it opened, so she could read for an hour.

For weeks leading up to that day, she contemplated going through old newspapers from the day she was taken. As much as she wanted to read about her own disappearance, she feared reliving the months that immediately followed her kidnapping. She worried that perhaps her parents had never looked for her, even though she knew that wouldn't be true. But after the things she'd done and all the time that had passed, she seriously doubted they could accept her back as the young woman she'd become.

On this morning, her birthday, she finally decided she'd take the plunge. As she looked through the local newspapers from August 3 of that year, she found nothing. Then it dawned on her that the story would have been published the day *after* she was taken. She pulled the local paper from August 4. On the front page, she looked into the eyes of the eleven-year-old girl she vaguely remembered. The young girl looked so happy. Maggie remembered the family party where the picture had been taken a month before her disappearance. But now, four years later, she barely recognized herself.

She stared at the photo of Maggie Clarke, wishing she could go back in time and take back all she'd lost. The girl looked so sweet and innocent. Maggie knew the picture showed a girl who was carefree and in love with her life. Then she shifted her eyes to the story, and the headline practically slapped her in the face. It read:

GIRL, 11, KIDNAPPED FROM PLYMOUTH
MEETING MALL

Eleven-year-old Maggie Clarke disappeared on August 3 from the Plymouth Meeting Mall. The young girl was on her way to get a slice of pizza, her mother told reporters. "She was only gone for a couple of minutes. I don't know where she is. If anyone knows where our Maggie is, please call the police." Lorraine Clarke, the girl's mother, sobbed when interviewed outside her home early the next morning. Maggie Clarke is five feet tall and weighs eighty-two pounds. She has black hair and blue eyes. She was wearing denim jeans and a pale pink blouse at the time of her disappearance. She was last seen inside the food court at the Plymouth Meeting Mall. Anyone who has information should call the Plymouth Township Police Department.

Maggie hadn't noticed the stream of tears running down her face. She felt as though she was a third party to the information as she tried to absorb the article about herself. Maggie continued searching through other papers. Her picture had been plastered all over the front pages. Her mother and father were interviewed several times. Maggie didn't remember her parents looking as old as they did in the photos. The most troubling realization was that Maggie no longer felt attached or connected to them. Her heart broke as she stared mournfully at the two people who were once her parents: they were now strangers.

Maggie found articles written about her every few days for three weeks following her disappearance. She was saddened that each time an article appeared, it was hidden a little deeper in the paper. Finally, her disappearance was nothing more than a brief update that simply said that the search parties had ceased until more evidence turned up. She read all of the articles twice. The one common thread, aside from her parents, was a Detective Rae Harker. Judging from the picture in the paper, he looked like a large man—someone criminals wouldn't want to mess with—and Maggie wondered how long he looked for her and how much he knew about her.

Looking back, Maggie felt downright stupid. She had lost her life trying to impress a bunch of snot-nosed classmates who excluded her from their lame little group. She would give anything to reverse time.

The gnawing grip of regret settled into her bones, and a veil of darkness fell over her.

Maggie quickly left the library. By the time she found Juju in an alley off Kensington Avenue, she was practically hysterical. Her sobs came in loud, gut-wrenching waves. Juju was alarmed, thinking that something horrible had happened to Seth.

"What is it? What's wrong?" Juju asked.

"My mom and dad looked for me, Juju. They looked for me and never found me. I should have never left my mom. I should have stayed with her and my brother at the mall," she sobbed.

Juju didn't know how to respond. Then it came to her. "That means they still want you. Right?"

"No! Why would anyone want me? Look at me. Look at what I've become!" she yelled, gesturing to her short shorts and the low, plunging neckline of her shirt that revealed her boobs.

"You didn't become a hooker, Maggie. They made you one. This isn't your fault, and I'm sure if you called them, they would want you to come home."

"Did you forget what they did to Cali because she was going to call my parents? They drowned her to death. They put her in a cage and drowned her. Rock would kill them or me. He would tell John William or Myles, and they would destroy my entire family," she wailed.

Juju understood the evil Rock was capable of when someone stole a twenty-dollar bag of dope. She considered Maggie's fear and realized that her friend was probably right. She'd watched Rock slice a man's thumb off for stealing from him.

"I think you're right, Maggie. I know you love your family, and Rock can be ruthless. For now, you need to go on living. But someday, I bet anything you'll be home with your family again," Juju offered.

"I wish I could believe you. I hope you're right, Juju."

As the girls parted, Maggie headed toward the center of Kensington in her Daisy Dukes and a padded bra. She looked down at the four-inch heals she was wearing. The faux leather was worn and chipped, the sides of the shoes were cracking, and all of it repulsed her.

Chapter Sixty-Two

Rob and Keith Clarke sat at the dinner table after the dishes were cleared. Finally, Lorraine walked over to them carrying a small cake with four candles, one candle for each year Maggie had been missing. Rob sighed heavily as he gave his thoughts over to the daughter he missed and loved so dearly.

Each year on Maggie's birthday, Lorraine served a cake. They never sang happy birthday; it was a time for the three to remember what they'd lost.

"Happy birthday, baby," Lorraine said, before cutting into the cake.

Keith, Maggie's brother, now eight years old, looked to his father. Then he turned back to his mother, whose head was bowed as if she was in deep prayer.

"Mommy, why do we have a cake for Maggie when she isn't here anymore?" Keith asked.

"Well, because it's important that we never forget her, son. You two loved each other very much. She was a great sister to you," Lorraine reminded him *again*.

"Yeah, you tell me that all the time. But I don't remember her. Sometimes I wish she was never here 'cause you always talk about her and not me." He sniffled, feeling overshadowed by a ghost he'd long forgotten.

"Don't say that, Keith! I wish every day that she was here with us. And you know, just because we love Maggie doesn't mean we love you any less. We love you both the same," Lorraine reassured him.

"Keith," Rob said somberly, "it's just that Mom and I had two great kids. But one of them went away, and when you have kids, you love them like no one else in the world."

As soon as the Clarkes finished eating their cake, Keith ran off to his bedroom. Lorraine and Rob sat together silently, each of them alone with haunting memories of Maggie.

"How is it possible that I can miss her more as time goes on?" Lorraine asked Rob.

"I know, sweetheart. I know exactly how you feel. For me, it's because I think about the things she'd be doing as each year passes. High school, dances, parties…" He paused, dreaming of what could have been, what should have been. "We would be starting to think about college. It's overwhelming, and it's the worst burden any human being can carry through life."

Lorraine broke down and cried. Rob stood slowly and pulled Lorraine to her feet. The Clarkes stood in the kitchen, holding onto each other, both wishing they could be hugging their child.

"I still think she's alive," Lorraine said, breaking the silence.

"I don't know, Lorraine. Sometimes I let myself think so, too. But then I worry that if she is still alive, she is being tortured. I don't know which is worse for me: the permanence of death or the prolonging of the agony. It slashes my heart to shreds to think about either," Rob said with raw sadness.

"I know. Rae Harker told me that when he found out his daughter had been killed, relief and devastation overwhelmed him. He said they were the two hardest emotions he's ever had to deal with at the same time. I think you're right, Rob; it's this internal conflict. I don't want her to be alive and suffering, yet another part of me, a selfish part, wants her to come back no matter what has happened to her. It makes me feel like a horrible mother," Lorraine cried.

"You're not a horrible mother, Lorraine. You're human, and you're a great mother," Rob said, rubbing her back.

At eight o'clock that evening, Rae Harker rang the Clarkes' doorbell. Rae visited them at least two times a year, without fail: on Maggie's birthday and on the date she disappeared.

"Hi, Rae," Lorraine's voice was sullen when she opened the door.

"Hey, Lorraine. Just wanted to stop by and see how you're doing," Rae said.

"We're doing the best we can, as usual. Any word? Any new developments?" Lorraine asked with hope.

"No, sorry to say, there aren't. I'm sure you read about the twelve-year-old girl that has been missing for three days. The one who they think was taken from Love Park in Center City," Rae said.

"Yes, I've been watching it on the news. What the hell, Rae? What's wrong with people in this world?" she asked, not expecting an answer.

"I wish I knew. But, you know, I was thinking about you and Rob. Maybe you two should think about contacting the missing girl's parents. I mean, unless you've been through it, it's hard to imagine what they're going through. I can hook you up with a couple of cop buddies down on the Philadelphia force, if you're willing to talk to the parents," he said.

Rob had overheard Harker from the living room and walked up behind his wife. "I think it's something we should try to do, Lorraine. It won't bring Maggie back, but maybe we can help someone else while we're living this nightmare. Remember how hard it was in those first months? Breathing, eating, sleeping—even blinking—was an effort. Maybe we can make a difference. Something to make Maggie proud that we're her parents," Rob offered.

Lorraine hesitated, looking from Detective Harker to her husband. "OK. We'll give it try. Reach out to your cop friends. Tell them if the girl's mom and dad need to talk, we're here for them."

Detective Harker stayed for a short visit. When he left, Rob went up to bed, but Lorraine sat on the sofa. In the silence of her home, for the first time, she accepted the idea that she could help others through their tragedy. If she were lucky, maybe by helping others, she'd actually begin to heal. Not forget Maggie, but begin to heal.

Chapter Sixty-Three

Juju was standing only five feet away when she heard Maggie tell a man sitting in his car that she wouldn't get in. "I don't get into cars. If you want something from me, we have to go back into the field behind these buildings," Maggie stated, pointing off to her right.

Juju couldn't hear what the man said; his words were jumbled. But she watched Maggie take a step backward as he sped off.

"What was that about?" Juju asked Maggie.

"Remind me to tell you later. I have to keep moving. It's been a slow night, and at the rate I'm going, I'll be out here until tomorrow morning trying to make my quota. My feet are killing me, and I'm just tired. Why do men like these stinking high heels? Why can't they be turned on by slippers?" Maggie joked.

"I don't know why. Because they've all been trained to like chicks in fuck-me pumps. Anyway, when are you comin' over?" Juju asked.

Maggie rubbed her temple. "In the morning. That's when I'm always over, Juju," she said, jabbing Juju in the belly.

The next morning, as soon as Juju set a cup of coffee in front of Maggie, she asked, "So what is it you were going to tell me about the guy in the car last night? You looked scared out of your mind."

"Ugh! That's because I *was* scared out of my mind. I have this thing about getting into cars with men I don't know. I get this intense fear that seizes my entire body. I read about stuff like this. I think I have post-traumatic stress disorder," Maggie explained simply.

"Huh? Post what?" Juju asked, her face scrunched in confusion.

"Post-traumatic stress, it's what happens to people when they have been through something really bad. I think it comes from John William forcing me into his van. So now, every time a john wants me to get into his car, I freak. I can almost always convince them to go into

251

the field, but every once in a while, like that guy last night, they get pissed off," Maggie rambled.

"Aren't you afraid Armando will find out about this?" Juju asked, concerned for Maggie's safety.

"Yeah, I am. But I'm more afraid to get into a car with a john than I am of being caught by Armando. It's everything I can do not to run in the other direction. I can feel myself start to panic. I break into a cold sweat. It's a horrible feeling, and it gives me the creeps. Don't tell anyone; I don't need it getting around," Maggie stated, suddenly feeling vulnerable even talking to Juju about it.

Maggie was petrified to do anything wrong, worried that Armando would put her back in the box in the upstairs closet or something even worse. The thought of getting into a car with a stranger terrified her. She was afraid every time she walked off with a john that he was going to hurt her. She was frightened that the other girls would do something to get her in trouble. But the worse fear of all was her constant worry that Thelma would do something to harm Seth.

The months passed quickly, and before Maggie knew it, it was Thanksgiving. She tended to think about her family more during the holidays than at any other time of the year. On the morning before Thanksgiving, Maggie, Seth, and Juju were sitting on the curb in front of Seth's elementary school. The girls still met him every morning; it had become a ritual. When Seth finished his doughnut, Maggie stood. "OK, Seth. You have to get into school now. I won't see you tomorrow or Friday because it's Thanksgiving, and you're off from school," she informed him.

Seth clung to her. "I hate it when I don't get to see you, Aggie. Thelma said I ain't good enough to have Tanksgiving dinner. I have to stay at home with her. I hate it there, and I hate Thelma," he yelled, frustrated.

"I know you do, but this is just temporary. Before you know it, we'll be living together again, and you won't have put up with Thelma anymore," Maggie said.

"Fine." Seth pouted. "But I hope she doesn't keep hitting me. I hate it when she hits me. It's better when she just makes me stay outside. Even being cold doesn't hurt as much as when she whacks me," he whined.

Maggie fought her natural urge to walk to Rock's house and beat the shit out of Thelma. Afraid Seth would see her anger and that would scare him more, she put on her sweetest smile. "Does Rock see Thelma hitting you?"

"Yeah, she puts out her hand, and he takes off his belt and gives it to her. Then she hits me with it. See?" Seth said, lifting the back of his shirt.

"Holy shit!" Maggie blurted, staring at the marks on his back.

She leaned into Seth, taking him into her arms. "I won't ever leave you. I'm going to get you out of there. Do you believe me?" she asked, fighting back tears.

Seth nodded. Then with his head hung low, he walked into the elementary school, where he would spend a few painless hours before he would have to go home for the long, four-day weekend.

Chapter Sixty-Four

It was Thanksgiving, which meant nothing to Rock and the men who hustled the girls. While they allowed the women to cook a dinner in the house, they were expected to work that night. It was a busy night for prostitutes in Kensington, where the population of addicts and degenerates meant there were more people out on the streets with a reason to party rather than spending time with their families giving thanks.

Juju was among the partiers. She'd sold her dope within a few hours and decided to stay at Needle Park and drink beer with some of her pusher friends. She had just guzzled her fifth beer and was drunk. Juju stood and staggered over to three guys she knew from the streets. She heard one of them say, "The really hot one," just as she approached.

"Yeah, that chick, Maggie. I know who you're talking about. She's gorgeous. Too bad she's a hooker or I'd have to charm her into being my old lady," one of the guys stated.

The others nodded in agreement. "Hey, Juju! You hang out with that girl, Maggie. Why don't you ever bring her out to party with us?" a good-looking, dark-haired teen called Bond asked.

"Maggie does her own thin', Bond. She's my friend and doesn't want to get caught up with any douche bags like you," she stated, her tongue loosened by liquid courage.

Bond laughed. "I don't know how she does it. All those assholes I see her talking to. Some are old, some are nasty, and others are just ugly," he told the others. "It must really blow to climb into cars with some jerk-off you don't even know. I hate dealing with some of those pricks here in the park, out in the open. There are some real shady characters," Bond said, looking at Juju.

Juju guzzled another beer and let out a long, loud, manly burp. "Maggie doesn't get into cars. She only does it with them where there are people nearby. She's not an idiot," she stated, flailing her arms in slow motion.

The alcohol Juju consumed removed all of the boundaries between her thoughts and the words coming out of her mouth. She was very drunk, and by the next morning, she wouldn't remember most of what she'd said.

But the boys had heard her loud and clear. When Bond left Needle Park, he walked down Kensington Avenue to find Rock. All of the hookers and dealers knew that giving Rock information regarding his business was valuable, and he always took care of those who watched out for his best interests.

"Rock, hey man!" Bond yelled and ran toward him.

"Yeah, 'sup?" Rock asked casually.

"Hey man, happy Thanksgiving," Bond said.

"Yeah, same to you. How you doin'? You need more dope?" Rock asked.

"Nah. I have about ten bags left. I'll probably need more tomorrow. Anyway, I ran into Juju down at Needle Park tonight. She was pretty drunk. Told us something about that girl, Maggie, of yours I thought you might wanna know," Bond said proudly.

"Oh yeah? What's that?" Rock asked half interested.

"She told us that Maggie won't get in cars with her johns. She's refusing them. Tells them she'll take them back to the field, but if they won't go, she turns down the trick," he stated.

"Hmm, that's interesting. Little bitch would only give hand jobs when she first started. Got away without me knowing it for a while, too. Why would Juju tell you this? She's friends with the little ho."

"I told you, man. Juju was drunk. I ain't never seen her that drunk before. Anyway, I just thought you'd want to know. You know, so you can check it out. I'm watching out for ya man, and makin' sure if I hear anything you should know, I come and tell ya. That's all," Bond said, nervously waiting for validation that he'd done a good deed.

"Yeah, man. I appreciate that," Rock said. Then Rock stood and gave Bond a gangster handshake.

Rock got back to the house of whores just when Armando was kicking one the girl's asses because she talked back to him. Armando looked over as his boss took long strides through the living room. Rock's jaw was set hard, and his demeanor revealed his burning fury.

"'Sup man?" Armando asked as he shook Rock's hand.

"Word on the street is your bitch, Maggie, is at it again. Bond told me that she's turning down johns if she has to get into their cars. I want to know what's going on. I'm gettin' tired of this shit, Armando. You all need to learn how to tame your bitches. Now, get on it and let me know what you find out," Rock told him and left the house.

On his short drive home, Rock wondered what he would do with Maggie if what Bond had told him turned out to be true. He couldn't put up with the shit she was dishing out. Otherwise, the rest of the girls would think they could do whatever they wanted. Maggie had to be put in line...the hard way.

Chapter Sixty-Five

The next evening, Armando confirmed the rumor about Maggie and went over to Rock's house to discuss the matter.

"Hey, Rock," Armando called as he walked through the front door.

"Hey, man. What'd ya find out?"

"Yeah, it's true. I sent one of our guys from North Philly over to see her. She wouldn't get in the car with him. You want me to handle this?" Armando asked.

"Yep, you take care of her. Don't kill her. This one has great earning potential. But this time I want you to break her in the right way. She needs to understand we make the rules, not her! Oh, and one other thing, I want you to do..." Rock dictated.

When Maggie returned to the house early the next morning, Armando was waiting for her. He held out his hand to take the money she'd earned and handed it to Diesel. Then he backhanded Maggie, and she flew sideways, landing on top of a couple of girls who were sitting on a mattress nearby.

Instead of helping, the girls pushed her off them and onto the floor. Armando stomped over and kicked Maggie in the gut. She barfed and fell lifelessly into her own puke, which clung to the side of her face.

"Get the hell up, you little bitch," Armando seethed.

Armando pulled Maggie up by her hair, and she ran behind him as he ascended the stairs.

"Please, Armando. I didn't do anything, I swear," she begged, but her pleading fell on deaf ears.

Once in the bedroom, he pushed Maggie onto the bed.

"Let's go. Get undressed," he ordered.

"Please, Armando. At least tell me what I did," Maggie pleaded.

"It's not what cha did, ya stupid little freak. It's what ya didn't do. Little Maggie doesn't get in cars with her tricks. Ring any bells?" he sneered.

"I'm sorry, Armando. It's just that when I was taken, the man who kidnapped me put me in a van, and now I'm scared to get into cars with people I don't know," she said, hoping to avoid punishment.

Armando started laughing. A first it was a giggle, but then it turned into a full belly laugh. His reaction led Maggie to believe that maybe he understood her dilemma. But then his laughter took on a sinister growl, which eventually became the dominant sound, Maggie knew she was fucked.

"Oh boy," he yelled, as his laughter waned. "That's a good one. Now take off your fuckin' clothes before I tear them off myself."

Maggie quickly undressed and stood before him naked.

"Come on," he said and headed for the closest.

"Oh no, Armando. Oh, please don't put me in the box. Please. I'll try to do better," she promised.

"Bitch, please. Ya ain't gonna try to do nothin' better. If I ever decide to let you outta there, you're gonna do every damn thing I tell ya to. This ain't no negotiation, you idiot," he spewed ruthlessly.

In the closet, Armando unlocked the box. "You getting in yourself or do you need me to throw you in there?" he half asked.

Trembling, Maggie sat on the edge of the vertical box; slowly, she slid herself into it until her bare feet hit the bottom. Then she squatted into a ball.

"I'll see ya when I see ya," Armando said with a big grin on his face.

As Maggie sat, cramped at the bottom of the wooden box, she knew this was only the beginning of her punishment.

Chapter Sixty-Six

A day later, the box opened, and Maggie, who was sore and exhausted, looked up.

"Let's go. Give me your hands," Armando instructed.

With effort, Maggie raised her hands above her head and struggled to stand. Armando hoisted her out as if she was weightless. In the bedroom, she stood, but was unable to extend her body upright.

"I'm sorry, Armando," she cried, fearing what was to happen next.

"No, you ain't sorry. If you were sorry, you wouldn't have done what cha did in the first place," he snapped.

Armando unbuckled his belt and slowly removed it from his waist, purposely making time drag on. It was all about breaking her down so she wouldn't dare disobey him again. The first lash landed across the front of her thighs. Each lash that followed was harder and left her aching. After several minutes and, with Maggie huddled on the floor, he walked over and opened the bedroom door.

Trinity and two other hookers walked into the room. Armando handed the belt to Trinity first. With great excitement, Trinity began swinging the belt at Maggie. Each thrash landed in a different place on her body. Maggie looked at her for pity, but Trinity's expression only showed disdain and the need for vengeance.

"All right, 'nuff," Armando told her.

Maggie's body felt as if she'd been stung by a million hornets. *It's over*, she thought. But then Armando handed the belt to the second hooker, and when she finished, the last hooker took her turn at "taming the beast," as Armando called it.

When it was all over, Maggie was unable to stand or move any part of her body. Armando grabbed her under the arms and took her back to the closet.

"I think ya need a little more time to figure out who the boss is 'round here," he taunted.

He slid Maggie into the box. Her legs folded under her, further irritating the fresh, pulsating welts. Maggie cried, not so much from the pain in her skin, but the pain in her broken heart. As her sobs became deeper and she let her emotions go, she felt as if all of her blood was circulating around her brain and her head was going to burst open. When she finally stopped crying, she sat in a heap at the bottom of the vertical box and waited.

The next day, Armando came back and pulled Maggie from her prison. As she emerged from the box, its rough wooden sides scraped her exposed skin. It felt as if she was being massaged with sandpaper. When she was back in the bedroom, Armando propped her up on an old chair in the corner.

"Don't move a muscle," he told her, as he walked out of the bedroom to execute Rock's other idea.

Maggie was too weak to move anyway. She could barely hold her head up. When the bedroom door opened again, Armando shoved Seth into the room. He walked in behind the young boy, who was already crying and shaking. Behind Armando, the three hookers followed.

"Aggie!" Seth screamed and ran to her.

But before Seth could reach Maggie, Armando grabbed a handful of hair from the back of his head, bringing the boy to an immediate halt. Seth cried harder and reached up for Armando's hand to try and pry himself free, but Armando pushed the child full force into a table next to the bed.

Armando proceeded to slap Seth repeatedly. As Maggie looked on helplessly, her blood started pumping through her battered body, and soon her pain was replaced with high-voltage energy she couldn't control.

"Just leave him alone! He's only a little boy!" Maggie screamed. Then she turned to Trinity and the other two hookers. "Stop him. What's wrong with you?" she shouted, with judgment dripping from her words.

For the briefest moment, Maggie saw what she believed to be sympathy on Trinity's face as she watched Seth get a beating. Then Armando turned to the three girls and told them to "let loose."

Trinity hesitated, but Armando pulled her forward. "What's wrong wit' cha, bitch? You was liking it when you were beating on Maggie. Now unless you want to switch places with her, you'll do what I tell ya," he threatened.

Trinity turned to Maggie with a sorrowful look before she landed the first kick into Seth's back. The girls each took their turns, doing as they were told, knowing the dire consequences of not following orders. After many minutes, Armando told the girls to leave the room.

Seth was lying on the floor, whimpering and barely able to move. It was too much for his tiny body to take. Armando grabbed him up from the floor and threw him onto the bed. He pulled a switchblade from his pocket, and the shiny blade sprang to life. Armando put the knife to Seth's neck. Maggie looked on, helpless and full of self-loathing because her fear of getting into cars with strange men had cost the person she loved most his life.

Chapter Sixty-Seven

Armando glared at her, the blade pressing into Seth's throat as his eyes bugged out with paralyzing terror. Armando pressed harder, and the sharp blade drew blood to the surface of Seth's neck.

"I can kill him right now. Ain't nobody gonna miss his scrawny white ass. Nobody but you, that is. What cha think I should do? Now let's see, should I kill him or let him live? That's the real question. And the answer, well, that all depends on you," he said slowly, adding to Maggie's dread.

"I'll do it, Armando. I don't care. I won't ever lie to you again. I'll get into cars. I don't care what happens to me. Please just leave Seth alone. Pleeease," she begged.

"Well, now, here's how it's gonna work. *If* I let this useless piece of shit live, you're gonna do whatever I want you to. If I ever hear that ya lied to me again, I *will* kill your sweet lil boy here," he stated with utter certainty.

"OK, OK," Maggie wailed, unwilling to lose the only family she had left. "I swear. I'll do whatever you want, and I'll never lie to you again."

"Good. Now get your ass into the shower. Then you can have something to eat. You're back out there tonight. In fact, I'm gonna go wit' cha just to be sure you do as you promise," he mocked.

Running purely on adrenaline, Maggie stood and walked into the bathroom. She turned back to Seth from the door. "I love you," she said genuinely.

Seth met her eyes. "I love you too, Aggie," he said, between chest-pulling sobs.

Maggie watched as Armando pulled Seth off the bed and led him out of the bedroom. As Maggie turned on the shower, she wondered, *how did Armando find out about me not getting into cars? The only one who knew was Juju. Oh my God, Juju!*

Chapter Sixty-Eight

———————◼———————

That night, Armando trailed ten feet behind Maggie on Kensington Avenue as she faced her greatest fear. When her fourth customer pulled up to the curb, Maggie leaned into the car.

"How much for regular?" the seedy young man asked.

When Maggie told him the price, he said, "Get in."

Maggie reached for the door handle, and it felt as though the metal was burning through her flesh. She looked over her shoulder and saw Armando watching her intently. She flashed back to what he had done to Seth, and with courage she didn't know that she had, Maggie pulled the door open. Every muscle and nerve in her body twitched as fright clamped down on her senses.

"Are you getting in or what? I don't have all night," the john said. "Let's go!"

Overwhelmed by a sudden urge to run away, Maggie looked back at Armando just as he started to walk toward her. She took a deep breath, held it, and slid into the passenger seat of the car. As the man pulled away, she looked out her window. Everything was a blur, and she was sweating profusely. The man reached over and put his hand on her inner thigh. His fingers felt like daggers on her skin, and she flinched.

"Oh, you wanna play hard to get, huh? That's good. That's very good. I like games." He pulled into an abandoned lot. "Come on; let's get into the backseat," he told Maggie.

Maggie reached for the door handle, but it was missing. Panic rose in her gorge, but she focused on Seth. *Don't freak out*, she told herself, *Seth needs you to be brave.*

Maggie looked over at the stranger who was watching her with a slimy smile. "That's been broken for a while. Doesn't matter, though. I want you to climb over the seat. That way I can get a look at that sweet ass of yours," he stated in a disturbingly perverted voice.

As Maggie hoisted herself over the front seat, she spotted door handles on both rear doors. Her anxiety subsided slightly. At least there was a way out of the car. Then she imagined that Armando had followed them to make sure she did what she'd promised. This thought allowed her to relax. *If Armando is watching, he'll never let this low-life pig steal me,* she decided.

Maggie's john had reached up her short skirt as she was climbing into the back. Her senses fully awake, she was repulsed by his touch and by the things she was doing. It was as if curtains had opened and she was peering into the window of her life since she'd been taken. The reality rocked her to the core. Instead of giving into her fear and disgust, Maggie grew stronger, fiercer, and made up her mind that she was going to find a way out. She didn't know when, and she couldn't conceive of how, but she believed that a way out would come to her.

As the man slid on top of her and mauled her, Maggie lay lifelessly, unwilling to participate. She didn't care what he wanted from her. She no longer cared what any of the men wanted from her. Maggie decided that very night that she would take her life back. This potent thought calmed her. She felt powerful as the belief took root in her heart.

When the slob finished, he drove her back to Kensington Avenue. He stopped next to the curb, close to where he had picked her up. She was no longer a naïve girl.

She turned to the slime ball. "Give me my money," she stated in a hard voice.

The man handed Maggie the cash, and she floated out of the car. Armando watched, realizing that something about her had drastically changed; it was visible. Her demeanor and strut made him uneasy. He didn't understand the depth of agony Maggie had suffered at the hands of the sex traffickers. Therefore, Armando could never grasp the strength of her will to emancipate herself from the physical and mental slavery that had been consuming her.

Maggie had finally left the kidnapped child behind her. In less than an hour, in a moment of clarity, she'd become a woman who wouldn't quit. As she swaggered down the street with her head held high, she remembered what Cali had said right before they drowned her: you are the one among us who will survive. Her fearlessness grew with each deliberate step. People who had seen her on the streets before now watched a woman on a mission.

Maggie was no longer afraid of the monsters who had been weighing her down; she was going on the greatest journey of her life. Destination: freedom.

Chapter Sixty-Nine

———————————◼———————————

"What the hell did you do, Juju?" Maggie accused.

"Well, good morning to you, too. What's your problem? Where have you been?" Juju asked, still trying to wake up.

"Oh, good you noticed I haven't been around for several days. Let's see, I was in the vertical box for a couple of days. Had the shit beat out of me by Armando and some of those whore bitches of his. Then, as if that wasn't bad enough, they brought Seth over to the house of whores and they beat the shit out of him in front of me. Threatened to slit his throat. And do you want to know why?" she asked, feeling betrayed by her only friend.

"Why?" Juju asked quietly, unnerved by Maggie's sudden aggression toward her.

"Because Armando mysteriously found out that I wouldn't get into cars with johns. Now let's see, since you're the only person I've ever told, I guess you're the one who told Armando. Or was it Rock?" Maggie accused.

Maggie didn't trust Juju anymore. She wanted her to know the pain she'd caused by opening her big pie hole and revealing Maggie's secret.

"What? No, I didn't tell either of them *anything* about you. Maggie, I would never do that to you," she pleaded.

The two girls stood staring at each other. Their eyes were locked, and Juju could tell that Maggie was different. She wasn't the same person. Juju quickly thought about what she'd done since she last saw Maggie. Then, like a bat out of hell, it came to her: *I must've told the guys at the park when I was drunk. Oh, fuck me! I've screwed the only person I love,* she thought with remorse.

"Maggie, please just sit down for a minute," Juju started. "I think I know what happened. I was at Needle Park on Thanksgiving. I was drunk, really drunk. Somehow, I must have said something about you to the guys." Juju's head dropped, and she put her hands up to cover her face. "I'm sorry, Maggie. I'm so sorry. I would never do anything to hurt you or Seth. You know that, don't you?" she asked, desperate not to lose Maggie.

Maggie could see the honesty and anguish in her friend. She began to soften. "Well, it was a really stupid mistake. You have no idea how horrible they were to Seth and me," she persisted, her anger fizzling out.

"No, I don't. The only thing I know is that I wish I could go back in time. I wouldn't have gotten so drunk. You have to believe me. I never tried to hurt you," Juju wailed.

Maggie sat and watched her friend break down right before her eyes. Juju's suffering gave her no pleasure. In fact, it made her feel protective. Then she thought about the night Armando put her out in the snow and the way Juju had carried her inside and taken care of her. Maggie realized that Juju had made a huge mistake, a mistake that could have been fatal for Seth and her. She walked over to Juju and put her hands on her shoulders.

"OK, Juju. It's going to be OK," Maggie assured her, softening at the sincerity of Juju's regret. "We all do shit we shouldn't do. But do me a favor?" Maggie asked.

"What's that?" Juju croaked.

"Don't get drunk anymore. And if you do decide to get drunk, make sure I'm with you to keep you from getting me in anymore trouble," she said, brushing the hair back from Juju's face.

Juju reached for Maggie and held her tightly.

"Thank you for believing me. I don't know what I'd do if anything bad ever happened to you. Before I met you, I was alone. I haven't had anyone in my life who has *truly* loved me. You're the first," Juju confessed.

Maggie realized how much the two girls had in common. While their backgrounds were different, their hopes were the same...to have people in their lives who truly loved them.

It wouldn't be long before Maggie learned just how much Juju loved her.

Chapter Seventy

———————— ■ ————————

The next day, Maggie and Juju met Seth on his walk to school. The long weekend was behind him, and his angst was apparent as he walked toward them.

"Hey, Seth," Maggie sang, as she bent down and cradled him in her arms.

"Hi, Aggie," he said, sniffling.

"What's wrong, little man?" Juju asked, poking him.

"Nothin'," Seth replied.

Clearly, Seth had a difficult weekend. After he was beaten in front of Maggie, Rock took him home. Seth didn't go into much detail about the cruelty Thelma showered upon him over the Thanksgiving break.

"I'm sorry they hurt you, Seth. I'm not going to let that happen again. Are you OK?" Maggie said, thinking of the beating he'd endured.

Seth nodded. "I'm OK," he gasped, as tears streaked his dirty cheeks.

"Did you have turkey for Thanksgiving?" Maggie asked cautiously.

"Uh-huh. Thelma put turkey in the dog bowl for me," he said, embarrassed.

Maggie's insides were twisted, and she used all of her self-control to hide her festering fury towards Rock and Thelma. "Thelma sucks, Seth," Maggie said with resolve. "Forget about her. Do you know what today is?"

Seth shook his head without enthusiasm.

"Today is your birthday. December 3. You're eight years old today."

Maggie took a broken crayon and a used piece of paper from his bag. She wrote 12/3.

"See, 12 is for the twelfth month of the year, December. And 3 is for the third day. Now, look at it closely. Do you see it?" she asked.

"One, two, three?" he said, afraid of looking stupid.

"Exactly. Twelve three. December 3. One, two, three. Isn't that great?" she gushed.

Seth remained unemotional. "Sure, that's great," he told her, more relieved that he'd answered her question correctly. The kids at school and Thelma always told him he was stupid, and Seth had started to believe he was dumb.

"We bought you a present," Maggie said, hoping it would make him feel better. She pulled out a small box wrapped in newspaper.

Seth held it in the palm of his hand, looking at it closely; slowly, a spark of excitement began to surface.

"This is for me?" he asked, with a glimmer of hope in his voice.

"Yep, it's from me and Juju. We bought it especially for you," Maggie explained. "Go ahead and open it."

Seth tore the paper off and looked at the miniature, plastic, toy soldier.

"Wow," he breathed. "Some of the kids at school have these. But this one is the best one ever," he stated, turning the toy over in his hands to inspect it.

"This one is special, Seth. I told the man at the drugstore all about you. I explained how brave you've been. I told him you're the most courageous eight-year-old in the whole world. Then, guess what happened? The man at the store went into the back and brought out this soldier. He said *this* soldier was a war hero, and since you're so brave, we should buy it for you. It's the only one like it anywhere," Maggie lied.

Maggie wanted to give Seth hope, make him feel special. Her heart ached for the small boy whom she loved as her own.

"Really? That's so cool. I'll keep him forever and ever," Seth promised.

By the time the two girls left Seth, he was in high spirits. Maggie and Juju always made him feel better. They made him feel like he mattered—especially Maggie. She was the only constant in his life. With Maggie, he felt like he belonged. She was the only sense of "home" he'd ever known. Seth believed everything Maggie told him. He knew that one day they'd be together. He dreamed about Maggie coming to take him away from Rock and Thelma.

Seth couldn't know what Maggie would have to do in order to make his dream come true.

Chapter Seventy-One

It was just before sunset, and Maggie was trolling Kensington Avenue for business. She passed old buildings occupied by shady businesses. The whole city seemed to be in a state of hopelessness. People came and went, and the city just got older and more decrepit. The structures continued to stand, but only because they were made of brick and mortar. Paint peeled from the buildings; black grime from city living and neglect covered the red brick. The sidewalks were an obstacle course of uneven cement slabs. Yet no one seemed to notice. Kensington's residents were poor, stoned, or homeless. None of them had asked for the life they lived. It was as though hell had seeped up from the bowels of the earth and covered the city like a wet wool blanket.

Maggie watched two other hookers walking toward her. The larger girl, Legacy, wore her jeans two sizes too small, strangling her large thighs and making her belly plunge over them in a blob of fat and flesh. Her tight, fake-leather jacket grabbed her just above the belly button, which accentuated the extra pounds of flesh around her middle. The smaller girl, called Froggie, had her hair pulled back in a tight bun, a hairdo that put far too much emphasis on her bulbous nose and buck teeth. Maggie knew the girls were hookers who used drugs heavily.

As Maggie got closer to them, she could see the craziness in their eyes. They strutted aggressively, and she sensed that they were going after someone. When they were almost upon her, Maggie stepped to the side, closer to the building, to let them pass. But they didn't walk by. Legacy landed the first punch in Maggie's gut.

"You stealin' our dope, bitch? You think 'cause you white and tight it give you a right to take shit from us?" Legacy accused.

"I don't know what you're talking about. I didn't steal anything," Maggie gasped.

"Fuckin' liar," Froggie rasped in her deep, dark voice. "We gonna fuck you up."

"I didn't steal anything!" Maggie wailed.

Legacy punched Maggie again, just skimming her cheekbone. On instinct, Maggie began to flail her fists at the larger girl. She managed to connect with Legacy's collarbone. Froggie grabbed a handful of Maggie's hair and pulled her down to the ground. The two girls began to kick her, and Legacy dropped on top of Maggie and held her down while she punched her. Maggie continued to kick at them, keeping her hands up to cover her face. She squirmed, wiggled, and bucked to shake Legacy off, but her sheer weight kept Maggie pinned in place.

As the girls beat on her, a crowd began to close in. Men were laughing as other hookers looked on, just shaking their heads. Some of the strung-out girls yelled, provoking Maggie's attackers to continue. The noise from the crowd was deafening to Maggie. Then, a distinctive voice cut through the onlookers. It was growing closer, and it was really, really angry.

"I will fuckin' kill you whore bitches," Juju barked, as she stood over the rubble of bodies.

Legacy looked up and stood quickly. "Who the fuck you talkin' to, skank?"

Juju went into her stance—arms spread, hands wide open, palms facing Legacy. She put her dominant leg behind her and leaned into her left leg. "Leave her alone," Juju warned.

"Are you kiddin'? Who you think you scarin', trash?" Legacy sneered and moved toward her.

Juju closed her hands into fists but didn't budge. Legacy charged at Juju with her hands in the air, ready to deflect Juju's fists. When Legacy was close enough, Juju planted her left foot and brought her right foot forward, connecting with a front kick between Legacy's legs. The large girl went down to her knees, and Juju nailed her in the face with one blow. Legacy was lying on her side on the verge of unconsciousness when Froggie began a slow growl at Juju.

Froggie sprang off Maggie and attacked Juju head on. Juju was rattled by the unexpected assault. She stumbled backward. *Find your center*, she reminded herself, and calmly went back into her defensive position. When Froggie was close enough, Juju lifted her back leg, swept it around, and knocked Froggie's legs out from under her. Froggie dropped to the ground on her left side. She tried to spring up again, but Juju locked her fingers together and brought her hands down hard on Froggie's forehead.

With Legacy and Froggie sprawled on the sidewalk like road kill, Juju rushed over to Maggie. The crowd continued to hoot and holler as Juju knelt next to her. "Are you OK?" Juju asked.

"Who, me? Sure, I was just about to kick their asses when you showed up," Maggie said with a weak smile.

"Come on," Juju told her, helping her up from the ground.

Once they were away from the crowd, Maggie asked, "Are you crazy? Do you know the shit storm you just brought on yourself?"

"Fuck them, Maggie. Once I heard you were getting your ass whooped, which, by the way, *you were*; I didn't care what happened. Anyway, those pricks don't scare me," she stated.

"I know, Juju. But you know how the hookers operate. If they get the others against you, it could be trouble. Hookers fight hookers, and dealers fight dealers. I don't have to tell you. Now what are we going to do?" Maggie asked, relieved that Juju intervened, but fearful that her friend would face retribution.

"I'll figure something out. Don't worry about it," Juju said confidently.

Chapter Seventy-Two

The two girls had been in Juju's apartment for less than an hour when there was a loud banging on the door. Juju slid the chain into place and opened the door a smidgen. "Open the fucking door," Rock said.

"It's Rock. Just be cool," Juju told Maggie.

Juju opened the door and let Rock enter. "What the hell were you thinkin', Juju? You know how this shit works," he growled, pressing Juju against the wall.

"Look, Rock, they were two on one. Those ho bags where beating the shit out of Maggie. It was an unfair advantage," she said.

"Oh, yeah, so pulling out that kung fu shit of yours ain't no unfair advantage. I have two bitches that are all screwed up now. I wouldn't care, except that now they can't work tonight. So you tell me, how am I gonna make up the money ya cost me with your little karate moves?" Rock snarled.

"Maybe those bitches will have to work longer to make up for their losses," Juju countered, not backing down.

Rock huffed. "You're lucky you didn't get your ass kicked. The other girls coulda jumped in on ya. Then I'd have two hookers and a pusher down. This ain't no good for my business. You need to let Maggie handle her shit by herself."

Maggie felt herself becoming defensive of Juju. "I was handling my shit, Rock. I was minding my own business. They accused me of stealing their dope. I don't *use* dope, and everyone knows that."

Rock moved away from Juju and toward Maggie. "Oh, now you gettin' all brave with me. You best watch what you say to me, girl, or ya ain't gonna be happy."

"I'm just saying, Rock. It's not Juju's fault," Maggie explained, pretending to heed to his warning.

Rock snickered. "You just better keep your little friend here contained. Ain't no tellin' what those bitches will do now," he warned Maggie.

Rock walked toward the door. Before leaving, he turned to Juju. "As for the profits I lost, you better get your ass out there and start selling more dope. Otherwise, you'll answer to me," he said in a menacing voice.

After Rock left, Juju slid down the wall and sat on the floor. Maggie went over and sat beside her. "Well, this isn't good," Maggie said, stating the obvious. "You should have just let them kick my ass. Now you're in trouble because of me." Maggie was brimming over with guilt.

"Nah. I ain't in trouble. I'm not scared of those losers or Rock," she blurted, sounding braver than she felt. "You just need to stay on alert. The best way for them to get to me is to mess with you."

Maggie was overwhelmed with emotion. The dominant feeling was love for Juju. She had risked a lot by jumping into the fight. She knew that Juju loved her, but out on the streets, it was easy for people to hunt someone down and sabotage them. They would have to be very careful until the incident blew over.

"You were like a little ninja out there," Maggie offered with a smile.

"Yeah, well, Sensei taught me well. Maybe you should think about learning how to defend yourself. No telling if I'm going to be around the next time someone screws with ya," Juju advised.

"I guess it can't hurt. Are you volunteering to teach me?" Maggie asked.

"Sure. I can try. I mean, from what I saw, you're pretty uncoordinated," Juju teased.

"Oh yeah?" Maggie responded, pretending to put Juju into a headlock.

Juju looked up at Maggie, and as Maggie's grip loosened, she raised her head and planted a kiss on Maggie's lips.

Maggie was taken back. "What's that about?"

"Really? Are you that oblivious?" Juju asked.

"About what?" Maggie questioned.

"Um, news flash: I'm into girls," Juju told her.

"You are? How come I didn't know that?"

"'Cause you aren't into girls, right?" Juju asked, hoping for the answer she wanted.

"Um, I don't think so. I'm not into guys, either. I just do what I do. Never really gave it much thought. Besides, I've never been attracted to anyone like that," Maggie stated.

"You ever kiss someone you love? You know, I mean like a real kiss?" Juju prodded.

"No, I can't say that I have. Sex isn't something I feel; it's just something I do," she explained.

Juju leaned forward and kissed Maggie again. This time, it was a passionate kiss. She parted Maggie's lips with her tongue, and the two girls shared a moment. Maggie jerked away when Juju slid her hand up her shirt.

"I'm sorry, Juju. It's just not me. I love you, but not like that," she explained.

"Yeah, it's cool. But when you fall madly in love with me, don't come cryin'," Juju said, disappointed.

As Maggie walked back onto Kensington Avenue, Juju played heavily in her thoughts. She didn't want Juju to stop loving her, but she really didn't feel anything when they kissed. *Was her ability to be in love also stolen? Was there anyone out there in the world that she would ever want?*

Maggie wondered just how much had been stolen from her by the predators who took her youth and innocence. Lost in her own thoughts, she looked up. Trinity was standing in her way.

Chapter Seventy-Three

"Well, if it isn't Miss High-and-Mighty," Trinity mocked. "Screw you, Trinity. What do you want?" Maggie countered.

"I saw your little bull dyke hittin' Legacy and Froggie. Ya know, there's gonna be revenge. No one beats on my friends and gets away with it," Trinity threatened.

"Maybe you should tell your friends that I don't do drugs and that I didn't steal their stuff. What's your problem, Trinity? I never did anything to you, and all you ever do is try to make my life suck more than it already does," Maggie spat back at her.

Trinity glared at Maggie. "Who the fuck ya think told 'em you stole their shit?" she asked, egging Maggie on.

"You're a bitch, Trinity. I'm sick of you. Maybe I'll start treating you the way you treat me," Maggie told her, standing her ground and fighting the urge to punch Trinity in the face.

"You best think twice about fuckin' wit' me. Ya don't know what you're getting into. Ya don't know nothin' 'bout what it takes to survive," she hurled.

"Oh, so now you're the authority on pain and suffering. Listen, Trinity," Maggie said, taking a step closer to her. "I've survived more shit in my life than you'll ever know. Just 'cause I'm white doesn't mean I haven't had a hard life. You think you're so damned tough. Well, I got news for you: you aren't. I can tell you stories that'll make your fingernails curl. I've seen more death and violence than you can know. So just stay the hell away from me, and I'll stay away from you," Maggie growled in a low, throaty voice.

Trinity drew back slightly, just enough to let Maggie know that she'd had an impact on her.

As Maggie started to walk away, a slow simmer began in Trinity's stomach. She was accustomed to being the bully and wasn't happy that she had lost the ability to intimidate Maggie. She liked messing with the little bitch. It made her feel better, stronger. It gave her a sense of power. She didn't want to lose the only power she had on the streets. *The bitch will have to be put in her place*, Trinity thought.

Just as Rock had predicted, a couple of weeks later, after they'd healed fully, Legacy and Froggie went looking for Juju. The twosome had been planning for weeks how they would rock her world. Their plan included other people, and because the people they hung out with were also violent by nature, they agreed to help for a price.

It was a busy Saturday evening for Juju when Legacy and Froggie approached her. "Well, look who it is. If it isn't Bruce Lee," Legacy sang, as she shuffled by Juju a little too closely.

"Beat it, bitch. I'm working and don't need any of your bullshit," Juju said nonchalantly.

"Ha! You're fuckin' kiddin' me, right? You think you gonna get away with the shit ya pulled on us a couple of weeks ago? Nah, that ain't gonna happen," Legacy told her.

Juju finished her sale and turned to face Legacy. "Look, it was nothing personal. You ganged up on my friend, and I was just levelin' the playin' field. Two against one ain't so fair. Ya know what I'm saying," Juju said, sizing up both girls.

"Yeah, but ya know, that ain't how me and Froggie see it. You ambushed us, took us by surprise. We don't like no surprises. You feelin' me?" Legacy asked with unnatural calm.

Juju started to back away. Legacy's posture signaled that something bad was about to happen. Just as Juju started to go into her stance, she backed into two overgrown men. Juju spun around, taking in their size, and dread washed over her. She looked around for someone she could call on to help, but no one was there. One of the men seized her shoulders. She tried to pull away, but he was too strong. She looked into his face to try to talk her way out of it, but words escaped her as she became blinded with fear.

"What? You ain't got nothin' to say now? You were a real big ass when ya assaulted us, but now ya can't do nothin'. Now it's your turn to see what it feels like to be surprise attacked," Froggie rambled in her raspy voice.

Legacy struck the first blow to the side of Juju's face. The two girls took turns hitting her while Shrek I and Shrek II kept her from getting loose. When the girls were finished letting off steam, they turned to the Shrek twins. "You know what to do now," Legacy commanded.

One of the men put out his hand, and Froggie laid a one hundred dollar bill on his palm. Juju was beaten and sobbing, her head hanging. Legacy bent down and looked up into Juju's face. "You *real* ugly when you cry, bitch. You better cut it out before the boys here decide to kill ya after takin' what they want from ya," she tormented.

Juju didn't have it in her to beg. She had never begged for anything in her life, and she didn't plan to start now. Instead, Juju pulled strength from deep within and spit in Legacy's face. "Fuck you," Juju said breathlessly.

Legacy wiped the spit with her hand and swiped it across Juju's shirt, "No, baby, it's fuck *you*. Enjoy it now," she sang and walked off with Froggie.

The two Shrek's pulled Juju to her feet. "We gonna have a real good time tonight. Don't worry," the smellier one promised.

Chapter Seventy-Four

The men shuffled Juju along to a condemned house on the next block. One of them kicked in the plywood covering the back door. Once inside, they turned on a flashlight and pulled Juju into what looked like an old living room. In the middle of the floor was a dusty, old rug, "Put her over there," said the man with the flashlight.

The other man, whose grip was like a vise on her arm, walked her over and pulled her arms behind her back. Before she knew it, a rope was tied around her wrists. One of the men forced her down onto the carpet. Crazy thoughts ran through her head...they were going to shoot her, slit her throat, burn the house down with her in it. Her chilling thoughts were endless and scared her more than she wanted to admit.

She felt herself sliding across the floor as one of the men pulled the rug to the other side of the room. Then, her legs were forced apart and tied to a radiator. She was lying on her back, and now, as the reality of what they might do to her began to seep into her brain, she started to panic. The sound and feel of her clothes being torn from her body made her blood run cold.

When she finally dared to open her eyes, the two men were standing over her. One was already naked from the waist down. He hovered over her for an extended period before he straddled her torso and finally sat his big, fat ass on her abdomen. He began to pull on her nipples while the other one talked.

"Here's how it's gonna happen. We're gonna get what we want from you. If you act nice, we'll let ya live. But if ya act like you don't want us, we gonna kill ya. Now, when we finished playin' wit' cha, you ain't never gonna bother Legacy or Froggie again. You understand?"

"Yes," Juju managed. "Please, you don't have to do this. I'm gay, all right?"

"Oh, well, that's very special. You gay! Well, tonight you straight, and tomorrow you can be gay," he told her, laughing.

The man sitting on Juju's abdomen reached behind him and shoved his fingers into her vagina. Her attempts to free herself only enhanced the sexual experience for the two men. When they finished raping her, the men left her lying on the floor without a saying word.

Juju lay still, shocked and traumatized, unable to move a muscle. The only thing she was capable of doing was willing Maggie to find her.

It was midnight when one of the other drug pushers found Maggie and told her about Juju. "Yeah, they took her into an abandoned house. They came out, but she didn't. Do you want me to show you where?" he asked.

Maggie ran at top speed to the house where they'd left Juju. She crept around to the back of the house and, seeing the opening, she entered. Maggie moved through the darkness until finally the boy who was with her struck his lighter. They moved slowly until they came upon Juju.

Maggie rushed over to her friend and put her head on her chest to listen for a heartbeat. "Juju, it's Maggie, I'm here. You're going to be OK," she assured her. They untied the ropes that bound Juju, and the two of them helped her out of the house.

Once they were in Juju's apartment, Maggie turned and hugged the boy who had helped her. "Thanks," she told him and softly closed the door.

Turning her attention back to Juju, she helped her into a loose T-shirt and got her into bed. Maggie slid under the sheets with her friend. She held Juju tightly and stroked her hair. After a few hours without any response from Juju, Maggie got out of bed. She rolled up a towel and placed it under Juju's knees to elevate her legs. She had read that it enhanced blood flow to the brain for people who are in shock.

Maggie carried a pot filled with water and ice cubes over to the mattress. She grabbed a T-shirt from the closet, soaked it, and then began to run the wet shirt over Juju's face. She massaged her temples and finally, she forced Juju to take small sips of water. After what seemed like an eternity, Juju began to respond. She was blinking at a normal pace and turned her head to make eye contact with Maggie.

Tears streamed down Juju's face. "It was horrible."

"I know it was. But you're going to be OK. You need to give yourself time. You're going to heal from this," Maggie promised.

"I was a virgin. I messed around with a couple of girls before, but I never had sex," Juju wailed.

"I'm so sorry, Juju. The price you paid to defend me was too high."

Juju closed her eyes and embraced the clutches of sleep that comes from pure mental and physical exhaustion. Right before she dozed off, she mumbled, "I would do anything for you, Maggie."

Maggie kissed Juju's cheek and climbed into bed next to her. *Tomorrow, we will start over again*, Maggie told herself.

Chapter Seventy-Five

In the months following Juju's rape, Maggie spent hours trying to help her overcome the mental anguish of the assault. It made Maggie wonder how she, herself, was able to cope with being violated at such a young age. She knew that her abduction had tainted her view of the world, and after months of trying to talk Juju off the ledge, she finally opened up and confided in detail about her own experiences.

Juju had heard bits and pieces of Maggie's story, but now she heard the whole, horrible truth. Maggie shared things with Juju that she never thought she'd tell anyone. To hear of the ongoing horror Maggie and Seth had endured gave Juju strength and put her own circumstances into perspective. Juju never realized how bitterly awful Maggie's life had been. As Maggie recounted the past five years of her life, it was simply devastating. But it was this intimate information that made Juju feel as though someone understood the depth of her own despair.

Over the next month, Juju slowly came out of her funk. The experience would change her forever, but she was well on the road to recovery. With the worst behind them, the two girls fell back into their "normal" routine.

Maggie's own situation at the house of whores had become more tolerable. With young girls coming in and older girls moving out, she found her place among them. A few of the new girls even looked up to Maggie. She was pretty, smart, and carried herself differently than the other prostitutes did. Maggie still had that special something about her, and as she came into her own, a certain charm and sophistication prevailed. As time went on, Armando allowed her to take more liberties. He even let her sleep at Juju's every now and again, but only after dropping off her nightly earnings.

On the flip side, Seth seemed to be sinking into a deeper, darker state of mind. Seth had violent thoughts about Thelma, which he shared with them when they met him before school. He began to talk more openly about the abuse Thelma laid upon him. Thelma either treated him like an animal or she completely neglected him. Seth talked about running away, but Maggie knew the risk was far too great. He wasn't old enough to make it on his own, and if Rock caught him, he'd kill him for sure. Maggie wondered if there was a way she could find Seth's parents. He was still young enough to be reunited with his family, although he didn't remember his parents. But if she could locate them, maybe they could get him out of his ruined life.

Maggie spent hours at the library looking through all of the Philadelphia newspapers, starting on the day she and Seth met in the back of John William's van. There was nothing on Seth. She searched the whole year he was kidnapped. Again, nothing was reported. It was as if Seth never existed. She thought that was odd, since she was able to find her own story so easily. Finally, letting go of the possibility that Seth could return home, she turned her attention to another idea: maybe she could convince Rock to allow Seth to live with Juju. After all, Seth was unwittingly a drug runner for Rock. He wasn't a pusher on the streets, but he did provide a valuable service to Rock.

Shortly after Maggie's sixteenth birthday, Seth's situation became desperate. The girls met up with him on his way to school. Seth was holding his right arm up with his left hand and walking very slowly. The girls rushed to him, and their mouths dropped open when they spotted the arm he was holding. It was broken three inches above his wrist, making his hand sit higher than the forearm.

"Seth! What happened, sweetie?" Maggie asked, trying unsuccessfully to hide the alarm in her voice.

"Thelma caught me stealing food from the trash can in the kitchen. She said I'm a thief and a sneak. She told me I had to be punished. Then she made me put my hand on the counter and she whacked my arm with a baseball bat. It hurts so much, Aggie." He cried in her arms like a newborn baby.

"I know it does. But don't worry; we're going to get you taken care of," Maggie assured him. Juju hadn't moved. Her eyes were locked on the mangled arm. "Juju, I need you to go find Rock. Fast!" Maggie commanded.

"What? Sure," she said, coming to her senses. She ran down the street in the other direction.

Maggie helped Seth sit on the sidewalk under the shade of an old tree. She wanted to hold Seth, but was afraid she'd hurt him more. Instead, she rubbed his small back with the palm of her hand. "Everything will be OK," she said in a calming voice. "Things are going to change. I promise."

Seth looked up at her, his face displaying nothing but sadness and defeat. "I hope so, Aggie. Thelma keeps sayin' she's gonna kill me someday." He paused and swallowed loudly enough for Maggie to hear him gulp. "I think she is going to kill me. She's the meanest person ever. Even meaner than John William."

In that moment, Maggie wished she possessed magical powers so she could wipe Thelma off the face of the earth. To get Seth's mind off his pain, Maggie reminded him about *Harold and the Purple Crayon*. "If you could create everything you ever wanted, what would you draw?"

"I would draw me living with you somewhere safe. We could play games and eat," he said.

Maggie thought about how simple it was for Seth to define happiness. Safety, love, and food were all he wanted. Not too much to ask. Most kids his age wanted things, but all he wanted was stability. His idea of getting everything he wanted had nothing to do with desires but rather, with the purest basic human needs.

As Maggie reflected on Seth's wishes, Rock pulled up next to the curb with Juju in the passenger seat. He got out of his car like a slug and walked over to them. "What's all the fuss about?" he asked, eyeing Seth's arm.

Maggie had already decided to take the high road. Pissing Rock off wouldn't get Seth the immediate help he needed. "Well, we need to get Seth to a doctor. As you can see," she said, pointing at his wrist, "his arm is broken."

"What did you do now, boy? Man, you're a pain in the ass," he hissed at Seth.

Seth remained silent, his fear of Rock transparent.

"Come on, Rock. You know Seth didn't break his own arm. He needs help," Maggie persisted, wanting to relieve the child of his suffering. "Besides, if he goes into school like this, they will send him to the hospital. The doctor will call protective services. Then, they'd go out to your house, and you could get in a lot of trouble. I mean, it's not like you have adoption papers for Seth or anything. You'd have to explain why he's living with you. They'd want to question Thelma, too." Maggie knew that he paid off the principal at Seth's school, but she was gambling that he wasn't paying off anyone at the local hospital.

"Oh, yeah? How do ya know all this stuff?" Rock asked, intrigued that she would consider the outcome.

"Because I read. There are all kinds of things in the newspaper. The point is, Seth needs to go to a doctor."

"Yeah, I have a fella. He's a doctor. He helps when I need him. We can take the pain-in-the-ass there; see if he can fix him up," he yammered.

Maggie spoke with urgency. "We need to get him there now, Rock."

"OK, get him in the car. You're coming too," he said, looking at both girls.

Maggie sat in the backseat with Seth lying across her lap. Forty-five minutes later, they pulled into a long gravel driveway, and Rock parked the car. As they walked to the front door of the house, Maggie noticed that trees surrounded them. The last house she'd seen was more than a mile down the road. *Definitely not in the city anymore*, she thought.

The two girls helped Seth into the house. Maggie didn't know what to expect, but it was a very normal, well-kept, two-story house, not much different from the house in which she'd lived with her parents. Rock's friend, George Percy, who was referred to as Dr. Purse on the streets because of all the money he had, led them to a bedroom on the first floor.

"What's your name?" Dr. Purse asked, bending down to talk to the boy.

"Seth," he whimpered.

"Nice to meet you, Seth. My name is Dr. Purse. Seth, I'm going to get your arm all fixed up. You'll be better before you know it," he said in a voice that gave Seth comfort. "Let's get you up on the table," he instructed as he pulled over a step stool.

Seth climbed up on the stool with help from Maggie and sat on the edge of the gurney. Maggie looked around the room, which had been turned into a mini trauma center. Dr. Purse, who had worked in private practice for many years, ran a business out of this house that catered to pimps from the surrounding area. Dr. Purse had convinced himself that he was doing something good for mankind by helping people who needed him the most, but the vast amount of cash he made treating his patients also gave him a very comfortable lifestyle. George Percy lived in a two-million-dollar house in a ritzy neighborhood in Villanova, Pennsylvania with his wife and five children.

Maggie and Juju shared a look of relief as Dr. Purse talked to Seth in a reassuring voice. He left them in the room, and when he returned, his nurse, a thin, pretty woman was following him. After the nurse cut Seth's shirt away, Dr. Purse looked at the fracture carefully. Looking up at his nurse, he said, "It's obviously broken. Let's get an x-ray and we'll take it from there. Let me give this little guy something for the pain." It took only seconds for Seth to ease into la-la land after Dr. Purse gave him an injection.

The nurse turned to Maggie and Juju. "Do you want to help me?" she asked, her smile lighting up her face.

Maggie and Juju nodded and stepped to either side of the gurney to help. They both silently wondered where they were going as they passed several closed doors. At the end of the hallway, which ran the entire length of the house, the nurse opened a door, revealing a stark white room with a large x-ray machine in it.

It took a couple of hours for Dr. Purse to do his magic, setting the bones just right, and then the three of them left the house with a groggy Seth wearing a hard cast on his arm.

As they drove back to Kensington, they were all silent. Seth slept peacefully. After twenty minutes, Maggie finally asked the question that was burning inside her. "Rock, Seth really isn't good for Thelma. I mean, this time it was only a broken arm, but you never know what she'll do to him next time. Seth knows Thelma hates him. Thelma told Seth she was going to kill him someday. I was thinking maybe he could move in with Juju. He could still work for you. At least you'll know that he'll stay alive, and he is good for your business. No one would ever suspect a kid." She held her breath.

Rock pulled over to the side of the road and came to a screeching halt. "Bitch! Have you lost your damn mind? That boy belongs to Thelma," he growled. "Ya ain't got no right tellin' me what I oughta do!"

"Sorry, Rock. It was just an idea," Maggie said, hoping he would drop it.

Juju chimed in, picking up the slack and trying to divert Rock's annoyance onto herself. "I don't know, Rock. Sounds like it could be very profitable for you. Seth will be out of commission for a week or so. At least with me, you won't have to worry about this kind of shit."

Rock stared at Juju, and she watched him until she saw his face soften.

"I'll think about it. Now shut the fuck up," he mumbled, turning the volume up on the radio.

Chapter Seventy-Six

A week later, Rock found Maggie working on Kensington Avenue. He rolled down the window of his car and glared at her. "Get in!"

Maggie's heart seized. She wondered if she was in trouble for something. She quickly got into the front passenger seat.

"I thought about what you said about Seth. I think ya might be onto something. So here's what we're gonna do. I'm taking you out to one of those houses, like the one you lived in with Seth. We're gonna take a look at some of the kids, and you're gonna pick out a kid for Thelma to replace Seth," he said, a smile forming on his lips.

"But...but...Rock, why does Thelma need another kid—"

"If you want Seth to live with Juju, that's what ya gotta do. Besides, I need to make sure to keep my business a secret. So the way I see it, if you do the pickin', that makes you as guilty as me. I consider it insurance," he explained cynically.

Rock had realized that by letting Seth live with Juju, which was no problem with Thelma because she hated the kid, he would lose leverage with Maggie. He needed to ensure that Maggie was in the game. Otherwise, she could easily take the boy and run.

Maggie hesitated for a brief moment. If she did what Rock wanted, Seth would have a chance at a better life. But in the process of saving Seth, she would be putting another child in danger.

"This ain't rocket science, girl. Ya either want to help your little friend or ya don't. Besides, Thelma wants a girl this time. The choice is yours. I'll give ya 'til tomorrow to decide. Come find me before noon. Now get your ass outta my car and get back to work," he said coldly.

Back on the street, Maggie staggered around in a daze, forgetting she was supposed to be working. The dilemma of saving Seth's life at

299

the cost of another child's was staggering. She couldn't wrap her mind around having to make such a horrible decision. Finally, after a few hours of self-torture, she went looking for Juju. When she found her, Maggie broke down into tears.

"What's wrong?" Juju asked, worried.

Maggie explained the proposition Rock had offered. "How can I make this decision? If I choose to leave Seth there, Thelma will eventually kill him. But if I pick another kid for her to destroy, then it will be my fault. Rock said it would make me part of his disgusting business. I don't know what I'm supposed to do," she wailed, throwing herself into Juju's arms.

"Maggie, you need to think about this the right way. If you agree to pick the next kid, you'll be saving her from the life she's living as a human sex toy. Right? I mean, you told me about what it was like to live in captivity. I know what you're doing now doesn't thrill ya, but ya do have a little more freedom. Remember what happened to Cali and Max," Juju said.

"I do remember what happened to them, Juju! There's not a day that goes by that I don't think about Max and Cali. But what about all the horrible things Thelma will do to this new kid? Am I supposed to pretend like bad shit won't happen to her at the hands of that bitch?" Maggie countered.

"Maybe Thelma would treat a little girl better. Maybe she just hates boys. You don't know. If I were you, I would agree to do it. At least you'd be saving one of them. If things stay the same, then Seth and some little girl you don't even know will both have a chance of dying. You have a chance here to save one life. If things turn out well, you could actually save two lives. Think about it," Juju said, trying to influence her friend's decision.

"I never thought about it that way. I guess you have a point." Maggie sat on a bench and looked up at the sky. She willed the heaven above to help her make the right choice. Juju had made a really good point. If she could help Seth, that was better than not helping anyone.

"OK. You're right. But here's the deal. If I agree to do this, then you have to promise we'll meet this little girl every day before school, just like we do with Seth. That's the least we can do. We'd have to keep an eye on her. Deal?" Maggie asked.

"Deal," Juju said with gusto.

Maggie found Rock before noon the following day. He was surprised that she approached him with such confidence. He'd been certain that she would reject his offer.

"Hey. OK, I'll do it. I'll pick the girl for Thelma, and Seth gets to live with Juju. That's the deal, right?" Maggie asked, clearly surprising Rock with her decision.

"Yep, that's how it'll work. You and me will take a little trip tomorrow," he explained.

Maggie nodded. "What time do we leave?"

"I'll be over to pick you up at seven tomorrow morning. Be ready," he ordered.

"Yeah, I will," Maggie told him, and then she walked off to look for customers.

Chapter Seventy-Seven

Maggie and Rock left the house of whores shortly after seven the next morning. They drove for an hour before Rock parked his car. He leaned over to Maggie. "Take the blindfold off. We're here," he grumbled.

Maggie whipped off the rag that had shielded her vision. She held her hand over her eyes until they adjusted to the light. Once her eyes focused, Maggie looked around. They were in an abandoned commercial complex. The buildings looked like no one had stepped inside of them for a thousand years. Weeds and ivy almost covered the face of the buildings. She felt as if she was in a jungle except for the cracked asphalt, which seemed to go on for miles. Maggie slipped out of the car and followed closely behind Rock. He stopped before they reached a metal door on the side of the building. "Just keep your fuckin' mouth shut. You only talk to me when I ask you questions. Ya fuck this up, and I'll kill ya and that little bastard of yours," he threatened, referring to Seth.

Maggie nodded numbly. Once they were inside the building, her stomach clenched at the smell of corruption. All too quickly, she remembered the retched stench of these places—a mixture of rotten men with their liquor- and smoke-ridden breath and children doused in cheap perfume and cologne. Her adrenaline began to pump rapidly, and she had an overwhelming urge to turn and run out the door.

Rock gave her a scathing look. "Don't forget what I just said," he warned.

He shook the hand of the man who had opened the door for them. "Hey, man," Rock said. "Julius is expecting me."

"Yeah, he told me. Go ahead up. He's waitin' for ya."

Rock led Maggie down several narrow corridors, which had no doors or windows, until they finally came to a long flight of metal stairs. Maggie realized that if she had to run out of the building, she wouldn't know which way to go. The hallways had intertwined and crossed over other halls. It felt as if they were rats in a maze.

At the top of the stairs, they entered a room with black lighting. Maggie felt the little hairs on the back of her neck stand up, and a chill raced up her spine. The tiniest gasp slipped through her lips; it was just loud enough for Rock to hear, and he turned to her.

"I'm warning ya. I'll leave your nasty ass here if you screw this up. Pull yourself together," Rock hissed through clenched teeth.

Maggie sat next to Rock on the sofa against the far wall. Five minutes later, a large door opened, and a man walked across the room to Rock with his hand extended. "Hey, Rock. Good to see you again," Julius said with a seedy smile.

"Yeah, same here. This here is one of my bitches. She's gonna help me pick one," Rock explained.

Julius eyed her lustfully. "She's pretty fuckin' hot. You sure you don't want to do a trade instead?"

Rock looked at Maggie and grinned. Her heart began to rattle against her rib cage, and her face felt like it was on fire as she flushed with panic.

Julius stepped closer and sniffed her hair. "How old are you?"

A lump clogged Maggie's airway, and she stared at Julius in silence. Rock slapped her on the back of the head. "The man asked you a question, bitch. Answer him," he directed.

"Sixteen," Maggie whispered, forcing the word through her lips.

Julius stepped closer and pulled Maggie to her feet. Rubbing his hand down Maggie's back and over her ass, he pulled her to him and locked his body against hers. His eyes flicked over to Rock. "Before we move on, I wanna have a piece of this fine ass."

"Yeah, man. Go ahead. But you need to do it here," Rock told him.

Rock wasn't nuts about Julius taking a free piece of ass that he owned. Julius didn't give anything away free. But Rock had called in a favor so he could get Thelma another rug rat. Still, he wasn't about to let Maggie go off with Julius; he needed to protect his property. It was a filthy business, and deception was widespread. It was just part of the game.

Rock looked at Maggie, his eyes flat. "Let's go, girl. Take your fuckin' clothes off and get on with it." Then Rock turned his attention to Julius. "You got protection with ya?"

Maggie was no good to him on the streets if she caught a disease.

Julius nodded with hungry eagerness, getting all revved up for Maggie and her powerful beauty. She stood in the middle of the room naked, and Julius looked her up and down, absorbing the perfect body that matched the stunning face. "Let your hair outta that ponytail," Julius instructed.

Maggie let her jet-black hair fall. It had been a long time since it was last cut, and it hung to the small of her back. "Oh, yeah." Julius breathed heavily and quickly undressed.

"Come on, bring it over here," he told Maggie, pointing to the sofa.

Maggie glided over calmly, using her best hooker attitude to disguise her fear. The fact that Rock hadn't left the room gave her some comfort. As she stood facing Julius, he tore open a condom and handed it to her.

"Here, you put it on me," Julius said, taunting her.

After Maggie slid the rubber on, he spun her around, locked his arm around her waist tightly, and bent her over the sofa. He entered her from behind. Maggie held in her screams of rage as Julius sodomized her in the darkened room with Rock watching. When Julius finished, he pushed her face-first into the back of the sofa cushion. Then he turned to Rock. "All right, now we can get down to business," he stated, with a satisfied grin.

Maggie quickly grabbed her clothes and dressed. She rushed over to Rock, conflicted that she somehow felt safer standing close to him. They followed Julius into another dimly lit room. They stood in the center of the room for the briefest moment before the room went pitch black. Maggie held her breath and then, to her surprise, one light popped on against the wall. The light was inside a glass box, the size of a large coffin, and inside the box stood a young girl.

Another light came on in a glass box to the right, with another young girl inside. In all, there were three glass boxes against each of the four walls. When all of the boxes were illuminated, Maggie looked around in pure terror as twelve girls between the ages of nine and eleven stared back at her with big, fearful eyes.

"OK, I want all of you to stay perfectly still," Julius told the children. "Don't move until I tell ya to move."

Rock dragged Maggie by the arm to get a closer look at each child. Their sorrowful expressions made her want to set all of them free. In each of them, she saw herself and the others she had lived with at the prison. Her heart ached with sympathy. They walked back to the middle of the room, and Rock whispered, "So? Which one? Which of these *innocent little creatures* are you going to pick?"

Maggie looked around the room; her mind buzzed as she thought about all of the things these children were being forced to do. Her vivid memories of sex traffickers made her stomach churn. She recalled her fear and feeling of worthlessness as people looked her over as if she was a piece of meat. She continued to stare in silence, yearning for her family again, just as she had done in the first months after John William kidnapped her. She wished there was something—anything—she could do to help the children who watched her with guarded anticipation.

"Hey!" Julius screamed at a girl who slumped to the floor of her box from exhaustion. "Get the fuck up or you'll be sorry," he threatened.

Rock looked in the direction of Julius, and while both men had their backs turned, a nine-year-old girl behind them gave Julius the finger and then quickly dropped her hand back to her side. Maggie had been staring directly at her. She was impressed by the girl's nerve and was drawn to her instantly. She was a fighter and a little brazen. Maggie thought she was perfect. Unlike Seth, the girl had brass balls, and she'd need them to survive the wrath of Thelma.

When Rock and Julius turned around, Maggie shifted her gaze to a different box so they wouldn't catch her staring at that little girl.

"Well? Which one is it?" Rock pressed, growing impatient.

"That one." Maggie pointed. She walked over to the girl and stood close to the glass as Rock turned to Julius to negotiate the sale. When neither of the men were watching, Maggie gave the girl a slight nod, and the little girl raised her eyebrows in response, as if they were speaking a secret code of honor.

"How much?" Rock asked.

"Twenty grand," Julius responded.

"Twenty grand? Ya gotta do better than that, man. I was thinkin' more like ten grand," Rock countered.

Julius held Rock's gaze. The girl was worth a lot to Julius, so Rock was going to have to lose something if he wanted to get a better deal.

Julius pulled Rock over to the side of the room.

"I have an idea. I'll give her to you for ten grand, but I'm gonna need a little something in return," Julius stated.

"Like what?" Rock asked, visibly annoyed.

"Like that bitch of yours over there, for starters," Julius said, pointing at Maggie.

Maggie didn't know what the two men were saying, but it was clear she was a part of their conversation. Her mouth went dry, and she instinctively wrapped her arms over her chest. After several more minutes, the two men shook hands. Rock walked toward Maggie with a disturbing smirk.

"I got me a deal," Rock told her.

Something about Rock's posture told Maggie that trouble was coming her way. She willed herself to speak, but couldn't form any words.

Finally, words erupted from Maggie's lips. "Can we leave now?" Her voice trembled.

Rock's face stayed firm. "I'm leaving now, but you ain't."

"What?" Maggie shrieked. "Rock, you can't leave me here. Please take me with you."

"I made myself a good fuckin' deal. That's what I did," Rock mocked.

Maggie lunged forward and clung to Rock.

"Please, Rock, oh please don't leave me here. I've done everything you wanted. Please don't do this to me," Maggie begged.

Rock laughed, pushed Maggie backward, and she fell onto the floor.

"Didn't anyone ever tell ya not to make a deal with the devil?" Rock ridiculed.

Then he hacked up phlegm and spit on her. "Ya dumb bitch. Thought ya were so smart, huh? Thought ya could get away with your bullshit. Well, ya ain't that smart now, are ya?"

Maggie scampered across the floor and wrapped her arms around Rock's ankles. "Noooo. Oh, please, no. I don't want to stay here," she cried.

Julius had walked over to them, followed by two of the men who worked for him.

"Get her outta here," Julius instructed.

The men pried Maggie off Rock and dragged her toward a door. The whole time, Maggie was screaming and fighting to break free. She turned back to Rock, who was leaving through the door they had entered.

"Rock!" Maggie screamed at the top of her lungs as the door slammed behind him.

Chapter Seventy-Eight

———————————————————————

Maggie was taken down several flights of stairs to a corridor with rooms on either side. As they passed each room, Maggie noticed the various children inside. The realization of what had just transpired had yet to settle in her mind. It was as if she was living in a real-life horror film.

The two men stopped at a door, unlocked it, and shoved Maggie inside. She lost her footing and fell face-first onto the hard industrial tile floor. She rolled onto her back quickly, just as the men slammed the heavy door and threw the deadbolt.

Maggie sat up slowly, looked around the room, and her eyes landed on a little girl huddled in the corner with her knees tucked tightly to her chest and her forehead resting on them. Maggie inched her way over to the little girl until she was kneeling in front of her.

"Little girl?" Maggie whispered.

The child finally raised her head, and when she did, Maggie recognized her as the child whom she'd picked for Thelma. Stunned, Maggie fell back onto her ass. Rock had not only left Maggie there, but he hadn't taken the little girl home with him.

"Why are you still here?" Maggie finally managed.

"'Cause that asshole you came here with left without me," the girl hurled.

"I'm sorry," Maggie stated mournfully. "We're going to be all right," she added, trying to calm the girl's fear as much as her own. "My name is Maggie. What's yours?"

"Joey."

"How old are you?"

Joey thought for a moment, the memory leaving her with great despair. "Nine. My bitch mother traded me for drugs and a case of beer on my birthday."

Oh shit, Maggie thought. Then the enormity of what had transpired pushed through her consciousness, and Maggie began to sob. Joey shifted closer to Maggie.

"Don't cry. They don't like it when we cry. Besides, if you're a crybaby, they make you take pills to make you stupid. Some of the other kids have to take them all the time, and they can hardly even talk," Joey warned.

"You're right, Joey. Crying isn't going to make this any better." Maggie sniffled, forcing her emotions aside.

Maggie was struck hard by the information Joey had shared. Under John William, they didn't force the kids to take drugs; it was a choice they could make on their own. She understood quickly that she would have to keep her wits about her to have any chance of surviving.

Maggie got to her feet and walked to the door. She peered through the window in the door and noticed a small girl looking back at her from the room across the hall. As she watched the girl, it was like looking into a mirror and seeing her past life. *Why did Rock do this to me?* Maggie thought. She had allowed Rock to deceive her. He had fooled all of them, and now she was back in the hands of sex traffickers.

The questions and thoughts stifled Maggie's ability to remain calm. She told herself to breathe. Her eyelids spontaneously blinked faster, as if flicking away her horrifying reality. She realized that she had brought this situation on herself by being outsmarted—by making one wrong decision. She had been so focused on saving Seth from Thelma that she hadn't seen Rock's true intent. He had played her for a fool. The enormity of her situation crushed against her ribs as the pain of regret surged through her body, ripping through her nerve endings like a tornado.

Several hours later, Maggie was startled by the sound of the deadbolt on her door sliding back. A white man in his mid-twenties stood staring down at her. His head was shaved, and his beard almost touched his chest. His eyes were black, and his small mouth was too tiny for his round, pudgy face.

"Let's go," the hideous man commanded.

Maggie slowly rose to her feet and hesitantly walked toward the door. She stole a glance in Joey's direction, but the young girl refused to make eye contact with her.

"Move it, slut!" the man screamed.

Maggie hurried to the door. The man snatched her up by the arm and pulled her along. Maggie didn't have to guess where the man was taking her. She already knew what would be expected as he led her back up the stairs to the upper floor of the dilapidated warehouse.

Maggie felt a heavy shroud of sorrow wrap around her soul for making the wrong decision. Once again, the urge to go back in time and recant a horrible decision consumed her, its broad tentacles latching deep inside her psyche. How could she have been so naïve? Why did she ever trust Rock? What would happen to her now that she was back with sex traffickers? What would happen to Seth? Would she ever see Seth and Juju again?

Chapter Seventy-Nine

T he men who worked for the sex traffickers had stripped sixteen-year-old Maggie of all her clothes. She struggled in vain as they tied her arms and legs to the bedposts in a windowless room inside an abandoned warehouse.

"Please, you don't have to tie me up," Maggie pleaded. "I'll do whatever you want me to do."

Her begging was met with ugly laughter. The two men left the room, slamming the door behind them.

A few minutes later, four men in their early forties entered the room, which was illuminated by candles. Maggie strained to watch them through the eerie darkness. The men were whispering; they all carried beer bottles. She could tell by their staggering gaits that they were drunk.

"Well, look what we have here," Ernest, the most vocal of the pack, announced as he stepped closer to Maggie.

His friends, Ivan, Damon, and Conway, gathered around the bed where Maggie lay in bondage.

"Please," Maggie uttered.

"Oh, shit! It speaks," Ernest said, laughing.

"I'd suggest you shut the fuck up," Conway said, leaning into her. "Otherwise, we're gonna hurt you real bad."

Maggie was utterly helpless. She'd been through a lot, but being back in the hands of sex traffickers was more than she could comprehend.

"I wish they hadn't taken her clothes off," Ivan said, slurring his words. "These dudes really blow. We told 'em we wanted her dressed. Fuckin' bullshit."

"Did they put the bag in here?" Ernest grunted.

"Yeah, that's it over there," Damon said, pointing.

The four grown men had brought toys along with them.

Ernest carried the bag over and dropped it at the foot of the bed. After unzipping the bag, he reached in and pulled out nipple clamps. Maggie's eyes bulged as Ernest opened the clamps and placed them on her nipples. She resisted the urge to scream as the clamps dug deeply into her sensitive skin.

Ivan began to grunt and clap rapidly. He bent over Maggie, grabbed the chain that connected the clamps, and gave a quick yank. Maggie let out a yelp as pain shot through her breasts.

A moment later, Conway took a vibrator out of the bag and turned it on. Holding the vibrator against Maggie's lips, he ordered, "Suck it, bitch!"

Maggie hesitated for a brief moment, long enough to piss Conway off.

"You fucking whore. I said suck it," Conway yelled, shoving the vibrator into Maggie's mouth.

Maggie gagged when Conway pushed the device to the back of her throat. The four men watched in amusement as she tried her best to do what she was told. When Conway removed the vibrator and stepped away, Damon reached into the bag and then moved closer. Before Maggie knew what was happening, Damon had shoved a ball gag into her mouth.

"That's to keep you from distracting us with whatever whore bullshit comes out of that mouth of yours," Damon told her.

Maggie pleaded with her eyes and in return received a hard slap in the face from Damon.

"Don't even look at us, bitch. You're not good enough to breathe the same air, you understand?" Damon seethed.

Maggie nodded but went into a state of panic. *Are these guys going to kill me?*

As the hours wore on, Ernst, Ivan, Damon, and Conway became more aggressive with Maggie. At first, they took turns having sex with her.

Maggie lay still after they'd finished. Then Ernest grinned.

"Time for some fisting. How about it, boys? Who wants this one?" Ernest asked.

"Me!" Ivan called, moving quickly to Maggie's side.

Maggie watched as Ivan slathered gel on his hand. Then he inserted his fist inside of her. She arched her back, fearing that he was tearing her insides apart as he moved his fist in a circular motion. When Ivan finished, they used toys on her. The men took turns having sex with her again, and to Maggie's disbelief, Conway gave Damon a blow job. These middle-aged men were harsh and kinky.

During the torturous hours, Maggie tried to think about Seth and Juju, but the things the men were putting her through made it hard to focus on anything but her immediate pain.

After five hours of sexual assault, Maggie hoped she would die. But instead, the four men stopped, packed their bag of toys, and left her tied to the bed, bloodied and bruised. Maggie's body was limp and broken.

To ease her sorrow, she thought about Seth and Juju, and hoped they were wondering where she was. As she remained still, staring up at the ceiling, a man named Brute entered the room.

"Damn, girl, those fuckers are nuts. You gotta be beat," Brute said jovially.

Maggie's eyes followed him as he cut away her bonds. Her arms and legs were exhausted from being tied for so long, and she was barely able to move them.

Brute reached his hand out, and Maggie grabbed it. After Brute steadied her, he threw a blanket around her shoulders.

"You'll need a shower before your next client," he sang, as if he was doing her a favor.

Maggie hung her head. The thought of more torment was unbearable. She began to wobble. Brute put his arm around her shoulders to steady her, and Maggie began to cry.

"None of that, now. You've got work to do, missy," Brute stated as he led her to a bathroom with shower stalls.

As Maggie let the warm water wash over her, she yearned for the bony fingers of death to take her away from her hell on earth.

Chapter Eighty

For the next month, Maggie's nightmare continued. She no longer thought about getting away or going back to her old life. She preferred to think about death. But she couldn't figure out how to kill herself. The traffickers were always around, always looking in on the kids or having sex with them between clients.

Six weeks after Maggie was left at the warehouse, the traffickers told her to put on the clothes she'd been wearing when she arrived. Brute stood in the doorway of her room while she changed, and when she finished, he led her up a different set of stairs.

Maggie looked around as she entered a large, dimly lit room.

"Sit over there," Brute instructed, pointing to a chair in the corner.

As Maggie sat waiting and no one came, her anxiety grew. She hadn't been in this room before, and she worried about what that meant. In the middle of the room, there was a bed, and at its foot was a tripod with a camera attached. She looked at the camera, remembering the first day of her captivity. The memories filled her mouth with sour bile.

Forty-five minutes later, the door opened. Maggie held her breath. She gawked as Rock strutted into the room and gazed at her.

"Ya like your new home?" Rock asked.

"No," Maggie said, starting to cry. "I want to go back with you."

"Oh yeah? Now all of a sudden ya like bein' wit' Rock, don't ya?"

Maggie nodded. "Please, Rock. Don't leave me here. Take me out of here," she pleaded.

Rock rubbed his chin as he considered what she was asking. "I'm not sure. Ya might need a little more time to think 'bout what ya really want. I mean, ya haven't been here that long, and well, I got me a couple new girls since ya been away."

What Maggie didn't know was that Rock had negotiated a deal with Julius. In order to buy Joey for ten grand instead of twenty, Rock agreed to leave both girls there for six weeks to make up the difference. Rock believed it would serve two purposes: pay for the new kid for Thelma and tame Maggie. It had worked.

Maggie stood and walked to Rock. When she was in front of him, she tilted her head and looked into his eyes. Then she slowly leaned in and kissed Rock. He responded as he parted her lips and drove his tongue to the back of her throat. Resisting the urge to vomit, Maggie willed herself not to pull away. When their kiss ended, Rock watched Maggie closely.

"Please, Rock," she whispered. "Please take me back home. These men are nothing like you. They're vile and nasty. I'll make you feel really good if you just take me out of here."

"OK, baby, Rock will take ya home," he said.

Rock took Maggie's hand and led her out of the room. A few minutes later, they met with Julius in another part of the warehouse.

"Where's the kid?" Rock asked Julius.

"Waiting down by the door. You can grab her on your way out," Julius said.

The two degenerates shook hands, and Rock led Maggie toward the exit, where they saw Joey waiting with one of the guards. As they approached, Maggie gave Joey a smile. Joey moved deliberately toward Maggie and stood next to her. Then the girl reached out and took Maggie's hand.

Rock watched them closely. *Little bitch better cozy up to Thelma like she is with Maggie*, he thought.

Joey had light-brown, wavy hair that hung to her shoulders. Her eyes were the palest green Rock had ever seen. Beyond the intriguing color, he saw a fire there that made it impossible for him not to be drawn to her. She was as pretty as Maggie was, just a whole lot younger. He hoped Thelma would love her; otherwise the kid was in for some hard days.

Oh well, Rock thought, *that's the kid's problem. If Thelma doesn't like her, Joey will just have to deal with it.*

Chapter Eighty-One

Outside the warehouse, Maggie and Joey quickly climbed into the backseat of Rock's car. Once they were inside, Rock walked away from the car to talk to two men who were standing outside the door of the building.

Relief washed over Maggie, and she began to relax. The thought of returning to Kensington thrilled her. She was determined to obey Rock and do whatever he wanted so he would never send her back to the sex traffickers again. At least being a prostitute in Kensington gave her some freedom. Besides, hooking on the streets was far less violent than anything she'd experienced in the last six weeks.

Maggie looked over at Joey, knowing their time alone was limited.

"Joey, we only have a minute to talk, so I want you to listen. You're going to live with a woman named Thelma. You have to be strong and do what she tells you to do. Make sure you're polite and offer to help her around the house. They're going to send you to school. I'll be there every morning before school to meet you. No matter what, you can't let the guy that bought you—or his nasty wife—know that I come to see you. OK?" Maggie said in a rush.

"Do you promise to meet me?" Joey asked, feeling a bond with Maggie.

"Of course I promise. I'm even going to bring two friends with me, Seth and Juju. You're going to love them. Just remember, I'm going to do my best to watch out for you. All three of us will," Maggie stopped talking as Rock opened the car door.

Rock threw two T-shirts into the backseat, "Cover your eyes," he instructed. Maggie put Joey's blindfold on and then her own. Rock started the car, and they drove off. Joey held on to Maggie for dear life.

Her experiences with the sex traffickers left her hardened, yet she was still a frightened nine-year-old girl.

A while later, Rock parked in front of his house. "Take the blindfolds off," he told the two girls.

Joey stretched to see out of the car window. She looked at Maggie. "Are we here?"

"What's this 'we' shit? Maggie, get your ass out of the car and get back to your house," Rock barked, as he left the car.

Maggie gave Joey a quick squeeze and whispered, "Be brave. That's why I picked you; because you were the bravest girl in that shit hole."

Rock swung the back door open and waited while the girls got out. "Let's go," he told Joey.

Joey was pouting when she walked into the house where Thelma was waiting. "Well, ain't she just the prettiest thing you've ever seen?" Thelma squealed. "Come over here and let me get a better look at you," she said to Joey.

Remembering what Maggie had told her, Joey walked over to the sofa and stood in front of Thelma. She wondered if there was something wrong with the lady. Thelma's eyes were red and glassy. "Come on over here and give your mama a hug," Thelma said, opening her arms.

Joey was repulsed by Thelma's metallic breath, a mixture of drugs, cigarettes, and lack of dental hygiene. *Just do what Thelma tells you*, she reminded herself. Joey leaned in, put her small arms around Thelma's thick neck, and gave her a hug.

"Aww, look at that Rock, the girl already loves her mama. Now, why don't you be a good little girl and go into the kitchen through that door and fetch your mama a cold beer from the refrigerator?" Thelma said.

Joey fumbled her way around the back of the house and found the kitchen. She pulled out a cold beer and returned to the living room. Joey handed the beer to Thelma.

"See! Now that's the kind of kid I like. She's smart, Rock. Not like that fuckin' idiot ya brought home last time," she pointed out.

"Good, baby. I'm glad you're happy. I'm sure Joey is probably hungry. How 'bout if I go get us a pizza and we can sit down like a family and have dinner?" he asked in a charming voice.

"Yeah, you go do that. While you're gone, me and this little princess will get to know each other. Did she bring any clothes with her?" Thelma asked.

"Nah. Just what she's wearing. I'm sure ya got shit upstairs she can use," he said.

"Yeah, we'll go up and see while you're gone," Thelma agreed.

That night, while lying in bed, Joey waited for deranged men to come into her room as they had in the place she'd just left. To her relief, no men ever came. When she woke up in the morning, after sleeping through the night for the first time that she could remember, she looked around the small room, wandered out into the hallway, and found the bathroom. Joey already felt a sense of freedom. Her heart felt lighter, and she made her way downstairs to find Thelma passed out on the sofa.

Joey walked into the kitchen and filled a glass with water from the faucet, and then she walked quietly to where Thelma lay sleeping. Joey stood over the woman for only a brief moment before Thelma's eyes bolted open. Startled, she sat up abruptly. "What the fuck?"

Joey jumped back and met Thelma's stare. Then she gave her a small smile. "I brought you a glass of water," she explained, pushing the glass toward her.

"Oh, thanks." Thelma took the glass and guzzled the water. "Next time, don't be sneakin' up on me like that." Thelma rubbed her temples with her fingers and looked up at Joey. "That was very thoughtful. Go on now and get yourself dressed," she said, and reclined on the sofa again.

Joey rushed up the stairs to her bedroom. She wondered if perhaps someday soon she would go to live with Maggie, the girl who helped get her out of that awful place where she was living. Joey allowed herself to feel hope, something she hadn't felt in a long time. *Maybe things will be different now, and I'll get to live like other kids*, Joey thought.

But Joey had yet to see the *real* Thelma.

Chapter Eighty-Two

It had been more than five years since Maggie was stolen from her family. Over the last year, Lorraine and Rob Clarke had become advocates for families of missing children.

They had just returned from the city after sitting for hours with a couple whose child had been taken just two days earlier. Detective Harker went to see the Clarkes each time a local child went missing. They tried to visit as many people as they could, but work and taking care of Keith made it impossible to meet with everyone in crisis.

"What's going on in this world?" Lorraine finally asked, more to herself than to Rob.

"I don't know. But at least we're doing something with our own loss. We're helping people to cope. In a weird way, I find comfort in helping other people. I wish there was more we could do," he said, feeling the enormity of other people's losses on his shoulders.

"Rob? Do you still wonder where Maggie is?"

Rob let out a loud sigh. "I don't know, Lorraine. I know you want to believe she's still out there and someday we'll find her, but I'm not so sure anymore. There are days when believing she's dead is more comforting than hoping she's alive."

"What do you mean? How can you think that way?" Lorraine asked desperately.

Lorraine needed Rob to believe they'd find Maggie someday. His belief fed her own belief, and she wasn't willing to give up hope that they'd see Maggie again. In fact, it was hope that kept her alive and functioning. Without hope, Lorraine was sure she would shrivel up and die.

"Look, we've seen so much tragedy over the last year, all those parents and their missing kids. It just seems like we would have heard something by now. When I let myself believe that Maggie's alive, then it tears me up to think about what's happening to her. You heard what that little Smith girl said when they found her—she was tortured and starved. What if the people who took Maggie are doing the same thing to her? How can I get out of bed in the morning knowing my kid is suffering like that?" Rob asked.

"The Smith girl was taken by a neighbor. He watched her for years. That sicko fantasized about her. Maggie wasn't taken by a neighbor," Lorraine debated weakly.

Rob took his wife into his arms. "We don't know that, Lorraine. The only thing we know is that she may have been abducted by sex traffickers," Rob reminded gently.

The two of them shared an unimaginable pain that only parents of missing children could know. All of the false leads that had given them temporary relief and optimism had led to dead ends. Then the cycle of grief and loss started all over again, as if it were the first day Maggie was gone.

Rob pulled away first. "We need to eat something before Rae Harker gets here."

Lorraine nodded and went to the kitchen to make them sandwiches. Now that Rob and Lorraine were heavily involved in working with families of missing children, Rae stopped in once a month, sometimes more frequently, to find out what they were able to uncover from the distraught parents. It was often in the small details, which many families didn't think mattered, that the police found their best leads.

The Clarkes had just finished eating when the doorbell rang. Rae Harker greeted the couple and casually walked into the kitchen, opened a cabinet, and took out a mug for coffee. For more than five years, Detective Harker had spent a lot of time with the Clarkes, and he was no longer a stranger in their home. He finally settled down at the kitchen table with Rob and Lorraine.

"Well, something significant happened today," Rae reported.

Lorraine sat forward, leaning on her elbows with anticipation.

"The Philly police busted a house where they found a dozen or so underage prostitutes." He watched as Lorraine's eyes widened, and he gently laid his hand over her wrist. "Maggie wasn't there. However, the girls they found could provide us with more information on the other kids that have gone missing," he stated.

Lorraine slumped in her chair. "How do you know none of the girls are Maggie? Did you ask them? Maybe she's been brainwashed to lie!"

"I know because all of the girls are either Latino or black. There weren't any white children recovered from the home," Rae said in an even voice. He knew how Lorraine tortured herself over the possibility that Maggie was still alive. He always made it a point to be sensitive when supplying information to her.

"Oh. Where was the house?" Lorraine asked sadly.

"It was in North Philly. They're still holding the girls at the police station. I've been told they're all in their early to middle teens. There were four men in the house when they busted in, and they're all being held for questioning. From the information they've gotten from the girls so far, it sounds like these are the four men who forced them into prostitution."

"I hope all of those sick bastards burn in hell. Is there anything we can do to help?" Rob asked.

"Well, actually, I was thinking that if I can swing it, maybe you could talk to one or two of the girls they rescued. They may be more inclined to tell the parents of a missing girl what they know than they would be to talk to the police. Do you think you'd be up for it?" Rae asked.

"Why us? I mean, talking to the families is one thing, but talking to these poor, innocent girls seems a little out of our league. Were just regular people. How would we know what to say?" Lorraine asked nervously.

"Think about it. Let's say someday we find Maggie. We know she would have information that could help other people. You would know what to ask her. You've been at this for a long time, and from where I sit, there aren't any other parents who have been as involved as you two have been," Detective Harker explained.

"He makes a good point, Lorraine." Rob slid his chair over and put his arm around his wife. "What if we can save just one other child? What if another couple could do what Rae is asking us to do and they said no? Wouldn't you want them to try if it meant finding more kids? Maybe even our own child?"

Tears dripped from Lorraine's chin, and she wiped them with a new sense of bravery. "OK, fine. We'll do it. I just hope we find out something that's going to help," she told them.

"Good! I'll make some phone calls and give you a buzz in the morning," Rae said. He rose and shook hands with both of them. He pulled Lorraine into him. "If I can make this happen, you're the one person I think can make a difference. I wouldn't have asked you if I didn't believe that," he assured her.

Lorraine was the kind of woman that people trusted. Her genuine and candid nature made her likeable and easy to engage. She had been great with the families of missing children. She gave them hope for a successful recovery. She was a natural at helping people learn to cope. Lorraine was oblivious to the comfort that she gave to the other parents. But Rae Harker knew all of this about Lorraine.

Lorraine's unrelenting belief that Maggie would come home made all the difference. Rae just hoped that one day he could make Lorraine's dream come true.

Chapter Eighty-Three

Two days later, Rob and Lorraine drove to the Philadelphia police station in Center City. Only one girl was willing to talk to the Clarkes. Lorraine's nerves started to get the better of her when a fifteen-year-old Latino girl walked into the room and sat across from them. The first thing Lorraine noticed was how old the girl's eyes were. It was as if she was staring into the eyes of a sixty-year-old woman.

"Hello. I'm Lorraine, and this is my husband, Rob."

"I'm Crista," she announced. "The police said you wanted to talk to me."

There were several moments of uncomfortable silence as Lorraine and Crista watched each other closely.

"Your turn to talk," Crista told her with an attitude.

Lorraine smiled at her warmly. "Well, Rob and I have a daughter named Maggie. She was taken from us over five years ago. We talk to a lot of other parents whose children are missing. I thought maybe you could tell us something that would help us find our daughter." She smiled as she watched Crista soften just a tiny bit.

"Like what?" Crista asked.

"Well, like maybe you know of other places where girls are being kept and forced to..." Lorraine's voice caught in her throat.

"Forced to have sex with a bunch of disgusting slobs? You can say it. I've been doing it for three years now. I don't have anything to hide. In fact, I'm good at it," Crista said.

"Well, I'm sure you did what you needed to do to survive. I respect you for that," Lorraine told her.

"Oh yeah? You respect me for spreading my legs and giving sloppy blow jobs?" Crista taunted.

"I respect you for doing whatever was necessary to live through your ordeal. Look, nothing you can say will shock us. I understand you're angry, and I don't blame you. But we're angry too. Somewhere out there, our child may be doing the same things you had to do. We just want to help," Lorraine said in a raised voice. She was beginning to lose her cool.

"Oh yeah? So you're saying that if your kid comes home, you're not gonna care about all the shit they made her do? Humph. Bullshit. I never thought my parents would care, either, but I see the way they look at me. I know they hate me now," she said, her voice rising.

"That's not possible. A parent can't hate their own child for something that's not their fault. I'm certain your parents love you. They're just confused. It's hard to imagine someone doing horrible things to your kid. Maybe you have to tell them what you need. What you lived through is unthinkable, and this is in no way a comparison, but it's not easy to be on our side, either. We sit and pray and wait for news that never comes…"

Lorraine broke down and bawled. Sobs racked her body.

"Is she OK?" Crista asked Rob.

With tears streaming down his face, Rob turned to Crista. "You're the closest we've come to knowing what it would be like to find our own daughter. We were hoping you might be able to help. That's all," he explained gently.

Crista sat back in her chair and watched carefully. She wanted to be 100 percent certain that this lady wasn't fucking with her. Crista and the others had been saturated in paranoia by their pimps. They were always on the lookout for someone trying to set them up and get information they shouldn't be giving. It was ingrained in her—in all of them. When she was certain, she finally spoke. "OK, so you said your daughter's name is Maggie, right?"

Lorraine's head popped up as if she were a turtle coming out of its shell. "Yes, why? Do you know her? Have you seen our daughter?" Then Lorraine reached into her purse and pulled out a picture of Maggie for Crista to look over.

"Nah. I never saw her. But before they moved me to North Philly, they kept me in a house in Camden. There was chick there named Shana. I got pretty close with her, and she was always ranting about some chick named Maggie. She lived with her in Pennsylvania or some shit like that. She said Maggie was kidnapped from some mall. Is that your daughter?" Crista asked.

Lorraine nodded sadly. "Yes, it is. We knew she was held here in Pennsylvania for a while. The police had arrested your friend, Shana, and found out that they had been held together at some point," she confessed.

"Well, did you know that Shana thought Maggie was special? Bitch was all kinds of jealous of your kid. Apparently, Maggie got the attention of some guy named Myles, who ran the place. Soooo, he dumped Shana and made Maggie his new girl," Crista said, as if it was completely normal and she thought the information would make the Clarkes feel better.

Rob's hands were on his lap under the table, and he instinctively curled them into tight fists. It was incomprehensible that some man had made Maggie his *new girl*. She was only a child. In the meantime, Lorraine made a mental note. Myles was a name she'd give to Detective Harker.

"We didn't know this, Crista," Lorraine finally said.

Crista felt the sadness and loss of the two grown-ups who sat in front of her. They really did love their daughter; that was clear to her. So she decided to continue. "Well, from what Shana told me, Maggie was one strong bitch. She would read all kinds of books some perverted doctor would bring her. She helped Shana out a couple of times when her customers hurt her real bad. Anyway, Shana said all the other kids loved Maggie. I can't remember their names, and she talked mostly about Maggie anyways, 'cause even though she said she hated her, I could tell she liked her too. She was just jealous that she wasn't as smart as Maggie."

Crista watched as Lorraine and Rob sobbed for the child they loved. Finally, unable to remain silent, Crista blurted, "The last time Shana saw Maggie, she was still alive. Who knows? Maybe she still is."

"You're right, Crista. Maybe she is, and someday she'll come home to us just like you're home with your parents," Rob offered.

"Yeah, maybe she's out there somewhere. Hey, do either of you have a cigarette?"

"No, we don't smoke, and you shouldn't either," Rob added.

Crista looked at him with an amused grin, and he realized how stupid it was for him to scold her for smoking after all that she'd been through.

"I'm sorry, Crista. I don't mean to preach. It's the father in me," he said softly.

"Yeah, I get it. Anyway, is there anything else you wanted to talk about?" Crista asked.

Lorraine shook her head and pulled herself together. "Nope, not right now. But if anything comes up, could we get in touch with you?"

"Sure. My parents said it was OK for me to talk to whoever I needed if it helps put this thing behind me. Ha! They don't know shit if they think I can put something like this behind me. It's a part of me now. You know, after a while, it doesn't seem so bad to be a whore. Guys used to pay a lot of money for me—not that those assholes ever let me keep any of it. Anyways, do you think you could give me your phone number? I kinda like talkin' to you guys. Maybe you can give me advice on how to handle my parents. I mean, they think I'm the little girl I was before I disappeared. I ain't nothin' like that person. I had to leave her far behind if I wanted to live..." Crista's voice trailed off as she thought of the pretty, sweet girl she once was.

By the time they rose to leave, a bond had formed. Each of them walked away with new insight. As Lorraine walked out of the police station, she touched the small piece of paper with Crista's phone number on it.

Right before Lorraine got into the car, she turned to Rob. "If Maggie ever comes back to us, I don't think she'll be the person we knew. Crista has helped me to see how all the corruption and exploitation changes a child. We need to do more, Rob. We need to start helping these kids make their way back into society. There has to be more we can do."

Chapter Eighty-Four

Seth felt like he was living in a dream. He had been living with Juju for almost six months, and Maggie was there whenever she wasn't working, which made him feel as if she lived there too. He and Joey had become close friends.

Seth was working for Rock, and all the exchanges of money and drugs were coordinated through Juju. After a couple of months, Juju talked to Rock. "So, we need you to give Seth some money for his work. I mean, I can't afford to pay for everything. Maggie chips in a little, but you know Armando is tight with his allowance to the girls," Juju explained.

"We didn't have no deal on the boy getting paid. You and Maggie should've thought about how you were gonna feed him before ya cut a deal. So, I ain't cuttin' no deal wit' cha now," Rock told her. "I don't care if that little shit stain starves to death. He ain't my problem."

Juju wasn't surprised by Rock's response; she'd expected as much. Plan B was for Maggie to find out if Armando would increase her allowance a little. Maggie wasn't looking forward to asking him, but she figured it was worth a try. Maggie approached Armando on a rainy Thursday morning. "Hey, Armando," she sang in a sweeter voice than normal.

"What the hell do *you* want?" Armando asked defensively.

"I wanted to talk to you about my allowance."

"What about it?"

"Well, I was wondering if you could increase it. I need to help Juju out with some of the expenses for Seth," she said honestly.

"Ha! You're fuckin' kiddin' me, right? Get the fuck outta my face before I knock the shit out of you. I don't care about Juju and that little asshole kid of yours."

Maggie remained silent and angrily left the house. When she walked into Juju's apartment fifteen minutes later, the two girls looked at each other, and Maggie shook her head.

"You know what? This is a bunch of bullshit," Maggie said, stomping her foot. "We're making these jerks a lot of money, and they won't share any of it with us. This is really pissing me off."

"Yeah, I agree. We know Rock isn't going to give me a bigger cut of the profit from selling, and I can't charge more for my dope to keep more money 'cause I'll price myself out. My customers will buy from someone else," Juju said thoughtfully.

Then an idea began to form in Maggie's head.

"That's it! I know what to do. I'll turn a couple of extra tricks a week and just keep the money. You know, nothing big, just two or three tricks would give us enough money," Maggie said with confidence.

"Um, yeah, that sounds like a shitty idea. Do you know what would happen if Rock ever caught you doing that? It's happened before, and he found out about it. The girl disappeared, and we never saw or heard about her again. That's too risky. There's no way you'll keep it a secret. They have a lot of people who work for them, and you never know who's watching you," Juju warned.

"I would never tell anyone, so there's no way Rock would ever find out. That girl must've told someone what she was doing, and that's how she got caught. I mean, the new girls would never get away with it, but Armando only cares that I meet my weekly quota. I think the risk is low. We both keep our traps shut, and no one knows any different," Maggie persisted.

Maggie felt an obligation to Seth, and it was her intent to keep him safe, fed, and loved, just as she had promised him. If it meant taking a small risk to earn a little extra cash, then that's what she'd do. She told herself that it wasn't like she was stealing from Armando. After all, it was her body being sold and her skill earning the money. The way she saw it, she was the one who was being robbed, not Rock or Armando. With her mind made up, Maggie assured Juju that everything would be fine.

That very night, Maggie sold herself to one more customer before finishing her shift. When she was done, she went to Juju's apartment and gave her the thirty dollars. Then she walked back to the house of whores to give Armando her earnings. He took the money and counted it in front of her, something he did routinely with all of the girls. Content because Maggie had earned her quota, Armando walked into the room where the other men sat drinking and smoking.

Well, that was easy, Maggie thought as she stretched out in her "spot" on the dirty living room carpet. *Piece of cake.*

During the months that followed, Maggie turned a couple of extra tricks each week. This made her capable of earning enough money to help Juju with the expenses. The two girls even were able to stash away a bit of money for the future. Everything seemed to be working as planned, and Maggie was proud that she was able to help all of them.

One Sunday afternoon, while they were eating Chinese takeout in Juju's tiny apartment, Maggie talked about expanding her profits.

"Look, Juju. No one is even noticing a couple of times a week. It's really simple; if I just turned one extra trick a day, it would give us extra money. We could save it all and someday get the hell out of this rotten place. No one has noticed me doing it so far, and they're not gonna notice if I do a couple more," Maggie explained.

"What happens if you get caught? Huh? What will happen then?" Juju argued, with no chance of winning.

"I won't get caught. I have it all figured out, OK?" Maggie insisted.

Maggie truly believed she could do it without anyone noticing. But Maggie was dead wrong.

Chapter Eighty-Five

Maggie was turning an extra trick every day and, as a result, the girls were able to save a little money. They were even able to buy Seth some secondhand clothes dirt cheap. It was on Maggie's birthday, when she went back to the house of whores wearing jeans and boots that Juju had bought with some of their savings, that Armando became suspicious. The men who ran the house never gave the girls enough money to buy things on their own. Clothes were bought at rock-bottom prices when the men decided that a few new items were necessary to keep the customers attracted.

Armando may not have noticed had it not been for the younger girls ogling and commenting on the new items Maggie was wearing. But the real giveaway was that Maggie tried to downplay the gifts. Armando pretended not to notice Maggie secretly hushing the others. He knew something wasn't right, and it all added up to another deception by Maggie. The next evening, Armando secretly followed Maggie. He watched her take johns back into the tall grass of the open field, and he counted them. When she came home that night and handed him her earnings, she was one trick short of his count.

Armando spent the next week watching and counting until he was sure about what Maggie was doing. Only then, did Armando have a private sit-down with Rock. He told him everything he'd found out.

"We can't have this shit goin' on. The others will catch on, and before we know it, they'll all be scammin' too," Armando said. "I think it's time we talk to some of your associates. She's young enough that we can still sell her or maybe even get a good swap for her."

"Yeah, that's not a bad idea," Rock agreed. "We can't be havin' this bitch stealin' from us. Besides, she's marketable. I just need some time to get everything hooked up. In the meantime, keep your eye on her."

As Rock drove back to his house, his thoughts were racing, and he was furious that Maggie had deceived them once again. He'd already given her too many chances. The time for her to go had arrived. Before Rock went into the house where Thelma and Joey were waiting for him, he thought, *after I eat dinner, I'm going to make a call to New York; see what that bitch, Maggie, is worth.*

Rock dialed the number and then sat back in his chair, waiting for the phone to be answered. On the third ring, the man picked up. "Myles," the voice announced.

"Myles, it's Rock. How you doin', man?"

"Rock, it's been a while. How've you been?"

"Good, man, good. Hey, ya remember our last transaction? That girl, Maggie, I bought from ya a few years back?" Rock asked, knowing damn well that Myles would remember her. Maggie had the type of beauty that no man could forget.

"Yeah, sure. I remember her." Myles thought about little Maggie. She'd been his favorite for quite some time. So sweet and innocent. Of course he remembered her. There'd been many others since Maggie, but she would always stand out in his mind.

"Well, I got a little problem. Bitch gave us some shit in the beginning. Lying and doing things she shouldn't. We took care of all that. Things have been good for some time. Now we just found out she's scammin' us. She's turning extra tricks and keeping the dough. Ya know what happens when one of the bitches does this and gets away with it," Rock remarked.

Myles smiled on the other end of the phone, thinking of clever little Maggie. She always was a smart one. "Yeah, I understand. Once one gets away with it, they all think they can do it. So why are you calling me? What are you looking for?"

"I'm looking for a buyer," Rock stated. "I'm gonna need a good price for her. Remember, I paid ten grand for her just three years ago. I'm looking to double my money, at least. I've trained her, and she's even hotter now than she was then," he said, trying to talk up the sale.

Myles thought about it for moment. "OK, I'll see what I can do. No promises. You're asking for a lot of money. Remind me how old she is," he said.

"Seventeen. But I'll tell ya, she's one fine-looking bitch," he said enthusiastically.

"Seventeen? Rock, you must be smoking crack. Twenty grand is a lot to expect for a seventeen-year-old. I don't care how hot she is," Myles told him.

Rock could feel the muscles in his calves tensing into tight knots. He knew Myles was right, but he couldn't just let Maggie go, and he couldn't keep her in the house with the other girls; not anymore. She'd killed the little trust he had in her.

"She'd make a good porn star," Rock said without thinking, desperate to get a good price for her.

"Hmmm. That's not a bad idea. Let me make some calls and see if there's any interest. I want you to take some pictures of her and send them to me right away."

"Pictures. Yeah, OK. I'll take some pictures and get them out to ya tomorrow. I'll be talkin' to ya."

Rock hung up the phone and called Armando. "I need you to get me pictures of Maggie. I want hot, sexy pictures. Get her a couple of those 'fuck me' outfits. I'll be over later tomorrow. Make sure it's done before I get there," he ordered and hung up the phone.

The next morning, Armando woke Maggie up early. "Come on, let's go," he told her.

She followed him up to a bedroom on the second floor. *Ugh*, she thought with deep disgust, *the scumbag wants sex*. She was surprised when she entered the bedroom. There were red satin sheets on the bed, and across the room, several sexy outfits were spread out on an oversized chair. *Oh great! Now he wants sex* and *for me to dress up. Yuk!*

"We need to get some pictures of ya. Sexy pictures," Armando stated.

"For what?" Maggie asked, surprised.

"Bitch, who the fuck are ya questionin'? Get your smelly ass over there and put on one of those outfits I bought ya. Then go comb your hair and put on some makeup I left for ya in the bathroom. Hurry up!" Armando yelled.

When Maggie emerged from the bathroom ten minutes later, she looked like a Victoria Secret model.

"Get yourself over here on the bed and do some poses," Armando stated coldly.

Maggie did as she was told. Armando told her how to pose—raise your arms, spread your legs wider, push your hair out of your face, take your bra off, pull your thong over...the instructions went on and on. The photographer must have taken a hundred pictures of her.

When they were finished, Maggie put her clothes on and went back downstairs. She nervously noticed that none of the other girls were being taken upstairs for pictures. Why only her?

She thought about it for a few minutes and then let the worry slip away, convincing herself that everything was fine.

Chapter Eighty-Six

Three days later, the phone rang. Rock answered. "Yeah?"

"It's Myles. The pictures were fabulous. You were right, she's even better looking now," Myles confirmed.

"Good, good. Do you have a buyer?" Rock pressed, wanting to ditch the small talk.

"Let's just say I have someone who is very interested."

"Oh, yeah? They're going to put her in porn movies, then?" Rock asked curiously.

"Not exactly. They're looking at her for a snuff film," Myles said casually.

Fuck. That sucks, Rock thought. *They're gonna buy her and kill her in a porn film. Oh, well! As long as they pay me my price, I don't give a shit.* For Rock, everything came down to money. All of his decisions were based on how he could make the most money possible.

"So what now?" Rock asked.

"We wait. I'll let you know when I hear back," Myles said.

The next day, Myles extended an offer of five thousand dollars for Maggie.

"What the fuck is this? I paid ten grand for her. Why the fuck would I sell her for five?" Rock asked, outraged.

"Because she's seventeen years old, and all they're going to do is make one film with her, and she'll be dead. I'm sure you made your fair share of money off her over the last three years. You've made back that ten thousand many times over."

"How much is your cut?" Rock asked.

"It's 15 percent. It ain't much. I'm not in this particular deal for the money. I'm just trying to help two people I know make a deal," he said.

"Five thousand ain't enough. I need at least ten," Rock told him.

"Fine. I'll call my contact. I'll let you know."

Rock sat forward in his chair and slammed his fist on the top of the table. He was angry that Maggie had betrayed him yet again, and in the long run, he would lose money. But keeping her put too much at stake. She had to go as soon as possible.

A week later, Rock went to see Armando to let him know he'd made a deal to sell Maggie for eight thousand dollars. Armando was disappointed at how little they'd gotten for her. Rock gave Armando explicit instructions. "I'll be driving her up to New York in two days. Make sure she's here and ready to go. I'll pick her up in the morning."

Rock wasn't any happier about the sale than Armando was. From a business standpoint, it was a stupid move. But when he took in the bigger picture—the larger implications of Maggie's actions—he knew it was something he needed to do. On his way back to his own home, Rock drove slowly down Kensington Avenue. Sitting at a traffic light, he noticed a crowd had gathered on the sidewalk next to a car with its windows open, blaring music. A group of men were bouncing around, hooting and hollering. When Rock took a closer look, he saw Maggie. She was pole dancing on a street sign.

Rock parked his car and watched from across the street as Maggie worked the crowd of men. She shimmied up the pole effortlessly and moved to the music. Her long, lean body was magnificent as she smoothly and eloquently became one with the pole. Rock was captivated by her elegance and sensuality, her muscles tensing and relaxing. Her body appeared to be flawless. He had to admit that she was a good pole dancer.

When the music stopped, Maggie led one of the men behind the building. She returned fifteen minutes later and took a second man behind the building. When she came back the next time, the music was screaming from inside the car again, and Maggie did her pole routine. *Well I'll be damned*, Rock thought, *she found a way to boost her own business*. As the other prostitutes watched and threw annoyed glances, Maggie was the center of attention for the paying customers.

Rock thought about Maggie's fate. She was so talented and attractive, a real money-maker. It seemed such a shame to throw all that potential money out the window for a measly eight thousand bucks. He sat in his car for over an hour, watching the men feed off her. The other hookers were practically turning green with envy. There had to be another way for him to salvage her. He needed to think of something spectacular. Rock remembered what he had learned as a young man from Thelma's father. You must always think in terms of money, even if it means doing something you've never done before, the old man told him. This is a tough business, and only the men who understand human nature will succeed.

Rock watched for a while longer, and then slowly the idea formed in his mind. He played the idea out in his head as if he were watching a movie. Then he decided.

Rock knew exactly what he was going to do with Maggie.

Chapter Eighty-Seven

———————————————■———————————————

"The deal is off," Rock told Myles. "I have something else in mind for Maggie."

"Well, I can appreciate that, but you do know you've put me in a bad situation. My client is going to be very unhappy. I had to work some difficult angles with this low-life to put this deal together," Myles responded.

"I know, I know. I appreciate all you've done. But the girl is worth too much to me. Tell your client I'll make it up to him another way, another time. But Maggie ain't for sale. I got new information that gave me a solution to my problem. I didn't have this info when I called you. I'll be more than happy to pay ya for your time. We've known each other a long time, and I've never backed out of a deal. I hope we can continue to do business in the future," Rock said.

"All right, well, I hope you're making the right decision. Maggie is a smart girl, and you have your hands full. As for my time, let's just keep it at *you owe me*. I'll call some other business owners and see if I can find a girl for this snuff film. Whatever you just found out about Maggie saved her life. Like I said, she's a smart girl. I'd keep my eye on that one, if I were you," Myles warned him.

"Yeah, man. I hear ya. Hey, thanks for your help. Let's stay in touch."

Rock sat back in his chair, and relief washed over him. He knew it was bad business to cut a deal and then back out of it at the last minute. He also knew he'd only get away with doing it once before no one would do business with him. *Maggie better come through*, he thought, or *I'll kill her myself.*

The next person Rock called was Armando. "Did you tell Maggie we were taking a little trip?" Rock asked.

"Yeah, I told her. The bitch was full of questions. I had to slap the shit out of her to make her stop talkin' and told her to be ready to go when ya get here," Armando said, sounding like a tough ass.

Rock smiled as he held the phone to his ear. "Yeah, she ain't like the others. That one has a mind of her own. Well, were gonna keep her with us. I have another plan for her. I'm gonna move her out of the house to make sure none of the other bitches pick up her habit of scammin' us."

"What's your plan?" Armando asked, shocked. He did not want to lose the income he made off Maggie.

"I'll explain it to ya later. I'm going to Juju's to talk to Maggie now, so she ain't gonna give ya no shit. Don't worry. I'll make sure ya see some green from what she earns. I'm gonna give ya 5 percent," Rock explained, sensing what Armando was thinking. Rock needed to keep his crew of men happy; after all, they dealt with the day-to-day bullshit of the business.

"Yeah, yeah, OK, Rock. That sounds good. Just let me know what you need me to do," Armando said, relieved.

"When she comes back today, all ya gotta do is make sure she puts on the sexiest outfit ya got. Have her put it on, and give her something big to wear over it. Something that's easy to take off," he said.

Rock left the house and went to Juju's, where he knew he'd find Maggie. When Juju opened the door and Rock stepped inside the tiny studio apartment, Seth jumped to his feet and ran to Maggie. He placed his whole body behind hers and poked his head around her side to keep an eye on Rock.

Noticing the boy's fear, Rock chuckled loudly. "Relax, boy. I ain't here for you."

"So, what are you here for?" Juju asked with apprehension.

"I'm here to talk to Maggie," Rock said. The serious tone in his voice sent chills up Maggie's spine.

"Su...sure, Rock. What's up?" Maggie asked nervously.

"Come on. We need to take a little ride," he responded mysteriously.

Maggie and Juju exchanged worried looks, both wondering if Rock had found out that Maggie was turning extra tricks. After giving Seth a hug, Maggie followed Rock outside and slid into the front seat of his car. Rock turned and swung a forceful backhand at her face. He wanted to scare her and put her on notice that what he was about to say wasn't an option.

"I know what you've been doing," Rock said and went silent.

"I...I...I don't know what you're talking about," she stuttered, blood dripping down her chin from her split lip.

"Oh no? Ya don't know you've been scammin' me? Turning out extra tricks and keeping the dough?"

"I can explain, Rock. Juju and I didn't have enough money to buy food for Seth and pay all the bills. I gave Armando my nightly quota. I never came up short on that," she pointed out.

"Your nightly quota is a minimum of what I expect ya to earn. Do ya think I pay for your skank ass to live for nothin'? For you to go behind my back and steal money from me?" Rock yelled.

"No. I'm sorry," Maggie replied timidly. But she was starting to burn up inside. Maggie knew how much money they made off her. She resented Rock, Armando, and all of the others for exploiting her and the other girls.

"So what now?" Maggie asked, not wanting to prolong whatever punishment was coming to her.

Her mind was racing, and she had a gripping fear that Rock would sell her back to the sex traffickers.

"I saw you dancing on the street pole the other day," he stated evenly.

"And?" she asked, rattled.

"And I've decided to put that skill of yours to good use. I'm taking ya out to a strip club. The manager there is gonna give ya an *audition*. We're going up there this afternoon. I expect ya to perform. You understand me?" Rock said in a coldblooded voice.

"But I'm not a stripper, Rock. I only know a couple of moves I learned before I came here—"

"Shut the fuck up!" Rock yelled. He grabbed a fistful of her hair and pulled her face close to his. "Listen real good. We're gonna go to that bar, and you're gonna dance like your life depends on it. *Because it does*," he threatened.

Maggie's fear of being on a stage started choking her—not so much her fear of stripping but that Rock said her life depended on it. *What did he mean? Would he kill her if she didn't get hired?* The pressure mounted, and her stomach felt like she was riding on a roller coaster. Maggie willed herself not to throw up.

"I'll pick ya up at the house at two o'clock this afternoon. Be ready. That means be standing on the sidewalk waitin' for me," he instructed. "Another thing…get your ass back to the house *now*."

Rock nodded toward the car door, silently telling Maggie to get out. She couldn't resist the urge to ask the question burning inside of her. "What did you mean when you said my life depends on it? What's gonna happen if this guy doesn't like me?"

"Let's just say I have an offer on the table. Someone who's lookin' to buy ya from me, and I'll leave it at that," he said, hoping his lie would pay off.

Maggie rushed out of the car and ran back to Juju's apartment. She threw open the door and burst into tears.

Alarmed and instantly frightened, Juju went to her. "What happened? What did he want?"

"He wants me to audition at a strip club. He said my life depends on getting hired. He found out I've been skimming money," she said, bawling.

Juju quickly reflected on all the warnings she'd given to Maggie. But she decided it wasn't the right time to preach. Instead, she wanted to be strong for Maggie.

"Yeah, well that motherfucker doesn't know who he's messin' with. You can dance like there's no tomorrow. You ain't got nothin' to be worried about," Juju said angrily.

Maggie took her hands away from her face. "Do you really think I'm good enough?"

"Do bears shit in the woods?" Juju asked.

Maggie smiled through her tears; she was half laughing and half crying. Then she was suddenly struck by the memory of Cali. She'd taught her how to dance well. Cali would want her to be strong. Slowly, she began to fill with confidence, and her tears subsided.

At two o'clock that afternoon, Maggie got into Rock's car. His tires screeched as he pulled away from the curb, and he drove to Double Visions.

Chapter Eighty-Eight

I t took a moment for Maggie's eyes to adjust from the sunlight to the darkness of the bar when they walked into Double Visions. She looked around the large room, her eyes pausing on the four men sitting at a bar that wrapped around a stage. Then she looked at the stripper dancing on the stage. She was wearing only a thong, and she appeared to be in a trance as she swung her hips slowly back and forth.

Rock moved up to the bar and stood.

"What can I get you?" the bartender asked, eyeing them.

"We have an appointment with Jay," Rock announced.

"What's your name?"

"Rock."

"Yeah, OK. I'll let him know."

As they waited, Maggie fidgeted, and Rock sat on a barstool watching the stripper. He'd called the day before and talked to Jay, the bar manager. Apparently, he was the guy who made all the decisions when it came to hiring dancers. Rock knew little about Jay, but he did find out from him that Double Visions let the girls keep their tips without paying the house a percentage. The thought of keeping all of Maggie's tips was appealing to Rock, and that had been the deciding factor on which strip club to choose.

Only a few minutes later, a tall man with salt-and-pepper hair and glasses came up the steps in one corner of the room. He strode over to Rock and Maggie, reeking with authority.

"Hey, Rock. Good to meet you," Jay said, extending his hand.

"Yeah, man. Same here. This is Maggie," Rock said, gesturing behind him.

As if Rock wasn't there with them, Jay walked over to Maggie and shook her hand. "Hey, Maggie. Good to meet you. Before we get started, I need to make sure you're eighteen," Jay stated.

Maggie nodded but remained silent.

"Great. Then you have ID I can see?" Jay asked.

Maggie reached into the pocket of the trench coat she was wearing and gave Jay the fake ID that Rock had given to her for the audition. It was a Pennsylvania driver's license that had been expertly converted with Maggie's picture and the name Maggie Brown. Jay looked it over, satisfied that it was a real license, and handed it back to her.

"All right. Let's go downstairs to my office," he told her.

Rock slid off the barstool to follow.

"Nah, man. You need to stay here. We don't allow boyfriends in there during the interview. In fact, no boyfriends are allowed in the bar during a dancer's shift. You gonna be OK with that?" Jay asked.

"Um, yeah, sure. I'll wait up here, then," he said. He gave Maggie a look of warning.

Maggie followed Jay downstairs. To the right was a large dressing room where two girls were sitting in front of mirrors applying makeup, lots and lots of makeup. They looked up and watched her in the mirror as she walked by. She followed Jay down a short hallway and into his office. Inside, a beautiful blond-haired woman sat in a chair next to Jay's desk. Jay sat behind the desk and said, "This is Shiver. That's the name we use for her here because the men say when she dances, it makes them shiver from head to toe. Shiver helps me with all of the dancers. Keeps things in order and prevents the girls from trying to make money on the side doing the kind of shit I don't allow in my bar."

Maggie gave her a broad smile, and Shiver was drawn to her. It wasn't just Maggie's youth and beauty, but a certain vibe the girl gave off that put Shiver at ease. She rose to her feet and gave Maggie an embrace.

"It's nice to meet you, Maggie. We want you to relax," Shiver said, sensing Maggie's tension.

While Shiver talked to Maggie, asking questions about her dancing experience, Jay watched her closely. Her face was beautiful, and her blue eyes were phenomenal, almost unreal. It made him wonder if she was wearing colored contacts. But her hair was in a sloppy bun on the top of her head, and the trench coat was baggy, making him doubt that she was the whole package. But that was exactly Rock's plan. He intentionally had her look the way she did, and Maggie had been told exactly what to do when the time came.

"Part of our interview is to get to know you, and the other part is to be sure you have the right look. Shiver and I will need to see you in a thong and bra. Are you wearing those?" Jay asked.

Maggie nodded, and then said, "Yes. I actually wore one of my favorite outfits."

"OK, great. Let's get to it then," Jay said nonchalantly.

Maggie unbuttoned her trench coat and let it fall to the floor at her feet. She was wearing a deep-purple, satin, push-up bra, her breasts forming perfectly round mounds above the cups, and a matching thong with rhinestones. On her legs, she wore sheer, white, thigh-high stockings with satin tops. The purple and white contrasted wonderfully against her skin tone, making her appear as if she radiated light. Jay and Shiver looked her over, and when their eyes rested upon her face, she removed the hair tie that held her messy bun in place. Her long, silky black hair fell below her waist. She was exquisite. Perfect. Too perfect to look natural. When neither of them said a word, Maggie reached behind her and unfastened her bra. As it fell away, her firm, round breasts remained in place, standing boldly at attention.

After several moments, Jay spoke. "OK, that's great Maggie. Can you turn around?"

As she turned, the muscles in her thighs rippled, and when he looked at her tight ass, without an ounce of fat, he instructed her to put her trench coat back on.

"So, I heard you telling Shiver you stripped before? I didn't catch what bar that was at," Jay probed.

"Oh, I was telling Shiver I used to strip at small private parties. I've never danced in an actual bar before," Maggie offered.

"Was there more involved than stripping?" Jay asked.

Maggie smiled. "Do you mean was I getting paid to have sex?"

Jay nodded.

"No," Maggie stated, feeling as though she was telling the truth, since she never got to keep any of the money the sex traffickers made from her.

"All right, good. I don't tolerate prostitution in my bar. If I decide to hire you, and you're caught having sex with our customers, and by sex I mean regular sex, hand jobs, blow jobs, all of it, you'll be fired. Do you have any questions?" Jay asked.

"Nope. I'm good," Maggie told him.

"OK. Let's go upstairs, and we'll have you dance, so we can see what you can do," Jay told her.

When they reached the bar, Jay went over to Rock. "Hey, Rock. I'm gonna need you to step outside. We want Maggie to dance for us. It'll just be one song, and then I'll send her out."

Rock stood slowly, put his hand over his money on the bar, and jerked his arm back. He shot an angry look in Maggie's direction and left the bar. He wasn't used to rules and people telling him what to do. Once Rock was gone, Jay gave the DJ a signal to begin a new song.

"You're up," Jay told Maggie.

Shiver squeezed Maggie's hand. "Just get lost in the music. You'll be great. Go get 'em."

Maggie started out slow and kept rhythm with the beat. When she shimmied up the pole, her strong calves made it look effortless. She swayed and flowed to the music. The few people who were watching her were mesmerized.

When the song was over, Maggie felt euphoric. Her movements had come so naturally. She barely realized that the men around the bar were staring at her. When she got off the stage and walked over to pick up her coat, Shiver pointed behind her. "They want to give you money," she said, feeling happy for Maggie. She'd seen enough to know that Maggie had the basic pole moves mastered, and with a little coaching, would be a superb dancer.

Maggie walked to the four men, one by one, who were holding out dollar bills for her. As she stopped in front of them and held out her hand, each of the men paused before placing the bill in her palm. Jay had to refrain from laughing. Then he made eye contact with Shiver and gave his nod of approval. When Maggie got back to Shiver, she was excited.

"OK, our first order of business is to teach you how to collect tips," Shiver teased.

"Why? What did I do?" Maggie asked, nervous she'd done something terribly wrong.

Shiver took Maggie's hand and pulled her along into the lap dance room. Inside the large room, there were double-wide seats separated by privacy panels. Shiver whipped off her tank top and let her bra drop. Her breasts, much larger than any Maggie had ever seen, popped out like two melons.

"OK, now I want you to be one of the guys sitting at the bar."

Maggie giggled. "All right."

"Well, hold out your dollar for me," Shiver said, egging her on.

Maggie put a dollar bill between her middle and index finger, just like the men had done with her minutes before. Then she was gripped, as Shiver made eye contact with her, making Maggie feel as though she were the only human being left on earth. Shiver pressed her boobs together with her hands, snatching the dollar bill between her breasts.

"See, the men want to put their dollar bill between your boobs."

"Oh! Wow, I feel like an idiot," Maggie admitted.

Shiver laughed and put her arm around Maggie's shoulder. "I think you're going to do just fine here. Welcome to Doubles."

Chapter Eighty-Nine

—————————◼—————————

Maggie rushed outside where Rock was waiting.

"They hired me," she gushed, feeling relieved.

Rock smiled. "Good. It's a good thing for you this worked out. I'm makin' some other changes too. You're moving in with Juju, for starters. The other thing is, instead of trolling the Avenue, I'm gonna set ya up with clients in the apartments we use for our hourly customers. I'll tell them you're a stripper, and that'll bring them in. This way I can keep track of your tricks so ya can't rip me off anymore."

Maggie thought about what Rock just said, and her excitement mounted at moving in with Juju and Seth. It didn't matter that they would be living on top of each other in the small, rundown, studio apartment. The only thing that really mattered was they would be together.

"Sure, Rock," she said casually, trying to hide her excitement. "I'll do whatever you want."

"Damn fuckin' straight you'll do whatever I want," Rock mumbled as he walked toward his car with Maggie following closely behind him.

During the drive back to Kensington, Rock explained that he would be "loaning" her money for new costumes, and she would have to pay it back.

"Armando will drop ya off and pick ya up for your shifts. Don't even think of pulling any funny shit 'cause I'll have people on the inside watching ya. No lying, no stealing, no bullshit, or you and your friends will pay the consequences. This is the last chance you're gonna get," he warned.

Maggie watched out the window of the car as the road raced by them. She remembered when she was a little girl, staring out the window, watching the scenery whiz by when her parents took Keith and her to New York for a day. Back then, the road was leading her on a magical journey to a big city filled with excitement. Now, as the trees became a green blur, her heart ached for the life she'd lost, and she wondered if she'd ever have that exhilarating feeling again.

When they got back to the house of whores, Maggie walked into the shared living area and began to gather her measly belongings, while Armando and Rock talked privately in the other room. Finally, the two men emerged. Armando told Maggie how everything was going to work.

"You're gonna work the latest shift ya can at Doubles and as many of them as ya can get. When ya ain't dancin', you'll be entertainin' some high-end clients," Armando said.

By high-end clients, Armando meant people who were willing to pay by the hour.

Maggie nodded. "Right. Can I go now?" She was chomping at the bit to get back to Juju's and tell them her news.

Rocked pulled out his handgun and placed it against Maggie's temple. "One more thing," he added. "If ya try to run or contact anyone, remember that I'll kill you, Seth, Juju, and your whole fuckin' family. There ain't nowhere ya can hide from me."

The seriousness with which Rock made his threat made Maggie's insides quiver. She knew Rock's long reach and was certain he'd kill all of them if she dared to try to escape his clutches.

"Be back here at seven o'clock tonight. I got your first client lined up," Armando chimed in.

Once outside, Maggie tore down the street toward Juju's. When she got to the apartment, she burst through the door, bending over to catch her breath. Juju and Seth sat on the mattress, the small television blaring cartoons into the tiny space.

"What happened, Aggie?" Seth squealed, running to her.

"I just got the best news ever," Maggie managed between breaths.

"What? What is it?" Seth asked, waiting in anticipation to hear the good news.

"We are all going to live together," she revealed, a single tear gliding down her cheek.

Seth threw his arms around Maggie's legs and hugged her tightly. Juju walked over, beaming, and put her arm over her friend's shoulder.

"How the hell did you pull that off?" Juju asked, hoping it was for real.

Maggie winked at Juju. "Oh, it just worked itself out. We can talk about all that later."

It only took a second for Juju to catch on that Maggie didn't want to discuss it in front of Seth. She hoped her friend hadn't made a bad deal or taken on more than she had bargained for. Later, when she learned the truth, she was surprised by Rock's actions—pleasantly surprised, of course—but she felt there must be more to it than he'd let on to Maggie.

Later that day, before Maggie was to return to the house of whores to meet Armando, the three took a bus into South Philly for an early dinner. Maggie had wanted to try a particular place she'd overheard some of the other hookers talking about.

Thirty minutes later, Maggie, Juju, and Seth were standing outside the Melrose Diner on Snyder Avenue. The building looked as if it were made of glass and aluminum foil. There was a clock shaped like a coffee mug set in the middle of the restaurant sign.

Inside, there were red vinyl benches, Formica tables, and lots of chrome. The floor was black-and-white checkerboard tile. This wasn't a restaurant made to recreate the past; it was a real part of old South Philly, and aside from a few upgrades, the place had remained the same for over fifty years.

The waitress, a woman clearly in her late sixties, moseyed over to the table and greeted them with a welcoming smile. "Well, now. Welcome to the Melrose Diner. Have you dined with us before?"

Maggie politely responded, "No ma'am. This is our first time. We heard wonderful things about this place."

The waitress nodded and gave them all a hearty smile. "You heard right. Everybody who knows goes to Melrose," she recited loyally. "That's our motto here. Take a look at the menu, and I'll be back to see how you're doing in a couple of minutes."

When she walked away, Seth leaned over to Maggie. "Can you read it to me, Aggie?"

"What do you mean? You can read it yourself," Maggie responded in a happy voice.

Seth opened the menu and began looking through it. When the waitress came back to take their orders, Seth was last. "What can I get cha, hon?" she asked Seth.

He opened the menu and pointed to a picture of a Belgian waffle with home fries and bacon.

"Can I have everything in this picture?" Seth asked.

"You sure can. Good choice, little man." She rushed off to put in their order.

Maggie and Juju exchanged concerned glances. Maggie leaned into Seth. "What's going on? How come you pointed to the picture?"

Seth's eyes instantly turned red as his tears began to spill over. "'Cause I can't read," he stated sadly and pressed his chin into his chest.

When Maggie put her arm around him and pulled him into her, Seth began to cry openly. "Thelma wouldn't let me do any homework. She wouldn't help me. Said I was a stupid idiot. I-I-I just don't know how to do it," he stuttered.

"Don't your teachers notice?" Juju asked.

"They don't care either. They say just as long as I'm being good and actin' like a human bein'," he said, repeating the words his teachers had impressed on him over the years, "then I can stay outta trouble."

Maggie gently lifted Seth's chin with her hand. "No one knows you like I do. You're a smart boy, and when you grow up, you can be anything you want to be. You don't have to be upset. I'm going to teach you how to read. Trust me."

Seth put his arms around Maggie's waist and held onto her while he sobbed, and his tension melted away. He hated being the stupid kid in class. He wanted to be like everyone else. He pulled away from Maggie and looked up at her. "When will you teach me?"

"We'll start today," Maggie promised.

Chapter Ninety

———————————————————————————

Maggie and Juju took Seth straight from the Melrose Diner to the library in Kensington. As they walked up the steps, Maggie heard children laughing and yelling. She peered in the direction of the high-pitched voices, and her eyes fell upon a small group of young boys. They were pointing and laughing. She heard one of the voices above the crowd. "Seth, what cha goin' in there for? You probably don't even know what a library is. You're too stupid to read."

The group of boys began chanting, "Seth, Seth, you have nasty breath; your mother was too stupid to put you to death. Seth, Seth, you have nasty breath; your mother was too stupid to put you to death."

Juju started to step toward the boys, but Maggie gripped her shoulder. "No, let me," she said.

Maggie bent down to whisper in Seth's ear. "Do those boys go to your school?"

Seth nodded, blood rushing to his face in blotchy circles as his embarrassment mounted. He looked as though he was going to cry again.

"Do they tease you like this all the time?" Maggie asked, feeling the enormity of the burden Seth had been carrying.

"Yeah. Sometimes it's worse. When we're at recess, they chase me around and throw the basketball at me. I told them it hurts when they hit me with the ball, but they won't stop," he confessed.

"I see. I want you to wait here with Juju," Maggie instructed.

"No, Aggie! Please don't say nothin'. They'll be meaner to me," he begged.

"It'll be OK. I just want to talk to them. I'll be right back," she responded.

Maggie walked over to the boys with her head held high and her back perfectly erect.

"Hi, guys. My name is Maggie. I'm Seth's sister. I heard you teasing him. Why are you doing that?" she asked sweetly.

"'Cause he's a stupid idiot. He can't even spell or read or nothin'," one of them reported.

"Yeah, and he always smells like poop, too!" a different boy chimed in, as they pushed each other and laughed. "We think he eats his own poop," the boy continued, impressing his friends with his remarks.

"Well, that's interesting. Let me ask you a question. How would you feel if everyone picked on you for no reason? I mean, Seth is quiet, but he isn't stupid, and he definitely doesn't smell or eat his *poop*. In fact, I think that anyone who does what you guys are doing to Seth is very mean. How about if you cut him a break?" she said.

The boys noticed the tension in her voice.

"Why don't you all run home to your mommies and tell them what you do to Seth? Hey. Maybe, I'll go tell your parents what you're doing. How about that? Now, I think that's a great idea," Maggie said, tapping her chin with her index finger.

The boys grew nervous. "Let's go, guys," one of the boys said. He started walking away from the library.

"Oh, boys? I know where all of you live. So unless you want me to go talk to your parents, you will *stop* picking on Seth. Understand?" Maggie asked. "Stop being so nasty!" she added in a powerful voice.

Maggie made all of them a little worried. None of them answered her. They walked away whispering to each other, and Maggie knew she had only gotten Seth a temporary reprieve from his tormentors.

"What did they say, Aggie?" Seth asked when she returned.

"Not much. But I'm hoping they'll leave you alone for a while," she said.

Seth ran his hand through his golden-blond hair, "Probably not. They like pickin' on me. When I grow up, I'm gonna be strong with big muscles and kick the shit out of all of them."

"Shit, huh? Where did you learn that?" Maggie asked with a smile.

"Juju."

Maggie turned to her friend. "Oh, great. So Juju is teaching you how to curse. Way to go, Juju!" she said, giggling.

Maggie turned back to Seth. "You know...when I was your age, the kids at school picked on me too," she confessed. "I was always left out of everything. On the day that John William took me, I had talked my mom into letting me go buy a slice of pizza on my own at the food court. I wanted to show the girls who left me out that I was independent. Trying to get even with them cost me my family," she finished sadly.

Seth's eyes bulged from their sockets. Maggie realized that she'd scared him without intending to.

"I have an idea. How about if Juju teaches you how to kickbox?" Maggie said with excitement.

Juju lit up. "Yeah, dude. I can teach you how to protect yourself from those little creeps."

"Really? I'm gonna learn to read and fight? Yay!" Seth announced, bouncing up and down. "I love you, Aggie."

"Really, dude? What about me? Where's my love?" Juju teased and started to tickle him.

Seth was giggling so hard that he was gasping for air when Juju finally stopped. Maggie watched them, her feelings of love running deeper for the two people whom she considered her only family. She extended her hand to Seth, he grabbed it, and she led him into the library.

Learning, she knew, was the only way to break the cycle. This was the one gift she could give to Seth that no one would ever be able to take away from him. She was reminded of her own parents and the gift of learning they'd given her.

For just a few minutes, she allowed herself to think about Lorraine and Rob Clarke. She wondered if they still missed her. So much time had passed that her memories of them had become foggy, almost surreal. She still missed her parents—their good natures and loving ways. Her life was so different now, and she was so far removed from the world she'd once known. Her dreams of being reunited with them, once so strong and vivid, had diminished. Now it seemed as though those dreams had belonged to another person.

Chapter Ninety-One

Maggie had two weeks before she began working at Double Visions. In the meantime, she spent her days and evenings meeting men at the "apartment." The hours between four and seven o'clock in the evening were quiet, and she spent much of that time with Seth at the library. Just as she thought, Seth was a smart boy who only needed someone to teach him. In a few short weeks, he'd already shown his capacity to learn new things.

"Aggie, do you remember what your mom and dad look like?" Seth asked her one day.

"Sort of. I mean, I do remember, but it was a long time ago. Why?" she asked.

"'Cause I can't remember my mom and dad at all. Do you think they loved me?" he asked.

"Are you kidding? Who wouldn't love *you?*" Maggie grew serious. "I'm certain they loved you, and they still love you."

"Then hows come they never look for me?" he wondered aloud.

"We don't know they haven't looked for you. In fact, I'm sure they did. But you were too little when John William stole you from them. You don't remember where you lived. A while ago, I looked to see if I could figure out where your parents live. But I couldn't find them anywhere around here," she told him.

"Maybe they moved," Seth offered.

"You might be right. But maybe you weren't born around here. We don't know what your last name is, and that makes it really hard to find them," Maggie said softly, pulling him closer to her.

"Do you think if we ever find them, they'll want me to go back and live with them?" he asked.

"Of course. You're their son," she stated, believing she was telling Seth what he wanted to hear.

"Well, I hope they never find me then. I don't want to leave you and Juju and go live with them. I don't even know them. You won't let them take me away, will you?" he begged.

"Seth. Even if your mom and dad were to find you, we'll always be family," she said, trying to reassure him.

"If your mom and dad find you, will you go live with them?" Seth asked.

"I haven't thought about them finding me in a long time, Seth. I mean, I don't know what I'd do. I'll be eighteen years old soon. I'm almost an adult." Maggie gave it serious thought for a moment. "You know what? Maybe I would go live with them if I knew Rock wouldn't do anything to hurt us," she said.

"What would happen to me, then?" he asked, fear creeping into his voice.

"You'd come with me, of course!" she said sincerely.

"But what about Juju? Would she come with us too?" he asked, wringing his fingers together and looking over at Juju to see if she was worried too.

"Sure. We'd all go together," Maggie pledged.

Maggie didn't want Seth to worry. The bullies at school were enough for him to handle.

"Hey, how are the kids at school treating you?" Maggie asked, realizing that he hadn't mentioned them lately.

"They haven't been bothering me as much since Joey punched one of them in the nose," Seth said, giggling.

Maggie laughed with him. Hearing how Joey had stuck up for Seth gave Maggie some comfort. At least he had one person on his side at school. Maggie worried about him all the time. She was intimately aware of the trauma Seth had lived through with John William and all the strange men. He'd been broken as a small child, before he had even developed a mind of his own.

"Good ol' Joey. She doesn't take crap from anyone," Juju piped up.

Seth, Maggie, and Juju met Joey every day before school started, just as Maggie had promised her. In the beginning, Joey had an easier time with Thelma then Seth ever had, but as time went on, Thelma became more abusive toward her. Joey simply dismissed the verbal assaults, but some mornings she had fresh bruises on her arms or face.

Once, when Joey had a black eye, Maggie pulled her aside.

"What happened? Did Thelma do this to you?" she asked.

"Yep. She's a crazy bitch," Joey announced casually.

"I'm sorry, Joey," Maggie had offered, feeling personally responsible for the child's living situation.

"It's OK. One of the girls that I used to live with, in the place where you got me from…she used to beat me up all the time. Then, one of the older girls taught me how to fight when everyone else was asleep. So the next time that girl hit me, I kicked the shit out of her. And, like I told ya before, it's better than those old men havin' sex with me. I'll take a couple of slaps and punches if it means I ain't doin' that no more," Joey had explained.

"Aggie?" Seth whispered softly, interrupting Maggie's thoughts.

"Yeah?"

"I think someday I'm gonna marry Joey," he said with a mischievous smile.

"Seriously, dude, this is the shit you think about?" Juju teased.

"What Juju means is that you're ten years old. We think you have plenty of time to figure that out," Maggie explained, shooting Juju a scolding look.

"OK," he giggled, "but I'm tellin' ya, someday she's gonna marry me."

Maggie hoped that one day they'd all be happy. Maybe they'd each get married and have children of their own in a place where drugs and sex didn't dominate. She had high hopes for all of them and believed the day would come when they could say good-bye to the mean streets of Kensington.

Chapter Ninety-Two

———————◼——————————

Maggie's first night at Double Visions was nerve-racking. She showed up for her shift an hour early, just as Shiver had instructed, so she could get ready and meet the other girls. When Maggie entered the dressing room, she winced, as scowling looks fell upon her. Most of them stopped what they were doing, sat perfectly still, and watched her, secretly wishing she wasn't the new girl and she would just go away.

"Girls, this is Maggie. She starts working here tonight," Shiver said, making eye contact with each of the eight strippers.

All of the girls except one glowered at Maggie. Annoyed by her beauty, even in worn-out street clothes, they all knew she'd be spectacular once she was in makeup and costume. The catty group turned without acknowledging her.

"Girls! Really? Are you fuckin' kidding me?" Shiver shrieked.

Shiver turned to Maggie. "They'll be fine. Just takes them a little time to warm up to newbies. Doesn't help them that you look the way you do, but it's sure going to help you, sugar," she said.

Maggie nodded, but inside, she was fuming. She couldn't care less what the bitches thought of her. She wanted to scream, "You all should be nervous because I'm here to make money, and we can do it together, or I'll do it on my own."

Shiver saw the fire in Maggie's eyes and knew immediately that she'd find her way among the girls, who could be more competitive than professional athletes. One of the girls finally walked over to Maggie and introduced herself.

"Hey, Maggie. I'm Chelsea," she said, extending her hand. "You can use the chair next to me. There are only nine of us working tonight, but on the weekends, there could be up to fifteen of us in here. So sometimes we have to use each other's spaces. You can keep your shit in one of the lockers over there," she told Maggie, pointing to a wall lined with lockers.

Shiver smiled to herself as the two young women starting chatting. Feeling as though Maggie could handle herself, she left her in the dressing room with Chelsea. Maggie purposely walked over to the open seat next to Chelsea as gracefully and sensually as she could. She didn't want enemies, but she wasn't about to take any crap from the other dancers.

Maggie sat down and watched the other girls in the mirror. Most of them were average looking, nothing overly exciting stood out about them. A couple of the girls were quite pretty, not as tall as Maggie was, but just as lean. Several of them had fake boobs that were so big they appeared unnatural. All of the other girls except for one had tattoos and body piercings. *Just your typical night at the neighborhood strip club*, Maggie thought, amusing herself.

Maggie noticed that one of the girls was wired and jittery. The girl had to be a meth head, she thought. She bounced around from girl to girl, giggling over nothing and lighting one cigarette after another. Her jaw was grinding from left to right, right to left and, every so often, she'd sniff the air while contorting her face like a shriveled prune. Maggie found her repulsive and kept telling herself, *don't make eye contact...don't make eye contact.*

Damn it! Maggie looked up at exactly the wrong moment and made eye contact with the meth head.

"Hey, man. My name's Crank. Man, you're fuckin' hot as shit! So, um, you wanna do a little toot before you go upstairs?" she offered.

Maggie thought how appropriate and inappropriate the girl was for taking that particular stage name. Maggie smiled like an innocent, precious young girl. "Oh no, thank you, Crank. I don't really care for it."

"Yeah, OK, that's cool. Hey listen, don't say nothin' to Jay or Shiver about me offering you dope. They'll kick my ass outta here if they catch me using in the club," Crank stated.

"Nope. Your secret's safe with me," Maggie told her, both amused at and astonished by Crank's odd behavior and movements.

"Cool. OK, well, I'll be watching you when you get upstairs. Everyone will be," Crank said, leaning into Maggie's personal space.

Maggie backed away in response. "These bitches are just pissed 'cause you're gonna be earning a lot of dough. If you can dance, then they're gonna shit sea horses," Crank whispered in a voice loud enough for Chelsea to hear too.

It wasn't long before Shiver came back into the room and stood next to Maggie.

"OK," Shiver said. "Let's go over makeup. Honestly, if I were you, I wouldn't overdo the makeup. You have natural beauty. I want to teach you a little bit about accentuating those gorgeous eyes and pulling those high cheekbones forward."

Maggie was amazed at how easily Shiver taught her how to apply makeup. Then she changed into one of the costumes she'd brought with her. Shiver and Chelsea looked her over.

"You look perfect!" Shiver exclaimed. "Now, we need a stage name for you. Is there a name you'd like to be called?"

Maggie hadn't thought about it before that moment. As different names ran through her mind, she settled on the thought of Cali, who had taken care of her and taught her how to pole dance. Then her memories of Max rose to the surface of her consciousness. She arranged and rearranged the letters of their names in her head.

"How about Climax?" Maggie asked, looking from Shiver to Chelsea for a reaction.

They nodded their heads.

"Well, it's different. I like it and Climax suites you well. The men will love it," Shiver said.

Chelsea nodded. "I like it, too."

Forty-five minutes later, one of the bar staff entered the dressing room and yelled, "Crank and Climax, head upstairs. Your set is coming up."

Upstairs in the bar, Shiver stood with Maggie while she waited for her cue to go onstage.

"OK. You're gonna be fine. Just relax," Shivered whispered, feeling Maggie's anxiety.

Then the DJ's voice came over the speakers. "We have a new dancer with us tonight. Double Visions would like to welcome Climax to our family," he said wholeheartedly, as if he knew Maggie.

As she walked to the center of the bar to take the stage, all of the bartenders turned and watched her. The customers perked up, as they always did, for a new girl. Maggie stepped up onto the stage and swallowed hard as she began to move to the song she had picked for her debut dance.

Maggie glided across the stage on her long legs. Then she stopped abruptly, grabbed the pole with both hands, and began to snap her hips from side to side. Her hands slowly slid down the pole until she was squatting, her knees spread wide. Then she arched her back and began to rise again slowly. Gripping the pole tighter, she hoisted herself up and began the slow, sleek climb to the top of the pole. She watched the men intently, making eye contact with as many of them as possible, while she reached behind her back and unsnapped her bra to reveal her breasts.

It was a sea of smiles around the bar as the men stared at Maggie in awe and fascination. Her movements were fluent as she worked the pole to the beat of the music. When the song finished, Maggie stepped off the stage gracefully and made her rounds at the bar. As she gathered her tips, she was overcome with excitement. She chatted easily with the customers, something she'd learned how to do well on the streets of Kensington. If you wanted to make money as a hooker, a lot of money, then being charming and knowing how to make men feel special was a sure way to keep a john.

Several of the other dancers had gathered around the bar to watch Maggie's debut performance. They'd all hoped she'd be a complete flop to offset her beauty. To their disappointment, Maggie was as fluent and graceful as many of the experienced dancers were.

When Maggie finished accepting her tips, she walked out from behind the bar. Immediately, a man approached her and asked for a lap dance.

"Of course I'll give you a lap dance. Just give me a minute to freshen up, OK?" Maggie stated smoothly.

"Sure, baby. I'll wait right over there," the man said, gesturing toward the entrance to the lap dance room.

Maggie rushed into the dressing room to find her only friend at Doubles.

"Shiver," Maggie whispered into her ear.

"Maggie, you did an awesome job. I told you they'd love you," Shiver complimented.

"Thanks. But I have a little problem. There's a guy upstairs waiting for a lap dance," she stated.

Shiver gently weaved her arm through Maggie's. "Let's go into Jay's office. I'll show you."

Maggie let out an audible sigh of relief, and Shiver giggled. "Relax, honey. It ain't nothing."

Shiver quickly showed Maggie how to perform a lap dance. "You can't touch him. You can hold onto his shoulders while you dance, but don't touch him anywhere below the shoulders. You're going to straddle him, and it'll be easier if you are on your knees. It's just a slow grind baby, back and forth, up and down, but don't actually grind on him...you sorta grind in midair. You also want to push your titties toward his face. At no time can he grope you. There's always one of the bouncers sitting just inside the room, so if you have any issues, you just get their attention and give them a nod. They'll know exactly what to do," she explained.

As Maggie climbed the stairs to go back into the bar, her heart was racing. There was so much to remember. It was much different than hooking, where anything goes. She strolled over to the man who was waiting for her. "OK, I'm all set now."

"Hell, as far as I'm concerned, you were set before you went to freshen up," he stated in a sleaze ball tone.

Maggie's nerves were getting to her, though. It wasn't the vulgar man who gave her the jitters; she was used to a lot worse from her johns. She was concerned about a few of the dancers who had been glaring at her as if they wanted to slit her throat.

Chapter Ninety-Three

Maggie wasn't imagining things. The other girls really wanted her to go far away and never come back to Doubles.

The man she led back to the lap dance room was a high-paying customer who always got his dances from Montana, the most experienced girl at Doubles. All of the other girls knew to stay away from Montana's regulars. She didn't hesitate to punch another girl in the face if she got pissed off at her. Most of the girls followed Montana's lead. If she hated a girl, then so did most of the dancers.

Montana watched Maggie closely, looking for her weakness, but there was nothing visible. Some of the girls would cover their mouths when they laughed to hide crooked teeth, or take painfully careful steps in their six-inch heels because they struggled for balance. Others put their skimpy dresses back on after they danced to hide a stomach that was poochy from giving birth or overindulging in fast food. But all Maggie showed was confidence, and she was clearly comfortable with every inch of herself. This just pissed Montana off even more. Her own areas of self-consciousness were the stretch marks on her breasts from her implants—she'd gone from an A cup to a D, and she didn't like how they jiggled when she walked. She also tormented herself about the pockmarks from teenage acne on her face. She had to fill the marks with makeup to make her skin appear flawless.

At the end of the evening, none of the girls acknowledged Maggie when she entered the dressing room. While the dancers chatted about their good and bad tippers of the night, Maggie minded her own business and changed back into her normal clothes. She didn't notice Montana's hateful stare. Grabbing her things, Maggie left the dressing room, headed upstairs, and out the backdoor where Armando was waiting for her in his car.

As she walked through the parking lot, she was slammed in the side of the face. Quickly regaining her balance, she found herself face-to-face with Montana. "Listen, you fuckin' bitch. You go near my regulars again, and I'll put a hurting on you that you'll never forget. You think you're hot shit, but you ain't nothin'. You better watch your back, girl," Montana threatened.

Maggie listened, but was still stunned from the unexpected blow to the head. She took a step toward Montana. "I don't know what you're talking about, and if you ever touch me again, you'll be sorry," she stated in a deadly serious voice.

Montana sneered at her and began to laugh. "You think you fuckin' scare me? Bitch, I will fuck you up so bad ain't no man gonna wanna look at you again," she stated evenly.

On the outside, Montana looked sure and poised, but on the inside, she was a bit intimidated that Maggie came back at her. None of the other girls had dared to stand up to her.

"Montana, I don't want any trouble from you or anyone. I'm here to dance, earn money, and leave. If your *regulars* want a lap dance from me, then I don't know what to tell you. Maybe you should use that *charm* of yours to keep them loyal. That is, if you have any charm. You're just a bully and..."

Maggie's words stuck in her throat when Armando approached the two girls. She'd forgotten he was waiting for her. He had seen her get slammed in the head. He would've jumped in to stop Montana if necessary; after all, Maggie wouldn't be any good to him with her face mangled. But he was pleasantly surprised to see Maggie stand up for herself.

"Maggie! Let's go. We need to roll out," Armando announced.

Both girls turned toward the domineering voice that sliced through the dark silence of the night. Montana turned and walked the other way, and Maggie walked over to the car.

"I see you got yourself an enemy already," Armando announced in an amused tone.

"Whatever. She was babbling about how I need to stay away from her regulars," Maggie started to explain.

"Bitch! I ain't your girlfriend, and I don't wanna hear about your fuckin' drama. All I know is, I don't give a fuck who wants to give you money. If I find out ya turn anyone down, you'll have more to worry about than that bony-ass bitch," he yelled as he turned the radio up to a deafening volume and drove them back to Kensington.

Back at the studio apartment, Maggie told Juju all about her first night at Doubles. "You know, it's crazy to think I'm excited about being a stripper. But compared to hooking, I feel like I'm getting a break. I know that sounds nuts. No one in their right mind would think that way; no one who was normal, anyway," Maggie confessed.

Juju laughed at her friend. "Tell me one fucking person who we know that's normal. I mean, I get what you're sayin' and all, but I guess normal just depends on what you're used to. Anyway, how were the other dancers?"

"Ugh! There's this nasty bitch, Montana, who sucker punched me in the parking lot on my way out to meet Armando. She was pissed 'cause one of her 'regulars' paid me for a lap dance. I probably gave ten lap dances tonight, so I have no idea which dude she's even talking about," Maggie explained.

"Did you fight back?" Juju asked with annoyance.

"Nah. I let it go, but I told her she better not ever touch me again," Maggie said proudly.

"You can't let any of those bitches get away with anything, Maggie. Once they know you won't fight back, they'll just keep riding ya. That's why I taught ya how to fight, remember?" Juju stated aggressively.

"Yes, Juju, yes, I remember. Trust me, if I need it, I'll use it. I'm just trying to fit in as much as I can. Besides, the last thing I need is to get fired from Doubles. I really believe Rock will kill me if I screw this up. I'll be careful, though. Stop worrying, *Mom*!" Maggie teased.

"Well, apparently someone has to be the adult around here. I mean, with you out all hours of the day and night. Who would've ever thought I'd be the responsible one?" Juju joked.

"Oh, isn't that a pile of crap. I'm the rational one in this house... well, apartment." She looked around her. "OK, shit hole," Maggie admitted.

"So, um, I have some news too," Juju told her, snuggling closer to Maggie on the floor where they sat.

"Oh, yeah? Did you win the lottery? Please tell me that you did."

"Not quite. But I met someone," Juju said, blushing.

"You mean like you met someone to date?" Maggie questioned.

"No, like I met someone to paint my toenails. Of course someone to date."

"Wow. That's cool. What's her name?" Maggie asked, trying to sound interested, but her stomach clamped down hard. She knew it was selfish, but she didn't want to lose Juju. Maggie started to squirm, and she couldn't make her eyes meet Juju's. She had decided that jealousy and fear were two emotions that didn't mix well.

"Her name is Rory. She's a couple of years older than me and so beautiful. I can't believe she's even attracted to me," Juju admitted.

"Seriously? Juju, you're hot. So did you go out on a date already?" Maggie asked cautiously.

"Not yet. We're planning on getting together late Tuesday night after I'm done selling," Juju said with excitement in her voice.

"Oh."

"Oh, what? Why aren't you excited?"

"I'm excited," Maggie explained. "It's just that I never really thought about one of us meeting someone else. It's just something I didn't expect."

Juju could sense that her news made Maggie nervous. Quickly realizing that Maggie might feel abandoned, she added, "It's only one date, Maggie. I'm not going anywhere. You know we'll always be family. You're like my sister, and Seth is like the little brother I never wanted," she declared, trying to lighten the mood.

The girls started to giggle. "I'm sorry, Juju. I'm being a jerk. It's just that this is the first time in a long time I had a family and somewhere to live of my own. I'm afraid of losing all of it," Maggie divulged.

Maggie and Seth were finally together in a place they called home. But things change, and life moves on…Maggie would soon find out that nothing ever stays the same.

Chapter Ninety-Four

On Maggie's fourth night at Doubles, she was relieved to see that Montana wasn't working. She had been avoiding her ever since the confrontation. She'd even asked Shiver to point out Montana's regulars so she could try to avoid them.

When Maggie sat down in the dressing room to put on makeup, she overheard the other dancers talking about a girl named Emma, who had danced at Doubles before and had just returned after a long absence. The dancers were clearly unhappy that Emma had come back. Maggie surmised by the way they talked that Emma was a club favorite, and the other dancers didn't like the competition.

Maggie had just finished pulling up her stockings and attaching them to the garter belt she was wearing when she looked into the mirror and saw the most beautiful woman she'd ever laid eyes on. She knew it had to be Emma. She was the same height as Maggie, but with long, satin, blond hair and piercing emerald-green eyes.

Emma strode through the room as if she owned the place. Maggie watched, fascinated by her beauty and self-assurance. Emma wore a steady grin as she flipped her long hair over her shoulder. She went to the chair next to Maggie and sat down.

Emma looked over at her. "I'm Emma. I haven't worked here in a while and don't remember you from when I was here before."

"I'm Maggie. This is only my fourth night," Maggie said in a lively voice.

"Let me guess. These bitches here hate you and treat you like shit. Right?" Emma asserted.

Maggie giggled. "Yeah, something like that."

"Well, that's because you're fuckin' gorgeous," Emma offered.

"Let me guess. They hate *you* because you're gorgeous?" Maggie countered.

"Yeah, something like that," Emma said, giggling.

Shiver walked into the dressing room and looked over at Emma and Maggie. She was pleased to see they were already talking to each other. The contrast between the two of them took her breath away, and she made a mental note to put the two girls onstage at the same time.

"Emma! How are you, sweetie?" Shiver sang.

Emma stood and embraced her. "You know, I've been doing OK."

"Well, Jay and I are thrilled to have you back. Our regulars have been buzzing about you since Jay put the word out that you were returning. I see you've met Maggie," Shiver said, giving Maggie's forearm a gentle squeeze.

"Yep, I sure did. And I see the girls are the same pack of jealous, cackling hens they've always been," Emma said, looking over Shiver's shoulder to make eye contact with some of them.

"Now, now, darlin', be sweet. You know it ain't easy keeping up your clientele. They all just wanna make money, just like you and me," Shiver said sweetly.

"Now, Shiver, you know I don't give a rat's ass about what any of the mean girls want," Emma reminded her. "So, when do I go on?"

"They'll be ready for you in about forty-five minutes. We're gonna send you out by yourself for the first song, then we'll send another girl in when the second song starts," Shiver explained.

Shiver turned to Maggie. "I'm sending you out with Emma tonight. I think the two of you will look magnificent together. Two opposite-looking beauties at one time. It's a good night for Doubles." She smiled.

As Shiver walked away, a thought popped into Maggie's head, and she turned to Emma without giving it any more consideration. "Hey, Emma, I was thinking we could team up and put on a show. You know, some kissing, undressing each other, that kind of stuff. I think we could make a lot of money."

Emma's flawless smile spread across her face. "Yeah, let's show these girls how it's done. You dance good?"

"I think I'm pretty good. The men like the way I dance," she said bashfully.

"Well, great! Let's rock this fuckin' place," Emma roared with enthusiasm.

Emma did her first return dance, solo. The men were in high spirits to see that she was back, and Maggie was happy for her new friend.

When the next song started to play, Maggie stepped up on stage and grabbed the second pole. After ten seconds, the two young women were entwined in a mass of silky hair, flesh, and muscle. It was the kind of show men fantasized about. With these two dazzling creatures touching each other, the clients went wild, and as a result, their tips were generous. After their first performance together that night, they spent some time at the bar having drinks and getting to know each other better.

"So how did you end up at Doubles?" Emma asked Maggie.

"Well, the money is really good, and my pimp thought this would be an easy way to supplement our income. I do some hooking on the side. Rock, that's my pimp, sets me up with guys, and I meet them at a couple of places Rock owns," Maggie explained, as if it were nothing.

"You're OK with hooking?" Emma asked.

"Let me tell you, it can be a hell of a lot worse. My family sort of lost me when I was a kid. I ended up living in pure hell. Lots of horny adults out there—if you know what I mean. So dancing here and turning some tricks during the week is a hell of a lot easier than walking the streets looking for customers or being held in captivity and sold to different men every night," Maggie confided with an odd sense of distance.

To hear Maggie talk as though she was giving the details of some other person's life made Emma more curious about her new friend. Emma recognized the pattern—Maggie's life was too painful to claim as her own, yet it was the painful memories that forced her to tell others about it. As a victim, Emma understood the connection and the distance with which Maggie described her life.

Emma really liked Maggie and decided to do everything in her power to keep her as a friend. It wasn't easy to find friends when she was trying so hard to remain unnoticed in society. Only in the darkness of the bar was there a chance to stumble upon someone who would actually care. The two girls didn't have much in common, their childhood stories veered in two different directions, equally heartbreaking. But they shared the same emptiness; the loneliness in the pits of their stomachs when they lay alone in bed at night, waiting to be rescued by sleep.

As time passed, Emma and Maggie began performing lap dances together for clients, earning a lot of money with each act. The two girls thrived on the sense of power their performances gave them, and they looked with satisfaction at the other dancers who had cast them aside.

Emma and Maggie became the show of all shows at Doubles. And, to make things even better, one night after dancing a few sets together, Emma introduced Maggie to Vincent and Tony, two men Emma knew and trusted—two very dangerous men whom Maggie would get to know much, much better.

Chapter Ninety-Five

———————■———————

Tony and Vincent were the Consiglieri, advisors to the Godfather of the Italian mafia in Philadelphia. They were childhood friends of Salvatore, the Underboss and son of the Godfather. When Maggie was introduced to the two men, she had no idea who they were and did not know their affiliation with the mafia. Because Emma had so much trust in them, it was natural for Maggie to like them and get to know them better when she was working at Doubles. Both of the men liked Maggie. She was innocent, yet she was bright, and the combination of those two traits intrigued them. Maggie unknowingly pulled at Tony's heart. She reminded Tony of his wife, Kay, who he loved with his entire being. The two women didn't look alike, but they shared the same mannerisms and way of talking.

When Emma was working, Tony and Vincent would hang around to talk with Maggie between her sets. They never asked her for a lap dance, and when she danced, they threw money onto the stage from their seats; they never stuck money between her breasts, as they did to the other girls.

Tony and Vincent knew Emma through Salvatore, and he had asked them to keep an eye on her. "Make sure she gets to her car safe and that no one gives her a hard time," Salvatore had instructed.

It was a Wednesday night at Doubles, and the bar was unusually slow. Emma and Maggie had just finished their set. Emma was giving a lap dance, while Maggie sat between Tony and Vincent at the bar.

Curious about her, Tony asked, "So Maggie, tell us somethin' 'bout cha. Like how ya became a dancer for 'xample. See, Vincent and me here, we don't understand why a smart girl like you is strippin'."

Maggie couldn't help but be amused by their South Philly accents, but she didn't want to be rude and openly laugh at them. "Well, I've been in the sex business for a long time. Since I was a young kid, actually, and, dancing here, I can earn good money, plus I don't even have to have sex with anyone," she explained.

Vincent made a facial gesture as if he'd just smelled a pile of steaming-hot shit. "What cha mean when ya was a young kid? You're still young. How fuckin' young could you've been?" he asked.

Maggie let out a long, gradual breath. "I was eleven. I was sort of 'taken' from my family. I haven't seen my mom and dad since that time. Now it's been too long, seven years. So much has changed; I wouldn't even know how to talk to them. Besides, I'm eighteen now. I'm an adult," she said, hoping they'd let the subject drop.

"What cha mean, ya was taken?" Tony pressed, wanting to know what happened.

"I was taken by a man named John William. Or at least that's what we called him. I was at the mall with my mom, and he took me," she said, exasperated.

Tony leaned in a little closer to Maggie. "So is what you're tellin' us is dat this asshole, John William, took ya and had sex wit' cha when ya were eleven years old?"

Maggie stared into the glass of soda on the bar in front of her. She considered how much was too much to tell them. But they had been so nice to her, and she'd spent a lot of time with them at the bar over the past months. Deciding that it would be fine, she took the plunge. "No, John William took me, and I was forced to have sex with a lot of different men…women, too. They would come and buy us. You know, there were a lot of kids there, and these freaks would come in and pay to have sex with us."

Tony replied without thinking, "You're fuckin' jokin', right, Maggie? 'Cause we ain't got no tolerance for grown people who wanna have sex wit' little kids…"

His voice trailed off as he noticed the horrified look on Maggie's face. She'd trusted them and told her secret.

"I'm sorry, Maggie. It's just dat it's unthinkable to know there are people out there doin' this stuff to kids," Tony explained.

"It's OK, you guys. Really," Maggie assured them. "It's a difficult thing to wrap your mind around. Sometimes, when I'm alone, I wonder how I even lived through all of it. If I let myself think about it too much, I feel so lost and alone. But you know, I have some good friends now—*like the two of you*—and I live with my friend, Juju, and my little man, Seth."

"Oh! We didn't realize ya had boyfriend. Does Seth treat ya good?" Vincent asked hopefully.

Maggie started to laugh. "No, Seth isn't my boyfriend. He's more like my little brother. He's eleven years old. He and I were both taken by John William on the same day. It's a pure miracle that we've been together this whole time. I guess we were just meant to be with each other. You guys would love Seth. He feisty and funny." Then her voice grew darker. "He's been through a lot too. I mean..." She hesitated for a moment. "He was only seven years old when they started to sell him. He's been through some pretty horrible things. You know?"

Maggie looked from Tony to Vincent, waiting for acknowledgment so she didn't have to explain.

"Yeah, we know what you're talkin' about. It just ain't right. So this John William guy...is he still alive?" Vince asked.

"I have no idea. I was sold to Rock four years ago. I haven't seen any of them since they took me from the house where they kept us," she admitted.

"Wait!" Tony yelped. "What do ya mean sold?"

"Oh, I feel like an idiot. I'm sorry. Just forget it," Maggie begged, realizing that opening her pie hole could get her into a whole bunch of trouble. She looked deeply into Tony's eyes. "Please, Tony. I've said way too much already. Please. Maybe someday, when my life is different, I'll tell you all the gory details. But until then, it's safer for me and the two of you if I keep certain things to myself."

Of course, Maggie had no idea that Tony and Vincent were at the top of the Philadelphia mob. She didn't know about the long-reaching arms they had in the corrupt world around her. She couldn't have known that Tony and Vincent were far more powerful and merciless than any of the people who had ruined her life.

Chapter Ninety-Six

When Maggie wasn't at the go-go club, she was either entertaining clients that Armando arranged for her, or spending time with Seth. Maggie didn't kid herself; she was still a hooker, even though the johns were provided for her. She was just not the kind who had to hustle men on the streets. There were two apartments where she worked most often, and both were in Kensington, not far from where she lived.

In many ways, when Maggie met johns in one of the apartments, she felt as though she was still a small child in the hands of John William. The men who were willing to pay by the hour tended to want more from her then the average guy on the street did. Many of them were kinkier and more perverse. Often they'd want to role-play with her. Maggie found herself pretending to be their mothers or sisters, innocent schoolgirls, nurses, disciplinarians, or victims. She did everything from tying them up and hitting them to being tied up and subjected to their every sexual fantasy. She truly hated that part of her life.

One rainy Tuesday afternoon, Maggie was scheduled to meet with a new john. She sat on the old sofa in the small living room of Rock's tattered apartment, waiting. Finally, she heard a soft rap on the door. Maggie hesitated for a moment and then opened the door.

"Hi, baby, I'm Maggie. You here for a date?" she asked, trying to hide her dread.

"I don't really think I'd call this a date. My name is Colby," he said, extending his hand. "I just moved into town. I don't really know anyone here in Kensington, and I've been kind of lonely. I'm just looking for someone to hang out with, and people around these parts aren't too friendly…or sober," he said, trying to make her laugh.

"Oh. Well come in and we can get started," Maggie said mechanically.

Colby walked over to the sofa and sat. Then he reached into the backpack he'd brought with him and pulled out a thermos of coffee and two paper cups. Maggie sat next to him and watched him intently. She was trying to figure out what kinky thing he was into. Did he want her to pretend to be a waitress? Maybe he wanted her to pretend she was working as a barista.

Colby looked over at Maggie. "Cream and sugar?"

"Yeah, that'd be great. Um, you do know if you drug me or anything, my pimp will find out. I have other johns coming in this afternoon. I mean, you do know I'm a sure thing. You don't have to drug me," Maggie offered, getting a little worried.

Colby laughed. "I'm not going to drug you. Watch."

Colby took a big gulp of coffee from each of the cups. Satisfied that the coffee was harmless, Maggie picked up one of the cups and sipped on it.

"So, what would you like me to do for you?" she asked.

"I want you to talk to me. That's all," he stated.

"OK," she said, drawing the word out. "Well, let's see. You know what I do for a living. So why don't you tell me what you do?" Maggie asked, searching for conversation.

"I work with kids," Colby said bluntly.

"What kind of work with kids?" Maggie asked. She had been with many men who supposedly "helped kids."

"Kids that end up on the streets. Doing things they don't want to do." He paused, letting his message sink in. Less than thirty seconds later, he saw that Maggie finally grasped what he was saying.

"Oh, you mean underage kids. Runaways?" she asked.

"Yeah, runaways. Kids like you. I want to help," Colby explained.

"Well, first, I'm not a kid. I'm eighteen years old. And second, there are certain people who will kill you if they find out you're trying to mess with their business," Maggie stated with as much confidence as possible.

"OK, well where I come from, we call those people maggots. The thing about maggots is that when you drench them with hot water and bleach, they die," he said with a smile.

Maggie looked him up and down. "This is a dangerous game you're playing. If my pimp found out that you're telling me these things, he would probably kill you himself. The people you're fighting aren't the type to let anyone take anything from them. I don't know who you are or where you came from, but my advice is to get the hell out of this place," Maggie warned.

"I'm not trying to get anyone hurt, I'm—" Colby started to explain.

Maggie didn't give him a chance to finish. "Like I said, you should just get out of here before it's too late. Otherwise, you're just going to hurt people," she barked.

Colby was shocked. He figured Maggie was in her late teens, and he was pleasantly surprised by her view of the world around her—and even more by her concern for his safety. He was a complete stranger to her. "You're right, Maggie. Thanks for the tip," he said with sincerity.

Maggie's nerves got the better of her, and Colby watched as she fumbled toward the door on her high heels. Colby stayed planted on the sofa. "I paid for an hour, and I'm not leaving until the hour is up," he told her.

"Fine. Then we can sit here and not talk to each other. If you want sex, just tell me what you're looking for. Otherwise, I got nothing more to say," Maggie insisted.

"I think you have a lot to say, Maggie. I've seen you going to the library, caring for that little boy, giving dollar bills to some of the homeless people when you think no one is watching. A person in your profession doesn't do that stuff if she chose this life. You didn't choose this life. Did you?" Colby persisted.

"What's your point?" Maggie asked, remembering the final warning Rock gave her.

"My point is that you and I could work together. Maybe we could help each other and at the same time get some of these young kids off the street," he pleaded.

"No. No way. There is nothing I have that you need," she said dismissively.

"I don't believe you. I think you have more to offer than you're willing to admit. Look, I've taken a big risk coming here and talking to you. I've watched you over the last six months to be certain you were the right person. You don't use drugs; you don't drink; I know you work at a go-go bar and entertain johns at this apartment and another apartment four blocks from here. You meet a little girl every day before she goes to school, and she clearly adores you, just like the young boy who lives with you. I can help," Colby said, trying to get through to her.

Maggie sat with her hands in her lap. She refused to speak. Forty minutes later, after sitting in silence, Colby grabbed his things and walked toward the door. "My hour is up. I hope you'll think about the things I've told you. I'll see you again," he said.

When Colby left and closed the door, Maggie remained on the sofa, her hands trembling in her lap. She was confused by all of the things Colby had told her. What if he was working for Rock? Was she being tested?

There was no doubt she wanted to help other kids. She'd wished a million times over that she could rescue all of them from the life they'd been given. Then she thought, *there is no way I can take a chance and betray Rock. He'd kill me and everyone I know, for sure.* But Maggie couldn't help but fantasize about helping some of the younger kids on the street. She thought about the twelve- and thirteen-year-old girls who were hooking because they had no other way to live or they'd been taken from their families, just as she had been.

Her mind whirled. *There is no way I can take a chance and betray Rock again. Is there?*

Chapter Ninety-Seven

———————◼———————

Before Armando picked Maggie up to take her to Doubles, she rushed back home to tell Juju and Seth all about Colby. She repeated everything he'd said to her.

"So, what do you think?" Maggie asked them.

"What if he works for Rock?" Seth asked first.

"Yeah, Seth's right. He could be setting you up. You know he'll fuckin' kill you if he finds out that you're giving out any information about him," Juju confirmed.

"I know. I thought of that, too. There's just something about this guy that seems legit, though. If he is for real, we might be able to help a lot of kids—our friends on the streets," Maggie said.

"Aggie, I think we gotta know more about this guy. What's his name again?" Seth asked.

"Colby," Maggie reiterated.

"Yeah, we gotta find out more about this Colby guy," Seth repeated and turned to Juju to back him up.

Juju rubbed her temple. "Well, I think we should see if he comes back to meet you again. If he's for real, then the next time you see him, we'll have questions for him. Oh, I know! Tell him you wanna see his ID. Ask him who he's ever helped. Tell him you wanna look shit up in the newspaper, and he's gotta tell you on the spot. He can't come back a week later, after he had time to research stuff."

"That's a good idea, Juju. If he really does help kids, he should be able to name at least one that he saved," Maggie said thoughtfully. "You're a lot smarter than you look," she teased her friend.

"Yeah, well, you smell a lot worse than I thought you would," Juju poked back.

Seth stood by and laughed at both of them.

"I don't know what you're laughing about, Seth. Your breath smells like shit," Juju added.

Seth had thrived after moving away from Thelma and into the loving care of the two teen girls. He had turned eleven and entered the fifth grade. Seth had become an avid reader, and as a result, he had accelerated in his schoolwork. He was five feet tall, about seven inches taller than most of the boys in his class. Shedding his tiny stature had helped him to claim a place among his peers. He was a very good-looking kid. Many of the girls his age had secret crushes on him, but he was devoted to Joey; the two were inseparable. Joey's light-green eyes shimmered with adoration for her "boyfriend," Seth; and he'd sworn his loyalty to her. When Joey showed up at school with a swollen and blackened eye after Christmas break, Seth rushed to her side.

"What happened to you?" Seth asked with despair in his voice.

"That bitch, Thelma, walloped me 'cause I complained that I didn't get any Christmas presents. Doesn't matter, though, 'cause I slipped some extra cocaine into her beer, and she dropped off to sleep like a load of shit. Then I raided the refrigerator and watched Christmas movies all day," Joey explained.

"We need to get ya outta there, Joey. Aggie got me away from her and Rock," he said with determination.

"How come you call her Aggie and not Maggie?" Joey wondered aloud.

"Don't know. I guess it's just what I always called her. She's my Aggie. 'Cause when I was little I couldn't say Maggie, and then I just never stopped calling her that. Anyways, I think we should talk to Aggie and see if she can help you too. You know, just like she helped me," Seth offered.

"I don't know, Seth. You know what an asshole Rock can be. It ain't like he's gonna like me leavin'. I keep Thelma busy so she stays outta his hair. That's what I heard him tell one of the jerk-offs that works for him," Joey explained.

It didn't matter what Joey said. Seth decided that when he got home that afternoon, he was going to talk to Maggie and Juju.

"But Aggie," Seth shot back after explaining he wanted Joey to live with them. "How can you say no? Maybe if you ask Rock, he would let her," he whined.

"It's not that easy, Seth. Rock doesn't do things just to be nice. I'd need something to bargain with, and right now I don't have anything he needs."

Maggie peered at Juju, who was listening intently. "Juju knows how Rock is. Tell him."

"Maggie's right, Seth. Rock doesn't do anything that isn't good for him. When it comes to Thelma, he won't do a thing that would piss her off. In a couple more years, when Joey is a little older, Thelma will want a younger kid anyway," Juju stated with certainty.

"Well, I think you're both being jerks. We have to do *something* to help Joey. Remember how mean Thelma was to me? Remember all the bad things she did to me?" Seth pleaded.

"Yeah, we remember. But Thelma did things that were way worse to you—" Maggie began to explain.

"Well, if you won't ask Rock to let her live with us, then I'll ask him myself," Seth said, pouting.

"No. You won't ask Rock anything. Do you hear me?" Maggie yelled.

It was the first time Maggie had ever raised her voice at Seth. Her instincts to protect him went into overdrive. She was pacing the studio apartment, her fingers roughly combing her hair back. Maggie's reaction made Seth nervous, and he went to her.

"OK, I won't talk to Rock. But you have to promise we'll try to do something to help Joey," Seth said in a small voice.

Maggie took Seth into her arms. "I promise that if there is a way to help her, we will."

This made Maggie think about Colby's offer. It was time to find out who Colby was and what motivated him. Aside from potentially being one of Rock's employees, he could be some kind of pedophile. If he checked out, though, they all might have the opportunity for a better life. Maggie picked up her coat and walked to the door.

Chapter Ninety-Eight

When Lorraine and Rob Clarke weren't working, they dedicated their time to helping missing children and their families. They had teamed up with Crista, who was a source of hope for them, and had set out to help others. The Clarkes and Crista met with children who had been found or returned to their parents. Not all of them had horror stories. Some had been taken by a parent during a custody battle. Others had been stolen and kept in captivity but had not experienced unwanted sex or violence. The children who had been abused were the hardest to help. They were also the children who needed the most help.

One morning at two o'clock, the phone rang.

"Hello?" Rob rasped.

"Rob. It's Rae Harker. The Whitpain police just found a missing girl. They haven't verified her identity yet, but she told them that she was taken five years ago," the detective said. "We need your help. They want you to go in and see what she'll tell you. They found her in the basement of an abandoned house in Norristown. No one else was there at the time, so they don't have any suspects. We need to find out what she knows. There could be others," he said.

"Holy shit!" Rob blurted. "OK, we'll get dressed and head over to see her."

Lorraine was already pulling on her jeans.

"I'll call Julie to come over and stay with Keith," Lorraine said.

When the Clarkes arrived at the hospital, Detective Harker was standing outside the girl's room with a uniformed police officer.

"Thanks for coming. I know this is outside of our normal procedure, but I wanted the two of you to talk with her as soon as possible," Harker explained.

Inside the room, every light had been turned on, even the bathroom light. Rob cast a glance at Rae Harker, who whispered, "She feels better with the lights on. I'm assuming, since they found her in a dark basement, that she's afraid of the dark."

Lorraine rushed over to the girl's bedside. "Hi, sweetheart. My name is Lorraine, and this is my husband, Rob. I don't want you to be scared or worried. We're just here to help you," she said in a calm voice that did not betray the panic coursing through her body.

The girl was scared out of her mind. Her eyes kept darting from Lorraine to Rob to Detective Harker.

Without taking her eyes off the young teen, Lorraine said, "Men, we're going to need you to step outside. OK?"

Rob and Rae exchanged a knowing look and left the room.

"OK. Now it's just us two girls here," Lorraine announced.

The young teen immediately began to loosen her grip on the blanket.

"Can you tell me your name?" Lorraine coaxed, placing her hand on the girl's shoulder.

"Kelly," the girl answered in a small voice.

"Kelly, it's nice to meet you. I want you to understand that you are safe here," Lorraine assured her.

Kelly looked around the room and then she met Lorraine's eyes. "What do you want from me?" Kelly asked.

"I don't want anything, honey. I'm here to help you. Do you remember being down in a basement?" Lorraine asked.

"Yeah, I've been down there since they took me," Kelly said.

"Do you remember where you were when you were taken?"

"Yeah, I was playing dodge ball. I was playing with my friends. After it was over, I was walking home because it was time for dinner," she said.

"Do you know who your parents are?"

"Yeah. I know who they are. Will you get them?" the frightened teen asked.

"Sure, but you'll have to give me some information to help the police find them. Do you think you can tell me what happened to you?" Lorraine asked gently.

Kelly nodded.

"Before you start, I need to have one of the female officers come into the room so she can write things down that will help the police find your mom and dad. Is that OK?"

Kelly nodded again.

The policewoman sat in the corner of the room, trying to go unnoticed while Kelly told Lorraine her story.

"I was walking back to my house and took a shortcut through the woods. I took the shortcut every day; all the kids did. Outta nowhere, this big guy was standing in front of me. He had a rag tied around his face, and all I could see were his eyes. He grabbed me, and I saw him raise his arm. There was a needle in his hand, and then I was in the basement on a mattress. My hands and feet were tied up so that I couldn't run," Kelly stopped and watched Lorraine. Kelly was certain she'd heard her gasp.

"When I woke up, I was only wearing my underwear, and I started crying, and some guy came down the stairs and got really pissed. He was yelling at me to shut up," Kelly explained with distance in her voice.

"Then he took off my underwear, and I was crying harder, but he just laughed at me. He said the more I cried, the harder he got. It didn't take me too long to figure out what he meant by that. So he had sex with me and then kept coming back to do it again. After a while, other men had sex with me too. Lots of men..." Her voice trailed off as she fixed her gaze on a spot on the wall across from her bed.

"If this is too much for you, Kelly, we can take a break. It's OK. Do you want to take a break?" Lorraine asked, feeling like she was suffocating in the details Kelly had shared with her. Lorraine imagined that Maggie had suffered the same fate. It was unbearable to think about Kelly in this situation, but to think about Maggie in this way was torture.

Kelly shook her head. "I wanna tell you 'cause I wanna see my mom and dad."

Lorraine nodded.

"They kept me there for a long time. I remember I was eleven when they took me. I was in fifth grade. I think I've been gone for five years 'cause I counted five times that I heard Christmas music on the radio they played upstairs. So I think it was five years," Kelly explained.

"OK, is there anything else? Do you know any of their names?" Lorraine pressed.

"I know the guy who fed me was called Slim. There was a guy named Animal, who was really mean to me all the time. The guy who liked to hit me when he had sex with me was called Axe. That's all I know. There were a lot of other guys, but I never knew their names. I wasn't allowed to talk to anyone except for Slim. I think he was the boss of them. There's one other thing." Kelly hung her head, her chin touching her chest. "I had a baby there," Kelly whispered, avoiding Lorraine's eyes.

"What happened to your baby?" Lorraine asked, horrified.

"They took it from me as soon as it was born," Kelly said, crying. "I never even got to see it."

"I'm so sorry, sweetheart. We're going to do everything we can to help you. I want you to know that you're not alone anymore," Lorraine said in a soothing voice.

"Can I see my mom and dad now?"

Lorraine looked over at the policewoman and gave her a small nod. Then she leaned over and gave Kelly a long embrace. Right before Lorraine left the room, she turned back. "Kelly? Did you ever meet a girl named Maggie? She's my daughter."

"No, I've been alone since I was taken. Did someone steal her, too?" Kelly asked grimly.

"Yes, someone took her, but I know that one day we're going to find her. You take care of yourself, and I'll be back to see you soon," Lorraine said in a cheerful voice, not wanting to upset the girl.

As Lorraine left the room, the policewoman stood and walked over to the bed. "Kelly? Can you tell us your last name and your parents' names?"

While Kelly gave the policewoman that information, Lorraine stepped into the hallway. She collapsed against Rob and sobbed. She cried for Kelly's lost youth and the baby that had been taken from her. Then she cried for Maggie, the child she'd lost and had yet to find. The regret in her heart was a constant pain, reminding her of how she'd failed to protect her daughter.

Chapter Ninety-Nine

When Maggie arrived at the apartment, Colby was waiting for her. He gave her a warm smile as she approached. "Hello, Maggie."

"Hi," Maggie responded dryly.

Maggie led him into the apartment and over to the sofa. She watched Colby carefully. He took off his jacket and gingerly laid it over one of the chairs in the small living room.

"Have you thought about what I told you last time?" Colby asked.

Maggie nodded. "How am I supposed to trust you? How do I know you aren't a friend of Rock's?"

Colby considered her question. "You're right. You know nothing about me."

"Exactly! So how about if you tell me about someone who you helped, and I'll see if your story checks out," Maggie offered.

"Well, I'll tell you what you need to know, but you have to remember that I work undercover. If you blow my cover, there'll be really bad consequences for me and the others who are working to help kids like you," Colby confided.

"So how will I know for sure who you really are?" Maggie asked.

Colby began to talk about some of the kids he'd helped over the past year. As he spoke, Maggie wrote down the names and places. He talked for thirty minutes, and then he stopped and waited.

"How old are you?" Maggie wondered aloud.

"I'm twenty-five. Why?"

"I was just curious," Maggie said.

"How old are you?" Colby inquired, wanting as much information about her as possible.

"I told you the last time you were here that I'm eighteen. I just turned eighteen in September. I'm an adult," Maggie informed him, as if he wouldn't figure that out for himself.

"So how did you get here?"

"I walked," Maggie joked sarcastically.

"That's not what I meant. How did you end up in Kensington working for Rock?"

"Who said I work for Rock?" Maggie asked.

"Well, you asked me how you could be sure I wasn't working for Rock, so I figured that's who your..." Colby's voice trailed off. He did not want to offend her.

"That's who my pimp is? You can say it. I mean, we both know why we're here in this apartment," Maggie said.

"OK, sure. Your pimp," he said.

Maggie hesitated. She thought carefully. She liked Colby. He was kind and soft-spoken. He had a reassuring quality that made her want to trust him. She wanted him to be the real deal in the worst way. He was confident and carried himself differently than the other men did. Simply put, Maggie couldn't find anything sleazy about him. In the end, though, she had to protect herself and Seth. She couldn't take any chances until she knew for sure that Colby was who he said he was.

"Oh, look at the time," Maggie said and stood.

"Yeah, my time is up. So, I'll come back and see you in a couple of days?" Colby asked hopefully.

"Yeah, sure. It'll give me some time to look into things and ask some people about you," Maggie told him.

"Asking questions about me isn't a good idea," Colby stated, alarmed. "If it gets around what I'm trying to do here, I would be in danger. You know better than I do what these scumbags are capable of."

Maggie remained silent as she opened the door. Before leaving, Colby turned to her. "I can help you. I promise I'm not screwing with you. I really do want to help you find a way out of this crap. Just think how much we could help others if we teamed up. We can beat these bastards. We can bring kids back to their families," he pleaded.

Maggie made no commitments. Colby reached out to touch her hand, but Maggie immediately withdrew from his touch. Her reaction was a sure sign to Colby that he hadn't gained her trust yet. But he intended to try to make her believe in him.

When Maggie was done meeting with her clients, she hurried over to the library to research some of the stories Colby had shared with her. She found some of the articles in old newspapers. Some of them referred to children who had been found and returned to their parents, but as Colby had told her, the people who had helped find them were not named. The articles all referred to undercover agents—all except for the very last story.

Maggie found a quote from a Detective Rae Harker, the same detective she'd read was involved in her own disappearance. She wrote a few notes about him. Then she starting reading everything she could get her hands on about Detective Harker.

Chapter One Hundred

At Doubles that night, Maggie sat with Emma in the dressing room. Emma had been through a lot of bad things in her life, and as Maggie told her about Colby, she listened intently. Later, in the bar, unbeknownst to Maggie, Emma explained the "Colby situation" to Vincent and Tony.

"Yeah, Rae Harker. We know 'bout him. Never met him, though. We got some cops we know. We'll ask around about him," Tony offered.

"Good. Thanks," Emma said. "But remember, she's vulnerable—she's a sitting duck—so don't let on why you're asking. I don't want that asshole Rock to find out."

A few nights later, Tony confirmed that Rae Harker had checked out with their source inside the police department.

"The guy works wit' some other people who work on the streets. Our source said this Harker guy is one of the good ones. Devoted his life to helpin' kids after his own daughter was taken and killed, a real fuckin' shame. They didn't know no guy named Colby, but I'd tell Maggie to find a way to get him to admit that he works with Harker. Otherwise, there ain't no way of knowin' if the guy is for real," Tony explained.

Vincent added, "If there's anything we can do to help, ya need to let us know, Emma. Maybe we could get her away from that Rock-head fella. You know, we can be pretty influential when we wanna be," he joked.

"Yeah, I know you two could make a mother turn on her own children," she retorted.

"Now, I wouldn't go that far. Tony and me here are just two nice guys that take care of what needs to be taken care of," Vincent bantered.

"Uh-huh," Emma retorted, eyeing them as if she were a mother hen. "Well, this needs to be Maggie's call. She's got a young boy she takes care of, so you have to be careful."

An hour later, Emma pulled Maggie aside as she was leaving the lap dance room.

"Hey, girl," Emma sang. "I did some investigating about that Colby guy."

Maggie's eyes widened.

"Relax," Emma cooed. "It's all good. It was very discreet. Anyway, I found out that Rae Harker guy is for real. He's been helping kids ever since his own daughter was taken. They found her dead, and he's been an advocate for missing kids ever since. Anyway, he works with undercover people on the streets. So, if you can get Colby to talk about Harker, I think you can feel safe that he's for real."

"Where did you get all this information?" Maggie asked, still skeptical.

"That doesn't matter, Mags. All that matters is you got something to go on now," Emma told her sternly.

"Wait! Did you just call me Mags?"

"Yeah. Why? You don't like it? I won't call you that if you hate it," Emma said.

"No, I love it, actually. My friend, Cali, who I told you about, she used to call me Mags. It feels like a hundred years since I've been called that," Maggie said, feeling the pain of losing Cali all over again.

"Oh, OK. Well that's what I'll call ya, then," Emma responded, feeling awkward that she'd brought up memories of Maggie's past. "You sure it ain't gonna make you sad?"

"Yeah, I'm sure. Thanks for checking things out for me. No one knows I was asking, right? Rock will kill me if he ever found out what I was doing," Maggie said with desperation in her voice.

"No one knows shit, Mags. Just do what you gotta do. It's all good," Emma reassured her. "I got your back."

Maggie didn't know what "I got your back" really meant coming from Emma, but a sense of security washed over her. She knew that Emma hadn't shared everything about her own life. Maggie was certain there were details that Emma kept to herself, secrets that she'd never want anyone to know. Maggie was right.

As Maggie left Double Visions that night, Tony and Vincent trailed behind her. Armando peered through the open window of his car at the two men who were walking behind Maggie as she approached the car. As the two mafia men passed Armando, they glared at him with contempt. Tony couldn't help but make a comment just loud enough for Armando to hear.

"Hey, Maggie, if ya ever need help, ya know we'll be there for ya!"

"Um, thanks, Tony. Have a good night," Maggie responded, feeling Armando's anger rise as she stepped into the car.

Armando looked over at her. "What the fuck did those two Guido's mean by that? What kind of help are you tellin' them you need?" he asked, leaning in closer to her.

"Nothing, Armando. They didn't mean anything by it. They're probably drunk," she rambled.

But Maggie had never seen Tony or Vincent get drunk in the bar. Sure, they had a few beers, but they were always in control of what was going on around them. Maggie respected them for that, not realizing that in their line of business, the only time they'd dare to catch a buzz would be in the company of other mobsters. In public, they remained in control at all times. "Yeah, well, ya better keep your shit together, bitch, and that means keeping your fuckin' mouth shut. Rock will cut those two pricks down in an instant. Then their deaths will be on your filthy hands," Armando threatened.

As Armando put the car in drive and left the parking lot, Tony and Vincent watched his taillights disappear. Through the open car window, they'd both heard the conversation between Maggie and Armando.

Finally, Vincent turned to Tony. "Hey, Tone, ya think that was a threat? That lousy, low-life, rotten spick bastard doesn't know who he's fuckin' wit'."

"Yeah, I know, Vin. But remember, the family comes first. We can't go startin' shit wit' out talkin' to Salvatore first. I don't see him bein' too agreeable 'bout us takin' up arms over one of the girls that works here. Ya see what I'm sayin'?"

Vincent let out a long sigh. "Yeah, but don't forget, Salvatore met Emma here. He might be more understandin' than you think."

"Yeah, maybe. Let's just keep dis to ourselves for now. OK, Vin?"

"Sure, Tony. But I don't like that asshole."

"I don't like him much either, but like I said—"

"I know, I know," Vincent interrupted. "The family comes first. Always has and always will. That's what we're all about."

"Right, Vincent. That's exactly right," Tony confirmed. But it didn't stop him from worrying about Maggie's fate at the hands of the prick that had just driven off with her.

Chapter One Hundred One

———————————◼———————————

When Seth woke Maggie up the next morning, her head was throbbing. During the entire ride back to Kensington, Armando had berated her. He'd promised to hurt Seth if she dared to do anything other than what she was told to do. She'd stayed up for hours imagining the horrible things he'd told her would be done to Seth.

"Come on, Aggie. I have to get to school. I'm gonna be late," Seth ragged at her.

"All right, all right. You're such a little nag," she said dramatically.

Juju sat on the edge of the mattress and handed Maggie a cup of instant coffee. "Rough night?"

"Yeah. Armando lost his shit on me. He can be such a jerk," Maggie reported.

"Oh yeah? What'd he freak out about?" Juju asked.

"Oh, these two guys at Doubles said if I ever needed anything, they'd help me. He overheard them in the parking lot." Maggie lowered her voice to a whisper. "Armando threatened to hurt Seth if I didn't do exactly as I was told. I stayed up practically all night worrying about it. I wonder if my life will ever be my own. I mean, sometimes it feels like this will never end. I can't see any way out of it. I'm eighteen. I have a lot of years left in me before I'm not useful to them in this business. By that time, I'll be a dried-up old hag."

Just then, Seth raced out of the bathroom. "Come on, you guys! We need to leave," he demanded.

The two girls quickly pulled on warm clothes and left the apartment. Seth was in a particularly talkative mood that morning.

"Aggie, it's going to be Christmas soon, and I wanna buy Joey a present. I was thinking I could buy her something to keep her hands

403

warm. She always shoves them in her pockets and says they're freezing," Seth explained.

"I think we can manage to buy her a pair of gloves. We can probably get her a scarf and hat to match. How's that sound?" Maggie offered.

"Oh, man, really? That would be great. 'Cause you know she's my girlfriend, and I need to take care of her. Mr. Jenson, my gym teacher, says good men treat women nice. Anyways, Mr. Jenson says if we work really hard, we can do whatever we wanna do," Seth said.

"Well, Mr. Jenson is a very smart man. But I think when he says good men treat women nice, he means that you need to show them respect. It's not really about buying presents for girls," Maggie explained.

"I know that, Aggie! I'm not stupid, you know. I just wanna buy her a present so she knows that I love her," Seth stated in a serious voice.

"Well, listen, little man," Juju butted in, "I don't care what Maggie says. I want people to buy me presents. I want everyone to buy me presents," Juju yelled, opening her arms to encompass the entire world.

"I don't know if we'll have enough money to buy you anything for Christmas, Juju. After we buy Joey a present and me a present and Aggie a present, there probably won't be any money left to buy you anything. Right, Aggie?" Seth teased.

Maggie joined in on the fun. "You know, you're right, Seth. After you buy me that diamond necklace that I've been eyeing at the jewelry store down the block, there won't be any money left to spend on Juju. I know! We'll have no choice but to put coal in her stocking."

"Oh, really? That's the thanks I get for helping you two geeks?" Juju squealed as she ran after Seth and began to tickle him.

Seth was rolling on the ground, trying to get away from Juju. He suddenly broke into a coughing fit, and Juju backed off and helped him to his feet. His face was drained of color.

"Seth? Do you feel OK?" Maggie asked.

"Yeah, I just feel like my brain is spinning."

"Come over here and sit down," Maggie instructed, leading him to a bench. "Drink some juice." She handed a small bottle to him.

"I hate orange juice, Aggie. I don't know why you make me drink it," Seth complained.

"Because it's good for you, that's why. Now drink," Maggie commanded.

Juju was completely unconcerned. She always rode Maggie about mothering Seth too much. "You know, he's gonna grow up to be a pussy if you keep hovering over him all the time. He's a tough kid until you come around, then he turns into some needy little weasel," she'd lecture.

"Um, Seth, if you're done faking, can we get going?" Juju said, mocking him.

Seth turned and gave her a big smile. "I wasn't faking, Juju. That was for real."

"Yeah, sure. And I have a million dollars. That's for real, too. Come on before Maggie licks her finger and combs down your hair. You're smothering him again, Magster!" Juju teased.

"Ha! Very funny. I'm not smothering Seth. I'm simply concerned about his well-being. One of us needs to be mature here, and it certainly isn't going to be you," Maggie shot back. Then she poked Juju in the ribs. "And don't call me Magster again. It's an ugly name."

Maggie knew that was the wrong thing to tell Juju, who skipped ahead, chanting, "Magster, Magster, Maggie is the Magster!"

Juju stopped and turned to Seth. "What's up with the coughing? You've been having coughing sprees since I met ya. You're a little hacker, is what you are...keep you're damn germs to yourself," she teased

Seth giggled. He liked Juju's sense of humor, and he liked that she wasn't too serious about everything. Sometimes, though, when they needed to pay the rent and didn't have enough money, Seth thought Juju should be more serious. But even then, she would play it off and tell both of them to stop getting their panties in a wad.

"Who the hell else is going to rent this lousy rat nest? They'll get their money as soon as we can get it together," she'd told Seth and Maggie several times.

Finally, they spotted Joey walking toward them. As they got closer, they all noticed that she was limping. Seth sprinted over to her and gently seated her on the curb.

"What happened, Joey?" Maggie asked with alarm.

"Thelma happened. What else?" Joey said without emotion.

Juju bent down in front of Joey. "What hurts?"

"My ankle."

"Let me see." Juju got right down to business.

Joey lifted her pant leg, and Seth gently removed her worn canvas sneaker. Maggie could see the swelling even before Juju took Joey's sock off.

"Can you walk on it?" Juju asked.

"Yeah, if I walk really slow," Joey explained.

"Good. It's probably just sprained. You guys stay here, and I'll run to that drugstore a couple of blocks back and get something to wrap it with," Juju said.

As Joey, Seth, and Maggie sat on the curb talking, a car came to a screeching halt in front of them. Startled, Maggie looked up. Rock was getting out of his car.

"What the hell are you two doing with Joey?" he demanded.

Maggie spoke before the others had a chance. "Juju and I were just walking to meet one of her customers, and we saw Joey limping down the street. We made her stop and sit on the curb. It wasn't her fault. I think she has a sprained ankle. Juju ran to get something to wrap it with," Maggie explained, hoping he'd buy her story.

Rock looked closer at Joey's ankle. "What the fuck did ya do now?"

"I didn't do nothin'. It was all Thelma's fault. If she wasn't so high all the time, maybe she'd stop batting me around," Joey screamed.

"Who the hell are you yelling at?" Rock asked, his expression turning deadly. He stepped closer to Joey and gave her a hard slap on the top of the head.

"Owww!" Joey cried.

Seth jumped to his feet, forgetting how cruel Rock could be, and stood in front of Joey. "Leave her alone!" he said in a steady voice.

"You're fuckin' kiddin'. Sit the hell down before I break you in half, you little moron," Rock warned.

When Seth didn't back down, Maggie stood quickly and planted herself between the two. "What's up, Rock?" she asked.

"Get in the car. We gotta talk," Rock commanded.

Maggie scurried into the car as horrible thoughts about Seth bounced inside her head—the same awful thoughts that had kept her up the night before.

"I understand two men offered to help ya last night. You and me are gonna take a little ride 'cause I need to understand what cha told them to make 'em think ya needed protecting," Rock said. Red-hot anger seeped from his words.

Maggie remained silent. She was buying time. She needed to come up with a lie that Rock would believe.

Chapter One Hundred Two

———◼———

"I'm waitin', bitch! You better start talkin' fast," Rock exploded. "It's not a big deal, Rock. Some of the other girls told me if I make up a sob story, the men at the bar would give me bigger tips. All I told those two guys was that my parents died suddenly, and I was left all alone with no family. I told them I was trying to save money so that someday I can pay for college," Maggie said.

"What's that gotta do with offering ya help?" Rock said, smelling a lie.

"That's what these guys do. All of them are the same. They want to come into the bar and rescue the girls. It's all just a part of their fantasy. They think it will make me pay more attention to them. Besides, they were drunk, Rock," Maggie lied.

"Well, Armando didn't think they were drunk, and he took it as a threat. Here's what I'm gonna do. I'm gonna cut ya some slack this time, but only 'cause I ain't got no proof that ya told those two idiots anything about me or my men. But here's what you're gonna do. Tonight when you go back to that bar, you're gonna tell those two Italian pricks that if they so much as look in Armando's direction again, they'll be dead," Rock snarled. His brow was scrunched as he pushed his face closer to hers and waited.

"OK, Rock. I'll let them know. I swear," Maggie promised.

"Good. And another thing. If I find out you're lying and plottin' to leave, I'll kill Juju and Seth. I'll let ya live so that you can regret your decision to fuck me over for the rest of your pathetic life. Then I'll sell your filthy ass to the nastiest dudes I can find. I know a lot of them, too. Now get the fuck outta my car," Rock demanded.

Maggie quickly grabbed the door handle and shot out into the street. Rock got out and glared at Maggie over the roof of the car.

"Don't say I didn't warn ya. There ain't gonna be second chances this time."

Maggie nodded and rushed back to Seth and Joey.

"What did he want?" Seth asked, feeling protective.

"Nothing you need to worry about. Everything's fine," Maggie assured him.

Seth challenged her. "I don't believe you, Aggie. I can tell you're upset."

Just then, Juju returned with an elastic bandage to wrap Joey's ankle. She looked from Maggie to Seth and back. The tension was palpable.

"What's going on? What did I miss?" Juju asked.

"Rock just made Aggie get in his car, and she came back upset," Seth snitched.

Juju studied Maggie's face. Seth was right; something was wrong.

"Everything OK?" Juju asked her.

"Everything's fine," Maggie stated calmly.

Juju knew that Maggie would talk about it later. "Little dude, she's cool. Let's take care of your *girlfriend*, Joey."

Juju's comment brought a smile to Seth's lips. Then Seth started barking out orders. "You need to be really careful with her. Her ankle already hurts, and I don't want you to make it hurt more."

"Really, Seth? Yeah, 'cause I went all the way to the drugstore so I can buy this 'thing' so it would hurt Joey more," Juju shot back. "How the fuck does this thing work?" she asked, looking at Maggie and hoping she'd take over.

Maggie stepped in and took the bandage from Juju. "Give me. I know how to use it. Just sit back and learn from the master," she bragged.

As Maggie wrapped Joey's foot and ankle with the bandage, she explained that it couldn't be too loose or too tight. The other three watched as she applied the bandage like an expert.

"And you know all this from...?" Juju asked.

"Well, I learned it from books, but there have been times when I actually had to practice the technique," Maggie explained.

"I remember," Seth said sadly. "You always had to fix Shana after men did bad things to her."

Maggie hadn't thought that Seth remembered much of their life under the control of John William. But now she realized that she'd been fooling herself. *How do you forget living in the bowels of hell? How do you pretend that all the pain and torture never existed?*

"That's right," Maggie answered, not wanting Seth to feel dismissed. "I had to learn a lot of things so I could help Shana."

Joey broke the silence. "My ankle feels better. Thanks, Maggie."

Then Joey turned to her left. "Thanks, Juju, for getting the bandage."

Juju beamed at her. "Hey, whatever I can do to help. You two better get your asses into school before you're late."

As Maggie and Juju walked past the drug addicts, hookers, and homeless people on their way back to their rundown apartment, Maggie relayed the things that Rock had told her. The information made Juju squeamish. She didn't want any of them to be back on Rock's bad side. There was no telling what would happen if Rock felt threatened.

"So these two guys at Doubles…what do you know about them?" Juju asked.

"I know they're really nice guys. I know they live in South Philly, and they come to the bar a couple of nights a week. They know Emma really well…the dancer that I partner with. I never found out how Emma knows them. Do you think I should ask her?" Maggie wondered aloud.

"Nah, it doesn't really matter who they are, anyway. You just need to tell them not to make any more comments in front of Armando. Make sure they know you're serious," Juju said.

A few nights later, when Maggie saw Tony and Vincent sitting at the bar, it made her nervous. She liked the two men—they were nice to her—and she didn't want to tell them to stay away from Armando. Maggie was afraid she'd scare them off if she became high maintenance. But she knew it was important for them to know the truth.

Maggie finished her first set and collected her tips around the bar. She made her way over to a barstool between Tony and Vincent. She slid onto the seat. "Hi guys. How are you?"

"We're good, little Maggie. How are you?" Tony asked. He'd been in good spirits all day.

411

"Well, I actually wanted to talk to you two. You remember the last time you saw Armando in the parking lot? You know, the guy who picks me up every night?" Maggie reminded them.

"Sure, we know him. That flamin' fuckin' loser who wears that stupid smirk on his face. I'd like to rip his lips off every time I see him," Vincent said.

Maggie smiled at the sheer negative energy the men held for Armando.

"Yes, him, the one with the smirk. Well, he was really mad after you left." Maggie paused, and Tony filled the empty space.

"Oh, he was? What'd he do to ya?" Tony asked.

"He didn't do anything. But listen, you guys...I know you are trying to help, but I'd rather you didn't," Maggie said politely.

"We ain't tryin' to cause ya any problems," Vincent explained.

"I know, but it just makes things...it makes things...harder for me. So please don't say anything else to him, OK?" Maggie asked in a cracked voice.

"Yeah, sure, Maggie. We'll keep our traps shut as long as ya promise to tell us if ya find yourself in trouble. Deal?" Tony countered.

"Deal," Maggie said and flashed her brilliant smile.

When Maggie left them to get ready for her next set, Tony looked over at Vincent. "Somethin' ain't smellin' right, Vincent. The girl looked like she was gonna shit a brick. We need to be more careful around that asshole that picks her up."

"Yeah, I hear ya, Tony. I saw it too. Anyway, we can't be startin' no shit wit' out talking to the family first. We can let it drop for now, but somethin' is wrong. We'll see if Emma can get it outta her. What if this is da guy who takes little kids?" Vincent took a long swig of his beer. "All I know is we better not find out dat bastard is hurtin' her."

That night when Armando waited for Maggie's shift to end, he saw Tony and Vincent walking to their car. Neither of the men threw a glance in his direction, even though they both were acutely aware that he was there in the parking lot.

"That's right, motherfuckers. Just keep walking before you find yourselves dead," Armando said under his breath.

Chapter One Hundred Three

———————◼———————

"What are you so happy about?" Juju asked Maggie.

"I think I have a date with Colby today. I was starting to think he wasn't coming back to see me. But Armando calls him the Kensington Kook, and he said he was coming to see me today," Maggie explained.

"Why does Armando call him the Kensington Kook?" Juju asked, distracted by the label.

"I don't know. Some crap about how no one ever sees him around, and then all of a sudden, he shows up outta nowhere and wants to buy a date with me," Maggie explained.

"Maybe Armando is setting you up...trying to make you think he doesn't know the guy," Juju said.

"I never thought of that. You might be right. But this time, I have my plan in place. I'll be testing Colby instead of the other way around," Maggie bragged.

"Good. Stick to your plan, and even if he knows this Harker guy, don't tell him too much yet," Juju warned.

In the late afternoon, Maggie sat on the edge of the sofa waiting for Colby to arrive. At exactly four o'clock, there was a light knock at the door. Maggie opened the door slowly. The dull-yellow light from the fluorescent bulbs in the hallway ceiling cast an eerie glow on Colby's skin. A chill ran up Maggie's spine as she realized that this man might either help her or get her killed.

"You look like you just saw a ghost. Why so worried?" Colby asked.

"It's my nature to worry. It's not like I'm working in a convent. In this business, you can't trust anyone. Come on in," Maggie said as she opened the door wider so Colby could enter.

"How have you been?" Colby asked, making small talk.

"Why do you care?" Maggie shot back.

"Whoa! Easy does it. I'm just trying to be nice," he soothed.

"I don't need *nice*. I need honest," Maggie fired back.

"Right. All right, well I haven't been around in a couple of weeks because I was in New York. I was helping with a rescue," he said nonchalantly.

"A rescue? What kind of rescue?" Maggie asked.

"The same kind I'm hoping to do here in Kensington. If you'd help me, that is," Colby said. He smiled warmly.

"We keep having this discussion, Colby. I keep telling you, I have no way to know who you are. And even if I was sure you were here to help, I'm not saying I *would* help you," Maggie added, covering her ass if he really was working for Rock.

"Well, how do you want me to prove it to you, Maggie? What do you need from me so you'll trust me?" Colby asked patiently.

"Tell me about Rae Harker," Maggie said. She held her breath, waiting for his answer.

"Ha! OK. You want to know about Detective Harker. He's a good, honest man. I've worked with him on a couple of cases over the last two years. After his own daughter was kidnapped and found dead, Harker dedicated his career to finding missing children. I worked with him about year ago. We busted a house in North Philly that was running an underage prostitution ring. Found eight girls. They had been taken from their families years earlier." Colby sat back and waited.

Bingo! Maggie thought. That was the same information she'd read about Harker. It also matched the information that Emma had provided to her about the detective. Colby watched the visible transformation as Maggie started to recognize the truth. Suddenly, she leaned into him a little closer. She let her arms, which were always folded over her chest, relax by her sides.

"Maggie, I'm the real deal. I know you have to trust me; but the truth is, I have to be able to trust you, too. The way I see it, we're both in the same boat. Agreed?" Colby asked leaning closer to her.

"Yeah, I guess so. But it's still going to take me some time," she cautioned him.

"I have time. I don't have a whole lot of patience, but I have time. So when can we get started?" Colby pressed.

"Started on what?" Maggie shrieked.

"Get started on getting you and the others out of this place," he said in an attempt to give her hope.

The vein on Maggie's neck began to rapidly pulsate. Of course, she wanted to get out of her situation. But she wondered where they would all go. She couldn't go home, not after all that had happened. She would love to see her parents again, but too much time and abuse had put that dream to rest. She didn't want to disrupt Rob and Lorraine Clarke's life any more than it had been already. She wondered for a moment what her younger brother, Keith, was like. Seth had long since replaced the brother she once knew and loved. She believed that Keith's life had been great, full of love and happiness, just the way her parents had treated her.

"I think we need to take this one step at a time, Colby. I mean, you're expecting a lot of things to happen. You're making it sound so simple," Maggie cautioned.

"Nothing about this process is going to be simple, Maggie. We have a lot of work ahead of us. It will be like sailing through shark-infested waters on a blow-up raft. For now, all I need you to do is answer my questions honestly. As we move further into this process, the questions will become harder and more personal," Colby warned, pausing to give Maggie time to process what he was saying.

"I see. Well, if I decide to help, how will I know that I'll be safe?" Maggie asked.

Colby took her hand in his. An electric wave fired from Maggie's fingertips, energizing her whole body. She wanted to pull her hand away from him, but she couldn't let go of the feelings that his touch released; it felt magical. Maggie flushed with embarrassment, and she hoped that Colby wouldn't notice.

As it was, he didn't notice at all; he was too caught up in the realization that his heart was jack hammering and his lungs felt as though they were constricted. The two sat together, waiting for the other to pull away. They might have sat on the sofa for all eternity if it hadn't been for a loud banging on the apartment door.

"Open the fuckin' door!" Rock hollered.

Chapter One Hundred Four

"OK, I'll be right there," Maggie yelled back.

She ripped off her shirt and looked at Colby with wide eyes. "Take your shirt off," she whispered, "Hurry up!"

Maggie stood and stared at Colby, who was naked from the waist up. For a moment, she was distracted, taking in every inch of him. He had a broad chest and rock-solid biceps. His stomach looked as though someone had carved the muscles that ran from the top of his rib cage all the way down to his pelvis. Colby's pants hung just below the hipbones and revealed the sculpted V where the muscles converged between his hips.

Rock pounded on the door again, snapping Maggie out of her stupor. "Bitch, ya better open this door now, or I'll break it the hell in!"

Maggie grabbed the knob and pulled the door wide open. Rock stalked through, grabbed Maggie under the chin, and pushed her up against the wall. Colby rose from his spot on the sofa, and Rock looked him over.

"Sit the hell down," Rock ordered.

Colby sat on the edge of the sofa. "What's going on here? I paid up front for a full hour."

"You'll get your full hour, but right now I need to talk to this stupid whore," Rock said, tightening his grip on Maggie.

"Wh-h...what, Rock?" Maggie managed.

"What? That asshole kid of yours talked Joey into running away. I wanna know where she is. Now!" he demanded.

"I-I don't know. You have to believe me, Rock," she gasped through the stranglehold he had on her.

Rock loosened his grip just a smidgen. "Talk!"

417

Maggie pulled air into her lungs in short, curt breaths. "I don't know what you're talking about. You need to let me talk to Seth. He would never do anything to deceive you. This is probably just a misunderstanding. Please, just let me talk to Seth, and I'll come find you. I swear."

Rock looked her over. "You have an hour to find me, and you better have the information I need. You hear me?" he grunted.

"Yes, yes, I hear you. I'll find you in an hour," Maggie promised.

Rock took one more glance at Colby before he left. Once the door closed behind him, Maggie slid down the wall and sat on the floor in a heap.

Colby moved to her quickly. "Are you OK? Did he hurt you?"

Maggie looked up at Colby, her mascara racing down her cheeks with her tears. "I'm fine. I need to leave and find Seth," she stated.

"I'll help," Colby offered.

"No, you can't come with me. You should know a john would never help a hooker. I'll see you another time, but right now I need to take care of my kid," Maggie told him.

Maggie quickly put her shirt back on, grabbed her purse from the floor, and flung it over her shoulder. Taking one final look at Colby, she left the apartment to find Seth.

She ran the four blocks back to their studio apartment and pushed the door open with a bang. Juju and Seth jumped from where they were sitting on the floor.

"What the hell's wrong?" Juju asked, alarmed.

Maggie looked straight at Seth. "Where's Joey?"

Seth, in a state of shock, drew in a breath. "I don't know, Aggie. I swear, I don't know," he said.

Maggie knew he wasn't lying. "When is the last time you saw her?"

"Friday at school. Why?" Seth began to walk back and forth in the small room. "What happened to her?" he screeched, desperation dripping from his voice.

"I don't know what happened to her," Maggie said.

"But today's Sunday, Aggie! Has she been missing all weekend?" Seth bellowed.

"I don't know. Rock thinks she ran away from home and that you know where she is," Maggie told him.

"All right. Here's what we're gonna do. Let's go find Rock and tell him Seth hasn't seen Joey since school on Friday," Juju suggested.

Seth ran to the door and then turned to the two girls. "What if Rock doesn't believe us?" he asked with apprehension.

"He's gotta believe us. We don't know shit. He'll see that. Let's just go," Juju said, following Seth and Maggie and pulling the door shut behind her.

They walked to Rock's house in silence, each of them lost in thought—in fear, actually, that something unthinkable had happened to Joey. Only when they were standing in front of Rock's house did Juju break the silence.

"You guys, we need to be prepared to fight. Do you understand? If Joey ran away, Rock won't believe that we don't know anything about it," Juju warned.

Seth listened with a deep sense of sorrow. "I don't care about Rock. I just wanna find Joey. We gotta find her 'cause I know something bad happened to her. I can feel it," Seth said.

Maggie instincts were telling her the same thing. "OK, let's go in and see Rock," Maggie said, walking up the steps to the front door with a greater sense of urgency.

Maggie knocked at Rock's front door while the other two stood beside her. Thelma got to the door first and immediately scowled when she saw Seth. "What the fuck you want?" she greeted.

"We're here to see Rock," Maggie informed her.

A second later, Rock came up behind his wife.

"Let 'em in, Thelma. They're gonna tell us where Joey went," he said.

"Oh. You the bastards that took my baby?" Thelma asked.

"No, we didn't take her!" Seth blurted.

Rock grabbed Seth by the collar of his shirt, but the young boy wasn't the same little rag doll he'd once been, and it took a little more effort to make him wince. Rock put his nose against Seth's. "Unless ya want trouble that ya don't know how to handle, ya better settle down, boy," he seethed.

Maggie pulled on Seth's arm to bring him into her. She put her arm over his shoulder and looked at Rock, her eyes begging for mercy. "We need to talk to you, Rock."

Rock watched her intently. Finally, he said, "Yeah, you better have somethin' good to tell me. That's all I know." He led them down the front hallway and into his office.

Maggie's stomach was churning. *How were they going to talk their way out of this one?*

Chapter One Hundred Five

———————◼———————

"**B**ut Seth doesn't know where Joey is," Maggie stated. "I don't believe him. Look at him...I can't even stand the sight of him," Rock shot back at her.

Rock had been interrogating Seth for the past thirty minutes. Seth, who was worried sick about Joey, had broken down and started to cry. Then he turned angry and began to argue with Rock. That's when Maggie stepped in to deflect the fury building behind Rock's simmering eyes.

Finally, unable to stand by quietly, Juju asked Maggie and Seth to wait for her outside. When they were gone, she turned to Rock. "Have you looked down in the basement? Remember the things Thelma did to Seth?" she reminded him.

"What are ya sayin', Juju? Are you tryin' to say that Thelma is crazy?" Rock roared.

"No. What I'm saying is that Thelma likes to party...sometimes a little too much. She could have put Joey down the basement and just forgot," Juju stated cautiously, not wanting to become the focus of his aggression.

"Fine! Go and look down the basement and come back and tell me if she's down there," Rock said.

While Juju was gone, Rock thought about Thelma. He decided that Juju could be right; Thelma may have done something with the girl and forgotten it. He thought back to Friday night, when Thelma and her girlfriend had been pretty fucked up. He had left them a lot of dope, and by the time he got back to the house, a little past one o'clock in the morning, the two of them were still going strong. He remembered what Thelma had asked as she looked directly into his face. "Is that you, Rock? Is that you, baby?"

Thelma was so high she couldn't even be sure that he was her husband. That was a first for her. Rock thought back to when he and Thelma were young, before the drug use. She had been such an innocent girl. But over time, drugs and alcohol had won the race. Her addiction had built slowly over a three-year period. Now, her sole purpose in life was to get rip-roaring hammered every day.

Juju stepped back into the office, interrupting Rock's thoughts. "Well, was she down there?" Rock asked with mocking sharpness.

"No, but that doesn't mean Thelma didn't do something to her. You know Thelma ain't right when she's on a heavy binge," Juju said.

Rock gave her a hard look—the kind of look that let her know she was on thin ice and needed to be careful about what she said next.

"All I'm sayin' is that we should look around a little bit. I'm just bein' realistic, Rock. Look, I know Joey didn't run away, 'cause if she did, Seth would know where she went. When Maggie asked him about Joey, I could tell by the look on his face he didn't know nothin'. So? Can we look around a little?" Juju asked apprehensively.

Rock considered what she was saying. He didn't like it, but he also didn't like the thought that Joey was somewhere in his house dead and rotting.

"Yeah, OK. But listen real good. I don't want Thelma to know what you're doin'. So if she asks, I'm payin' you to clean up around here," Rock warned.

"OK, I'll go get Seth and Maggie—" Juju started.

"Nah, I don't want that whore and that little asshole in my house. You can look inside. Tell the two of them to keep searching the neighborhood. Tell 'em to ask people if they saw her," Rock instructed.

When Juju went outside to tell Maggie and Seth the plan, she found them huddling close together next to a large tree. The temperature was below freezing, and the wind was whipping, making it unbearable to be outside for a sustained period.

"Fuck! It's freezin' out here," Juju said.

"No kidding. What took you so long?" Maggie asked, her teeth chattering.

"I convinced Rock to let me look around his house. I thought maybe Joey was down in the basement, but she ain't. So now he's gonna let me take a look upstairs and all. I told him Thelma could've gotten real fucked up, and maybe she put Joey somewhere," Juju explained.

"Good. Let's go back inside. I'm freezin'," Seth announced.

"You can't," Juju told them honestly. "Rock is being a dick. He doesn't want either of you inside the house. I'll tell ya what. You guys cut through the back and head down to the deli on Kensington near Somerset. I'll take a look around and then meet you there."

"I'm not so sure about leaving you here by yourself. What if something happens and we're not around?" Maggie asked.

"Nothing is gonna happen. You're such a worrywart. Now go! If you cut through Rock's backyard, it'll be quicker," Juju suggested.

"Come on," Seth told Maggie, pulling her by the arm. "I know how to get there."

"You have to be careful," Maggie instructed Juju before leaving her. "Rock isn't exactly trustworthy. If you don't meet us in forty-five minutes, we're coming back."

"I'll be fine. Now just go before we all freeze to death out here," Juju said, wrapping her arms tighter around her chest.

As Maggie and Seth reached Rock's backyard, the wind howled. They felt as if they were being sliced by razor blades. They clung to each other, struggling to walk against the strong wind. Then, to their disbelief, they felt sleet. Suddenly, they were inching through driving sleet and rain.

Seth pulled Maggie toward a small shed. "Come on, hurry up! We can go in there until it stops," Seth yelled over the strong wind.

Seth pushed the slide bolt to the right. Opening the door quickly, they stepped inside and pulled the door closed behind them. The temperature inside the small space wasn't any warmer, but at least they were out of the cutting wind and hammering sleet. Inside, the space was dark, the only light coming through tiny holes in the weathered old roof. Maggie could just about see the old paint cans and garden tools scattered around the shed. She led them over to the middle of the shed, and they crouched down together, trying to keep each other warm.

In a barely audible voice, Seth whispered, "Aggie, what if Joey is dead?"

"She isn't dead, Seth. Don't think that way. We're going to find her," she responded, attempting to keep his hope alive.

But Maggie had been thinking the same thing. Now, Seth was feeding her own fear that they had lost the girl forever.

"Ohhhhh."

"Did you hear that?" Seth asked.

"Hear what?"

"Ohhhhh."

"That! Did you hear that sound, Aggie?"

"Ohhhhh."

"There it is again!" Seth said with alarm.

"It's just the wind, baby," Maggie assured him.

"Ohhhhh."

"That's not the wind, Aggie," Seth insisted as he rose and strained against the noise of the howling wind to listen for the sound he'd heard.

"Ohhhhh."

The sound was faint, but Seth pushed deeper into the shed, struggling to hear it. He followed his instincts to the back of the shed.

"Ohhhhh."

"Over here!" Seth yelled.

Maggie moved quickly to his side. A large, canvas, drop cloth was spread over something. They pulled the canvas back, and underneath was a child's plastic toy box. Seth gave Maggie a grave glance as she moved forward and opened the lid. Inside was Joey, curled up in a fetal position.

"Oh my God," Maggie said.

Seth rushed in. "Joey? Joey? Can you hear me?"

Joey opened her eyes just a tiny bit but then closed them again.

"Help me," Maggie yelled over the whooshing of the wind, and the thrashing of sleet and rain, against the thin metal structure.

Seth maneuvered himself around the piles of junk, and together they lifted Joey out of the toy box. Maggie motioned for Seth to lay her on top of the canvas, and then she wrapped the child in the stiff, cold fabric. She felt for a pulse.

"She's alive," Maggie told Seth. "Her pulse is weak, but she's still alive!"

Seth began to run his hand over the canvas feverishly, willing Joey to live and trying to warm her up.

"Ohhhhh," the soft sound came from deep in Joey's throat.

"No, don't touch her, Seth. I think it hurts. She might have broken bones," Maggie stated with authority.

"Stay with her," Maggie told the frightened boy.

He crouched next to Joey, afraid he'd lose her; he was scared that she was going to die while he sat there and did nothing to help her.

Maggie pushed the shed door open and raced around to the front of Rock's house. She banged on the door with a fierce intensity. She watched through the small window as Rock thumped down the hallway, mad as hell.

He swung the door open. "What the hell is your problem, bitch?"

"We found her. She needs help," Maggie screeched in a high voice.

Juju raced up the hall behind Rock. "What happened?"

"We found her," Maggie repeated. "There isn't much time. She needs a doctor."

Juju opened her hand and pushed it toward Rock. "I need your car keys," she said without thinking, caught up in the panic.

Rock let out a hearty laugh. "You've done lost your fuckin' mind. I ain't giving you nothin' of mine."

"Then drive us to Dr. Purse," Maggie said, remembering the doctor who had fixed Seth's broken arm.

Rock paused for a moment, and Maggie pressed further. "Joey will die, Rock. She barely has a pulse."

Rock had no attachment to Joey. His only motive at that moment was to protect his wife. It wasn't hard to get rid of a dead body, but with Maggie, Juju, and Seth knowing about Joey's condition, that option was just too complicated.

"Bring her out front. I'll drive," he commanded, his voice deep and burning with resentment.

They gently put Joey in the backseat of the car, still wrapped in the canvas drop cloth. Rock refused to allow Seth to go with them. Maggie had to assure him that she and Juju would take good care of Joey. She insisted that he go straight back to the apartment and wait there.

"I want to be with Joey," Seth shouted on the sidewalk, his voice overpowering the wind.

Maggie gripped him by the shoulders. "There's no time to argue. Do what I say. Joey needs a doctor right now, and cooperating is the best thing you can do to help her."

As Rock peeled away from the curb, he looked in his rearview mirror at Maggie. *She's a fine-looking bitch*, he thought.

Maggie caught him looking at her lustfully in the mirror. She looked down at Joey's small body and the ashen color of her skin. She looked up into the mirror again and made eye contact with Rock. *I hope you die*, she thought.

Chapter One Hundred Six

R ock had just put the car in park when Maggie opened the back door and, with Juju's help, gingerly lifted Joey out of the car. They rushed toward the back of Dr. Purse's house. Maggie rang the doorbell frantically.

A few moments later, his nurse opened the door. "Oh my, what do we have here?" she asked.

"We don't know what's wrong. We found her outside in a shed, stuffed inside a toy box," Maggie stated, glaring in Rock's direction.

"OK, well, let's get her into an examining room," the nurse said calmly.

When they got Joey into the room, they put her on the table, and the nurse removed the canvas drop cloth. The child was wearing jeans, a long-sleeved shirt, and a winter jacket that was too small for her. On her hands, the nurse could see cigarette burns and small cuts. She proceeded to cut away the child's clothing and discovered that she had small cuts all over her body, tiny one- and two-inch slices. Some of the cuts had begun to form scabs, but the deeper wounds were seeping and swollen.

The nurse pulled a sheet out of a drawer and draped it over Joey. Then she put a heated blanket on top of the sheet. "Dr. Purse will be in shortly," she informed them.

"Tell him to hurry up," Juju insisted.

Dr. Purse came into the room a few minutes later. "Rock, good to see you, my man," he said in a cheerful voice and shook hands with the ogre.

"Now what do we have here," the doctor asked, lifting the blanket and sheet from Joey.

"My goodness," he said with alarm, as he rested his hand on Joey's abdomen. "Let's take her temperature," he told his nurse. "How long has she been like this?" Dr. Purse asked them.

"We don't know for sure," Maggie responded. "It could've been a day or two."

"OK, I'd like you all to step outside while I examine her."

Dr. Purse was accustomed to tragic events in the lives of the children he treated. After all, his only clientele were pimps. The doctor bent over to listen to Joey's lungs with his stethoscope. Her breathing was so shallow that it was barely audible. He took a pin from his pocket and poked at her feet and hands, but she didn't react. He rushed over to a cabinet that contained bags of intravenous fluid. He pulled a bag from the left side of the cabinet.

"We're going to use warm, intravenous fluids on her," Dr. Purse said to his nurse.

"Her temperature is eighty-two degrees," the nurse informed him, and put her hands around her own neck, a nervous habit she had when she thought that one of the children might die.

"OK, we need to move quickly," the doctor said.

He inserted a needle into Joey's hand, and as the warm liquid started to enter her bloodstream, he removed the blanket and folded it to the width of her stomach. He placed the blanket on her core, grabbed another warm blanket, and did the same with the second one.

The nurse grabbed a third heated blanket and covered Joey from the waist down.

"No," Dr. Purse barked. "Take the blanket off her legs and feet."

"But they're blue, Dr. Purse. She's freezing," his nurse said.

"Take it off now. The key is to keep her core warm. If we heat up her extremities before her core, we can put her into shock and cause more damage. Now, let's take a look at these cuts and burns..."

The doctor felt a tingly sensation in his spine as he looked over each of the cuts. From what he could tell, she'd been cut with either a sharp knife or a razor blade. Some of the cuts were deep and required stitches; others were oozing puss, and he could easily see that they were infected.

Dr. Purse couldn't know that Thelma and her girlfriend had gotten so stoned that they decided it would be fun to see how much pain Joey could take. She was a tough little girl, and they wanted to see if they could break her. They had stripped her down to her underwear and tied her to the kitchen table. They started by burning her with cigarettes, but when she didn't beg for mercy, they decided to take turns cutting her with a razor blade. Joey had eventually passed out, so they had dressed her and put her in the toy box in the shed. They were only going to leave her there for an hour. But they forgot all about her as they continued to get blitzed. Thelma had no recollection of what she and her girlfriend had done that cold winter night, nor did she really care.

The doctor couldn't help but think of his own children, warm and safe at home with his beautiful wife, as he scrutinized each cut and burn on Joey's body. It had clearly been extreme abuse, one of the worst cases he'd seen since he began working for the criminals who were his clients. He took a deep breath and collected himself. "I'll need you monitor her to be certain her temperature rises. Oh, and please start the bag of antibiotics I left on the table over there. I'm going to talk to Rock," he said.

Dr. Purse went out to where Rock, Maggie, and Juju were waiting. "Well, there isn't anything you can do here. Best to just go home," he advised.

"Wait! What's wrong with her?" Juju asked.

"First of all, she has hypothermia, so we're going to warm her up and get her body temperature back to normal. I'm also going to give her antibiotics. A lot of those cuts and cigarettes burns are infected," he said casually.

"OK, thanks. Let's go," Rock said to Juju and Maggie as he started to leave.

"We can't just leave her here all alone," Maggie wailed.

"Um, yes we can. You heard the doc. Ain't nothin' we can do now, so there ain't no need in stayin' here," Rock ordered.

"Oh, please, Rock, let me stay with her," Maggie begged.

Rock watched Maggie as she pleaded with him to let her stay. He enjoyed watching her break down and become desperate; it made him feel powerful. He thrived on the grief and anguish of others.

Rock burst into hearty laughter that came from deep in his wretched soul. Then he stopped abruptly and stepped closer to Maggie. "Get your ass in the car before I fuck ya up so bad that even Dr. Purse, here, won't be able to save you. You gotta get back to work 'cause I need money to buy me the things I want," he growled.

Maggie looked at Dr. Purse.

"Joey will be OK. We'll take good care of her," Dr. Purse said in a reassuring voice. "It may be a while, and you'll need to pay for twenty-four-hour care for someone to be here with her, Rock. I'll call you when you can come back and get her."

"Yeah, yeah, if it weren't for Thelma, I'd let the little bitch die," Rock stated. "Do what ya gotta do to keep her alive. When she's older, I'll turn her out on the street, and she'll pay me back every penny it cost to save her life."

An hour later, Maggie and Juju walked into their apartment. Seth was sitting on the floor, his knees pulled up to his chest, and his arms wrapped around them tightly. He was rocking back and forth in a trancelike state. Maggie bent down and put her hand on the top of his head, "She's going to be OK, baby. The doctor is going to take good care of her," she explained.

Seth's jaw was clenched, his facial muscles tight. "What's wrong with her? What did Thelma do?"

Maggie wanted Seth to know the truth. There was no reason to hide anything from him. "Joey has hypothermia. That means she got so cold that it began to hurt her body. The doctor is warming her up slowly." Maggie paused for a moment. "She also has cuts and cigarettes burns on her body."

Seth sprang up from the floor. "Aggie! I told you we had to tell Rock to let Joey live with us. See what happened now?"

"We do see what happened," Juju erupted, stressed by the whole ordeal. "But that doesn't change anything, Seth. Rock does what he wants to do, and if we piss him off, he'll just make life harder for all of us. What would happen if we pissed him off and he said you had to go back and live with them? Huh? What would happen then? So stop blaming Maggie for the nasty things Thelma did to Joey. It ain't right!"

Seth, startled by Juju's reaction, felt immediately sorry that he'd attacked Maggie. "I'm sorry, Aggie. I'm not mad at you. I'm mad at Thelma," he said with remorse.

"It's OK, Seth. I know you're not really mad at me. Right now, we need to be patient until I can figure something out. I promise we'll do whatever we can to help Joey, but she'll probably have to live with Thelma for a few more years," Maggie admitted.

Maggie had reflected on what Rock had said in the doctor's office about Joey being turned out in a couple of years. She wouldn't be able to live with herself if Joey was forced to prostitute. She wouldn't wish that fate on anyone. Rock's words about Joey's future turned over and over in her mind, haunting her. She felt nauseous and feverish. She, too, felt as though they hadn't done enough to help Joey. Thelma had gone too far this time.

Joey would have died that night in a toy box in a cold, dirty shed, had it not been for Maggie, Juju, and Seth.

Maggie didn't know how to help her, but she had to do something before Joey died or was forced to sell her body to strangers. If that happened, it would be Maggie's fault, and Maggie would never be able to live with herself.

Chapter One Hundred Seven

It was a quiet Sunday afternoon when the phone rang. Rae Harker was calling to ask Lorraine and Rob to meet him at an address he gave to Rob without any other details. The detective needed their help.

Within a couple of minutes, Lorraine and Rob were in their car, starting the thirty-minute drive. Arriving at the address Harker gave them, they turned into a long, tree-lined driveway. Rob and Lorraine looked around in awe. Rob parked the car, and they sat looking at a breathtaking, three-story mansion with steep roof angles and a rugged stone exterior. The landscaping was flawless. Even the driveway looked like it was cleaned on a regular basis.

"This house must be worth millions," Lorraine said. "Who the hell are these people?"

"I'm not sure. Harker didn't give me any information other than what I told you already. He wants us to talk to the parents. The police found their kid, and things aren't going so well. I told him we would come and give it our best shot," Rob explained to her a second time.

"Well, with all their money, you'd think they'd have plenty of professionals to help them," Lorraine stated, already intimidated by the couple she hadn't met yet.

Rae Harker pulled up behind them and parked. Lorraine and Rob swiftly got out and met him as he walked toward their car.

"Thanks for coming. I can always count on you two," Harker said with sincerity.

"No problem," Lorraine said. "What do you need us to do?"

"The Wilsons have recently been reunited with their daughter, Darla. She was kidnapped when she was fourteen. She's been missing for three years. When they found Darla, she was institutionalized for three weeks before they could even begin to figure out who she was," Harker told them.

"Three weeks? Why so long?" Rob asked.

"Well, Darla was so strung out on heroin that it took a considerable amount of time to get her through withdrawal and sober enough to be released. Her parents, the Wilsons, need help coping with everything. They love their daughter, but they are confused about how to help her," Harker explained.

"How can we help, Harker? I mean, what are we supposed to do for them? Maybe some professional counseling would be better for them," Lorraine suggested.

"Let's go inside and meet them. Then you can tell me if you might be able to help. Sometimes all people need is one person to listen as though they actually care. That's where you two come in," Harker said. "You're the most caring couple I've ever met."

Humbled by the compliment, Rob and Lorraine followed Detective Harker to the front door. The Wilsons answered the door together.

"Detective Harker, good to see you again," Todd Wilson said. His voice was lifeless, and his wife stood behind him silently.

"Hello, Mr. and Mrs. Wilson," Harker said, "This is Lorraine and Rob."

"Please call me Wendy," Mrs. Wilson stated, addressing all three of them. "Would you like something to drink?"

"I would love a cup of coffee," Lorraine told her.

"Good. Let's go into the kitchen," Wendy said, walking toward the back of the house.

As Lorraine followed Wendy through the house, she took in the vaulted ceilings, immaculate furnishings, and the sunlight that poured in through massive, floor-to-ceiling windows. The home was spectacular. Every detail and piece of furniture harmonized. It was a home to be envied. As they entered a kitchen that was the size of the entire first floor of the Clarkes' home, Lorraine paused a moment to take in its beauty.

Wendy broke the silence. "Detective Harker tells us that you have a daughter who's missing."

"Yes, her name is Maggie. She's been gone for over seven years," Lorraine answered with deep sadness.

"It's unbelievably hard to manage," Wendy shared. "No one can really understand the hollowness when you have a child that's missing. It felt as if someone had reached inside of me and pulled everything out until I was nothing more than bones covered with skin. I couldn't eat, couldn't sleep. It became almost impossible to get out of bed in the morning."

"And now that Darla is back? How are you coping?"

Wendy took a deep breath and exhaled for several seconds. "I feel much the same as I did before she returned. To be honest, Todd and I aren't coping at all. I think we expected to get back the child who was stolen from us. But that just isn't the case. Darla has been through so much, and at this point, we aren't even sure *what* they did to her. The doctors have confirmed that Darla was sexually assaulted. She has several scars on her back, and when she walks, which isn't often, she has a limp. Before Darla was taken, she was a straight-A student and a strong athlete. She had a lot of friends. Darla was an outstanding swimmer, and her dream was to compete in the Olympics, she had real potential…"

Wendy's voice faded away as she thought about the child that Darla once was and the drastically different child who had come home to her.

"I don't mean to sound ungrateful. I'm delighted that we have Darla back with us. However, I wasn't prepared for her to be so different. What I'm really trying to say is that my thirteen-year-old Darla was frozen in my mind. You must think I'm a very self-centered woman for what I'm telling you," Wendy added shamefully.

"No, I don't think that at all. To be honest, I still picture Maggie as the sweet, eleven-year-old girl who was happy and loved to be with her family. I don't know that any parent is capable of imagining how a missing child is maturing," Lorraine said.

"I love Darla. I love her with all my heart. And I just don't know how to make up for the time we've lost. I want those years back. I want to pick up where our lives ended—from the moment she was taken from us. Now I have a daughter who is a heroin addict. Our doctor told us that she will probably fight addiction her whole life," Wendy said.

Lorraine leaned forward in her chair and took Wendy's hand. "None of this means that you can't recapture some of the past. I'm sure it won't be easy, but if you try hard enough, I think you'll make it work."

435

Still holding Lorraine's hand, Wendy stood. "Come with me."

Hand in hand, they walked up the ornate, marble, spiral staircase. When they reached the second floor, they walked to the second door on the right. Wendy opened the door slowly. The first thing Lorraine noticed was an in-home nurse, who turned and smiled at the two women. Then Lorraine spotted the back of someone's head. She was sitting in an oversized chair facing the window. Lorraine assumed that she was Darla.

Beyond the window was the largest and most elaborate swimming pool Lorraine had ever seen.

Wendy and Lorraine walked across the large room and stood facing Darla. Lorraine couldn't control the low, eerie sound that escaped from her throat. The breathtaking bedroom began to close in on her. It felt more like a dirty, damp, bug-infested crawl space as she stared at the young girl.

Darla's hair was tangled and knotted; she was catatonic and looked like zombie. Her eyes were unfocused and jumping around to different places on the window and wall. The muscles in her arms and legs hung and wiggled when she moved. She was drooling and making odd noises, soft moans, and grunts.

"Darla, this is Mrs. Clarke. She's come to visit," Wendy stated slowly in a loud voice.

Darla didn't acknowledge her mother. Instead, she spun into grotesque laughter as she rocked back and forth in her chair. It was then that Lorraine noticed her rotted teeth.

Dear God, what have they done to this child? How can you allow these monsters to walk your earth? Lorraine asked.

Tears spilled out of Wendy's eyes as she watched her daughter. Trying to give Wendy some comfort, Lorraine pretended as though Darla were perfectly normal. "Hello, Darla. My name is Lorraine. It's nice to meet you."

"Why is it nice to meet me?" Darla growled.

Lorraine braced herself. "Because I've heard all about you," she responded cautiously.

"What do you want from me? You wanna see my titties?" Darla offered, lifting her shirt spastically. Darla's bare breasts were scarred and tattooed.

"No, I don't. But I would like to know what that tattoo means," Lorraine responded, casually pointing to Darla's right breast.

Darla looked down at herself and stared at the tattoo. It was a circle with random, jagged lines and ink marks in the center. The young teen stuck her index finger in her mouth. "Oh, I know," she said. "The men who did it said every time I moved, they were gonna put more needles in my tits so I can remember to stay still when they were 'riding me like a bull.' When I was bad, they took out that thing with needles and pressed it into my tits. It hurt a lot, too. That's all I think it means. Hey, do you have any dope on ya?" Darla asked, hopeful.

Lorraine was stunned and speechless. It took a moment before she responded, "No, Darla. You are back home now, and you don't need to use drugs. No one here is going to hurt you."

Darla nodded, intrigued by the woman.

"Nobody wants to crawl into me? That's what Roger used to say," Darla told them.

Lorraine looked for a way to change the subject. "Do you see that pool outside?"

Darla giggled and flailed her arms.

"Well, you're going to swim again. Do you remember how much you loved to swim?" Lorraine asked.

"No," Darla responded. "But I wanna go in the water. I get clean in the water, and then I don't get hit 'cause I'm dirty."

After a few seconds, Darla returned to her delirious state. She stood and began to remove all of her clothes. The nurse jumped to her feet before Darla could remove her panties.

"Now, Darla, remember what we talked about. It's not appropriate to take your clothes off with others in the room. Why are you doing that?" the nurse asked, trying to push Darla to think in a rational way.

"'Cause I wanna show everybody my pussy," Darla responded with a victorious look on her face.

"You don't need to show people your private parts," the nurse assured her.

"Let's go back downstairs," Lorraine said quietly.

When they were out in the hallway, Lorraine turned to Wendy. "I'm so very sorry. What can I do to help you?"

"You can pray for Darla. Just pray that someday soon, Darla will be capable of regaining some resemblance of a normal life. I know that she'll never be the same. In fact, that's what makes her homecoming so bittersweet. She's still lost, and I'm not sure we'll ever find her again. The doctors say that between the drugs and severe trauma, Darla may never fully return. But we're hopeful that over time, she'll regain some of what she has lost," Wendy responded.

On the Clarkes' ride home, Lorraine told Rob all about Darla. "I've never thought about the person Maggie has become. I still see her as the daughter we knew. Even seeing Darla doesn't help. She's not like the other girls we've visited. She's so fucked up. I feel so guilty," Lorraine admitted.

"Why would you feel guilty?"

"Because when we pulled up to that mansion of a home, I thought to myself, 'How bad can it be?' I mean, they have everything money can buy. I just assumed that their daughter was back with them and able to enjoy all the things her heart desired. I feel like a total bitch for judging them the way I did. People with a lot of money hurt the exact same way as everyone else," she said, crying.

"Well, you're not alone. I had the same thoughts. I was ignorant enough to think that somehow their pain wasn't as real as ours was. But you know, the bottom line is that we are all more alike than we thought. So was Darla that bad?" Rob finally asked.

"Oh, Rob, it was just awful. The girl is a mess. She looks nothing like the pictures you saw throughout the house. I'm not sure how Todd and Wendy can stand it," Lorraine said. "I'm not so certain I would be able to function if Maggie ever came back to us in that condition. Everything she was is completely gone. The poor girl is acting out the things those bastards made her do. Her breasts are covered with awful scars. They would punish her by tattooing her breasts, by mutilating her."

For the rest of the drive home, Rob and Lorraine were lost in their own thoughts about Maggie. The beauty of the Wilsons' mansion faded; instead, they pictured dark angels soaring above the stone building—evil had claimed the entire family.

Finally, Lorraine gave voice to the question that was plaguing both of them: "What if Maggie comes home severely damaged and doesn't even remember who we are?"

She looked to Rob for comfort, but his only response was, "I don't know." Once again, he grappled with the question of which was better, Maggie being dead or alive. All Rob wanted was for his daughter to be at peace. If he only knew...

Chapter One Hundred Eight

Maggie worried about Joey obsessively after leaving her with Dr. Purse, a man she hardly knew—a man who didn't grimace when Rock spoke of turning Joey out to prostitute in a couple of years. Without seeing or hearing from Joey in almost a week, she worried that they'd been duped, and Rock was going to sell Joey or trade her to another pimp. Maggie wouldn't rest until Joey was back in Kensington and she could see for herself that the child was alive and well.

Maggie had finished an early shift at Doubles shortly before midnight. When she returned to her apartment Seth was sleeping on the floor with the television blaring. Maggie had just undressed when one of Juju's friends, another dealer, burst through the door, dragging Juju in with him.

Maggie looked up at her friend, who was splattered in blood.

"What happened?" Maggie screamed so loudly that Seth shot off the floor.

"It's her finger," Juju's dope-dealing friend explained. "They cut it off."

Maggie rushed over and led Juju to the mattress. "Seth, get me two towels. Hurry!" Maggie demanded.

Maggie unwrapped the shirt that Juju's friend had fastened around her hand. Maggie assessed the hand quickly. The pinky finger was missing. With blood gushing from the wound, Maggie wrapped the hand in a towel and ordered Seth to follow her.

Maggie and Seth hurried outside with Juju. Once they reached the curb, Maggie flagged down a cab. They jumped into the backseat. "Episcopal Hospital," Maggie ordered.

"As fast as you can drive," Seth added.

Juju lay across their laps in the backseat of the cab, while Maggie held her hand up in midair. When they arrived at the hospital ten minutes later, Maggie threw twenty dollars to the driver and rushed Juju inside. When the admitting clerk spotted the blood-soaked towels, she immediately jumped to her feet and brought a wheelchair.

"What happened?" the woman asked as she rushed Juju back to the Emergency Room.

"We don't know. She came home like this. I think she's in shock. She won't talk to us," Maggie answered.

Just then, a nurse entered the bay and moved Juju onto a gurney. "OK, well, we're gonna help her. You can go into the waiting room," the nurse said.

"No, we want to stay with her," Maggie responded.

The nurse, too tired from her twelve-hour shift to argue, gave in and nodded. "What's her name?"

"Juju," Seth told the nurse.

"Juju? Can you hear me, honey? You're at the hospital. Your friends brought you here, and you're going to be just fine," the nurse said.

The nurse moved around the bed and elevated Juju's legs. Then she put Juju's arm in a sling that hung just above the bed. She moved quickly, and Maggie felt comfortable that she knew what she was doing. The nurse left the room for a few minutes and came back with several blankets.

"OK," the nurse said to Juju. "We're going to keep you nice and warm. This will help stabilize you. The doctor is coming to see you in a couple of minutes. I'm leaving your friends here with you to keep you company."

When the nurse left the room, Maggie and Seth rushed to Juju's side.

"Can you hear us?" Seth asked in a scared voice.

Juju turned her head toward him. "Yeah, I can hear you."

"Oh my God, Juju. How did this happen?" Maggie asked a little too assertively. "Were you playing that stupid game again?"

Maggie figured that Juju had been messing around with some of the other dealers, playing the five-finger filet game. Players placed one hand down on a table with their fingers spread apart and used a knife to stab back and forth between their own fingers, trying not to hit a finger. Maggie had yelled at Juju several times for playing the game. "It's brainless and only dimwits play it," she'd said. "So knock it off."

Tears filled Juju's eyes, and she slowly shook her head. "No, it was Rock."

"It was Rock," Maggie repeated. "Why would Rock do this?"

"Last night, I lost five hundred bucks somewhere. When I brought him money at the end of the night, I let him know there was money missing. He went crazy. Accused me of stealing from him, even though I told him I didn't. One of his thugs was with him, and he held my hand down on the picnic table in the park. Rock took out his knife and cut my finger off." Juju paused for a long moment. "Rock said that every night I don't pay him his five hundred bucks, he'll cut off another finger."

"OK, we'll get the money. Don't worry. We have about one hundred and fifty dollars saved," Maggie said, trying to give her comfort.

Juju nodded, but she didn't believe Maggie could come up with a way to get the rest of the money.

"Don't worry, Juju. We'll protect you," Seth asserted. "We'll get the money some way, 'cause we can't let anything happen to ya." He laid his head on the edge of the gurney.

Hours later, the three left the hospital and headed back to their apartment. The next morning, as Juju slept, Maggie dressed and left the apartment. She was headed to the house of whores to find Rock. When she arrived, the look on Armando's face was one of pure contempt.

"What the fuck you doin' here?" Armando asked.

"I'm looking for Rock. I need to talk to him," Maggie explained in a calm voice, although her insides felt like they were doing the jitterbug.

Armando disappeared into the back room. A couple of minutes later, Rock emerged. He was wearing an evil grin as he approached. "I bet you're here about Juju, huh?"

"Yeah, I need you to give her more time to get your money. I don't know how, but we'll find a way to repay you the five hundred dollars," Maggie pleaded.

Rock scratched his temple. "I explained to her that she'll lose a finger every day that I don't get my money. The way I figure it, she has nine more days to find it before she has two stumps for hands."

443

Rock stood firm, his back erect and his chest puffed out. He clearly liked being in control. Maggie scrambled for a way to convince him to give her more time.

"You've known her for a long time, and she even saved your life once. Remember? Couldn't you just give us a few more days? Just this one time?" Maggie asked in a tone that revealed her despair.

"What's in it for me?" Rock asked, crossing his arms over his chest.

"I don't know. What do you want?"

"I'm not sure yet. But I'll tell ya what. I'll give ya three days to find the money, and later, when the time comes, I'll tell ya what ya owe me for bein' so generous."

Maggie knew it was a bad idea to make a deal without knowing what it was going to cost her. But the alternative was to allow Rock to mutilate Juju's hands. Her chest was tight. She deliberately paced her breathing so she didn't hyperventilate. She rocked side to side, considering her options. There was absolutely no one to whom she could turn. Sure, she had friends on the street, but they were either prostitutes or homeless. Finally, she agreed to Rock's deal.

"OK, you have a deal. Three days, but today doesn't count," she boldly demanded.

Rock's facial features remained rigid, as if he were made of granite. "Yeah, all right. Three days not counting today."

"OK. I'll see you in three days," Maggie confirmed.

Rock grunted and left Maggie in the living room. The other girls had sat there without uttering a word so they could listen to the conversation. As Maggie turned to leave, Trinity, the hooker who'd been so mean to Maggie when she'd first arrived at the house of whores, stood up.

"Looks like ya got yourself in a jam. We all see ya walkin' around this town like your shit don't stink. Well, I guess ya just found out there ain't nothin' special about ya," she said mockingly.

Maggie stepped closer to the girl who had caused her so much angst over the years.

"Really? I seem to recall Rock giving me exactly what I wanted. Maybe you should clean the wax out of your ears. Or how about minding your own damn business?" Maggie shot at her.

"Ha! Ya think ya just won wit' Rock? Ya just wait 'til a monf from now when he screws ya over again," Trinity threw back in a nasty tone.

"Oh, really, Trinity. Tell me, how long is *monf* anyway? The word is *month*!" Maggie said.

Trinity had her hands on her hips. Her nostrils flared. "Fuck you, bitch! Ya need to get the fuck outta my face before I pound ya to death," she threatened.

"You're right, Trinity. I'm sorry for whatever I did to you that makes you hate me so much. But you know, maybe you should think about us girls sticking together. Maybe if we stood united, we'd have more say in the things that go on around this town." Maggie turned on her heel and left the house of whores.

It wasn't Maggie's nature to mock people. She learned early on that all of the hookers were pretty much the same, including her. They all lived in hell. They were rarely excited or looked forward to the future. Maggie made it a point to continue to learn as much as she possibly could, but she was an exception. She looked forward to leaving the sex world behind her someday. She wanted to be prepared for what life might bring her, even though in her heart there was little hope that she'd make anything out of herself.

Trinity stood motionless for several minutes after Maggie left the house. At first, it was because she liked the idea of the girls sticking together. But when she saw Rock standing in the doorway, having overhead everything Maggie had said, she couldn't move because she was afraid of what would come next.

Chapter One Hundred Nine

———◼———

Later that day, Maggie answered a knock at the door of the apartment Rock owned. Colby was waiting in the hallway.

"Come on in," Maggie said, walking toward the cheap sofa.

"How've you been?" Colby asked. "The last time we were together, Rock busted through the door accusing you of knowing where some guy named Joey was."

"Joey is a girl. She's an eleven-year-old who lives with Rock and his wife, Thelma."

"Oh, so Joey is Rock's kid, then?" Colby asked.

"Yeah, something like that."

"Well, did he ever find her?" Colby pressed.

"Yeah, we found her. She got lost and hid in a shed. She fell asleep and was there too long and ended up getting hypothermia. The doctor said she's going to be fine, though," Maggie explained.

Maggie didn't feel guilty about lying to Colby. Her main objective was to keep herself and the others safe. Colby knew her story didn't ring true, but he was smart enough to know that he hadn't gained her trust yet.

"That's good news, right?" Colby asked.

"Of course."

Maggie wasn't inclined to tell Colby about Juju's ordeal with Rock. Maggie met and held Colby's eyes for a long moment, blushing. She liked Colby. She'd been attracted to him ever since she'd seen him without his shirt. But now, her eyes smoldered with intensity. She nervously began to touch her hair and smooth her skin-tight dress. As she looked Colby over, her legs began to wobble. Colby was just over six feet tall. He wore his dark-brown, wavy hair almost to his shoulders. He had light-brown eyes, full lips that revealed beautiful teeth, and a smile that made her want to melt into a puddle. There was no doubt that she was attracted to him. If she were truthful with herself, the more time she spent with him, the more she wanted him to like her.

However, the realistic side of Maggie kept gnawing at her. To believe that a normal guy would ever become intimately involved with a prostitute was insane. Maggie believed she was ruined, as a person and as a woman. She had convinced herself that no sane, stable man would ever want her. When she'd allow herself to imagine the future, she pictured spending her life with a fat, sleazy, slovenly man who was either into drugs or sex, but more likely both—the type of guy who went out and left his woman at home raising the children he'd never wanted. Because of this picture of the future she'd painted in her head, she'd decided to be single for the rest of her life. She rejected the idea of being controlled by anyone once she was old enough and could break free from Rock.

An hour later, after Colby left, Maggie walked back to her own apartment, preparing for the questions Juju and Seth would have for her. When Maggie walked into the apartment, Seth and Juju were lying on the mattress.

"Did you figure out how we can help Juju? And what about Joey? Did Rock tell ya anything about her?" Seth asked with urgency.

"Hey, sweetheart, you have a lot of questions," Maggie said, trying to avoid answering them.

"Well, what happened?" Juju chimed in. "Is Rock coming back to see me tonight? Oh, God, I just can't lose another finger."

"OK, you two, calm down. First, I got Rock to give us three days to come up with the money. So he promised to leave Juju alone for now. We need to figure out what we're going to do, fast."

"So I *am* going to lose my fingers. Maybe I can run; just leave Kensington and hide," Juju offered.

"That's our plan B, Juju," Maggie said slyly.

"What's plan A?" Seth asked.

"I'm going to talk to Colby. He came to visit me at Rock's apartment this afternoon, and I've decided to ask him for the money. He's the only person I can think of who might be able to help us," Maggie confided.

"What will you have to promise to get Colby to do that for us?" Juju asked, concerned that Maggie would go too far to help her.

"Well, we know he wants information about the guys who work for Rock. I'm sure that's what he'll want," Maggie said, as if it wasn't a big deal.

"But what if he works for Rock? What if Rock kills ya, Aggie?" Seth asked, alarmed.

"I don't think he works for Rock. I don't know why; I just think he's the real deal," Maggie said.

"What about Joey? When you talked to Rock, did he say anything about her?" Seth asked.

"I don't know anything about Joey yet. I didn't get a chance to talk to Rock about her, but I promise the next time I see him, I'll ask," Maggie reported. Then she continued, "I have a feeling that Joey is doing just fine, so stop worrying so much, OK?"

Seth wouldn't be able to rest until he knew for sure that Joey was better. An hour later, exhausted from the conversation with Juju and Seth, Maggie walked downstairs and stood on the curb to wait for Armando. She was distraught, wondering if any of them would come out of this alive.

Chapter One Hundred Ten

———————◼———————

When Maggie got onstage that night, it cheered her up to see Tony and Vincent sitting at the bar. It had been a while since she chatted with them, and seeing them was a welcome relief from the anxiety that had plagued her all day.

"Hey, guys! How are you?" Maggie asked in a chirpy voice.

"Well, look who it is, Tone. If it ain't little Maggie," Vincent commented.

"Yeah, how ya doin', Maggie?" Tony asked.

"I've been good. So where have you two been? I haven't seen you in a while."

"Ya know, here, there; we're busy men," Tony joked

"So tell us, how's dat asshole, Armando, been treatin' ya. He givin' ya any grief?" Vincent asked.

Maggie wished she could tell them what had happened to Juju and Joey, but she didn't want to get them upset again. She couldn't risk either of them saying something to Armando that would piss him off. Maggie was trying to stay on Armando's good side, especially with their current predicament.

"Who, him? Ahhh, he's been fine. I just stay away from him as much as I can," Maggie lied, trying to sound sincere.

"Yeah, well, dat ain't no way to live, little Maggie," Vincent chimed in.

"Ya know, there's a lot of crazy shit goin' on in this world," Tony added. "So tell us what cha been doin' then."

Maggie laughed. "I've been doing what I always do, working. I take as many shifts as I can get here and then, well, you know, make some more money when I'm not here."

Tony and Vincent knew exactly what Maggie was talking about. Emma had told them that Maggie was a prostitute and Rock was her pimp. Emma, a strong-willed, independent young woman couldn't wrap her mind around what Maggie was expected to do. She had confided in Tony and Vincent that she hoped one day to help Maggie and free her of the life she'd known since childhood.

Tony and Vincent had been stunned to hear what Maggie did under Rock's control. She was a sweet young woman—and smart, too. They figured Rock kept control over her by threatening Maggie and the little boy she lived with. The two men had made a commitment to each other that if and when Maggie ever asked for their help, they'd convince the family of the importance of getting involved. Until that day came, all they could do was be nice to her whenever they spent time with her at Doubles.

As the night wore on, Tony and Vincent were watching the dancers onstage and chatting with one of the bartenders when they heard a woman yelling in the lap dance room.

Montana came storming out of the room. Then, in the doorway, she turned back and yelled, "Don't forget what I just told ya, bitch. Ya work one of my regulars again, and you're gonna be fuckin' sorry!"

Maggie tried to leave the lap dance room, but Montana shoved her. Maggie flew backward and thought she was going to fall, but she was caught in midair. Emma had come up behind her. Holding Maggie up, she glared at Montana. "You sure you want to do this?" Emma asked, her emerald-green eyes suddenly turning deadly.

"Fuck you, whore!" Montana snapped, feeling a tiny bit of fear start to grow in the pit of her stomach.

As Montana glared at Emma, she could feel herself start to get jittery. There was something in those green eyes, something unrelenting and spooky; it was as if Emma could cut through steel with them. Finally, Montana broke the gaze and walked away.

"That's what I thought, bitch," Emma whispered, just loudly enough so Maggie heard.

"Thanks," Maggie said. "I do know how to fight."

Emma smiled, and her eyes filled with mischief. "Oh yeah. You know how to fight, huh?"

"Yes. I'm actually pretty good, too," Maggie bantered.

"Oh, I see. Well, maybe you should pull one of your well-planned moves on Montana," Emma suggested, still smiling brilliantly.

"Nope. I can't," Maggie told her. "If I get fired from here, there'll be hell to pay. Montana is just annoying. She doesn't scare me. I've stood up to people a lot nastier than her on the streets. You haven't seen a real bitch until you meet a woman with a quota to meet for her pimp. Those chicks will tear you up if you don't handle yourself right. So, I just let Montana mouth off because that's all she really does. She's a lot of bark but no bite."

"Yeah, like a rabid fuckin' dog," Emma added.

The girls laughed, and as they exited the lap dance room, Tony waved them over. "Looks like you two fighters can use a drink," he remarked.

Maggie giggled. "We aren't fighters. We're just two women who get bothered because *all the men want us*," she teased, not believing it.

Tony looked from Maggie to Emma and back. "Yeah, they do. You're absolutely right. They do."

As Emma chatted with Tony, Maggie couldn't help but wonder if what Tony said about her was true. If it was, then could it be possible for Colby to want her? She smiled just thinking about Colby until Emma broke into her thoughts.

"Uh-oh. See that expression on Maggie's face? That's a woman thinking about a man she likes," Emma tormented.

"Stop. I am not!" Maggie shot back, feeling silly as she heard her own words.

"Whatever you say, Mags," Emma continued. "Just remember, if there's someone you like, and they like you too, well then go for it. Just be careful who you fall in love with," Emma warned.

"Yeah, I know what you mean," Maggie responded.

But Maggie had no idea what Emma meant. She'd never been in love with anyone before. Sure, she loved Seth and Juju, but that wasn't the same as being "in love" with someone, as in a man—or in Juju's case, a woman.

Don't get ahead of yourself, knucklehead. Colby is on a mission to break down the prostitution ring in Kensington. Don't start thinking that he really likes you, Maggie reminded herself.

453

Maggie didn't know it, but at that very moment, Colby was in a restaurant alone, three towns away, fantasizing about Maggie in the same way that she was fantasizing about him.

Chapter One Hundred Eleven

I t was the evening of the third day, the day that Rock expected his money. Maggie hadn't seen Colby since the last time he visited, so there had been no way to ask for his help. It was just before seven thirty at night, and Maggie began to worry because she had to leave the apartment to go to Doubles with Armando. Juju had been crying off and on for most of the day, but once night fell, Juju began to think that maybe Rock would give her more time.

The hard knock at the door startled the girls. Maggie opened it slowly and saw Armando standing in the hall. "Let's go," he ordered.

When Maggie turned to grab her purse, Rock stepped into the apartment. Without hesitating, he walked over to Juju, pressed her good hand on the floor, and removed her other pinky finger. Maggie watched helplessly as he pressed his weight behind the knife, tearing away the tiny muscles and breaking through the bone. It sounded like small pieces of glass being crushed under a shoe.

Juju's screams were deafening. Blood gushed from her finger, and pain shot through her arm. Maggie ran to Juju and quickly wrapped a towel around her hand as Seth stood two feet away, gawking at Juju's severed finger lying on the floor.

"I gave you three days. I got nothin'. Tomorrow she loses another finger," Rock told Maggie.

Maggie, who was panicked and shaking, looked up at Rock. "We'll get you the money. Please, Rock."

"Pleeease, Rock," Armando mocked. "Please don't cut off any more fingers."

The two brutes stood in the small space and laughed. "Let's go, bitch," Armando said to Maggie. "You're gonna be late for work. Get your filthy whore ass movin'."

Maggie reached into her purse and gave Seth twenty dollars. "Take Juju to the hospital as fast as you can."

Maggie turned before leaving the apartment with Rock and Armando. The scene was heartbreaking. Juju was lying on the floor sobbing as Seth tried to get her to stand up. Both of them looked so wrecked and helpless.

Outside, before getting into Armando's car, Maggie spotted Colby watching them. For a fleeting moment, she wanted to run to him and fall into his arms. Instead, she pretended not to see him. Right before she bent to get into Armando's car, Maggie gestured toward the building where she lived. As Armando began to drive, Maggie turned just in time to see Colby sprinting across the street toward Seth and Juju.

Colby descended on Juju and Seth so aggressively that they immediately panicked.

"It's OK. My name is Colby. I'm a friend of Maggie's. What happened?"

"Somebody cut Juju's finger off," Seth announced, wanting Rock to stop hurting her.

"Let me help. We need to get her to the hospital fast."

Not wanting to waste any time, Colby got them into his car and peeled away from the curb.

Finally, Juju spoke. "Why are you helping us? What do you want?" she asked weakly.

"I don't want anything. I'm just trying to help you, that's all," he assured her.

"Can you help us get money so Juju doesn't get another finger cut off?" Seth countered, aching inside with worry.

Juju's eyes grew wide with fear. She couldn't go through this agony repeatedly. "I'll kill myself. It would be better than having to live through what he's doing to me," she said, disoriented.

"No one needs to kill themselves. I'm going to help you," Colby promised, feeling responsible for defending Maggie and her friends.

By the time Maggie returned home that night, Juju and Seth were sleeping soundly. Colby had stayed with them just in case they needed his help. When Maggie opened the apartment door, she was surprised to find him waiting for her.

"What are you doing here? How's Juju?" Maggie asked, curious about him and concerned about her friend.

"I took Juju to the hospital and felt like I should stick around with these two until you got home," Colby explained.

Maggie exhaled and sat beside Colby on the floor.

"Thanks for taking care of them. You know, I've been thinking. It may be time for the three of us to get out of this town. We have to get away from Rock, from this city…from this hell that we are living in," Maggie said.

Maggie had thought long and hard about what to do next. While she was worried about Joey, who still hadn't returned home, she needed to protect Juju and Seth. She realized that the path Rock was on could cost Juju her life.

Colby was surprised. "Well, let's think this through. If you run, there is a high likelihood that whoever did this to Juju will find you unless you get far, far away. How will you do that with no money?"

"I don't know. That's my biggest problem. We don't have enough money to pay Rock, and we don't have enough money to get the hell out of here. I thought maybe we could use the little money we have and take a bus somewhere. We could live in the woods somewhere. We'll figure out something. We have to. This is insane," Maggie said, as tears spilled down her cheeks.

"Tell me how I can help," Colby stated.

"Ha! You happen to have an extra five hundred dollars with you?" Maggie asked jokingly.

"Maybe I can help. If you can tell me what happened, then I'm sure I can find a way to come up with the money you need. As long as I know that it's not for anything illegal," he clarified.

"Right, just forget it," she said, wishing their problem with Rock would vanish.

"You might feel better if you talk about it. I'm a good listener," he said, egging her on.

"I'm sure you are," Maggie said and smiled.

"Come on. Give it a shot. You never know," he coaxed.

"Juju needs five hundred dollars to pay off Rock."

"Is Juju a prostitute?" Colby whispered.

"No, she's not a prostitute," Maggie told him.

"Well, what does she do for a living?" Colby asked casually.

"If I tell you what she does for a living, it could be dangerous for us and you," Maggie shot back.

"Why? Do you think I'll tell the police or something?" he asked.

"I don't know what you'll do with the information. I just know I have to protect Juju and Seth."

"I will never do anything to harm you or the others. I give you my word," Colby stated boldly.

For some strange reason, Maggie believed him. She needed someone who could help get Juju out of this horrible bind. She tossed the options around in her mind: *trust Colby or…or nothing*. Maggie realized that she didn't have anything to lose anymore by telling Colby the truth.

She took a deep breath. "Juju is a drug dealer. She's been selling since she was a young girl."

"Hmmm, that complicates things a bit," Colby mumbled.

"See? Exactly," Maggie responded, annoyed at herself for telling him.

"Maggie, chill out. I didn't say I wouldn't help you. All I said was that it complicates things. So what kind of trouble is Juju in?" Colby asked with a desire to help and gain Maggie's trust at the same time.

"Someone swiped five hundred bucks from her. When she told Rock she'd been ripped off, he cut off her pinky finger. Then he told her that she would lose one finger every day until she replaced the money. I talked him into giving us three days to come up with the money. Today was the third day, and she lost another finger," Maggie explained.

"Fuck! That's crazy," Colby stated. "I need time to think about it. It'll be OK."

"Nothing will ever be OK as long as we stay here. Tomorrow night, he'll come back and hurt Juju again. I can't take that chance. She's all I have, her and Seth. The three of us are the only family any of us has, and I won't let anyone destroy them without putting up a fight," Maggie stated bravely.

"I'll figure it out," Colby promised.

Maggie was surprised. "Are you saying you'll help us even knowing that Juju sells dope?"

"I'm saying I'll try my best. In my line of work, I spend time gathering information and feeding it to the appropriate authorities. But I think if you and I can agree to work together, maybe the agency would see the benefit in giving me the money you need," Colby said.

"Are you trying to buy information?"

"Well, technically, I guess I am. But it's more like a negotiating chip for me to use with the agency," Colby admitted.

"And you'll keep my identity a secret?" Maggie asked cautiously.

"Of course I will. I'm in the business of helping people, not hurting them. Besides, I've grown to like you a little," he ridiculed and put his strong hand over hers. "I'll have the money for you in the morning," Colby said definitively.

Maggie didn't look at him. She stared straight ahead at the wall in front of her. Colby could feel her doubt filling the room. She didn't believe him, and he knew it.

"Maggie?"

The sound of Colby whispering her name sent a delicious ripple of pleasure through her entire being.

"Maggie," he said again, gently placing his hand under her chin and turning her head to face him. "The money for Rock will be here in the morning. Please...I don't want you to leave. We have work to do together. We have other kids to save," he explained. Colby was avoiding the real reason he didn't want her to leave...he loved the sexual energy between them.

"What will I have to give you for the money?" Maggie asked.

"You don't have to give me anything. I just want to protect you. I want to keep you safe. All of you," Colby added, looking over at Juju and Seth, who were sleeping.

"Thank you," Maggie said in a strained voice.

"Then we agree that you're going to stay put for now. Right?" Colby confirmed.

"Yes, for now. But I can't promise for how long, Colby. None of us are really living. All we do is exist so that others can make their own lives better. And, after seeing what Rock has done to Juju, I know he is capable of doing worse things to any of us. I'm no different than a slave. I do the unthinkable. I sell myself, my body, and not because I want to.

459

It's not because I choose to do it. It's because I feel like I have no way out of this shit," Maggie confessed.

"Do you know who your parents are?" Colby asked. He, too, wanted her away from this life.

"Yeah. I know, but it's been too long. So many things have happened. I could never face them. I'm too ashamed of the things that I've done—that I'm still doing."

"Maggie, your parents would understand. You didn't pick this life."

"I'm not so sure they would understand. Besides, Rock would find them and me. He would eventually kill all of us. He's told me he'd kill all of us, and I believe him. I know he would do anything to keep what he believes is rightfully his. If I went home, and anything ever happened to my family, I would never forgive myself. Anyway, I have Juju and Seth to think about too. I just can't..." Maggie's voice trailed off as the image of her parents stood boldly in her mind's eye.

Colby stood and reached his hand out to Maggie. She placed her long, graceful hand in his, and he gently pulled her up. They stood facing each other. "Someday, I hope to change all of this for you. I will do everything in my power to see to it that you're reunited with your family again. When we take Rock and his pack of lame-brains down, then it will be safe for you to return home," he promised.

Maggie walked Colby the few feet to the door of the apartment. He hesitated a moment before he bent down and placed a soft kiss on her cheek.

"Things will change, and I will be here for you when you need me," Colby whispered. Then he left, closing the door behind him.

Maggie stood perfectly still. She held on tightly to the feeling of Colby's warm, soft lips brushing her cheek. It had taken all of her willpower not to reach out and grab onto him. She wanted to hold him. She wanted him to hold her. Then, feeling foolish, she banished the sensation. *A man like Colby would never be with a girl like me. I'm a hooker. He's just being nice. Don't over think his intentions*, Maggie told herself.

But as Maggie lay on the floor that night, trying to sleep, the only thing she could think about was Colby.

Chapter One Hundred Twelve

———————— ▬ ————————

Maggie woke the next morning to a soft knock on the door. She eased her way up off the floor and stumbled as she grabbed the doorknob.

"Who is it?" she said softly.

"It's Colby. Open up."

Maggie opened the door and smiled. Her long, silky hair was disheveled, and her eyes were puffy from sleep.

"Good morning," Colby said softly. "I've brought coffee and doughnuts."

Maggie opened the door wider to let him into the apartment. Each of them took a seat at the small folding table they used as a dining room set.

"Ah, coffee. Just what the doctor ordered," Maggie said as she reached for one of the cups.

Colby didn't respond. He just watched her from the other side of the table. Maggie took a long slurp of the coffee.

"Could you drink any louder?" Colby teased. "Do that again and you'll wake up Juju and Seth."

Maggie giggled. "Yes, drinking quietly. Now that's not something they taught me in charm school. I must've been absent that day."

Maggie reached across the table, grabbed one of the powdered doughnuts out of the box, and took a big bite. "Mmmmm, I wove powder doughnuts," she mispronounced with her mouth full.

Colby couldn't help but laugh at the powdered sugar she wore from cheek to cheek. "That's a good look for you. I guess you missed charm school the day they taught how to eat doughnuts daintily too."

"Yep, I know. I'm a hot mess. You should see me eat spaghetti," Maggie teased.

"It would be my pleasure. Maybe we can go out to dinner some-time. I'll take you to a wonderful Italian restaurant in South Philly. Now, that's where you get real spaghetti," Colby stated.

Maggie wiped her mouth on her sleeve. Had Colby just asked her out on a date? What was she supposed to say?

"Don't make me any promises you can't keep," Maggie finally managed.

"I never do. I'm always true to my word, which is why I'm here."

Colby reached into his pocket and took out a wad of money. "This is the five hundred dollars I promised you. Now you can pay that asshole off, and we can move on."

Maggie's mouth dropped open. "How did you get the money? What did you tell the agency I'd do for it?" she asked, suddenly fearful of what she might owe.

"I didn't promise them anything. I told them I needed it so I could spend more time with you. That's what they want me to do... spend time with you so I can get information," he said, covering up his lie.

"Really?" Maggie couldn't believe something was actually going their way for a change.

"Really what?" Juju asked from the bed.

"Colby got the money we need to pay Rock. Look," Maggie squealed, rushing over to show her friend the money.

"What do we gotta do for it?" Juju asked skeptically.

"Colby said we don't have to do anything."

The two girls turned to face Colby, who nodded and smiled at them.

Seth was still rubbing the sleep out of his eyes when he noticed the wad of cash Maggie was holding.

"Aggie! You got the money. How?" Seth asked.

Maggie looked over at Colby, and Seth followed her gaze. The boy gave the grown man a quick nod of his head, and Colby responded in the same way. Colby stood and walked toward the door. He could sense that the boy was nervous about his relationship with Maggie. She was the only mother Seth could remember, and he was feeling threatened by Colby's presence over the last two days.

"All right, you guys. I have to roll. I'll catch you later," Colby said.

"Wait!" Maggie jumped to her feet and strode over to Colby. She reached up and gave him a hug. "Thank you. Someday, we'll pay you back every cent."

"Don't worry about it. Didn't charm school teach you that money grows on trees?" Then he got very serious. "You need to be careful with Rock today, all right? Give him the money and get out of there."

Maggie didn't know that Colby had used his own money to pay off the debt. Colby wanted her to trust him not only because he needed information about Rock's shady, corrupt businesses, but also because he wanted her to stay close to him. He couldn't deny the way he felt about her anymore.

Maggie nodded, and after Colby had gone, she turned back to her little family. "We did it! We got the money. I'm going to get dressed and go to see Rock."

"There's something else, too," Seth gushed. "Joey came back to school yesterday."

"Thank God! How is she?" Maggie asked.

"Joey's doing real good now. She said the doctor was so nice to her that she didn't want to leave and wished he would've kept her there so she didn't have to go back and live with Thelma and Rock," Seth said.

"Well, we're gonna keep a close eye on her," Maggie stated with a feeling of renewal.

Maggie felt joyful. Joey was safe, albeit still living with Thelma, and Rock would leave Juju alone now that she had his money. She felt a stab of gratitude for all Colby had done to help them out of their predicament.

On her way to see Rock, Maggie stopped at a small grocery store to grab a loaf of bread. Inside, she noticed a tall, blond-haired woman, almost instantly she recognized her. "Emma. Hey, Emma, what are you doing here?" Maggie asked as they hugged.

"I live in Kensington, Mags," Emma told her.

"Since when? Why didn't you ever tell me you lived here?"

Emma chuckled. "Because you never asked me where I live. I'm about a mile from here."

Just then, a beautiful little girl walked up and tugged on Emma's shirt. "Hey, sweetheart, I want you to meet Maggie. But I call her Mags," Emma explained.

The young girl looked up at Maggie. "Hi. My name is Izzy."

Maggie bent down to be at eye level with the child. "Nice to meet you, Izzy. You look exactly like your mom," she said, beaming up at Emma.

"No, Izzy is my niece," Emma clarified.

"Well, then, you look exactly like your aunt," Maggie declared.

A tender smile played on Izzy's lips. "Everybody says that. Right, Aunt Em?"

"That's right, baby," Emma said with deep affection.

"OK, I have to get moving. I'm on my way to see Rock," Maggie said.

Maggie grabbed the loaf of bread and headed toward the register with Emma close behind her. When the clerk told her how much she owed, Maggie reached into her purse. She fumbled around inside, trying to dig out her wallet. Finally, she put the purse up on the counter and looked inside.

Maggie began to quiver and she broke out into a cold sweat. Her heart was pounding, and she kept looking inside her bag, willing her wallet to reappear. All she could say was, "Oh my God. Oh my God."

"What's wrong, Mags?" Emma asked.

"My wallet is missing. It had all of my money in it," Maggie cried.

"No worries. It's only money, girl. Here, I can cover the bread," Emma offered.

But Maggie wasn't worried about the bread. She was worried about the five hundred dollars that was in her wallet to pay off Rock. In that moment, Maggie's whole world came crumbling down on her, and now she truly had no one to turn to.

Chapter One Hundred Thirteen

———————◼———————

"You don't understand," Maggie explained to Emma in tears. "I just lost five hundred dollars. That money didn't belong to me."

"All right. Calm down. Maybe you left it at home," Emma said.

"No, no I didn't. I had it in my purse. I must have dropped it," Maggie said, her chest heaving as she wailed.

"I saw that man with the red shirt put his hand in your purse and take something," Izzy chimed in.

"What? What man?" Maggie asked.

"The man in the red shirt. He was standing behind you," Izzy explained.

Emma bent down and whispered to Izzy, "Is the man still in the store, Iz?"

"Unh-uh. He ran out of the store," the child explained.

Izzy's eyes welled up as she began to think she did something wrong.

"It's OK, Iz. It's not your fault," Emma cooed.

Maggie was pacing the small aisle of the market, frantically rubbing her arms.

Emma approached Maggie, "OK. Who did the money belong to?"

Maggie looked around the small store. She recognized a couple of hookers and a john from when she used to walk the streets.

"Let's get out of here," Maggie said.

Emma and Izzy walked a short block with Maggie, and turned into an empty alley. Maggie faced Emma. "The money belonged to Rock. My, you know...pimp."

Emma leaned in closer. "Tell him it got stolen."

Maggie quickly relayed the story about Juju and brought her up to date on everything that had happened. She even told Emma about Colby and how he had given her the money.

"Juju will lose another finger because of me. Shit, Emma, she's gonna lose all her fingers. I have no way to get another five hundred dollars. Getting it from Colby was nothing short of a miracle," Maggie said, defeated.

"I can help you," Emma told her.

"What do you mean?"

"I mean I have money, and I can help you," Emma stated. It had been a while since she was able to do something nice for someone other than Izzy. Emma really liked Maggie. She was one of the best people she'd ever met in her ridiculous, fucked-up life.

"Are you serious?" Maggie asked.

"Hell, yeah. We can walk back to my house, and I'll get it for you," Emma offered.

"I don't know when I can pay you back," Maggie said. She was desperate for the money, but didn't want to lose her only friend at Doubles over money. Besides, Maggie had noticed that the other girls were afraid of Emma, so she figured there was something about her that kept them in line.

"I know. Someday, when you have the money, you'll pay me back. Relax," Emma said with a shrug.

When they reached the house where Emma lived, Maggie stood on the broken sidewalk looking up at the porch.

"You wait here. I'll go get the money. I live with a group of people, and we don't bring others inside. House rules," Emma said.

A few minutes later, Emma came back outside. "OK, here you go," Emma said, handing her an envelope.

"How do you have all of this money?" Maggie asked, perplexed.

"Mags, I don't have a pimp. I get to keep all of my tips. Right now, I'm saving money so I can move Izzy outta here. I mean, it ain't so bad. I have one good friend in the house," Emma explained. Then she grinned. "You better shove that money in your pants so you don't lose it. Be careful and don't stop anywhere along the way," she teased.

Maggie took the envelope, slid it inside her jeans, and held her hand over it tightly. "I don't know how to thank you. You just saved a life," Maggie said.

"Ha! That's a first for me, that's for sure," Emma said, more to herself than to Maggie.

Emma gave Maggie a quick hug. "See you at Doubles. Get your ass down to that dick-head pimp motherfucker and then go home to your friend."

Maggie walked toward the house of whores. She was still stunned by Emma's generosity. She wondered what had happened to Emma to make her leave home. She knew Emma had run away when she was a young teen, but Maggie had never really pried into why she left home.

Before she knew it, Maggie was walking through the front door, and the first person she saw was Rock.

"Ya got my money?" he growled.

"Yeah, I got it," Maggie said, trying her hardest not to gloat.

Rock approached and took the envelope out of her hand. He immediately counted the money. "You one lucky bitch. How'd ya get the money?" he asked suspiciously.

"A friend loaned it to me," Maggie said.

"Who? What friend?" Rock pressed.

"Why does it matter? You have your money back."

Rock backhanded Maggie, and she fell to her knees.

"It matters 'cause I asked you a mother fuckin' question. Maybe ya forgot who your boss is. Now who gave ya the dough?"

Maggie was holding the side of her face. Her teeth felt like they had been hit with a hammer.

"A dancer I work with at Doubles."

"Oh, yeah? This dancer have a pimp? Maybe she be needin' someone to take care of her like you do," Rock said.

"No, she doesn't need a pimp. She's a dancer," Maggie countered.

Rock pulled back his foot and kicked Maggie in the upper thigh.

"Bitch, ya just ain't gettin' it, are ya? Just 'cause you're dancin' and working at the apartments don't give you any more privileges than these other nasty skanks. I'll put your ass back out walkin' that street in a fuckin' minute," Rock yelled.

"I'm sorry, Rock," Maggie breathed.

"Get the fuck outta my face before I give ya a full-on beatin'," he threatened.

Maggie got to her feet quickly and limped toward the door.

"Tell Juju she got lucky this time. She comes up short again, I won't be so nice the next time," Rock screamed.

Maggie limped the whole way back to her apartment. She would've crawled back there rather than stay one more minute with Rock. When she walked in, Seth ran to her. "Aggie, what took you so long? What did Rock say?"

Juju was lying on the mattress, looking at Maggie, waiting for her to answer.

"He said we're all good. It's all squared away," Maggie said.

But Juju could tell something was wrong. She noticed Maggie's limp when she walked across the room and the stress lines around her eyes. Maggie didn't like to talk about things in front of Seth. She tried to hide as much from him as possible. He was, after all, exposed to more ugliness than most kids his age were.

After Seth settled down and started reading a book, Maggie snuggled close to Juju.

"Sooo, how was your day?" Juju asked.

"We paid the dick his money. Today was a great day, Juju."

"It doesn't look so great by the way you're limping," Juju said.

"Oh, that? It's nothing. Just a part of being one of Rock's bitches," she said.

"You sure you're OK?"

Maggie sighed heavily, releasing the weight of the day. "I'm just peachy."

As Maggie got lost in her own thoughts, she remembered Emma and Colby. It had been a long time since she felt any hope, but she was feeling it now, and it was invigorating. As the small flicker of hope ignited deep inside, Maggie thought that perhaps her life was about to change.

She was right. Her life was going to change. But not in the way she'd hoped.

Chapter One Hundred Fourteen

The next morning, Colby showed up at Maggie's apartment again. Instead of allowing him into the apartment, she stepped out into the darkened hall.

"Colby, I really appreciate everything you've done. But you can't keep coming here. If Rock finds out you're coming here, he'll kill you," Maggie explained.

Clearly disappointed, Colby nodded. "OK. I get it. You've seen enough of me, right?"

"No. That's not it at all. I really like spending time with you, but Rock sees you as a client who comes to his apartment. If he catches you here, he might put things together and figure out that you're here to hurt him. I'm just trying to protect you and your agency," Maggie offered.

"You're right. From now on, I'll pay Armando to see you at the apartment," Colby said, and turned to leave. Before he headed down the stairs, he swung around to Maggie one more time. "Just so you know, I'm not here just for the agency. I happen to like you. I mean, I like spending time with you. I just wanted you to know that so you don't go on thinking that it's all about work."

As Colby disappeared down the stairs, Maggie stood staring at the spot where he'd been standing seconds before. His words played like a symphony in her ears...he really liked her. She stood in the hall smiling until Juju opened the door.

"Why are you standing there smiling like a goofball?" Juju asked.

"Oh, no reason...other than I think Colby likes me," Maggie sang.

"No shit. It took you this long to figure that out? I mean, really, Maggie. Are you that blind? The guy has been hanging around ogling over you for a week. He took care of me, brought you breakfast, gave us money. It shouldn't take a brick wall falling on your head before you get the message."

"What?" Maggie gasped, smiling brightly.

"There's something seriously wrong with you. Have you looked in the mirror lately?" Juju mocked.

"What?" Maggie said, giggling.

"Oh, forget it. Come back inside before someone sees you standing there and mistakes you for a crazy person with that stupid-ass grin on your face. For the record, it's obvious you like him as much as he likes you," Juju added as she walked back into the apartment.

Maggie didn't respond, but followed Juju inside.

"Who was at the door?" Seth asked.

"It was Maggie's boyfriend, Colby," Juju teased.

"Colby's not her boyfriend," Seth yelled, not wanting anyone to come between them.

Maggie didn't want Seth to feel threatened in any way and quickly agreed with him. "He's right. Colby is not my boyfriend. He's just a guy who's helping us out."

"See, Juju? You don't know everything," Seth commented, sticking his tongue out at her.

Juju got into a defensive stance. "Yeah? Come on, you little brat," she teased and proceeded to fall on top of him.

"Get off me, Juju. I'm trying to read," he said, giggling. "Aggie, tell Juju to get off me!"

"You two work out your own stuff. I have to get ready for work. I have some early appointments today," Maggie said. She enjoyed watching the two of them play.

Colby was Maggie's fourth customer that day. He came waltzing through the door and plopped down on the sofa next to her. "What's going on?" he asked.

"Ahh, work," Maggie reminded him.

"Right. Work. So about that…I was thinking maybe you can share the names of the women who work for Rock," Colby stated.

"Sure, why not?"

Maggie spent the next half hour telling Colby as much as she knew about the hookers who worked for Rock. When she finished, they sat together on the sofa, and Colby asked about Juju. When there was no more small talk left, Colby reached for Maggie's hand.

"I was thinking about that dinner I owe you," he mumbled.

"And?"

"Well, how about if we try to get away for dinner soon?" Colby asked.

Maggie angled her body toward Colby. "I'll have to let you know," she said, leaning into him closer.

Maggie felt a flurry of activity inside. Hormones were coursing through her body. Her skin was tingly, and just thinking about kissing Colby made her lips feel as though they were on fire.

Colby was fighting his own urge to kiss her. He didn't want their first kiss to be in the apartment where he had to pay to be with her for the hour. If it were ever going to happen, he wanted it to be special, so Maggie knew it was for real and not because of what she did for a living.

"OK, let me know," Colby said. He stood and walked to the door. Maggie followed him and wanted nothing more than to wrap her arms around him and hold him close.

"Will I see you tomorrow?" Maggie asked.

"Yeah, I'll be back tomorrow."

Colby's eyes were simmering with desire as he looked into hers. They both resisted the compulsion to touch the other. Finally, Colby placed his hand on the back of Maggie's neck as he tenderly pulled her closer to whisper in her ear.

"You're a really special person," he murmured.

The heat of his breath on her neck flared the passion inside of her. Then Colby left, closing the door behind him.

It was only fifteen minutes later when Maggie's next client knocked. She opened the door, still dazed from all of the emotions she was feeling about Colby.

"Hey, baby, you here for a date?" Maggie asked in a sexy voice.

"I sure am. Where's the bedroom?" the john asked.

"This way," Maggie said, leading him into the next room.

"All right, girl. You go ahead and undress while I watch ya. Then you can undress me," he said with a slimy smirk.

As Maggie removed all of her clothes and did the same for her john, revulsion replaced the good feelings she'd felt for Colby minutes earlier. The man stood naked in the middle of the bedroom. "Come on, get on your knees and suck me off," he commanded.

Maggie slowly went to her knees, all the while wanting to destroy the john who stood before her, waiting to take his pleasure. Having sex with strangers was a mechanical task that she never associated with emotion. But this time, it was different because of what she had just felt for Colby. This time she was overwhelmed with hate and resentment.

Maggie tried to make her mind go blank. She tried not to think about Colby or the boorish pig who stood in front of her, slobbering and grunting while he climaxed. But her ability to wipe her thoughts clean failed her. She wanted nothing more than to have Colby rescue her from the destructive world that was her life.

Chapter One Hundred Fifteen

On Maggie's nineteenth birthday, Detective Harker visited Rob and Lorraine. The detective popped in every year on their daughter's birthday, but this time he wanted to do more than just stop by and show his support.

"Rae, you never forget her birthday," Lorraine commented as she opened the door for him. "It's been eight years, yet you still keep coming."

"Yep, that's what I do best...I keep showing up," Rae remarked.

There was something in his voice. He wasn't quite as jovial as usual, and Lorraine recognized it immediately.

"Come on. Rob's in the living room."

"Good, because I need to talk to you two together," Detective Harker said.

Lorraine's insides twisted into a tightly wound knot. *Oh God, this is the moment we've been dreading for the last eight years. He going to tell us that Maggie is dead*, Lorraine thought.

Rob stood as soon as he saw the expression on Lorraine's face. "What happened? Did you find her?" he asked.

"No, no, it's nothing like that. I'm sorry, Lorraine. I shouldn't have done that to you," Harker said sincerely.

"Christ, you scared the shit out of me, Rae," Lorraine told him.

"Sorry about that. I have news about another child. I need your help because this kid is dealing with some serious stuff. We found her about a month ago. She'd been missing for two years. Turns out, her crack head mother sold her for some dope. Kid has been through hell. She was sexually and physically abused. Sometimes starved and sometimes left alone for days," Detective Harker began.

"That's awful. What the hell is wrong with people?" Rob asked no one in particular.

"Well, it doesn't get better. When we found her, she was pretty beat up. She stayed in the hospital for a short time until we could get her to talk to us. The kid told us that before she was sold, her mother's boyfriend used to have sex with her. So given that her mother is a loser and can't be trusted with the kid, we had to put her into the system. She's been living in an orphanage in Blue Bell," Harker explained.

"How old is she?" Lorraine asked.

"She's thirteen. Her name is Mara, and she needs your help," the detective told them.

"Our help? What do you want us to do?" Lorraine asked.

"I want you to go and talk to her. You've helped many girls just by listening. This kid is rebelling against everyone. They think she's a big problem, but I think she needs to meet people she can trust. I think you two are those people..."

Detective Harker let silence fill the room as he waited for one of them to speak.

"Well, I guess we could talk to her. I mean, I'm not completely following why you think we can make such a big difference. But OK. How about it, Rob?" Lorraine said.

"Sure, we'll try to help," Rob said slowly. "I'm with Lorraine on this one, Harker. I'm not clear as to why you want us to do this. Mara is already in the care of the state. I mean, if the psychiatrists can't help her, I'm not sure what we'll be able to do."

Detective Harker let out a sigh that sounded more like a huff. "If they can't get through to this kid, and they haven't been able to so far, she'll never get adopted. She'll spend the next five years in the system. She's been through enough. I think she deserves a chance at a decent life. Don't you?" Harker asked.

"Of course we do," Lorraine answered for both of them. "When do we meet her?"

"I've arranged for you to meet her tomorrow at the orphanage," Harker said. There was a victorious tone in his voice.

"Oh you have, have you? And how did you know we were going to agree to meet Mara?" Lorraine teased.

"Well, because I can always count on you two to help when everyone else tries to get as far away as possible. It's what makes you such great people," Harker said.

"I'll call Julie and see if Keith can go to her house after school, just in case we don't make it back home in time," Lorraine said.

Later that night, as Lorraine and Rob lay in bed, reading, Mara was six miles away thinking about how to kill herself. She didn't want it to be dramatic—just quick and painless. Her intense anger for all of the people who'd failed her was tormenting her. Mara saw no good way out of her misery, no escape from the demons that haunted her day and night. She often wished she'd never been born.

The Clarkes arrived at the orphanage ten minutes early the next morning. Detective Harker's car was already in the lot when they parked. It was a warm September day, and children were playing outside on the swings and kicking balls around in the grass. Lorraine noticed one young girl sitting alone in a corner of the brick building with her back against the wall. The child was crouched down and looked like a cobra prepared to strike at anyone who got close to her. Lorraine knew that girl was Mara.

Instead of going inside, Lorraine walked over to her. When Lorraine was five feet from the child, she crouched down in the same position, mimicking the young girl's stature.

"Are you Mara?" Lorraine asked.

The girl looked up. Her brow was furrowed, and her upper lip was raised in a foul sneer.

"My name is Lorraine. So, are you Mara?"

"Why?" the girl asked.

"Because I've come here to visit someone named Mara, and I think you look like a Mara," Lorraine explained.

"Ha. Oh yeah? What does a Mara look like?" she asked mockingly, throwing Lorraine a hateful glare.

"A Mara looks like she needs someone to cut her a break. She needs someone who can be trusted so that she doesn't have to carry the burden of her horrific past alone. A Mara looks like someone who needs a friend. She looks like someone who needs to be held and kept safe because her whole, rotten life has been nothing but a complete disaster, full of rotten, no-good people. A Mara would rather die right now than face anymore of her life alone," Lorraine said.

Angry tears streamed from Mara's eyes and dripped from the bottom of her chin.

"Can I sit next to you?" Lorraine asked.

"I guess so," Mara said sadly, beginning to soften.

Lorraine moved next to the girl and sat snuggly up against her. Then she lifted her arm and put it over Mara's shoulders. "See, I'm not so bad. You are Mara, right?"

Mara laughed through her sobs. "Yes, I'm Mara," she affirmed and continued to cry. After five minutes, while still bawling, Mara rested her head on Lorraine's shoulder.

"No one's ever taken care of me before," Mara confided.

"I know," Lorraine said.

"What do you want from me?" Mara asked.

"Nothing. I just want to sit here and hold you. I want you to know there *are* people who care about you," Lorraine said.

"Not likely," Mara responded.

"Well, I care. I'm someone," Lorraine said.

"I don't know. Just 'cause you come here once and are nice to me and all doesn't mean you care. Maybe you're getting paid to be nice to me like the other assholes around here," Mara answered brazenly.

"Oh yeah? If I'm like the rest of the assholes around here, then why do you still have your head on my shoulder? Besides, I don't work here, and I'm not getting paid by anyone to sit here with you," Lorraine countered.

Lorraine and Mara sat in the corner of the building laughing as Rob looked on from across the courtyard. His wife was such a natural with these kids, he thought, as he slowly made his way over to where the two were sitting.

"Hi," Rob yelled from afar.

"Come on over here," Lorraine yelled back.

When he reached the corner of the building, he squatted down in front of Lorraine and Mara.

"Hi, I'm Rob Clarke," he greeted, extending his hand.

Rob's formal approach struck the two of them as funny. Lorraine and Mara started to giggle, and that turned into full-blown belly laughs.

"Oh nice, nice. I'm the butt of your jokes already?" Rob kidded.

Lorraine and Mara didn't know why they were laughing so uncontrollably. Maybe it was to release the tension that had been building up inside of both of them for such a long time. Or maybe it was because they didn't know what else to do. But whatever the reason, the laughter brought the two of them closer. Even though they'd only known each other for ten minutes, they felt familiar with each other.

A couple of hours passed before Rob, Lorraine, and Mara entered the building together. Detective Harker and the others who worked at the orphanage had been sneaking glimpses of the three from a window. The doctor thought it was remarkable that the Clarkes were able to get Mara to open up so quickly. He believed there was hope that the girl could be "fixed," as he put it.

Mara gave Lorraine and Rob a hug before she left them to go to the cafeteria for lunch. When she was gone, Lorraine and Rob went to the administrative office to find Rae Harker. They found him in the hallway.

"Well, I see you made a new friend," Harker teased.

"We sure did. She's a wonderful girl, Rae. She's clever and funny. You'd never know it by looking at her serious expression," Lorraine babbled.

"That's good. Yeah, that's real good to hear, Lorraine. If we can get her help, then perhaps she'll have a chance at being placed in a foster home," Rae said casually.

"A foster home? I thought she was going to be adopted," Lorraine barked.

"First things first. If Mara gets placed in foster care, she'll have a better chance of being adopted," Harker explained.

"No! You can't put that poor little soul into another house where something bad could happen to her," Lorraine protested.

"Lorraine, foster care is progress for these kids," Harker explained.

"No, I couldn't live with myself if anything more happened to Mara. I...we...want to bring her home with us. We'll talk with Keith about it when he gets home from school. I'm sure he won't mind. After all, he'll have someone to share his chores with. If everything goes well then we can be her foster parents," Lorraine blurted out. She looked at Rob for a reaction, and he nodded at Harker.

Harker's smile lit up his face. "Yeah, that's what I figured would happen once you all met."

"Are you saying you planned for this to happen?" Lorraine asked with a smile.

"Well, let's just say I had a good feeling about the three of you," Rae said.

"All right, it's settled then. I'll call you tonight and give you a definite answer. If we're good to go, how soon would she be able to come home with us?" Lorraine asked.

"Let's go talk to the people in charge of this place and figure it all out," Rae said.

Detective Harker knew from the moment he met Mara that she and the Clarkes would hit it off—or at least, he'd hoped so. Mara desperately needed loving parents to guide her, and the Clarkes needed a daughter to help them heal. Over time, the Clarkes had seen many happy and tragic reunions between parents and their missing children. Harker doubted that they would ever see Maggie again. He also knew they wanted and needed to raise a daughter. He knew Keith was a good kid and wanted more than anything for his parents to find peace again. Detective Harker had gambled, and it had paid off big for all of them.

Just over a month later, the Clarkes picked Mara up and took her home. Mara was in awe of their modest home. Having been raised in the projects and trailer parks, the Clarkes house took her breath away. She was particularly quiet, taking in all of her new surroundings and following Lorraine around the house like a puppy.

Upstairs, Lorraine paused at the bedroom door before she opened it. As she stepped inside with Mara on her heels, she felt elated and deeply saddened. Lorraine had hoped that Maggie would be back in the bedroom someday, but she surrendered to the likelihood that Maggie would never return home.

"Wow, is this my room?" Mara asked.

"Yes," Lorraine responded with distance in her voice.

Mara looked around and noticed that the room was set up for a younger girl. The stuffed animals on the bed looked old and abandoned. "Whose room was this before?" Mara asked.

"It was my daughter's room. Her name was Maggie."

"Did Maggie die?" Mara asked, picking up on the change in Lorraine's demeanor and hoping she wasn't sleeping in a dead girl's bed.

"We don't know. She was stolen from us a long time ago."

"Oh, can I see a picture of her?"

Lorraine led Mara over to the dresser and grabbed a framed picture of Maggie that was taken just before she was kidnapped.

"She's very pretty. Look at those eyes," Mara commented.

"Yes, she was a beautiful little girl."

Lorraine realized this might all be too much for Mara, who had her own past that needed to be handled.

"Enough of this sad stuff, Mara," Lorraine blurted with a wave of her hand. "This is a happy time for all of us. Let's get you settled in, and then you and I can cook dinner together. Sound good?"

Mara's smile lit up the entire room. "Wow. Really? That would be great."

Lorraine was delighted. "OK. Well, I'll let you look around your room. We haven't changed anything since Maggie was here. I was thinking you and I could give it new paint. You can pick the color, of course, and then we can buy some cool posters to decorate it—you know, make it more suitable for a cool thirteen-year-old like yourself," she said with enthusiasm.

"I would love that," Mara said, excited.

Lorraine walked to the bedroom door. Just before she left, Mara called out her name.

"Yes?"

"If Maggie comes home, will I still be able to stay here with you?" Mara asked, fearful of losing the only good thing she'd ever had in her life.

"Are you kidding? Absolutely, you'd stay. Maggie would have loved you," Lorraine stated, realizing with a stab of guilt that she had just spoken about her daughter in the past tense.

After Lorraine went downstairs, Mara sprawled out on the bed. She looked up at the ceiling and smiled, happy about her good fortune. Mara's thoughts drifted to Maggie, a girl she'd never met, and she wondered if Maggie had been tormented the way she had been for so long. But Mara could never imagine how much worse Maggie's life had been, compared with her own.

Chapter One Hundred Sixteen

By Halloween that year, Maggie and Colby had worked out a routine that allowed them more time together. Two nights a week, Colby would go to Doubles and pay for a lap dance with her. Inside the semiprivate stall, Maggie would reveal secrets of the many girls working for Rock.

Although their attraction to each other continued to grow, neither of them pursued intimacy. In Rock's apartment, it seemed inappropriate to Colby to show his affection for Maggie. At Doubles, Maggie kept a cool space between them, since Jay, the bar manager, didn't tolerate any kind of sexual contact with the clients, not even kissing. She'd never make the first move anyway. Even though Maggie was experienced in having sex, she'd never kissed anyone passionately.

After almost two months of meeting in the lap dance room, Colby did what she had hoped he'd do. "Um, I was wondering. When you're done with your shift here on Wednesday, could I take you for that spaghetti dinner I promised you? You get done at seven on Wednesday night, right?"

"Yeah, seven. I'm working the early shift," she answered awkwardly.

"Well?" he asked.

"Well, what?" she responded.

"What about dinner?"

"Oh! Right. Yeah, I'd like to go out to dinner," Maggie answered, hoping he was asking her for a real date.

"Good. Then I'll pick you up at your apartment around eight o'clock?" Colby asked.

"That's probably not a good idea. I'll take the bus to the Melrose Diner, and you can pick me up there. Do you know where it is?"

"Sure, I do. I love the Melrose. Everyone who knows, goes to the Melrose," he recited, like a total geek.

"So I've heard…from the waitress who works there, who is, oh, I don't know, about a hundred years old," Maggie teased.

"Are you calling me old?"

"No, I'm just saying that if anyone else heard what you just said, they might think you're a nerd—you know, a dweeb, dork, dink, wonk…pick whichever one you like best," she joked, pushing her fingers through his hair.

Whenever Maggie and Colby had any type of physical contact, they shared a sensation that was as addictive as a needle full of heroin to a street junkie.

"I'm none of those things. I'm the coolest dude you've ever met. Don't try to pretend like you don't know it, either. That's exactly why you hang with me. You're cool by association," he sang.

"Oh, right. I'm cool by association? That's a joke," Maggie teased.

"Well, Ms. Cool, I need to head out. Your doorman over there," Colby said, gesturing to the man who sat by the door of the lap dance room collecting payment and keeping an eye out for the girls' safety, "just gave me the 'time's up' sign."

Maggie stood and walked back into the bar with Colby.

"So I'll see you on Wednesday night," Colby confirmed, as if Maggie could possibly forget.

"Yep. I'll see you at the Melrose."

Maggie headed back downstairs to change into a different outfit for her next set. As she entered the dressing room, Montana gave her venomous look.

"Oh, girls, look…it's Ms. Cool. At least that's what I heard her little boyfriend call her when I was in the lap dance room," she said sharply and began to laugh.

"Well, Montana, it's just a shame that you aren't capable of actually connecting with a man," Maggie shot back.

"Girl, you're a damn fool. You think that guy is actually interested in being serious with you? They all tell us what we want to hear to get what they want. You are stupider than you look," Montana screeched.

Maggie walked over to her own chair, sat down, and stared at herself in the mirror. Was Montana right? Was Colby playing her?

"Earth to Maggie," Emma said.

Maggie turned to her and smiled.

Emma stood with her hands on her hips. "Don't let that fuckin' bitch get inside your head. She doesn't know shit about shit. Montana is a jealous, crazy whore. Does that guy you were with tonight want you to dance for him?"

"Emma, that's Colby, and the answer is no, he doesn't want me to dance for him. He only wants to talk to me. I know him from Kensington," Maggie said.

"He must really like you if he pays you to sit there and talk to him," Emma reasoned.

"I guess," Maggie said with a smile.

"What?" Emma shot back.

"He's taking me to dinner on Wednesday night," Maggie announced.

"Aw, Mags, that's great. Are you excited?" Emma asked.

"More than you'll ever know. But Emma, there's this thing about what I do for a living that keeps nagging at me. How can a normal guy get past that?" Maggie whined.

"You won't believe the shit guys will get past if they're into you. Just go with it. Is this the first real date you've ever had?" Emma asked.

Maggie blushed. "Yeah."

"What are you gonna wear? That's what you need to be worrying about," Emma said.

"I don't know. I mean I haven't thought about that. I don't really have anything. I have my costumes for here, and I have my clothes for the men I entertain in Rock's apartment..."

Maggie's voice trailed off as she began to think through her wardrobe. "The clothes I wear when I'm not working are crap. I don't have anything that's decent. Ugh. Now what?"

"I'm sure I have something you can borrow," Emma offered.

"Are you kidding me? You do?" Maggie asked excitedly.

"Yeah, I do. You know, you worry too much. It's gonna give ya wrinkles, and then I'll have to find another hot bitch to do my dance routine with," Emma said.

"Ha! I'm about the only one in this place willing to dance with the likes of you. Not to mention, kiss you with that smelly breath of yours," Maggie poked.

The two girls laughed as they got ready to go back onstage. Emma's life had been full of people who hurt her, and it was nice to know a person who never expected anything from her but friendship. She was happy that she could help Maggie.

Emma felt a surge of peace when she was with Maggie, and she wondered if the young, dark-haired, blue-eyed beauty would ever find her way out of the life she was living.

Chapter One Hundred Seventeen

———————■———————

The next evening, Emma brought Maggie a beautiful, black dress for her date with Colby. When she pulled it out of her bag, Maggie gasped. "This is incredible, Emma."

"It was a gift from a guy I know," she said. "Try it on."

Maggie put the dress on and stared at herself in the mirror. She looked stunning. The dress was strapless, fitted through the bodice to accentuate her breasts and the skirt flared dramatically. The layers of expensive chiffon fell around Maggie's hips and graduated to longer lengths. The hem stopped just below her thigh, showing off Maggie's long, lean legs.

"This is gorgeous, but I can't wear it," Maggie said.

"Why can't you wear it? The dress looks like it was made for you," Emma said.

"But if anything happens to it, I can never pay you for it. This must've cost a fortune," Maggie said, thinking that it must have cost at least one hundred dollars.

Emma shook her head and smiled. It was a Gucci dress, and the price was well over six thousand dollars. At the time, she'd been stunned. But Salvatore, the man who bought the dress for her, didn't even blink when he handed the sales clerk his credit card.

"Stop worrying all the time. Who the fuck cares how much it cost? I got a great deal on it, and if anything happens to it…well, it's only a dress. Seriously, Mags. You need to get a grip on yourself. You worry about small shit. So what shoes are you going to wear with it?" Emma asked, trying to change the subject.

Maggie let out a small yelp. "OK, I'll wear it, then. I was thinking about wearing my patent leather shoes," she finished, as she dug through her bag for the heels.

Maggie slipped the five-inch heels onto her feet and looked at herself in the mirror. Emma walked up behind her and peered over her shoulder. "You look like a model. You're truly stunning, Mags. Colby's gonna lose his shit when he gets a load of you," she said.

Maggie met Emma's eyes in the mirror. "Thanks, Emma. You're a good friend."

"Ugh, none of that sappy stuff," Emma teased her. "Besides, maybe someday I'll need a favor."

On Wednesday night, Maggie stood outside the Melrose, waiting for Colby to pick her up. Everyone who walked by her turned to steal a glimpse of the raving beauty. When Colby pulled up, he scooted out of the car and went to her side quickly.

"My God, Maggie. You look beautiful," he said.

Maggie blushed. "Thanks."

There was a pregnant pause until Maggie said, "You look great, too."

Colby chuckled. "Well, we'd better get going. I made reservations for eight thirty."

"Where are we going?" Maggie asked.

"I'm taking you to Ralph's. It's the oldest Italian restaurant in the United States. I promised you a good spaghetti dinner, and I never break my promises," Colby said.

Maggie hadn't had a meal that divine since she was taken from her family. She loved Ralph's.

Colby leaned into Maggie and her body tingled all over. "I love this place," he said. "I hope you're glad you came."

"Oh my God, the spaghetti is so good. Almost as good as my mom's," she said mindlessly.

The comment about her mother made them both pause for a moment. She hadn't associated anything in her life with her family until now. It left her feeling empty, and Colby was quick to pick up the conversation.

"So, who's Seth staying with tonight?"

Maggie rubbed her bloated belly. "He's at the apartment alone, but Juju will get home around ten o'clock. He's pretty independent for his age. Not that he has a choice. Juju and I both have to work if we want to live in that Dumpster of ours."

Colby leaned over and put his arm around the back of her chair. "You're a kind person, Maggie. Not many people would've taken on the burden of a child that wasn't theirs."

"Seth is mine. I've had him since he was four years old. He was just a baby. Poor little guy has been through a lot. We both have. But in the end, we have each other," Maggie said.

Colby kissed Maggie on the cheek. The intimate setting of the restaurant made her feel like she was someone other than herself, someone normal. For a moment, she got lost in the feeling that she was free to do as she pleased. But soon enough, the image of Rock popped into her head, bringing her back to her present circumstances, and she felt powerless. The realization that she didn't even have the freedom to love a man shattered her mood.

Maggie edged away from Colby to put some distance between them.

Sensing that something was wrong, Colby shifted away from her. "I'm sorry. Did I say something that upset you?"

"No, it's just that this whole spaghetti dinner was great and all, but at the end of the day, I still sell my body to other men. I mean, I know you would never be with someone like me, but sometimes I get the feeling that you want to be closer..." She let the words swirl in the air.

"You're right. I do want to get closer to you," Colby admitted.

"That isn't going to happen, Colby," Maggie informed him.

"Why? Why can't it happen?" he asked sadly.

"I just told you why. Because my life doesn't belong to me. Just imagine seeing other men coming or going when you come to visit me at Rock's apartment. How would you be able to handle that?"

"I don't know that I could," Colby confessed.

"Well, that's exactly why nothing can happen between us," she said firmly.

"You might be right. But this can't be your life forever, Maggie. At some point, you have to get away from all of this. You're a beautiful, smart woman. You deserve better, and the sooner you begin to break away, the quicker you'll have a life of your own," Colby said.

"Are you here to rescue me?" Maggie countered. She looked at him warmly. "No, you aren't, because we both know there's more to it than just walking away from all of it. I'd need protection, and so would Juju,

Seth, and my family. For now, it's just too difficult. Someday, maybe, but not now."

Colby knew that she was right. Now was not the time. But soon, he hoped, the agency would bring Rock and his crew down, and Maggie would finally be free.

"You're right. Now isn't the right time. But that's what we're working to fix. You and I will bring these assholes to their knees, and then you'll have your chance to be and do whatever you want. I promise you that, and I—"

"Never break a promise," Maggie recited, finishing his sentence for him.

"That's right. I never break a promise," Colby said with certainty.

On the bus back to Kensington, Maggie realized that she'd fooled herself into believing that she was capable of having a relationship. Her desire to live a normal life and to be with Colby had muddied her judgment. During dinner, as Maggie observed the other "normal" couples sitting around them, she'd had a moment of clarity and knew she couldn't put Colby in danger with Rock. It was in that fleeting moment that Maggie decided to push Colby away until the day came when her life was her own. Then she wondered if that day would ever exist.

Chapter One Hundred Eighteen

———————◼———————

W hen Maggie walked into her apartment later that night, the scene was chaotic. Juju was crouched over Seth, who was hugging the toilet and barfing violently.

Maggie rushed into the small bathroom. "What's wrong?"

"I don't know. When I got home, he was complaining that he felt sick to his stomach and was cold and achy. Then, all of a sudden, he got out of bed and ran in here," Juju explained.

Maggie took over and knelt beside Seth as he continued to throw up. She stayed with him until he felt well enough to get back into bed.

"I'm freezin' Aggie," Seth told her through chattering teeth.

Maggie knew he had a fever. She could tell by how hot he was when she helped him back to the mattress. "Does anything else bother you?" she asked as she layered shabby blankets and towels over him.

"My whole body hurts," he cried, "and my throat feels puffed up inside."

"Juju, can you get the aspirin out of the drawer?" Maggie asked.

It wasn't until two hours later that Seth finally settled down and went to sleep.

"What do you think is wrong with him?" Juju finally asked.

"He's got the flu. I sure as hell hope the two of us don't get it. That jerk-off, Rock, would probably make us work even if we were on our deathbeds," Maggie remarked.

Juju giggled. "Yeah, he's such a dick. Hell, he made me work right after he cut off my fingers. I quickly became known as the eight-fingered dealer."

At that statement, Maggie stopped what she was doing and looked at Juju.

"You're so freakin' sick," Maggie bantered.

The two girls fell into laughter, and eventually Maggie told Juju about her dinner with Colby.

"So you really like him, don't you?" Juju asked.

"Yeah, I do. But there's no way I can get with somebody now. Colby admitted he wouldn't be able to handle knowing the stuff I have to do for a living. I can't blame him," Maggie said a bit defensively.

"Hey," Juju said, holding up her hands, "I'm not judging anyone. I'm a gay, eight-fingered, drug dealer. Need I say more? Judging ain't my thing," she teased.

"Yeah, speaking of gay, how's that girl you met? Are you still into her?"

Juju's face brightened. "Oh, I'm into her, all right. I think I'm falling in love, actually. She's smokin' hot. She's knows I ain't ever gotten with anyone yet, and she's not pressuring me or nothing. We hook up, but I'm proud to say we haven't done it yet," Juju offered.

"So, when do I get to meet her?" Maggie asked.

"Not until I know it's serious. Plus, it feels kind of weird, like I'm bringin' her home to meet 'mom' or something," Juju joked.

"Whatever, you smelly brat. You're so nasty. I would love to meet her when you're ready. I'm not trying to rush you, and it doesn't bother me a bit that you have another life that Seth and I know nothing about. Or that you're out with some strange woman who could be a rapist or a serial killer. Nope, doesn't bother me one little bit," Maggie sang.

"Ugh. OK, well, I'll see how it goes," Juju said.

Maggie turned serious. "Did she say anything about your hands?"

"Oh, you mean the fact that one day I showed up and only had eight fingers left? She sorta freaked the fuck out the first time she saw it. But she knows I deal, and she knows all about Rock. So, I think she's cool with it now; probably cooler with it than I am," she said regretfully.

That night, as Maggie lay on the mattress next to Seth, she thought about Colby. She hoped to be in love someday and even have a family. Then her thoughts floated to Rock, and the peaceful feeling washed away in a wave of anger. She had a chance at love with Colby, and in her mind, Rock was forcing her to pass it up. She boiled over with hatred toward Rock for the things he'd done to all of them. Then her eagerness to help Colby shut Rock down swelled inside of her, and it made her feel powerful. Maggie was getting her first little taste of sweet revenge.

To Maggie's disappointment, Seth was still burning up with fever the next morning. He was no longer vomiting, mainly because there was nothing left in him to vomit. He continued to complain about nausea, though. Over the years, Maggie had read several medical books. She knew that if Seth had the flu, his body would eventually heal itself. However, his suffering was unbearable for her, and she decided to make him as comfortable as possible.

"Juju?" Maggie said loudly to wake her up.

"Wha...what? What time is it?" Juju grumbled.

"It doesn't matter what time it is. Seth feels like crap, and I need you to run down to the store and buy a couple of things. Come on, hurry and get dressed," Maggie said.

By the time Juju left the apartment, Maggie was holding Seth up in a hot shower. He was complaining of body pain and a terrible head-ache. "I feel like there's a rat in my head sticking his teeth into my brain," Seth said.

"I know baby. We're gonna make you feel better," Maggie consoled him.

Just then, Juju walked through the apartment door, "I got all the shit on your list. Now can I go back to sleep?"

"No, I need your help."

Juju warmed a cup of water and mixed in the salt and baking soda, just as Maggie had instructed. When Maggie filled the bulb syringe with the liquid, Juju's eyes grew wide. "Ew, what are you going to do with that?"

"We're going to irrigate his nose," Maggie said nonchalantly.

"I'm not doing squat with that thing," Juju said, taking a step away from the syringe as if it had cooties.

Maggie gave her a scolding look. "I need you to help him sit up and hold him still for me. Jesus, Juju, don't be such a freak," she added.

Seth cried and struggled as Maggie shot the lukewarm solution up his nose, but he was too weak to fight both girls, and he finally gave in. When they were finished, Maggie applied a warm, damp towel to his head and continued to do so throughout the day. She had hoped that he would improve by the next morning and was surprised when he said that he felt the same as he had the night before.

Each morning during Seth's illness, Maggie left Juju at the apartment and she walked to his school. First, she'd meet Joey for a few minutes and then she'd let the school administrator know that Seth was ill. She was trying to prevent the school from calling Rock to report Seth's absence. To her disappointment, the administrator showed no sign of caring that Seth wasn't well and that he would miss school.

Six long days later, Seth still couldn't get out of bed. That's when Maggie lost her cool. Her stomach was in knots, and she couldn't get Seth out of her mind for a minute. She felt utterly helpless, just as she had so many years ago whenever John William would take Seth away from her for several hours. Quickly, her concern turned to unchecked worrying, which was driving Juju and her crazy.

"I don't understand it, Juju," Maggie whispered in the bathroom behind the closed door. "He should be getting better. He still has a fever. I think he needs to see a doctor, but the only one we know who can see him without asking a bunch of questions is Dr. Purse. But you know what that means, right?" Maggie asked.

"Yeah, we have to ask that dipshit, Rock, to help us out. I think we should wait a little. I mean, at least Seth can eat a tiny bit of food now. He stopped throwing up, and his nausea is a lot less. I think we should give it a couple more days. If he still has a fever, then maybe we can talk to Rock about taking Seth to Dr. Purse," Juju said.

Maggie gave it careful thought before she responded. "OK, we'll give it two more days. If his fever doesn't start to go down, I'm going to talk to Rock."

"He's such a dick," Juju commented.

"I know he is, but we have to do whatever it takes to make sure Seth gets better," Maggie mumbled, more to herself than to Juju.

Maggie worried about the price they'd have to pay for asking Rock for another favor. Then she lay on the mattress next to Seth and stroked his hair while she hummed "Rock-a-Bye Baby" softly in his ear as he drifted deeper into sleep.

Chapter One Hundred Nineteen

———————————◼———————————

Two days later, Seth was sitting upright and joking with Maggie and Juju. After nine days, his high fever had finally broken that morning. The girls were relieved to see him feeling better. He looked weak and frail, but Maggie knew that with food and rest, he'd feel better within days.

"Fuck, man, I'm glad Seth feels better. I was really worried about him," Juju finally admitted.

"I know. These past nine days have really sucked. Between work and taking care of Seth, I'm totally beat. All I want to do is sleep," Maggie commented.

Slowly, Seth was beginning to feel himself again. He went back to school, and he even surprised the girls one evening by heating up frozen pizza for dinner. He'd been getter stronger, and on the third day after his recovery, Joey showed up at the apartment in the late morning.

Maggie answered the door. "Joey? What are you doing here? Why aren't you in school?"

The young girl looked pale and nervous. "Seth is sick. He fell down in the hall on his way to math class. I couldn't wake him up. The nurse came and got him, and he's in her office. You need to come now 'cause they don't have a phone number to call you. The nurse asked me to come and get you."

Maggie shot out the door, still in her pajamas, and ran to the school with Joey. In the nurse's office, Seth was lying on a small cot. Maggie rushed over to him.

"Are you OK? What happened?"

"I'm fine, Aggie. I just got really tired, and then I was asleep in the hallway," Seth reported.

"He passed out," the nurse, Mrs. Booker, interjected. "Went completely unconscious, but he tells me that he was pretty sick the last week or so," she stated as she did a quick assessment of Maggie. Exceptionally exquisite was what ran through Mrs. Booker's thoughts as she gave Maggie the once-over.

"Yeah, he had the flu for over a week. He wasn't able to eat or drink much. He's been feeling better over the last three days," Maggie explained.

Mrs. Booker considered the information. "Maybe he's just dehydrated. I think you should take him home and make sure he eats and drinks lots and lots of fluids. I want you to buy Gatorade on the way home. That will work well for him."

Mrs. Booker paused. She watched Maggie stroking Seth's hair. The nurse had seen a lot over the last twenty years…broken families, abusive parents, unruly children. But she was intrigued by the genuine love and adoration Seth and Maggie seemed to have for one another. *It's refreshing to see a brother and sister so close*, Mrs. Booker thought. There were so many unhappy people in Kensington—many born into the hardness of poverty. Hopelessness and joblessness were the mantras in this town, and those two factors often brought out the worst in people.

Mrs. Booker had seen Maggie on the streets about a year ago, hooking. Maggie had a look and grace about her that was hard to miss and impossible to forget. The nurse figured that Maggie was prostituting to keep a roof over Seth's head. With that, Mrs. Booker knew very well, came heartache and pain.

Mrs. Booker watched as Maggie mothered the sick child. *How lucky the boy is to have a sister with so much compassion*, she decided. The nurse cleared her throat, and Maggie looked over at her. Mrs. Booker motioned with her index finger for Maggie to follow her into a tiny office. She closed the door behind them and turned to Maggie.

"I want you to take this," Mrs. Booker said, handing Maggie ten dollars.

Maggie's eyes revealed her embarrassment and relief. "Thank you."

"You're welcome. Now, I want you to buy him Gatorade and make sure he eats, too. I can see that the two of you are very close. He's lucky to have a big sister like you," Mrs. Booker commented.

"Seth's the most important person in my life. I'd do anything for him," Maggie said.

Mrs. Booker softly patted Maggie on the shoulder. "You're a sweet girl. You listen to me: if Seth has any more problems, I want you to come back and see me. Keep a close eye on him. I took his temperature, and he doesn't have fever, so I really think he is just dehydrated. If there's anything I can do to help, you come and see me, hear?"

Maggie nodded. Before leaving the nurse's office with Seth, Maggie said, "Mrs. Booker?"

"Yes, dear?"

"Thanks for being so kind to us," Maggie said.

It was rare for Maggie to encounter people who thrived on helping others. In Kensington, people were more likely to go out of their way to harm or exploit people.

"No problem. Now you take care of this little man," Mrs. Booker commented, gently stroking the top of Seth's head.

Maggie and Seth walked slowly back to their apartment. The autumn air was crisp. Seth was lethargic, and his movements were calculated, as if every step he took was painful.

"Seth? Are you OK, sweetie?"

Seth nodded. "I'm just tired is all. I wanna go home and get in bed."

The two stopped at a convenience store and bought Gatorade with the ten dollars that Mrs. Booker had given to Maggie. Once home, Maggie settled Seth onto the mattress, and he quickly fell into a deep sleep. About an hour later, Juju came home and, seeing Seth in bed, gave Maggie a curious look.

"Joey came and got me. Seth passed out at school. The nurse thinks he's dehydrated from being sick for so long. She said to let him rest and make sure he drinks enough. I have clients lined up, starting at two o'clock this afternoon, and my shift at Doubles starts at eight o'clock. Will you be able to be here with him tonight?" Maggie asked.

"Sure. I'll go out earlier today. Once I make my quota, I'll come right back and stay with him. What should I do for him?" Juju asked with apprehension, remembering the bulb syringe that Maggie had stuck up Seth's nose.

"Just make sure he eats something and drinks a lot. I'm sure he'll feel better in the morning," Maggie said.

When Maggie got home at three in the morning, Juju was waiting for her. She looked over as Maggie entered the apartment. Her face was a mask of worry.

"What's wrong?" Maggie asked.

"I don't know, Maggie. Seth started shaking on the mattress, and his eyes were rolling back in his head."

As if it was planned, Seth began to jerk on the mattress again. It looked as if someone was seizing his shoulders and shaking him. Maggie rushed over and sat next to Seth. She gently rubbed his arms, and she knew immediately what was happening.

Juju's eyes were bulging from their sockets. She stood watching with her arms wrapped around herself. "That's what he was doing... what's wrong with him?"

Maggie tried to keep her voice even so she wouldn't reveal the panic that was rising in her chest. "He's having a seizure. Just relax. He's going to be fine. Wet a towel and bring it over to me," Maggie instructed calmly.

Juju sprang to action, grateful there was something she could do to help. By the time she walked over to the mattress with the damp towel, Seth's seizure had ceased.

Maggie took the towel and gently wiped Seth's face and neck. He looked at her through tired eyes. "What's wrong with me, Aggie? I'm scared," he muttered weakly.

"You're going to be OK, sweetie. I'm here, and you're going to be fine," Maggie fussed.

Then Seth looked at her with confused and disoriented eyes. Maggie lifted his thin, long body and placed him on his side, to keep his airway open. A few minutes later, he was sleeping again.

Juju was horrified as she watched Maggie. "What the fuck, Maggie? What are we going to do? There's obviously something really wrong with him, right?"

Maggie looked up at Juju. "Yeah, something's wrong. We're not going to panic...that would just freak him out," she whispered.

"But what are we going to do?" Juju insisted.

"We're going to wait and see how things go. Just remember to stay close to him when it happens. You wanna be sure he doesn't hurt himself if he has another seizure."

Maggie got up and went into the cramped bathroom. Only then did she let herself cry, releasing all of the anxiety and dread that had gripped her. When she came back into the living area, her eyes were bloodshot and her face looked as if it were made of stone.

"You all right?" Juju inquired, taking in her friend's expression.

"I'm fine, Juju. It's Seth I'm worried about."

Chapter One Hundred Twenty

J ust as quickly as Seth's symptoms began, they stopped. The next morning, he was feeling much better. He was still zapped of energy, but his spirits were better, and he had some color in his face. The girls were slightly relieved but still cautious.

"I want you to stay in bed and rest today," Maggie told Seth.

"No, Aggie. I wanna go to school. I wanna see Joey. Besides, I feel better now," Seth insisted, nuzzling into her for a warm hug.

"You're a real charmer, aren't you?" Maggie said cheerfully, as she pulled him closer.

"Yeah, the other boys hate me 'cause all the girls love me," Seth remarked.

"Oh, really?" Maggie teased.

"Yeah, but ya know, I love Joey. I told ya, someday I'm gonna marry her," Seth said.

"You're twelve, Seth. It's a little too soon to talk about marriage. Besides, you need to do well in school. You want to go to college, don't you?" Maggie pressed.

"You didn't have to go to college," Seth protested.

"That's because I couldn't, and you know that. But it's different for you. You'll have the freedom to do whatever you want," Maggie reminded him.

"Well, once I'm bigger, I'm gonna kick Rock's ass so you can do whatever you want too," Seth said valiantly.

"Nah, I'll be a wrinkled-up old woman by then. Rock will be running away from me," Maggie kidded. "You go to college so you can get really rich, and then I'll come and live with you. How's that sound?"

Seth's face lit up like fireworks on the Fourth of July. "Yeah, I like that. We'll live together forever."

499

Maggie gave him a tight embrace. "You're the best man in my life," she whispered.

Seth gave her a Herculean squeeze and walked into the bathroom to get ready for school.

That night, while in the lap dance room with Colby, Maggie let her guard down and told him about Seth. Tears dribbled down her cheeks as she expressed her concern over his freakish symptoms. "I think he needs to see a doctor. I mean, he felt better today, but who knows? He had seizures, and I know that's just not normal," Maggie explained.

Colby listened, and his heart ached for them. Then he came up with an idea. "You said the nurse at Seth's school told you to go see her if there were any more issues, right?"

"Yeah, but there's only so much she can do," Maggie responded.

"How do you know? If she can draw his blood, I can get it tested. All you need to do is convince her to take blood and give you the vials. Then I'll bring the blood to a friend of mine who works in a lab. That way, you'll know what you're dealing with. How does that sound?"

"That sounds incredibly nice of you. OK, I'll do whatever it takes. You'll get me everything for the blood test, right?"

"You bet I will. Just so you know, this isn't the norm. I would never do this kind of thing for other informants I've worked with in the past," Colby said.

"So now I'm just another informant," Maggie said, smiling brightly, knowing it was far from the truth.

"Nah, you're just my best-looking informant," he teased.

Two days later, Maggie and Juju walked Seth to school. They stopped for a few minutes to chat with Joey and watched as the two walked into the school together. Maggie and Juju waited until they entered the school, and then they went directly to the nurse's office.

"Hello, Maggie," Mrs. Booker said, giving her a warm smile, and then concern washed it away. "How are you? Is Seth OK?"

Maggie returned the woman's smile. "Seth seems to be better than he was two days ago. But we're a little worried." She gestured at Juju. "Oh, I'm sorry; this is my roommate, Juju."

Juju said a quick hello and turned back to Maggie, who continued speaking.

"He had a couple of seizures the night he came home sick from school. He hasn't had any more since then, and he says he feels better, but I'm worried. It's not normal to have seizures, right?" Maggie said nervously, already knowing the answer.

Mrs. Booker was silent for a moment. When she spoke, her voice was calm and even. "There could be many reasons why someone would have seizures: epilepsy, high fevers, a bad infection, or something like a tapeworm. I don't want to jump to any conclusions. How else has he been feeling?"

Maggie rattled off his symptoms. "He's very tired all the time. He has night sweats, and then he's freezing cold. He's been complaining that his body hurts him...you know, like when you have a fever and get achy all over."

Mrs. Booker nodded. "I'm not a doctor, but it sounds like our Seth is showing signs of mononucleosis. You'll need to take him to your doctor and have a blood test done to know for sure."

Maggie sat down in one of the two chairs in the office and put her head in her hands. After gathering her courage, she looked up at the nurse. "Mrs. Booker, we don't have a doctor. I'm sure you can appreciate that we are on our own. We don't have the money to afford a luxury like a doctor."

Maggie paused, letting her words sink in, before she spoke again. "I do have a good friend who knows someone who works at a lab. He can get Seth's blood tested if someone can take his blood." Maggie sat back and watched as Mrs. Booker processed exactly what was being asked of her. Maggie silently prayed, *Please God, let her help us; please God, let her help us.*

Mrs. Booker sat behind her desk and stared down at the neat pile of papers in front of her. She'd done a lot to help the children of Kensington over the years, but nothing like this. This would be the first time she would do something that wasn't legal. She pondered that thought for a moment. Was it illegal? Then she shook her head to bring herself back into the present.

"I've never done anything like this before, Maggie. I don't have the tools to draw his blood," Mrs. Booker said.

Maggie opened her purse and pulled out a needle and three vials. She laid them on Mrs. Booker's desk and sat back in her chair.

"I won't ask who gave these to you," the nurse said.

"They came from the lab," Maggie responded. "They're all sealed, so they're sterile," she pointed out.

"Yes, I see that. Listen, honey. I haven't drawn blood in a long time. I'm not going to be very good at it," the nurse stated, feeling ashamed the second the words left her mouth.

Mrs. Booker wanted to help children. That was why she chose to be a school nurse in Kensington. She'd received other offers in affluent school districts in the suburbs, but her need to help the less privileged made her accept the offer in the shit hole town of Kensington.

"Don't worry about it. Just do your best. Look, Mrs. Bookman—" Juju said.

"Booker, it's Mrs. Booker," Maggie corrected.

"Right, Mrs. Booker. We need your help, and there ain't nobody else around this place we can ask. You're all we got, so if you don't help us, we're fucked," Juju said.

Mrs. Booker was amused by Juju's brutal honesty.

"So, let me get this straight. You need me draw Seth's blood, give you the vials, and not say anything to anyone about what I'm doing?" Mrs. Booker asked.

The girls nodded in unison. Maggie added, "We're just asking you to cut us a break. All we're trying to do is make sure that Seth is getting whatever he needs to feel better. That's all…"

"OK, fine. But don't you girls make me regret doing this. Don't breathe a word to anyone, you hear? Not even your friend in the lab," Mrs. Booker stated.

The girls lit up. "You got it," Juju confirmed. "We'll take the secret to our fuckin' graves."

Mrs. Booker smiled at both girls. She was doing something completely out of character, even for her. But she was certain that she was doing it for the right people.

Mrs. Booker picked up the phone. "Can you please send Seth down to my office?"

Chapter One Hundred Twenty-One

----------------◼----------------

Maggie and Juju stood in the nurse's office while Mrs. Booker drew Seth's blood.

"Why do I have to do this?" Seth complained.

"Because you may need medicine to take care of whatever it is you got," Juju fired back.

Seth had a death grip on Maggie's hand as Mrs. Booker inserted the needle. To her disappointment, she missed the vein. "Damn it," the school nurse breathed. "Sorry, Seth. Hold on. Mrs. Booker is a little rusty."

Seth wiggled in his seat and looked at Maggie with eyes that screamed, *Get me out of here!*

"It's OK, Mrs. Booker. He's OK," Maggie said, giving Seth a look that screamed, *Sit still, or I'm going to really make you squirm!*

Seth closed his eyes and bit down. He felt the needle go in again and waited for what seemed an eternity. Then he heard, "Got it!"

Seth opened his eyes as the blood gushed into the vial, and he watched Mrs. Booker fill the other vials with his blood. When it was finished, he looked at Mrs. Booker. "When I grow up, I wanna be a nurse like you," he said with a smile.

Mrs. Booker smiled back at him and patted his knee. "When you grow up, you can be anything you want to be. All you have to do is focus on what you want and believe. Put in the work, and it'll pay off. Trust me, sweetheart," the nurse confirmed.

Once Seth went back to his classroom, Mrs. Booker handed the vials of blood to Maggie. "OK, here you go. Remember not tell anyone I did this for you. I could lose my job, which in itself doesn't worry me as much as I would worry about some of these kids if I wasn't here to keep an eye on them," Mrs. Booker stated.

"That's not a problem." Maggie lowered her eyes to the floor and then looked up at Mrs. Booker again. "Thank you. I know what we asked you to do for us is a big deal. Juju and I just want Seth to get better, that's all."

"Of course you do, and so do I. Now, go on and get those vials to the lab," Mrs. Booker instructed, touched by Maggie's sincerity.

Maggie and Juju left the school and got on a bus that would take them into the city, to the Melrose Diner. They saw Colby walking down the street toward the diner long before he saw them. Maggie reached into her purse and pulled out the brown lunch bag in which the vials were stored. As he approached, Maggie walked to him and hugged him, her hand holding the bag in the center of her body. She pressed the bag into his stomach, and he reached in, squeezed the bag, and put it into the pocket of his leather jacket.

"How long?" Maggie asked.

"I don't know. I'll find out when I bring them the vials. I suspect no longer than a week to get the results," Colby responded.

There was no small talk between them that day. The tight lines around Maggie's eyes were a dead giveaway that she was stressed out. It wasn't easy to ask normal, everyday people for favors, as she had the school nurse. It was even harder knowing that at any moment, someone could make her life a living hell by telling Rock about all of the sneaking around she was doing.

Maggie said, "Thanks. I'll see you soon," meaning that she'd see him at Rock's apartment or at Doubles.

Juju raised her hand and gave Colby a small wave before they walked back to wait for the bus to take them into Kensington.

Sitting next to each other on the bus, Maggie focused on the hum of the bus wheels rolling forward against the road as she thought about Seth. The thought of him brought warm feelings of love and connection. He was a sweet child and so protective of Maggie and Juju. He was growing up to be a really nice guy. She felt a jab of pride knowing it was she, and to a certain degree, Juju, who had instilled in Seth the qualities that would make him a man worth knowing.

Suddenly, the thought of Joey popped into her head, and she felt deep gratitude to the young girl for keeping an eye on Seth. *Maybe Seth is right*, Maggie thought. *Maybe someday he and Joey will get married.*

Chapter One Hundred Twenty-Two

———————◼———————

At Doubles a few days later, Maggie gave Emma an update on Seth's condition.

"Well, it's good you're getting his blood checked. How has he been feeling for the last few days?" Emma asked.

Emma knew what it was like to be a teenager with way too much responsibility; she quickly remembered how difficult life could be.

"He's been good, seems to be getting back to normal," Maggie said with relief.

"You know, girl, you're nineteen years old, and you're gonna need to decide what you wanna do with your life. Look, you're one smart cookie. None of these other nitwits know the kind of shit you know. You kept yourself educated...that's cool shit," Emma offered.

"Well, I read a lot, that's for sure, but it doesn't mean I'm educated. It just means I'm informed," Maggie said.

"Bullshit! Go get your damn GED and go to college, just like you told Seth to do," Emma said.

"It's not that simple, Em. Sure, I could get my GED, but Rock would never let me go to college. It's not like I have any money to pay for it, anyway," Maggie argued, her voice trailing off.

"Rock's a brainless dildo! I want you to listen real good to what I'm about to tell you. If there ever comes a day when you can't handle Rock, then you need to talk to Tony and Vincent. I don't know if they could help you, but if there was ever a chance for someone to go up against that piece of stank dog shit, it's the two of them. You hear me?" Emma said.

Maggie considered Emma's advice. She couldn't see herself asking others to get involved with Rock because it wasn't just him they'd have

505

to contend with; there were all of the people who worked for Rock, too—dangerous people who wouldn't hesitate to kill someone.

"Yeah, sure. If it I ever get desperate enough, I'll talk to them," Maggie said, just to appease her friend.

When Maggie ran into Tony and Vincent at the bar later that night, she gave each of them a big hug.

"What's up, guys?" Maggie sang.

"Same ol' shit, little Maggie," Tony said, toying with her.

Vincent's eyes grew serious. "Emma told us your kid ain't been feelin' too good. How's he doing?"

Maggie lit up. "He's doing much better now. It seems like whatever he had is finally working its way out of his system. The school nurse thinks it might be mononucleosis."

"Hey, ain't dat the kissin' disease? What? Ya got a little Casanova goin' 'round kissin' all the girls?" Vincent joked.

Maggie laughed along with him. Then, curiosity peeked by her earlier conversation with Emma, she asked, "So what do you guys do for a living, anyway? We never talk about you. It's always about me."

Tony studied her body language and offered, "We're businessmen. We run a lot of businesses in Philly. Why, ya lookin' for a new job?"

"Ha! I'd love a new job. But for now, this will have to do. So what kind of businesses do you run?" Maggie probed.

"All different kinds. Ya writin' a book or somethin'?" Vincent poked.

"No, not yet. I'll tell you what, though. I could write a crazy book with all the things I've been through and have seen in my life."

Maggie pondered the idea of writing a book. She certainly read enough of them, but to write one would be much, much different. She put it on the bucket list that she kept deep in the recesses of her brain.

Tony's tone grew serious. "Is everything all right wit' cha?"

He sensed that Maggie had something she wanted to say. Maggie sat on the barstool between them. She thought about how difficult it had been working both jobs and trying to care for Seth. She didn't mind her job at Doubles so much, but she hated selling herself for sex. Even though she'd done it since she was a young girl, the anger and resentment never dulled. Some days, she'd sit and fester about John William. Maggie would always blame him the most for all that had happened to Seth and her. There were others, too, like Myles. She hated him with a deep passion. When she was alone in the quiet of the night, she'd pray for superpowers that she could use to obliterate both of those scum-sucking pigs from the face of the earth.

"Hey, ya all right?" Tony asked again.

Maggie came out of her stupor. "Oh, sorry. What did you say?"

"I asked ya if everything is all right," Tony repeated.

"Yeah, sure, everything's fine. I'm tired, that's all," Maggie said, trying to downplay her feelings.

"Well, dat look on your face a minute ago made me think ya wanted to rip someone's nose off," Tony said, studying her expression more closely.

"Nah, I wouldn't mind neutering a couple of people, but they can keep their noses," Maggie teased.

"Ouch!" Tony responded and grabbed his crotch.

Maggie giggled. "I wish I had enough power to get even with some people."

Vincent asked, "Don't cha wanna ever call your mom and dad? They gotta still be lookin' for ya."

Maggie shook her head. "That's not really an option. Like I told you, Rock is a dangerous man. It would be too big a risk. He would like nothing more than to have a reason to cause me more pain. I keep a low profile with Rock and his guys...I've learned the hard way how cold-blooded they can be."

Before Tony or Vincent could speak again, the bartender gave Maggie a nod, indicating that her set was about to start.

Maggie jumped off the barstool and said, "See you later," as she walked to the other side of the room.

Vincent turned to Tony. "Ya think it's time we talk to Salvatore about this Rockhead motherfucker?"

"Not yet, Vin. Emma was gonna tell Maggie to ask us if she ever needs our help. For now, we sit tight. We can't get involved until it's impossible for us not to get involved," Tony said.

"Yeah, you're right. But she's such a nice kid," Vincent commented.

The two of them sat silently, watching Maggie and Emma put on their show for the men who sat around the bar. Tony and Vincent wondered what would become of Maggie and whether there was any future for her to become something more than what she was.

Chapter One Hundred Twenty-Three

S eth's blood test results came back a week later. Colby scheduled an appointment with Maggie at Rock's apartment.

"There was no sign of mono," Colby explained. "Some of his counts, or whatever they are, were off, but nothing that showed he has a problem."

Maggie let out a long breath. "Thank God! I just want him to be well. He's such a good kid, and he's already had too much shit in his life. He deserves to feel good and be happy."

When Maggie looked up, Colby was smiling at her. His facial expression made her feel special and valued. It felt like that moment when the sun peeks up over the horizon to begin a new day.

"What are you looking at?" Maggie said, her pouty pink lips looking irresistibly tasty.

"Oh, just admiring the scenery. You're very special, Maggie. I've met a lot of people in my short career—people who have been forced to do what you're doing now—and they've all had good things about them. Most of them worked with me to get out of their own shitty circumstances. But you seem to care more about everyone else around you than you do about yourself. I think it's brave and selfless. But sometimes you need to consider your own happiness before others'."

"I do think about my happiness, Colby. It makes me happy when Seth or Juju or Joey has joy, and it gives me comfort to know that Rock will leave my family alone as long as I stay put. It's as simple as that. I'm not any kind of saint; I just know what it's like to feel raw fear— the overwhelming fear that eats away the lining of your stomach and makes you feel as though death would be a great relief. I've watched friends die. I know how it feels to lose someone that you love...someone

509

who you could count on and who counted on you...I was just a baby," Maggie finished, her eyes glistening with tears at the memories.

Colby grabbed Maggie and held her tightly. While he couldn't imagine the fear Maggie described, he was able to empathize with her.

"You're a good egg, Maggie. Someday you'll bring remarkable changes to the world," Colby assured her.

Maggie laughed. "Yeah, sure I will," she said, her voice laced with sarcasm.

"I know these things," he joked, rubbing an imaginary crystal ball. "I have the ability to see into the future."

Maggie wished that Colby was serious. She hoped with all her being that he was right, and someday she would find meaning in her life and the reason why God was punishing her.

During the next five months, everything went back to normal for Maggie, Seth, and Juju. All of Seth's symptoms had disappeared, and he was feeling better than ever. He had just come out of the shower with a towel wrapped around his waist. He was chattering about a project his social studies class was working on. In the small apartment, where privacy was nonexistent, Seth dropped his towel to the floor and started to get dressed.

Maggie had been reaching for a box of cereal from the counter and turned around just as the towel hit the floor. Seth was facing her as he continued to describe his role in the project. Maggie's eyes shifted down to his torso.

"Um, are you sure you actually washed yourself in the shower?" Maggie asked.

"Yeah, why?" Seth responded.

Maggie walked over to him to get a closer look. Seth's torso was covered in a red rash.

"Is that itchy?" she asked.

Seth looked down and studied the rash. "Nope. I didn't even know it was there."

"Oh great! Now you have cooties," Juju mocked.

Maggie gave Juju a stern look as Seth walked toward her like a zombie with his arms spread to give her a big hug.

"Ew," Juju squealed. "Don't touch me. I don't want to catch cooties."

By then, Seth was hugging her tightly, and Juju broke down laughing and pulled him into her. Maggie watched them with amusement, but her mind was drifting back to some of the articles she'd read when Seth was so sick.

"Come over here, Seth," Maggie said in a calm voice.

Seth obeyed her, still stark naked. He stood in front of her, knowing she wanted to inspect his rash.

"Aggie, it doesn't hurt, and it doesn't itch," Seth protested before Maggie began to look him over.

"That's fine, but I still want to see it. Do you know how long you've had it?" Maggie asked.

"Nope, this is the first time I've seen it," Seth responded, distracted by thoughts of getting to school on time.

"OK, get dressed. You have to eat breakfast before you go," Maggie told Seth.

Maggie knew what she needed to do. Colby was going to meet her at Doubles later that evening, and she decided not to dwell on it until she talked with him.

"Colby, I need another favor," Maggie started when they were alone in the lap dance room.

"Sure. What's going on?" Colby asked with concern.

"I need to have Seth's blood tested again. Can you hook me up with everything and get your friend at the lab to run tests?" Maggie inquired.

"That shouldn't be a problem. What's going on? Is Seth sick again?" Colby asked, a little worried.

"No, he feels fine, but he broke out in a rash. I need to know for sure what's going on with him and was hoping your friend could run some tests on his blood to see if there's anything unusual," Maggie explained.

A few days later, in the nurse's office at Seth's school, Maggie and Mrs. Booker looked at the rash on Seth's torso.

"Does it itch?" Mrs. Booker asked Seth.

"Nope. I'm fine. Aggie worries 'bout everything," Seth commented.

"Well, young man, you're lucky to have someone who worries about you so much," the nurse told him.

Mrs. Booker tied off Seth's arm in order to draw his blood again.

"I hate this, Aggie. Why do I have to keep getting these needles? They hurt," Seth whined.

"Because the only way we can treat whatever is causing the rash is to know what's causing it, silly," Maggie responded in a voice that told Seth he needed to stop complaining.

After Seth left to go back to class, Mrs. Booker handed Maggie the vials of blood.

"Let me know if they find anything unusual," the nurse instructed.

Maggie met Colby shortly after she left the school and handed him the vials of Seth's blood.

"I need to know the results as soon as possible. Something isn't right, and we need to get him medicine to make all this shit stop. Seth is so tired of being sick all the time," Maggie said before she left.

Colby went straight to the clinic and gave the vials to his friend, the lab technician, who asked, "What are his symptoms?"

Colby explained, "Several months ago, the kid was really sick. High fever and vomiting. Then he started to feel better. After a few days, he had a couple of seizures. He was feeling fine for months, but now he has a rash across his torso. My informant wants to know if you find anything unusual in his blood so she can get the kid the medicine he needs."

The lab technician wrote some notes as Colby described what had been going on with Seth. Then she picked up the vials of blood and gave Colby a nod. "I'll call you when I have the results," she stated.

Chapter One Hundred Twenty-Four

When Colby got Seth's blood-test results, he paid for two hours with Maggie at Rock's apartment. As he walked through the door, his grave demeanor revealed that he had something serious to say.

Maggie stood back and took a long look in his direction. "What's going on?" Her heart was racing as she watched Colby struggle with his own emotions.

"Seth's blood test results came back," Colby said.

He grabbed her by the hand and led her over to the old sofa. Once seated, he turned to her.

"What? You're freaking me out," Maggie said, not knowing what to expect.

Colby drew in a long, deep breath. "Seth has AIDS."

Chapter One Hundred Twenty-Five

It took several moments for Maggie to process what Colby had just said.

Seth has AIDS.

Seth has AIDS.

Seth has AIDS.

Finally, Maggie shook her head. "They must have mixed up his blood with someone else's," she stated in a small voice.

"No, Maggie. There wasn't a mix-up," Colby said.

Every fiber of Maggie's body was rejecting the news that Colby had delivered. She was trying with all her might to change what she'd just heard. Seth couldn't have AIDS. It wasn't possible. Ding, ding, ding... her mind had hit on the truth, and it was quite possible that Seth had AIDS. But she continued to reject the information.

"No, it must be a mix-up. We didn't ask for an AIDS test. Your friend must have confused Seth's blood with someone else's," Maggie ranted with an edge in her voice.

He could see her breaking down. "My friend at the lab asked about Seth's symptoms, and I gave her a rundown of the last five months. So, she decided to test him for AIDS," Colby explained.

Maggie refused to allow Colby's words to penetrate her brain. Pulling her voice from deep within her throat, Maggie asked again, "What did she say?"

When Colby swallowed, the gulping sound seemed to resonate off the walls around them. "The results showed that Seth has stage-three AIDS." He let his words creep into her conscious mind and waited for her next question.

"How many stages are there? I read about AIDS a couple of years ago. Aren't there, like, six stages?" Maggie's voice screeched with desperation.

Colby put his strong arm tightly around Maggie's shoulder. "No, Maggie. There are three stages." He paused, trying not to rush through the information. "Stage three is the worst," he said sadly.

Maggie leaned into Colby. Her chest heaved as the reality of the situation seeped into her emotional being. She lowered her head, and her tangled hair covered her face. As much as she wanted to argue that it wasn't true, Maggie knew the truth deep within her soul. She had brushed away the dark feelings over the last three years whenever Seth got sick. It wasn't until his illness five months ago that the seed of worry planted itself deeply in Maggie's belly. Even then, she continued to dismiss her dark thoughts, pretending that her gut feeling was all an illusion. She ignored her instincts, and now her world crashed down upon her like a block of cement.

Maggie cried for close to an hour before she could speak again. She looked into Colby's eyes, searching for a tiny glimmer of hope. But she saw nothing but sorrow there.

"What can I do for him? Is there medicine he can take?" Maggie managed.

"There's medicine to keep him comfortable, but the disease has gone too far. I'm so sorry," Colby said.

An hour later, when Colby was leaving, and Maggie's next client was entering the apartment, she realized that her life before this moment wasn't as bad as she'd thought. Before she learned that Seth had AIDS, there was a sliver of hope that one day, they'd all be free and maybe even happy.

She wanted to leave Rock's shabby apartment, her home of prostitution, but the ramifications would be too great. Now, more than ever, she needed to be there for Seth. At the end of the long afternoon, she trudged back to her apartment. Inside, Seth was sitting on the floor with an open book, working on his math homework. Maggie went to him slowly and sat beside him.

"How are you, sweetie?" Maggie asked in a gentle voice.

Seth looked up at her, the ache in her voice startling him. "Fine. What's wrong?" he asked.

"Nothing's wrong. I just wanted to know how you feel," Maggie said, not knowing how she would ever be able to tell him the truth.

Maggie lifted his chin. Noticing the first purple spot on his neck, she stifled a groan that was lodged in her throat. The mark wasn't there a week ago. Had she been so busy with her ridiculous life that she failed to see Seth degrading before her eyes? Guilt and remorse took hold of her. As she stiffened, and her eyes swam in a sea of regret, she began to rub his back softly.

"What's wrong, Aggie? You're scaring me," Seth said, his senses electrifying his body.

Juju had been lying on the mattress, watching and listening to Maggie and Seth. She, too, was able to see the physical transformation in Maggie, and knew that whatever it was, it had to be bad news. She moved off the mattress and onto the floor next to Maggie.

Maggie looked from Juju to Seth and took the plunge. "Your blood-test results came back today."

Maggie paused, trying to regroup. She willed herself not to cry.

"And?" Seth asked innocently.

"And...it shows you have AIDS," Maggie whispered.

Seth shrugged. "So? What does that mean? Do I gotta drink more Gatorade?"

Juju's eyes filled with tears, and she shot up and went into the bathroom. She knew, without being told, that it wouldn't be good if Seth saw either of the girls being overly emotional. Besides, she had to process what she'd just heard.

"Sure," Maggie answered. "Drinking Gatorade is good. But this disease is a really bad one."

Seth looked at Maggie, his blue eyes curious. "What does it mean? I'm gonna get better, right?"

"I don't know, baby. I just don't know a lot about it yet," Maggie said honestly.

Seth stared down at his textbook. "Is it something that the other kids in school can catch?"

"No, it's not like that," Maggie said with certainty.

"So what are we gonna do?" Seth asked, feeling the gravity of the situation, but not understanding what was happening to him.

"Colby is going to help us get some information on how we can help you. So, for right now, we're going to wait to hear back from him,"

Maggie explained, trying to buy time before having to fully explain AIDS to Seth.

Seth shrugged again. "OK." He went back to doing his math homework.

In the early morning hours, after Maggie returned home from her shift at Doubles, she sat on the bathroom floor with Juju and explained all that Colby had told her.

"Are you saying it's too late?" Juju finally asked, needing confirmation.

"Yes."

The two young girls sat on the cold bathroom floor and wept.

Juju finally spoke. "At least he isn't sick right now. That's good, right?"

Maggie nodded. She knew there was nothing good about what was going to happen to Seth. She'd read everything she could get her hands on, trying to find out if there was any way to stop the disease from advancing further. She held out hope that the diagnosis was wrong, but she knew that she was simply avoiding the truth.

Maggie and Juju moved into the room where Seth lay sleeping on the old mattress. They squeezed onto the single mattress on either side of him, and each put an arm over him. It was a sleepless night, as each of them swam in their murky thoughts of the future.

Chapter One Hundred Twenty-Six

———————■———————

Thirteen-year-old Seth's health declined over the next two months. It was as if once they knew that he had AIDS, someone had opened the spigot on his illness. The young boy couldn't walk a block without having to sit on the curb and rest. He had chronic diarrhea, and fever overtook him on a weekly basis. Seth had purple blotches on his torso, back, and neck. Maggie and Juju watched as the disease ate away at him, removing all signs of the young, adorable boy they'd raised together over the past five years.

Seth's health was so fragile that Maggie went to talk to Rock about his condition. She walked into the house of whores just as Armando was dragging a new girl upstairs. Maggie's thoughts shifted to when she'd arrived at the house. The days she'd spent in the vertical box in the closet. The humiliation and dehumanization that had taken place to break her in. Her heart melted for the poor young girl with big, brown, innocent eyes who was being dragged up the steps. She gave the girl a knowing look, but she was as helpless as ever to change anything.

Rock stepped into the room and stopped in his tracks when his eyes set on Maggie. "What the fuck are ya doin' here?"

Maggie didn't hesitate. She dove right in. "We found out a couple of months ago that Seth has AIDS."

"Yeah? Dat ain't my problem," Rock said.

"Well, a couple of things. First, it's impossible for him to walk around and collect money from your dealers. It's physically impossible," Maggie began.

Rock raised an eyebrow skeptically.

Maggie didn't leave any time for him to object. "So, maybe you have someone who can replace him?" she asked sheepishly.

"Girl, you don't tell me how to run my fuckin' business. So the kid has AIDS. So what? Lots of people have AIDS," Rock stated.

"Seth is in the final stage of the disease," Maggie said, a tiny sob escaping from her throat.

The hookers who were listening gasped. All of them knew Seth. He was a good kid, and they saw him on the street all the time. Several of the girls put their hands on their chests and over their mouths, shocked at the news. Rock looked over at the girls, and without understanding the stages of AIDS, realized that it must be bad.

"So what does that mean? He's gotta get medicine? Are you here to ask me to pay for his fuckin' medicine? 'Cause if you are, you can turn the hell around and walk right back out that door before I give ya a well-deserved ass beatin'," Rock advised.

"No, Rock." Maggie stated assertively, her voice rising to just below a shout. "I'm not here for your money. Stage three means it's too late. The disease is eating his body. Every day, he gets closer and closer to death."

Maggie was about to scream at him and tell him what a piece of shit he had been to all of them. She wanted to lunge at him and rip his eyeballs from their sockets. But in a matter of seconds, she regained control and thought better of it. Striking out at Rock wouldn't get her what she'd gone there for.

Rock noticed the other girls waiting for his response. The last thing he needed was a whole group of unruly bitches to tame.

"I can have Joey pick up his route. Now get the fuck outta here and get back to work," Rock declared.

"That's not all," Maggie said. "I need time to spend with him. Between screwing every Tom, Dick, and Harry at your apartments and working shifts at Doubles, I don't have any time to spend with him." Her eyes bore into him as she pleaded. "I can't let him die like this, Rock. Not alone. He's only a kid. He deserves to have someone there with him..." Maggie paused. "To see him through this until he's gone."

Maggie's shoulders dropped, and her chest heaved. For the first time, she allowed others a real glimpse of what she was facing. A couple of the younger girls rushed up behind Maggie and put their hands on her shoulders. Rock looked around the room. He didn't want to see the little shit stain die, but shit happens; life happens. Regardless, he wasn't about to let her stop working. He and his men needed the income.

"Well, see, now that seems to be a personal problem. You ain't no good to me or that kid if ya ain't makin' money. You'll need to find a way to work it out or find me the money you'll be giving up," Rock grunted.

It was a small Latino girl who spoke first. "I'll stay out longer every day to turn two more tricks a day. Will that help?" she asked in Maggie and Rock's direction.

Rock eyed her; she had surprised him. Before he had a chance to respond, three more girls offered to do the same thing. Within a matter of minutes, all but three of the girls were offering up extra services to make up for Maggie's loss of income.

Rock glared at them as if they had gone mad. "If you fools wanna spend more time spreading your legs so this dirty bitch can have some time off, then be my guest. But let me tell ya, if any of you come up short, I will be your worst fuckin' nightmare." He turned his deep black eyes on Maggie. "Your shifts at Doubles stay."

Maggie nodded, and then he walked past her and left the house.

Once Rock was gone, Maggie turned to the girls. She'd been a friend to many of them. She'd helped most of them get acclimated to the streets. Maggie had treated the girls with respect and had given them a shoulder to cry on over the years. And unbeknown to any of them, she was helping to set them free as she provided information to Colby about Rock's organization. That part, taking down the whole organization, took years. It was important to make sure that when the time came, no man was left standing. Colby had assured her, though, that someday, Rock and all of his associates would cease to run Kensington.

Maggie hugged all of them, even those who didn't offer their services for her temporary freedom. Just as she was leaving the house, Armando was coming down from the second floor. He sneered at her. "That little bitch up there is almost as tasty as you were," he said, licking his fingers as if he'd just eaten something delicious.

Maggie's expression remained unchanged. Instead, she turned away and walked out the door. On her way back to the apartment, she stopped at the library. Seth had been talking about going to the seashore. He'd never been anywhere, and some of the kids at school had talked about it over the years. Earlier in the week, he'd said, "Aggie, do you think we can go see the seashore?"

Maggie had explained that it wasn't possible, but she felt guilty that she couldn't give him what he wanted. Instead, she stopped at the library to pick up a book on New Jersey. She and Juju were going to dress up in the bikini "work outfits" she wore at Doubles. They were planning to put a blanket on the floor of the apartment and have a picnic. Juju had even gotten her hands on a cheap copy of ocean sounds. They had it all planned out for him.

When Maggie returned home, Seth was bundled up on the mattress. He was cold all the time, and his shoulder and rib bones jutted out through his skin. Seth's facial features seemed to have faded away, leaving the shape of his skull to dominate beneath his colorless flesh. Only his eyes remained blue and radiant. Joey knocked on the door a few minutes after Maggie arrived home, and the three girls set everything up for their day at the seashore while Seth watched from the bed.

His breathing was raspy, and it took all of his strength to follow the girls around the small room with his eyes. Finally, Maggie walked over to the mattress.

"OK, are you ready for your day at the seashore?" Maggie sang.

Seth nodded, anticipation filling his eyes with wonder.

Maggie took off her robe to reveal her bathing suit, as the two other girls came out in their makeshift bikinis. Seth started to giggle, and they all joined in as they looked at each other. Maggie got Seth settled on the blanket and covered him up to keep him warm. They ate hot dogs and potato chips, followed by ice cream. Even though Seth ate very little, he reveled in the feeling of being at the seashore.

Maggie put her hands up in the air. "OK, now we need to go through our journey at the seashore." She had checked out an oversized picture book at the library for the occasion.

As she turned the pages of the book, Juju and Joey oohed and awed at the pictures of the beautiful beaches. There were pictures of several boardwalks with rides and people standing in line for french fries. Then, on the last page, was a picture of a huge elephant.

"What's that?" Joey asked.

Maggie read the caption. "It's Lucy the Margate Elephant." Then she looked over at Seth, who was staring at the picture intently.

"What?" Maggie said. "You like the elephant better than the beaches?"

Seth slowly shook his head. "I know that elephant. I've seen it before. When I was a little kid," he said. And for the first time since he'd found out he had AIDS, Seth began to cry.

Maggie watched Seth and looked at the elephant again. It was his first and only memory of his life before John William had taken him. A bottomless, gloomy, sadness penetrated her soul, and she felt as if she was plunging deeper into hell.

Chapter One Hundred Twenty-Seven

Maggie set out for the library first thing the next morning. She immediately began to research old newspapers from Margate, New Jersey. She went back to August 3, nine years prior. Nothing. She looked on August 4. Nothing. Then she looked at August 5, and there on the front page was a mother and father. The mother was crying, and the father looked to be comforting her. The headline read:

"Margate Mayor and Wife Plead for the Safe Return of their Child."

Maggie was whizzing through the article, looking for indications that their child was a boy. Bingo! She found it. It was a boy who was missing. Next, she glided through the paragraphs looking for the name of the child...Stefano Frey. Her excitement waned. No match.

Then Maggie stared hard at the picture of the missing boy. The newspaper had a black-and-white picture of a toddler in a sailor suit. His hair had been combed down, and he was wearing a sailor cap on his head. The boy had chubby cheeks, and he looked as though he'd been crying right before the picture was taken. *Shit, shit, shit*, she thought. *This isn't a picture of Seth.* He must have been taken to see Lucy the Margate Elephant on vacation. Her excitement, the only excitement she'd experienced since Seth became ill, vanished.

Later that night, in the lap dance room, she told Colby about Lucy the Margate Elephant. "I just wanted so badly to be able to let him see his mom and dad," Maggie explained.

Colby just listened in silence. The agony Maggie felt was palpable. She was tormented by the thought of losing Seth. He, too, had grown fond of the boy in the brief interactions they'd had over the years. Colby didn't dare ask how she thought Seth got AIDS; he was pretty sure he knew the answer.

Maggie left him and went downstairs to look for Emma. There was a lot of commotion among the girls. They all left the dressing room, one after the other. Maggie followed along, back up the stairs, and out the back door. She stood and watched as Emma was handcuffed and placed into a police car.

Maggie grabbed Shiver's arm. "What the hell is happening?"

"I don't know, sugar," Shiver said. "Something ain't right here," she said as she kept her eyes glued on Emma.

As the police car pulled away, Maggie could see that Emma's jaw was set hard. Her eyes looked as if they were glowing. Emma looked over at Maggie, who was crying, and she gave her a nod, as if to say thank you.

Word of Emma's arrest spread through the bar like an untamed forest fire. When Colby heard the news, he frantically looked around for Maggie, but couldn't find her. When she appeared on stage, Colby watched her closely. She looked as if she was running on autopilot. Her eyes were dull, and her movements were rigid.

Colby felt like a useless, dried-up piece of shit. First, Maggie's son, for all intents and purposes, was diagnosed with stage-three AIDS. Now, her closest friend at the bar had been hauled off in a police car. Not good; not good at all. He took a quick guzzle from the bottle of Budweiser sitting in front of him on the bar. There had to be something he could do to help get Maggie through all of this. There just had to be something. Then it came to him.

Two days later, Colby was in his car, driving to Margate. He set out to visit the Freys, the people whose son was stolen from them around same time that Maggie and Seth were taken. He'd found out that after the kidnapping of their child, the Freys, who were well-off, to say the least, had spent most of their time working to help missing and exploited children. They had agreed to meet Colby when he told them that he also worked to stop the criminals and pedophiles who snatched children from their families.

Colby pulled his car into the driveway of the Frey mansion. Before he was out of his car, a man and a woman in their mid-forties rushed out the front door to meet him. Even though both of the Freys were dressed in jeans and sweaters, Colby could tell they were from money.

They were perfectly groomed—perfect hair, nails, and jewelry. They looked athletic and healthy.

Colby extended his hand. "Mr. and Mrs. Frey, nice to meet you in person."

"Likewise," Mr. Frey stated, and gave Colby a welcoming handshake that immediately put him at ease.

It wasn't until they were well into eating lunch that Mr. Frey began to talk about their son, Stefano, who was taken. He informed Colby that their son had been playing with the dog in the front yard. Mr. Frey had gone back into the house to grab two glasses of lemonade. In the time it took Mr. Frey to return, Stefano had moved close to the road.

Colby thought about the mile-long driveway to their house. The boy had been taken just about twenty feet from the road. Mr. Frey was sprinting toward his son when he saw a man pick the boy up and run back to his vehicle. But it was too late; Stefano was gone. There was never a request for ransom, and no evidence turned up, other than a few tire tracks. The Freys both lived their lives trying to help other children, and they still blamed themselves for what happened to their son.

"He was the only child we had," Mrs. Frey explained. "After Stefano was taken, we couldn't conceive another child. At first, we believed that God was punishing us for acting so recklessly with our son. Then we got involved with missing and exploited children. We now realize that this can happen to the most overprotective parents. It's very difficult to lose a child and never know what has become of him. On our best days, we imagine him living with a family that wanted a child and paid some thug to steal one for them. On our worst days, we imagine our child being a drug addict or lying in a shallow grave where no one will ever find him. Being the parent of a missing child makes you appreciate time. Every minute, from the moment the child is stolen, feels like an eternity. Nothing ever tastes the same, looks the same, or sounds the same. All the little pleasures you enjoyed, even sex, become somewhat dulled and bland. However, helping others has enabled us to heal just enough so that we don't wish we were dead every day of our lives."

Colby was stunned by Mrs. Frey's openness with him. He was inexperienced in dealing with the parents of missing children. But now, Colby recognized how terrible it was for the parents, too. He hadn't given it much thought before Mrs. Frey enlightened him. What she described sounded like a slow, agonizing death.

Mr. Frey spoke next. "So, tell us why you're here. How can we help you?"

Colby coughed to clear his throat. "Well, I'm working with a young woman. She was taken when she was eleven," he looked down at his lap. "She was put into human sex trafficking along with four other children. Two of them, she watched die; and one was taken to another city. The youngest is a boy that she's been able to keep with her. Anyway, she just found out that her boy has AIDS. She was throwing him a special party. You see, he wanted to go to the seashore, but in her line of work, that's out of the question. As part of their party, she had gotten a picture book of New Jersey, and in it was Lucy the Margate Elephant. The boy said he recognized the elephant, and well, it's his first and only memory from when he was with his family. So the woman I'm working with, she went to the library and researched missing children around the date she and her boy were taken. That's how she found you. When it wasn't a match, she felt pretty badly. After she gave me your name, I looked you up and figured that even though you aren't the boy's parents, maybe you could give my informant a visit...it might help her. I mean, you know what it's like to lose a child. That's the way she feels now."

"What about treatment for the boy?" Mrs. Frey asked.

"He wasn't diagnosed until he was already in stage three," Colby said.

"Oh my gosh," Mrs. Frey said. Her hand sailed up to her mouth. "That's horrible. What an incredibly heavy cross to bear for this young woman. How old is she?"

"She's twenty," Colby said.

"What's her name?" Mr. Frey asked.

"I'm sure you can appreciate that we never disclose their names. It keeps everyone safe. But she wouldn't mind if you called her Jane Doe. She'd probably tell you she's been called worse," Colby said, and then wished he'd left off the last part.

Mr. and Mrs. Frey smiled at him anyway.

"I'm sorry. Jane Doe has a pretty good sense of humor. Up until lately that is, when she found out about her Baby Doe. It's amazing how resilient she and Baby Doe are after all that's happened to them," Colby said.

Mr. Frey leaned forward. "So how can we help the two of them? Are you looking for money so they can spend a weekend at the seashore?"

"No, no. I'm not looking for money. Jane Doe would never be able to leave for a weekend. Her pimp would surely kill her," Colby explained.

Mrs. Frey cringed visibly.

"Well, just tell us how we can help the two of them," she said with conviction.

"Like I said, I think if you just meet with her, maybe you can give her some comfort," Colby explained.

"We'd be happy to meet with her, I mean, Jane," Mr. Frey said.

"You'll have to go to her apartment. Baby Doe is too fragile to move right now. Besides, it's not as if she can take a few days off," Colby said, apprehensively thinking of this couple going into Kensington.

"You seem nervous, Colby. Is there something you aren't telling us?" Mr. Frey asked.

"Well, the Doe's live in Kensington. It's a rather seedy part of Philadelphia," Colby said hesitantly.

Mr. Frey's eyebrows rose. "Don't worry about us. We've seen a lot over the years. Shall we request a police escort?"

"That would just bring trouble to Jane Doe. Her pimp is very active and has many people in Kensington working for him. I was thinking we could get you into the apartment in the evening, when it's dark," Colby explained.

Mr. Frey put his thumb and index finger on his chin. "OK. What else? I can see there's something else by the look on your face."

"Well, you probably want to dress down. I mean no offense, but the two of you would stick out like a sore thumb in that neighborhood. I would suggest visiting the Goodwill store and getting clothes that make you appear..." Colby's voice trailed off. He suddenly felt as if he was asking too much of the couple.

"Appear poor?" Mrs. Frey finished.

"Well, yes. Poor or homeless would help you blend in," Colby finally admitted.

"Count us in. When?" Mr. Frey asked.

"As soon as possible," Colby responded.

"Fine. Give us two days to acquire our outfits. So we'll be there three nights from now. Does that work?" Mr. Frey asked.

"That would work great. Listen, I really appreciate your willingness to help. Jane Doe hasn't had too many breaks in her life. She's already drowning in sorrow over her boy. But remember, please don't ask too many personal questions," Colby cautioned them.

"Yes, we understand," Mrs. Frey said. "Would we be able to leave them some money? You know, for some items that may allow the boy additional comfort during this time?"

"I think that would be fine, but nothing excessive. If Jane Doe's pimp finds out she's spending a lot of money, it could raise suspicions. Our goal here is to help Jane Doe deal with everything that's going on with Baby Doe. She's extremely vulnerable," Colby said.

After Colby left the Freys' house, the couple sat on an overstuffed sofa in their large, plush living room. They were quiet for the better part of an hour. Mrs. Frey reached over and put her hand on Mr. Frey's leg. He looked up at her slowly and met her eyes.

"This is going to be different," Mrs. Frey began. "All of the horrible visions we've had of Stefano's fate will probably come crashing over us. We need to be strong for Jane Doe, but we need to be certain that when it's done, we don't dwell on whatever it is we're about to see."

Mr. Frey nodded in agreement. The Freys fell silent again, each pondering the circumstances they were about to face. The story Colby had shared with them about Jane and Baby Doe sounded horrid. However, they had dedicated their lives to making a difference. Over the years, they'd helped many children and families with monetary donations or by creating organizations in several states to provide the shelter and resources necessary to recover from the trauma associated with missing and exploited children. This would be the first time they were actually meeting two children who had never been found and returned to their families. Would they be able to come out of this experience and cope with their own loss again? That was the only question that plagued them.

Chapter One Hundred Twenty-Eight

———————◼———————

"Aggie, am I going to die?" Seth asked.

Maggie's breath caught in her throat. She felt as if she might suffocate to death. She shook off the gripping fear. Seth deserved to know what was *really* happening to him.

Maggie sat on the mattress next to where he lay. She took his hand into her own; it felt cold and bony. Pushing his long, blond curls from his eyes, she summoned the courage to give Seth the truth he desperately needed.

"Yes, sweetie, you are going to heaven soon," Maggie said.

Tears rolled down her cheeks as Seth watched her closely. Now he knew for sure that he was dying.

"Aggie?" he said, his voice cracking as the first hot tears hit the side of his nose. "What will happen when I die? I mean, what's gonna happen to me?" he managed.

"Well, you remember Cali and Max, right?" Maggie asked tenderly.

"Yeah, I remember them. They died, too. I remember being really sad."

"I know. It was a sad time for you and me, but they went to a better place. They went to heaven. In heaven, you can have all the things you want," Maggie said.

"But I want to live here with you," Seth sobbed.

"I want you to live here with me, too. But you know what?" she asked.

Seth shook his head.

"You're going to be with Cali and Max again. They're going to be waiting for you. I just know it," Maggie told him, putting her other hand to his heart.

"What about Joey? Who's gonna take care of Joey when I go to heaven?" he asked with dire concern.

"I'll take care of Joey. She and I will take care of each other. And then, someday, we'll go to heaven, and we'll all be together again," Maggie explained.

"Will you come soon?" Seth worried, not wanting to leave her.

"I don't know when I'll come to heaven. But when I get there, you better make sure you're waiting for me," Maggie said, trying to lighten his mood.

Seth turned his head and faced the wall. He was thinking about everything Maggie had just told him. He stared intently at the chipped paint inside the water stain on the drywall.

Seth turned to face Maggie again. "Thank you for always taking care of me. You're the best friend I've ever had."

Seth and Maggie sat together in silence. Juju, who had been sitting at the small table across the room, had been quietly crying. She wondered how they would get along without him. He'd been a big part of their lives. He was everything to Maggie. Juju considered the conversation she'd been having with her girlfriend and realized that now was not the time to move out and leave Maggie alone. She'd wait until things were better. But Juju knew that without Seth, things might never get better for Maggie.

Chapter One Hundred Twenty-Nine

The Freys arrived in Kensington at midnight. Maggie had worked the early shift at Doubles and had gotten home at eleven. Colby had told her all about the Freys, and she was anxious to meet them. He wouldn't be able to be with her, of course; they didn't want to sound any alarms for Rock.

Mr. Frey rapped softly on the apartment door. Maggie rushed to open it as Juju stood to the side.

"Hello, I'm Mr. Frey, and this is my wife," he said respectfully.

"Hi, I'm Jane," Maggie said and opened the door wider for them to enter.

Mr. and Mrs. Frey took in the sights around them. Only a few steps inside the open door, they were standing in a room no bigger than fifteen feet wide by twelve feet long. To the right was an old stainless steel sink and a small stove. Two cabinets hung on the greasy wall above the sink. One of the cabinets no longer had a door on it, and on the shelf sat one box of macaroni and cheese and a few cans of vegetables. Drip, drip, drip...the leaking faucet sang to Mrs. Frey as if the noise were being played in surround sound...drip, drip, drip. To the right of the kitchen stood a small folding table and a couple of beat-up chairs.

Shoved up against the wall to their left, under peeling paint, was a single stained mattress on the floor. There were no sheets on the mattress, and on top was a mound of old blankets and towels. For a moment, they all stood awkwardly, not knowing how to spark the conversation.

"Do you have a bathroom I could use? It was a little bit of a drive to get here," Mrs. Frey finally asked.

Maggie pointed to the door behind them. "The bathroom is through that door. You'll need to use the flashlight on the floor right there," she explained, pointing down at it. "There isn't a light," Maggie finished, flushing with embarrassment as she realized how minimally they lived.

Mrs. Frey entered the bathroom and closed the door. She shone the flashlight around the tiny room. There was a tub with a cheap shower curtain that looked as though it were made of plastic wrap. The toilet was old, and inside the bowl were years upon years of rust stains. There was no sink. A small mirror hung crookedly above the toilet. She thought of all the extravagant things in her own home, and a stab of guilt jolted up her spine. Shaking it off, she walked back into the only other room of the apartment.

"Thank you for coming all this way," Maggie began. "I know what Colby told you I needed, and it's true. We need advice on how to cope with everything that's happening right now. But there's something else I was hoping you could do."

"Sure, let's hear it," Mr. Frey said, willing to do just about anything after seeing the dismal circumstances in which these young people were living.

Maggie gestured toward the mattress and began to walk over. Mr. and Mrs. Frey followed.

"Hey," Maggie whispered to Seth. "Do you think you can sit up? There are some people here who might be able to help us."

Seth nodded. Up until this point, neither of the Freys realized that the child was lying under the pile of blankets and towels on top of the mattress. Seth put his arms around Maggie's neck, and she hoisted him up as Juju propped a pillow and old clothing behind him.

The Freys literally had to refrain from moaning aloud. The child was so thin. His bones were protruding, and they could see the purple blotches on his neck and wrists.

Mrs. Frey took a long, silent breath, filling her lungs with the stale air of the room.

"Hello," she said leaning down to look at Seth.

"Hi," Seth said shyly.

The Freys had read all about AIDS. They knew it wasn't transmittable by shaking hands or hugging, yet they both refrained from getting too close to the child. Mrs. Frey watched as Maggie fussed over the boy, holding his hand and rubbing his arm as she spoke.

Maggie began, "So, you see, I've read that you've become very involved with helping people find their lost kids. We were thinking," she paused and looked at Seth, "that maybe you could help us find his parents. You know, through all of the organizations you work with."

"I don't know if it'll work, but we're sure willing to try to help. That is what we do. We try to bring families back together. We hope to be reunited with our own child someday. How about you, Jane? Do you want to find your parents?" Mr. Frey asked.

"Now isn't the time. I work for dangerous people and well…it's just not the right time," Maggie said, sadness clouding her eyes. Maggie knew that in a matter of weeks, she could lose Seth to his disease. She found herself thinking of her own parents and brother more and more. "But we thought maybe if he could be reunited with his parents, it could bring…*closure* for him." Maggie whispered *closure* as if it were a very bad word.

"Of course, Jane. We completely understand," Mrs. Frey confirmed. "We're going to be staying in Philadelphia for a couple of weeks to see how we might be able to help all of you get through this," she vowed.

Maggie smiled. The couple watched the young woman. She was magnificent. Maggie radiated an inner and outer beauty that was almost blinding. While they were talking, Seth had fallen back into a slumber. He didn't have the strength to stay awake for more than ten minutes at a time. The Freys stayed awhile longer, getting to know Maggie and Juju. They found the two girls interesting and funny. Jane Doe seemed well educated even though she dressed like a streetwalker. She spoke eloquently and didn't use slang, unlike the Asian girl, who referred to herself as Cujo Doe.

An hour after they arrived, Mr. Frey stood to leave and pulled an envelope from his jacket pocket. He handed the envelope containing one hundred dollars to Maggie.

"Just a little money so you can buy Baby Doe things he might need to keep him comfortable," Mr. Frey said.

Maggie blushed deeply. She knew that they lived in a shit hole, and Seth didn't have even the smallest of luxuries to keep him comfortable. Grateful for the gesture, Maggie took the envelope and laid it on the floor next to the mattress.

Leaning over Seth, Maggie said, "The Freys are leaving. Do you want to say good-bye?"

Seth's eyelids fluttered a couple of times, and after a moment, he nodded. Maggie turned and looked at the couple. She pointed her chin toward the mattress.

"It was nice to meet you, Baby Doe," Mr. Frey said, his voice cracking. He was nervous and felt inadequately prepared to address the sick child. Seth smiled in response.

Mrs. Frey walked over to the mattress and looked down on the thin frame that lay beneath the tattered blankets and towels. *Get a fucking grip*, she told herself. *This is a dying child. Give him human contact.* She hurriedly sat on the edge of the mattress before she changed her mind.

"It was very nice to meet you. We're going to come back and visit you again. Would that be all right?" Mrs. Frey asked.

Seth smiled weakly and nodded.

Mrs. Frey involuntarily reached out and grabbed Seth's hand. "We will help you in any way we can, Baby Doe," she said.

She looked down at the boy's hand resting in her own. She almost got up, but looked down again, just to be sure she wasn't imagining things. On the inside of the child's wrist were two perfectly round birth marks that overlapped and looked like the number eight. She pulled the boy's wrist closer. Then she looked at her husband with unadulterated terror. Mr. Frey was swiftly at her side and looking down at Seth's wrist. *Oh dear God*, was all he could think.

Chapter One Hundred Thirty

——————————————

"Stefano?" Mrs. Frey said softly.

Nothing.

"Seth?" Mrs. Frey tried.

Seth's eyes popped open. *How does she know my name?* he wondered. He was sure that Maggie had said that the people visiting couldn't know their real names.

Mr. Frey looked at Maggie, who just stared at Seth and Mrs. Frey. She was confused. Then Mr. Frey explained, "Our boy, you know his name is Stefano. We used to call him Stef for short. He was only four when he was kidnapped. When you asked him what his name was, he would say 'Seth' because he couldn't pronounce 'Stef.'"

Maggie felt as if the bones had been ripped out of her legs. Juju rushed up behind her and steadied her. With Maggie rendered speechless, Juju took over. "Are you sayin' you think Seth is your kid?"

Mrs. Frey nodded as she looked into the eyes of the child she once held. In his eyes, she could see the past. Stefano had the exact same eye color as she did, and if she blocked out all the illness, she could see the eyes of her four-year-old boy. Mr. Frey was pacing the small room and raking his fingers through his thick head of hair.

Maggie forced herself to live in the moment. They had found Seth's parents. It was everything she'd hoped for and more. They were a nice couple who had dedicated their lives to helping others after Seth had disappeared. But she didn't expect to feel a tinge of nervousness at the thought of losing Seth to his parents. What if they took him from her now? What if she didn't get to spend their last days together? Panic rose and fell in her chest; it rose and fell again, a vicious cycle that was making her feel light-headed. *Find your voice...find your voice*, she willed herself, until a low gurgle started to make its way out of her mouth.

"How do you know it's Stefano?" Maggie finally managed.

"Because of the birthmark on his wrist," Mrs. Frey said unnervingly, lifting Seth's wrist.

There was a long stretch of silence, which none of them knew how to fill. The Freys had so many questions for Maggie. They wanted to know everything their son had been through and how the two knew each other. After a strained moment, Mrs. Frey spoke.

"Can we take him to the hotel with us?" Internally, Mrs. Frey was screaming, *this is my kid, and he's coming home with me!*

Before Maggie could answer, and to be clear, the answer was no—she didn't even know these people and wasn't about to send Seth with them—Seth lifted his head off the pillow. His bottom lip was quivering.

"I want to stay with you, Aggie," he said in a trembling voice.

Maggie rushed over to him and gathered him up in her arms. She rocked him back and forth. "Everything is going to fine, Seth. I don't want you to worry. You're not going anywhere. You're staying right here with me and Juju," she said and thought, *Oops, I just said Juju's name...tough shit.*

Maggie looked from Mr. Frey to Mrs. Frey, and reluctantly, they both nodded. Then Mrs. Frey stood and walked toward the door of the apartment. Maggie followed the couple out into the hallway.

Mrs. Frey looked at her, tears streaming down her cheeks. "Will you tell us your name?"

"Maggie. Seth has been with me since he was four years old. I love him. He's like my own child, but I want him to know who his parents are before...before it's too late. I don't want to fight with you over him. You have to understand there isn't much time left, and I don't want to spend it fighting. All I care about is that Seth lives his days out peacefully and surrounded by love," Maggie stated.

Mrs. Frey looked disheveled and battered. Maggie felt sorry for her and put her hand on the older woman's shoulder. "We'll figure it out. Together, we can do this," Maggie said with the wisdom of a fifty-year-old.

Mrs. Frey reached over and hugged Maggie close. "This is a lot for the mind to process. I'm so happy to finally have found him, and yet I know there's so little time left to love him."

Maggie nodded. She completely understood. Then she gave Mr. Frey a hug. "Come back tomorrow night, OK?"

The couple turned to leave when all they wanted to do was go back, grab their boy, and take him somewhere he could be cared for properly. As they walked down the hall toward the stairs, Mr. Frey turned. "We're thankful he's had you. We hope to better understand what his life has been."

Maggie nodded. "I'll tell you everything there is to know."

When Maggie was back in the apartment, Seth was awake and more aware than he'd been in a long time. "Were they really my mom and dad?" he asked.

"I'm not sure. I think they were. I mean, their story sounded real and all," Maggie rambled.

"Aggie, I wanna know them, but...but, you won't let them take me away from you, right?" Seth asked.

"Right, sweetie. I need you to focus on feeling better. You're not going anywhere without me," Maggie said, forcing a smile.

A few hours later, sometime during the early morning, Maggie and Juju fell asleep. They had stayed up for hours thinking through their options. If the Freys really were Seth's parents, they could easily take him home. Maggie had imagined finding Seth's parents and being happy to meet them, but then they'd go on their merry way, realizing that Seth belonged to her. She had raised him for most of his life, longer than his parents had been with him.

During the same hours, Mr. and Mrs. Frey lay awake in their hotel room discussing what they'd do. They wanted their boy back home with them. They loved him and had missed so much of his life. They could provide him with all the things he needed. They would get the best AIDS doctor on earth to review Seth's case and treat him. Maybe they could reverse the disease. Their hopes and thoughts about being reunited with their child were endless.

But shortly before the Freys fell asleep, Mrs. Frey told her husband, "We need to put our son's needs before our own. If we can do that, then surely we'll do all the right things for him."

But could the Freys actually put Seth's needs ahead of their own need to reunite with their son?

Chapter One Hundred Thirty-One

Maggie rushed into the lap dance room with Colby the next evening. She looked sleep-deprived and unkempt.

"What happened?" Colby whispered.

"The Freys say they're Seth's parents," Maggie told him.

"What do you mean? Why do they think that?" Colby asked, wondering if the Freys were lunatics.

"Seth has a birthmark on his wrist. Mrs. Frey recognized it and said she thinks Seth is her son."

Maggie went on to explain about Seth's name. Colby listened and wondered if it could possibly be true. What were the odds that he'd brought these people to their son, he wondered. However, as he listened to Maggie go over what had happened in her apartment, it all lined up and began to make sense.

"Maggie, you need to stay calm. These people have been searching for their child since the day he went missing. If they really are Seth's parents, then he and the Freys both have a right to know."

Maggie looked at Colby as if he'd just betrayed her. "But they can take him from me," she whined. "I...I don't want to lose him. Not now. He's sick, Colby. You know this. He's sick and he needs me," she argued.

"Yes, he does need you. But he also deserves to know that his parents love him and that they never stopped searching for him. It's not about what the Freys need or even what you need. It's only about what Seth needs. He's a very sick boy, and this may be the greatest gift you can give him," Colby said.

Maggie slouched in the seat next to Colby. Of course, he was right. She knew this without a doubt. But her heart felt as though it was being ripped from her chest.

"I'll tell you what. I'm going to drive over to their hotel now and talk to them before they go to your apartment tonight. Anyway, you can't just turn the boy over to them without knowing for sure that he's their son. That'll give you some time to wrap your mind around all of this. OK?" Colby said, lifting her chin from her chest and kissing her on the forehead.

"Yeah, OK," Maggie replied meekly.

At midnight, the Freys knocked on the apartment door. Maggie opened the door apprehensively, gave a small smile, and stepped aside for them to enter. Mrs. Frey rushed over to the mattress where Seth was sitting up.

"Well, you look like you feel a little better today," Mrs. Frey commented.

Seth smiled. He watched the Freys closely, waiting for a connection to them, a memory, to sense something familiar about them. Then Mrs. Frey said something.

"I don't know if you remember, but when you were little, you always wanted me to tickle the palms of your hands," Mrs. Frey said and demonstrated by etching small circles on his palm.

Bingo! Seth felt as though he was sucked back in time. He remembered. He used to love the feeling of his mother tickling the palms of his hands. His eyes brightened, and he looked to Maggie.

"I remember," he said, smiling from Maggie to Juju.

Maggie's heart melted. Seth's eyes had lit up with life. It was as if he was suddenly well again.

"That's wonderful, sweetie," Maggie said with sincerity as she moved closer to the boy.

Mrs. Frey felt hopeful and looked at her husband, who smiled at her with tears glistening in his eyes.

"Well, we talked to a man who's going to help us have blood tests done," Mrs. Frey explained.

"Why do we need blood tests?" Seth asked.

"Just to make sure that you are our son," Mr. Frey explained.

Seth shrugged. "OK, I guess so."

"Good," Mrs. Frey said. Then she looked over at Maggie. "We realize how overwhelming this may be for you. We owe it to everyone involved to be sure."

Maggie nodded and tried to push down the anxiety attack that wanted to overrun her body. Juju put her arm around Maggie's shoulder, and the Freys watched. They had questions they wanted answered.

"Maggie, we were wondering if you might be able to meet us somewhere tomorrow. Outside of the apartment, I mean. We'd just like to talk with you privately," Mr. Frey said.

Seth watched closely. "You should go, Aggie. You always tell me that when someone is sad, we need to do everything we can to help them. Mr. and Mrs. Frey look sad," he said.

Maggie giggled. "Oh, really?" She tousled his hair. Then she looked up at the Freys. "OK, tomorrow will be fine. Let's meet at the Melrose Diner. I can get there by eleven tomorrow morning."

The next morning as Maggie was getting ready to meet the Freys, Juju whispered that she wanted to tag along. Juju was worried about her friend, and she knew how troubled Maggie was over the thought of Seth going somewhere else to live.

"Juju, I'd love for us to go together, but someone has to stay here with Seth. We can't leave him alone. He can't even make it to the bathroom by himself. I'll feel better if I know you're here with him. Besides, the school nurse is stopping in to check on him, and she's going to take blood. I talked to her this morning," Maggie explained.

"OK, fine. But I want it on the record that I don't like this shit one fuckin' bit," Juju said, crossing her arms over her chest.

Maggie laughed. "You are one tough-ass bitch."

"You ain't seen tough yet, sister. Everybody better back the fuck off and quit being so pushy," Juju said. Then she got serious. "I can't bear to lose him either. I've grown to love the smacked ass. I mean, he's like a brother to me."

Juju walked slowly toward Maggie, who opened her arms and pulled Juju into her. The two young women stood in the bathroom, their official meeting spot, where Seth couldn't hear them, and held each other for several moments. Finally, Maggie pulled away.

"OK, no more of this shit. We need to keep it together. We've been through a lot, and Seth is counting on us to do what's right. Whatever we do from this moment forward is for him," Maggie stated.

The Freys were seated across from Maggie at the Melrose Diner. After they'd ordered, Maggie got right to the point.

"So you want information?"

"Yes, we want to know what happened to our...Seth. After he was taken...what happened to him?" Mrs. Frey asked.

Maggie explained how she woke up after being kidnapped and saw Seth in the back of the van next to her. She explained the years they spent in the prison and the house where Cali and Max died. She talked about Thelma and all of the horrible things she'd done to Seth and finished with how she, Seth, and Juju had come to live together. Mr. and Mrs. Frey sat with their mouths agape. It was worse than they had imagined. While Maggie told the story, the husband and wife cried and moaned.

"You said people forced you to have sex when you were kept in the prison and at the house. What about Seth? Is that where he caught AIDS?" Mrs. Frey asked, holding her breath.

"At first, they only took naked pictures of Seth. He was so little, and I guess, for some reason, the sick pricks who were paying to have sex with us didn't want a four-year-old boy. I'd say it was almost two years later when Seth told me that a man put his pee pee into his butt. He was a mess. I comforted him the best I could. My heart was aching. I begged John William, the man who stole us, to sell me more and leave Seth alone, but he just beat me for trying to tell him what to do. The people who owned us, made the men wear condoms with the girls because they didn't want us to get pregnant. But it was different for the boys. Max, the older boy who was with us, told Cali and me that they let those disgusting pigs do it without condoms. Max explained that they would be able to sell the girls for much longer than they could the boys. After a certain age, they'd either have the boys work in the business or kill them, depending on how 'agreeable' they'd been over the years. Max rebelled, killed some creep, and they killed him for it."

Veins were pulsating on Mr. Frey's forehead. "Was Seth raped more than once?"

Maggie nodded her head slowly as she looked down at her hands, which were resting on the table. "Yes. There were lots of men. I wouldn't even be able to guess how many times. I'm sorry. I tried to do everything I could to help him," she said remorsefully.

"Now wait a minute, Maggie. This is not your fault. Hell, if it weren't for you, we might never have been able to see our son again," Mrs. Frey said assertively.

For the first time since the Freys had arrived, Maggie felt as if the three of them were all on the same side—the only side that mattered to all of them: Seth's side.

Chapter One Hundred Thirty-Two

It took five days for the paternity test to come back. Mr. and Mrs. Frey drove to Maggie's apartment with the letter. Of course, they had opened the envelope, so they already knew.

Maggie was more comfortable with the Freys after their meeting at the Melrose Diner. They visited Seth every night. Now, as the Freys sat on the edge of the mattress, Maggie could sense that they were waiting to tell her something.

"So, we got the test results back today," Mr. Frey said in an even voice.

Seth locked eyes with Maggie. "And?" Seth pressed.

"It confirms that you are our son," Mrs. Frey said, trying her best not to scare any of them.

Seth pushed the covers back as best he could and with a little help from Mr. Frey, he swung his legs over the side of the mattress to rest his feet on the floor.

"So you're really my mom and dad?" Seth asked.

Maggie and Juju watched them, too stunned to utter a word.

"Yes, Stefano, we are," Mrs. Frey said.

Seth nodded. "OK, but don't call me Stefano. My name's Seth."

"You're right. I'm sorry," Mrs. Frey said. "We've looked for you from the moment they took you from us. Your father and I love you very much. We want to take you home with us. We want to take care of you." She looked at Maggie and Juju with gratitude. "Your friends can come and visit all the time."

Seth put his hands out, and Maggie helped him to stand. Adrenaline was racing through his body. He had to tell them what he wanted. He already knew that he was dying, and he couldn't imagine his life without Maggie, Juju or Joey. He steadied himself as he turned to face his parents.

"Thank you, but I want to stay with Aggie. It's not like I know you or anything. I mean, I know you're my parents, but I could never leave Aggie and Juju," Seth said sadly.

Mrs. Frey focused on Maggie. "It's not as if he has a choice. He's a child, a minor."

Maggie gestured for Juju to come over and hold onto Seth. Then she got down on her knees in front of the couple. "Please don't make Seth do something he doesn't want to do. I know you love him. He knows you love him, but the only family we've ever known is each other."

Maggie could hear Seth's lungs wheezing as he began to cry harder, and she jumped up and rushed back to him, urging, "OK, breathe slowly. In, two, three, four; out, two, three, four." She gently nuzzled his back.

"Aggie, please don't let them take me away," he cried. "I don't wanna leave you guys. I don't care how nice their house is. I just want to stay here with you and Juju."

Mr. and Mrs. Frey watched as Maggie comforted their child. Seth was completely at home in the loving arms of this stranger in the cramped, decrepit room they called home. Mr. Frey rubbed his wife's hand softly. Both of them knew it would be cruel to make him leave now.

Mrs. Frey rose and put her arms around her son, the son she'd loved, missed, and mourned.

"We would never drag you away from your family," Mrs. Frey said, choking back tears. "All we want now is for you to know who we are and that we love you."

Seth grabbed onto his mother and hugged her tightly as Mr. Frey stood and joined his family in the first family hug they'd shared in nine years. Mrs. Frey's emotions were raw, and as she looked from her husband to her long-lost son, she realized that her prayers had just been answered. For years, she'd begged God to be able to hold her boy and tell him how very much she loved him just one last time.

"I love you, Seth," his mother whispered.

"I love you too, son," Mr. Frey followed.

"I don't know if I love you. I don't really know you, but I think you're nice people. Especially since you're letting me stay with Aggie and Juju." Seth turned toward the two girls. They, too, were crying.

Maggie wiped her eyes. "Well, I think you two should stay in town. That way we can all be with Seth. You're welcome to come here and spend time."

Maggie looked at the two people who had brought Seth into her life. "I have both of you to thank for bringing this wonderful person into my life. I might have died long ago if it hadn't been for Seth. He gave me purpose and a reason to want to stay alive. Maybe by having him, you've given life to both of us."

Mr. and Mrs. Frey knew why their son loved this young, vibrant girl with all of his heart. She was caring and sensitive. She was tender and loving. She was Seth's mother. As hard as it was to accept, especially for Mrs. Frey, the couple knew that Maggie had raised their son and deserved to be called his mother.

"Thank you, Maggie," Mrs. Frey responded.

"Her name is Aggie," Seth joked.

"Yes, you're right. Thank you, Aggie. Mr. Frey and I would love to stay in town. We want to spend as much time with Seth as we possibly can. You've done a magnificent job with our boy, and we will always be grateful for the sacrifices you made to keep him with you," Mrs. Frey said.

Juju butted in. She couldn't take one more moment of all the emotions flying around the room. "Good! It's all settled then. Seth is staying put, and you two," she pointed at Mr. and Mrs. Frey, "can be a part of our family."

"OK, but let's start by everyone using first names. Now, let's see... we have the man of the hour, Seth, and Aggie and...what's your real name?" Mrs. Frey asked.

"Juju," she responded.

"OK and we have Juju. My husband's name is Ron, and mine is Juliet," Mrs. Frey said.

"I'll call you Juliet and Ron too, right?" Seth asked, feeling overwhelmed that they'd expect him to call them Mom and Dad.

Juliet stood tall, even though she wanted to drop to the floor in a heap and weep. "That's right, Seth. You can call us Juliet and Ron, too."

The boy smiled. "Good. Now that it's all settled, can someone—and when I say someone, I mean Juju—make me mac and cheese? I'm hungry," Seth said.

"Oh, now I'm the maid? You feel better for three seconds and you're trying to boss me around?" Juju joked, tickling Seth.

Seth started laughing and tried to get away from Juju. Then his laughter turned into an uncontrollable cough.

"OK, you two. Knock it off. Seth, you get back to bed. Juju! To the kitchen and cook," Maggie chimed in.

Juliet joined Juju in the kitchen that was eight feet from the mattress where Seth was settling in.

"Can I help?" Juliet offered.

Juju smiled. "Ya already have by not taking Seth away. I know it ain't exactly what ya wanted, but ya just made the two peeps I love most very happy."

Juliet had waited so long to see her son again. She'd imagined finding him and keeping him close to her so no one could harm him again. She had pictures in her mind of spending countless months getting to know him and helping him recover from his ordeal. As she reflected on what she'd imagined and the truth of what she was now living, a spark ignited. It wasn't how she'd played the movie in her head a million times, but it was something, and it was more real than she'd ever imagined. Her child was loved, and that fact was all that really mattered now.

Chapter One Hundred Thirty-Three

———————————◼———————————

Over the next week, Ron and Juliet arrived at the apartment every evening shortly after dark. They sneaked in warm blankets, pajamas, and pillows for Seth, Maggie, and Juju. They brought groceries to fill the two small cabinets in the broken-down kitchen. The girls were grateful for the help and the extra comforts as Seth slipped further away.

Unknown to Maggie, at the time the paternity test was performed, the Freys also had paid for AIDS testing. Their doctor, who went over the results with them by phone, said that Seth's CD4+ cell count of less than two hundred meant that his condition was incurable. The disease had won. In addition, their doctor confirmed that Seth had developed tuberculosis. The Freys were confused until the doctor explained that it was common for AIDS patients in Seth's stage to catch "opportunist infections."

"Seth's immune system was wrecked, which opened him up to different types of illnesses or cancer," the doctor explained.

The Freys had decided not to share the new information with Maggie and Juju unless it was necessary. The two young girls, especially Maggie, were drowning in grief. They could see the hard-set lines around Maggie's eyes and the tightness of her jaw every time she watched Seth without him knowing.

Maggie would gently slide under the covers with Seth and hold him closely. She would read books to him, and when he was awake, Maggie would tell him stories about her customers at Doubles, exaggerating most of them to make the boy laugh.

"Aggie," Seth managed one night, "you're the best friend I've ever had. I know that I'm going to die soon, and I already miss you. When

I'm gone, you'll take care of Joey, right? She ain't got no one who loves her 'cept for us."

"We don't need to talk about this," Maggie responded.

"But I wanna talk about it. Sometimes when I'm awake, all I can do is worry that Joey will be left all alone. I figure if you and Joey are together, then you can be happy with each other. Like we've been happy together," Seth insisted.

Maggie drew in a long breath. She had believed that by not talking about Seth's fate, it would somehow never become real. Looking into Seth's sunken eyes surrounded by white, ghostlike skin, Maggie could no longer avoid the conversation. She was overwhelmed with dread, knowing that if she didn't talk about death, it would come, and she would forever regret not giving Seth the last thing he needed.

Maggie stroked Seth's hair. "I promise I'll take care of Joey. I promise I will miss you for the rest of my life. I promise to always be the best and do the best I can for other people." A moan caught in her throat, and Seth put his weak hand over hers.

"It's OK to cry, Aggie. I'm sad, too. But after I'm gone, I gotta know that everything will be all right," he said in a weak voice.

"Everything will be fine," Maggie said, gulping.

"Fine how? Tell me, Aggie," Seth pressed.

"It's like I said. I'll take care of Joey and anyone else who needs me," Maggie confirmed.

"But what 'bout you? I want you to be OK, too," Seth said with the wisdom of a ninety-year-old.

"Ah, you know me. I can take care of myself," Maggie said bravely.

"But if you can take care of yourself, then hows come you still let Rock tell you what to do?" Seth asked.

Maggie thought about it for a moment. Seth was right. She was twenty years old and had failed to break free from the assholes who controlled her life, her every move. In her pursuit of saving Seth and Joey, Maggie had forgotten to fight for her own life.

"You're right, sweetie. I haven't done enough to free myself of that jerk," Maggie stated.

"Then what will you do?" Seth asked, wanting his Aggie to be happy.

"I don't know for sure. But I promise that I'll do everything I can to get away from all of it, including Rock," Maggie said with conviction.

"OK, but I'm scared to leave you alone. I'm scared for you, Aggie," Seth said.

"Look at you. You're the one who's sick, and you're worrying about me. You don't have to worry. I'm going to be fine, and I'll find a way. If I know you're worrying, it's going to make me worry," Maggie told him.

Seth laughed. "You're always worried, Aggie."

Seth lay back on the pile of pillows. He watched Maggie as she readjusted and started to read him another book. As she read, his thoughts wandered to when he was a little boy in his darkest hours living at the mercy of his captors. Maggie would hold him close after they'd hurt him and hum sweet songs. He would get lost in the vibration of her sound and feel as though nothing bad would ever happen to him again. Even though he couldn't comprehend death in its truest form, he knew he'd go away forever. Even that thought wasn't as frightening as being with John William or clients or even Thelma. Seth always found his peace in Maggie's arms, as he did now, and he came to the realization that he'd been given so much more than he ever knew.

Maggie left the words on the page and gazed into his warm, blue eyes.

"What is it?" she asked.

"It's nothin'. Except that I'm really lucky," Seth whispered.

Maggie was startled. Seth had lived such a tragic life. He had suffered so much pain and sorrow. She wondered if perhaps his mind was failing. How could Seth ever think he was lucky? Look what was happening to him...to her wonderful, sweet boy.

Seth could see that she was perplexed. "Aggie, we were really sad once. But we always had each other, right? You always loved me, right? That's why I'm lucky. 'Cause I never felt like I was alone."

"You're right, Seth. We've always had each other, and we always will," she confirmed.

Maggie felt ungrateful listening to Seth. He was right. They'd been lucky to have each other all of these years. With all of the horrors and torment, it was by sheer luck that John William had put them in the back of the van together, where they formed a bond that could never be broken.

Maggie began to hum as she softly rubbed his arms and shoulders.

"Just hold me, Aggie," the boy sputtered.

Maggie and Seth snuggled on the mattress and, for the next two hours, they didn't speak. They just held onto each other, feeling a love so pure that they knew they had received the greatest gift: love through the purest of all evil.

Chapter One Hundred Thirty-Four

Maggie awoke to the sound of Seth gasping for air. Startled, she jumped off the mattress, waking Juju with a start.

"What is it?" Juju asked, her heart racing.

"It's Seth. Grab some towels and wet them with warm water," Maggie commanded.

Juju called the Freys at their hotel. "It's Seth. You need to come now," she said.

Thirty minutes later, the Freys arrived at the apartment still wearing their pajamas. Juliet rushed over to the mattress and Ron followed. Maggie moved away from Seth to give them space to sit beside their son. Ron put his arm around Seth's shoulders as Juliet took hold of his small hand.

"Oh, God, please. We've just found him," Juliet cried.

Seth opened his eyes. "Hi, Juliet," he breathed, and moved his head up slowly to glance at Ron and give him an acknowledging wink.

By this time, Maggie and Juju were in the bathroom, crying tears of anguish that they didn't want Seth to see. The last thing Maggie wanted was for him to be scared to die. Juju had gone to Thelma's while they waited for the Freys to arrive and sneaked Joey out the back door while Thelma was passed out on the sofa.

"My baby, we're so sorry," Juliet offered. "We're sorry for everything that's ever happened to you."

"Will you guys make sure you take care of Aggie when I'm gone?" Seth asked in a small voice.

"Yes, of course we will," Juliet answered quickly.

"No, I mean you have to really take care of her, just like she took care of me," Seth pressed.

Juliet slowed her mind to listen closely to what her son was asking. Maggie was the center of Seth's universe, and had it not been for her, they might never have seen their son alive again. Seth had been blessed with the presence of Maggie for most of his short life. Juliet finally understood.

"Seth, we'll love Maggie just as you have loved her. Your father and I promise you that," Juliet swore through sobs.

"Thank you," Seth said.

Over the next hour, Seth's breathing became more labored. He was making an effort to keep his eyes open. Even at thirteen, he instinctively knew his life was just about over and that once he closed his eyes and gave in to the soft, deep sleep that beckoned him, he would never open them again.

"Juju," Seth called.

Juju approached the mattress quickly and knelt beside him.

"What's up, little man?" Juju asked, her voice cracking.

"You're the best sister ever. You should shower more, though, 'cause you're kinda stinky. I mean, ya smell like ass," Seth joked.

"Yeah, well, your breath stinks like elephant shit," Juju countered.

Everyone in the room joined in a mournful laugh, including Seth.

"Joey," Seth said as she moved next to him. "I'm sorry we never got married. But when you do, and you have a baby, can you name your baby after me?"

Joey nodded. She crawled on top of him and laid her head on his chest, which was all skin and bones. She could hear his heart pattering unnaturally fast.

"It doesn't matter who I marry. He'll never be as good as you," Joey assured him as her bottom lip quivered.

"Aggie promised me she'll take care of you," Seth said proudly, to let her know he'd hooked her up.

Joey lay with him for the next fifteen minutes, as all of them swam in their own silent thoughts and regrets.

"Aggie," Seth breathed. "It's been really hard to live, but I'm more afraid to die."

Maggie went to him and brushed his curls from his eyes. "I know, Seth, but you've always been brave."

"I love you, Aggie. I can't stay awake anymore. I don't think I'm gonna wake up again. Will you give this to Juliet and Ron so they can remember me? Tell them the story about it so they know what to do...for other kids, OK?" Seth asked, shoving something into Maggie's hand.

"I love you too, baby. I'm going to make you very proud. Having you made all the bad things worth it. I'm going to miss you so much. A day won't go by that I won't wish we were together," she said.

A tender peacefulness came over Seth as he listened to Maggie and believed that through her, he would never be forgotten. Seth closed his eyes, and Maggie rested her loving hand over his heart. Less than a minute later, Seth was gone.

Chapter One Hundred Thirty-Five

———————◼———————

Maggie clung to Seth with all her might as if she might keep him from dying.

"No, oh God, no. Seth. Please come back. Just for a little longer. I'm not ready yet," Maggie cried.

She was lying on the mattress holding Seth's dead body. Her grief exploded as her chest heaved, expanding and contracting violently. After a few minutes, Juju walked over to the mattress and pulled Maggie from Seth.

"Come here, Maggie," Juju said, giving her a bear hug to settle her trembling body.

Maggie reached over and pulled Joey into them. The thirteen-year-old girl felt as though she was falling into an endless black hole. Her loss was unbearable. Seth was her best friend, and she loved him. Joey's face and neck were blotchy, and the tears dribbled off her chin.

"What are we gonna do now?" Joey asked.

"I don't know," Maggie blubbered. "I just don't know."

Ron and Juliet Frey were huddled on the other side of the room. This was the second time they were grieving the loss of their child. It was an agonizing bereavement, and neither of them could believe what had happened. They were so grateful to be able to see their son again. But losing him again forever was a terrible blow.

Maggie came to her senses and felt something pricking the palm of her hand. She uncurled her fingers, and there sat the miniature, plastic, soldier. The toy Maggie and Juju had given to Seth when he was living with Thelma.

Maggie walked over to the Freys and held her hand out, palm up. "This is for you. Seth wanted you to have it. It was given to him several years ago. He had been living with that horrible woman I told you about, and his spirit was very broken at the time. I told him this soldier was a war hero, and I bought it for him because he was so brave. He wanted you to have it; he wanted you to be brave. This is Seth's only possession, and he picked you two to keep it for him...a sign that Seth loved you," Maggie offered. "He wouldn't ever give this away to just anyone. It was his way of saying that he was happy that you found him. He told me it's for you to remember him and to help other kids."

Juliet and Ron looked at the cheap toy soldier. *It was Seth's only possession*, kept bouncing around in Juliet's mind. *It's for you to remember him and to help other kids.*

Juliet grabbed Maggie around the waist and pulled her close. "Dear God, Maggie. You were a wonderful mother to our son. Ron and I, well, we want you to know it gives us comfort that you were with him when we couldn't be. We'll always be grateful for what you did for our baby."

Three days later, a group of people gathered at a gravesite in New Jersey, close to where Juliet and Ron lived. To avoid making Rock suspicious, Colby had given other undercover agents money to pay to be with Maggie for the entire afternoon. He couldn't risk Rock finding out that he and Maggie were working together.

Maggie, Juju, and Joey stood together on the side of Seth's coffin with their heads hanging low. The Freys stood next to them, with twenty other family members and friends. As the priest said his final blessing, Juliet handed Maggie a single white rose. Maggie looked confused.

"Place the rose on top of the coffin," Juliet whispered, her eyes teary.

Maggie stepped forward and gently placed the rose where she imagined Seth's heart lay inside the gray box. She placed her hand on top of the coffin and said a silent prayer.

God, please keep Seth safe in your arms. He's a good boy and didn't deserve all the bad things that happened to him. And God, please make John William and Myles suffer agonizing deaths. So many have been lost because of them.

Maggie turned and took her place, watching as others put red roses on top of the coffin and headed back to their cars. She noticed Juju grab a woman's hand. The woman put her arm around Juju, giving her comfort, and Maggie knew she was Juju's girlfriend. *It was so nice of her to come here for Juju*, Maggie reflected. The crowd had thinned, and Juju pulled on Maggie's arm.

"Maggie, this is my girlfriend, Rory," Juju said quietly.

Maggie turned to the tall, blond-haired, brown-eyed woman. "Hi," Maggie managed. "Thank you for coming."

"Hi. I'm sorry we have to meet under these circumstances. I wanted to be here for Juju," Rory explained.

"That's great. It's nice to meet you, and thanks again for coming," Maggie said absentmindedly.

When it was only the Freys, Maggie, Joey, Juju, and Rory left, Maggie asked all of them for a moment alone. She stared at the name on the shiny rock. Seth. No last name, no date of birth or death, only his name.

Maggie felt as gloomy as the overcast, sunless sky was. She didn't want to leave Seth there alone and imagined him when he was well. Her heart ached at the thought of going on without him. With her chin against her chest, she allowed herself to wail in the privacy of her own space and time. Her stomach twisted at the loss of Seth as her sorrow pressed in on her. She wrapped her arms tightly around herself. Then there was a gentle hand on her shoulder, and she turned to see Colby standing behind her.

"I'm so sorry, Maggie," Colby said in a solemn voice.

Maggie and Colby had only seen each other a couple of times at Doubles during the final weeks of Seth's life. While the Freys sneaked into the apartment every night, it was just too dangerous for Colby to be there too.

"Come on," Colby urged her, "it's time to go. You gave him all that you had, and he loved you more than he loved anyone else."

Maggie nodded. "I know. It's just that I never expected...I mean he always had bouts of coughing and...maybe if I had paid more attention, I could have saved him...gotten him medical attention before the disease took hold. I'll never forgive myself for not knowing, not doing more. He trusted me."

Maggie let out uncontrollable harrowing groans, and Colby snatched her up into his arms. Her body trembled as her despair took root in the center of her heart. She wanted to turn back time, she wanted Seth back in her arms and back in her life.

"N-n-nothing will ever be the same again," Maggie wailed.

"No, it won't," Colby told her with determination. "But you can and will make a difference. I'll see to that."

As Maggie walked toward the car, Colby had her wrapped in his strong arms. Joey scampered toward them as they approached Colby's car.

"Oh, Maggie," Joey whimpered, "what will we do without him?"

Maggie remembered her promise to Seth: to take care of Joey. She opened her arms and clutched the young girl to her. In silence, Maggie, Juju, and Joey slid into the backseat of Colby's car. As they drove away, Maggie took one last glimpse of the fresh gravesite, Seth's final resting place.

Chapter One Hundred Thirty-Six

<hr>

The night of Seth's funeral, Maggie was back at Double Visions, working. When she came out on stage, many of the onlookers felt a twinge of sadness as they watched her dance. Shiver had told several of Maggie's regulars that Seth had died. As Maggie went around the bar and collected her tips, many of the men gave her a little more money than usual, tipping her two or three dollars instead of one. At the end of her rounds, Maggie spotted Tony and Vincent watching her. They hadn't been back to Doubles since the police took Emma away. The only reason they had come in was to keep an eye out for Emma—on their boss's instruction.

Seeing them suddenly made Maggie miss Emma, as well, compounding her sense of loss.

"Hi, guys," she said in a low voice.

"Little Maggie, how ya holdin' up? Vincent and me, we heard 'bout what happened to your kid and came by to offer our condolences. Is there anything we can do?" Tony said.

"Thank you for coming to see me," she responded modestly. "It really means a lot. I appreciate everything, but there's really nothing anyone can do."

"We heard from some of the people here that the kid had AIDS," Vincent said wanting to know for sure.

"Yeah, he did," she said, gulping.

"How'd a kid that young get it?" Vincent pressed, wanting to hear it from Maggie.

"I imagine from when he was a small boy. There were so many men..." Maggie's voice trailed off.

"Holy shit. What da fuck is wrong wit' these rotten bastards? If I ever run into one of those mudder fuckers, they'll be sorry," Vincent exclaimed, forgetting about Maggie's feelings.

Maggie gave him a weak smile. "I don't doubt it, Vincent. But it won't bring Seth back to me."

"You're so insensitive, Vin. I mean, the girl just lost her kid, and you're talkin' 'bout the perverted dick bags that did this to him," Tony scolded.

"Ah, I don't mean nothin' by it, little Maggie. It just boils my blood, is all I'm tryin' to tell ya," Vincent said with remorse.

Maggie put her hand over Vincent's. "It's OK. I understand. It's not like I haven't given those assholes a lot of thought over the past weeks. I just figure someday they'll get everything they deserve."

Then she changed the subject. "So do you two know where Emma is? Since she was taken out of here by the police, we haven't heard anything from her," Maggie said.

"Nah, all we know is that Emma ain't comin' back for a while," Tony said.

"How long?" Maggie asked.

Tony fidgeted with the cigarette lighter sitting on the bar in front of him. "Don't know for sure. We ain't heard too much 'bout what's goin' on," he lied.

"OK, well if you see her, tell her that I would love to talk to her. Emma always seemed to relate to the things I've been through. I miss talking to her. I envy her strength. She doesn't take shit from anyone. I could use her 'fuck 'em all' attitude right about now," Maggie told them.

Tony and Vincent nodded, thinking about Emma. She was a straight shooter, all right. Emma would cut someone to their knees sooner than look at them.

"We'll tell her ya were askin' for her if we see her," Tony promised.

Tony reached up on the bar and grabbed a cocktail napkin. Then he gestured to the bartender for a pen. He scribbled something on the napkin and handed it to Maggie.

"We just came by to see how you're doin'. We don't get back here much, so if ya need anythin', ya just give us a ring," Tony said with a protective edge in his voice.

Maggie's eyes welled up. "Thank you. If anything comes up, I promise I'll call you."

As Tony and Vincent left Doubles, Maggie followed them to the door with her eyes. She put the cocktail napkin into the cup of her bra, recalling what Emma had told her: if there ever comes a day when you can't handle Rock, then you need to talk to Tony and Vincent. I don't know if they can help you, but if there was ever a chance for someone to go up against that piece of stank dog shit, it's the two of them.

For some reason that Maggie didn't understand, having their phone number made her feel as if she had a tiny bit of control. But that was nothing compared to the feeling of empowerment she'd have in the weeks to come.

Chapter One Hundred Thirty-Seven

"Is there anything else we're missing, Maggie? Are there any other people who work for Rock who could come back to bite us in the ass?" Colby asked with a sense of urgency.

It had only been ten days since Seth's funeral, but Colby and his agency were ready to move on Rock's businesses. Maggie was feeding into Colby's energy of eliminating Rock and his pimps and thugs once and for all. Now, more than ever, she wanted her freedom. Maggie wanted to begin her life anew, to make good on the promises she'd made to Seth.

"No, no one else I can think of. Just make sure Juju doesn't get busted. She knows what's going down, and I don't want the police to arrest her for dealing. You'll keep her out of trouble, right?" Maggie asked.

"Yeah, I have that covered. There's always 'special circumstances' we take into account. Juju wouldn't normally be one of those circumstances, but I told the agency you wouldn't talk unless she walked away from this whole thing clean. They gave me their word," Colby said.

Maggie nodded. "Maybe, when this is all over, we can go on a real date?"

Colby eyes turned mischievous. "Well now, Ms. Maggie. Aren't you getting ballsy all of a sudden, asking me out on a date."

A genuine smile broke across Maggie's face for the first time since Seth died. "Yeah, I guess I am. I've lost too much time with all of this bullshit—all of my childhood thrown away and then my teenage years. I'm working on saving my twenties."

Maggie grew serious. "I went to the free clinic in Center City. I got tested for HIV about a week before Seth died."

"Oh. Did you get the results?" Colby asked, her sudden somberness making his skin prickly.

"Yeah, I'm clean. I'm happy, but how is it that Seth could have gotten HIV in the few years he was exposed, and I can go all this time and not get it?" Maggie wondered aloud.

"You said they made the men use condoms, right?" Colby said.

"Right. But we didn't always use condoms for oral sex. Those bastards, including Rock, have been playing Russian roulette with my life, with all of our lives. I see things so differently now. I wish it didn't take Seth dying for me to stop being scared about what they'd do to me if I rebelled. What they're doing to me and the others is worse than death. I don't think they could make us suffer more. It's time for all of this craziness to stop. I'm taking my life back," Maggie stated with more courage than she actually felt.

Maggie wanted to have a life, and more than anything, she wanted to be away from Rock. But a seed of fear lay like a brick in the pit of her belly. She wasn't sure she'd know how to live normally. She may be book learned, but her daily life had revolved around sex.

Colby watched as she clenched her teeth tightly. "What is it? What's worrying you? Rock will stay in prison for a long time; you don't have to worry."

"I'm not worried about Rock. When this is all over, I don't really know how to start my life. I'm not sure what I'm supposed to do," Maggie confided.

"Don't worry, Maggie. You're a smart girl, and you'll have time to figure things out," Colby soothed, feeling her angst.

Less than a week later, Colby met Maggie in the lap dance room at Doubles. The two had been careful to use the seats farthest from other dancers and clients ever since Montana overheard them talking shortly after Maggie started working at the club. They sat side by side. Colby had never looked more serious.

"What is it?" Maggie asked.

"Everything will happen one week from today. They're going to take out all of Rock's houses," Colby said.

"Houses?" Maggie asked.

"Yes, we've been able to identify eight houses within a twenty-mile radius where Rock keeps girls," Colby whispered.

"By 'keeps girls' you mean prostitutes, right?" Maggie asked. Colby nodded.

"Why didn't I know this?" Maggie pondered aloud.

"We followed some of the men you told us about. We discovered that some were johns, but others were really working for Rock. Three of those people you identified led us to these other houses. The information you gave us is going to free a lot of young women, Maggie," Colby said.

Maggie nodded, but she was stunned by the knowledge that Rock had prostitution businesses all over the city. No wonder he was so powerful, she finally realized. Drugs, prostitution, porn...his empire was bigger than she'd known. Rock was a user of people, and his only goals were to make money and keep his pig of a wife happy. Maggie smiled, knowing that his days were numbered. She hoped that in prison, he'd get butt fucked every day for the rest of his life.

"OK, so this is good, right? You're happy. All the work we've done together is about to pay off," Colby reminded her.

"Yeah, I'm definitely happy," Maggie said, and then she paused. "I need to take care of Joey. That means I have to get her away from Thelma before this all happens."

Colby scratched his forehead. "I was going to arrange for child protective services to be there when we raid Rock's home."

Maggie shook her head. "No. She'll just be placed into another system. Her mother is useless. I'm going to talk to Joey tomorrow. I have an idea." She looked up at Colby. "An idea I don't want to share with you right now," she said firmly.

"S-sure," Colby stuttered, a little hurt that Maggie wouldn't share the secret.

Early the next morning, Maggie and Juju met Joey on her way to school. She ran to them, as she did every morning. But they noticed that she was trying not to put weight on her right leg. When she was close enough to them, they saw a fresh black eye.

"Did that bitch do this to you?" Juju asked.

Joey nodded with such bravery that Maggie pulled her over to the curb and sat down.

"Things are going to get better real soon," Maggie promised.

Maggie needed to be certain about Joey's mom.

"Remember when we met and you told me your mom traded you for drugs and beer?" Maggie started.

"Yeah, why?" Joey responded.

"Is that really what happened? Or were you trying to protect your family?" Maggie asked. She knew all too well how sex traffickers operated. They made sure the kids were always afraid to run by threatening to kill them and their families.

"Yeah. I hate her guts!" Joey exclaimed. The young girl's face turned bright red, anger welling up inside of her at the thought of her mother betraying her.

"I hate her guts, too," Juju interjected, getting angry with a woman she'd never met.

"Why are you askin' me that now?" Joey said.

"I just wanted to be sure because if a day came when you could go back to her, well, I just wanted to be sure, that's all," Maggie said, not wanting to divulge any information that could put Joey in danger.

Later that morning, Maggie made the phone call and held her breath, waiting for someone to pick up the phone.

"Hello?"

"It's Maggie."

"Hi, Maggie. How are you?"

"Juliet, I need your help," Maggie said with hope.

Chapter One Hundred Thirty-Eight

On the night of the big bust, Armando drove Maggie to Double Visions for her shift. Everything was set. She walked into the bar and found Colby.

"Let's go," Maggie said.

They left through the back door of the bar and raced back to Kensington. Colby dropped Maggie off near her apartment. She slipped into her building quickly and took the steps two at a time. Juju was waiting for her by the door. Maggie rushed into the apartment.

"You ready?" Maggie asked.

Juju held out her hands for Maggie's inspection. She wore large, ugly rings on each of her fingers.

"I'll take that as a yes," Maggie stated, her excitement building.

The two girls took back streets and alleys to get to Rock's house. They sat low in the grass behind the shed. Maggie looked at the watch Colby had lent to her.

"We've got twenty minutes," Maggie whispered.

The girls sat in silence. Their adrenaline was flowing. Maggie prayed that things would happen just as they had planned. At exactly 11:00 p.m., Maggie and Juju rose. They walked to the back door of Rock's house quickly, and Maggie fidgeted while Juju picked the lock. Once inside the house, they could hear the noise of the television coming from the living room. Maggie and Juju locked eyes. With a nod of their heads, the two girls stormed into the living room where Thelma was sprawled on the sofa, cigarette in hand, gazing at the television.

Thelma looked up, startled by the sudden activity around her.

"Who you motherfuckers think ya are, comin' into my house uninvited," Thelma growled.

"We're the bitches that came to watch you suffer!" Juju snarled.

Before Thelma could haul her body from the sofa, Juju landed the first kick into the woman's chest. Thelma fell back against the cushions, and Juju proceeded to slam punches into her face. As Maggie ran for the stairs to find Joey, she heard the sound of Thelma's nose breaking. A smile broke across Maggie's face.

Within five minutes, the girls were running out of the back door with Joey. Juju had left Thelma unconscious on the sofa. She wanted to beat Thelma until she was dead, but something Maggie said made her stop.

"That's enough. We have to get out of here. She'll get what's coming to her in prison," Maggie reminded her in a giddy voice.

The three of them ran as fast as their legs could move. They cut through a block of backyards and down a dark alley to an isolated street. They fled toward a parked car with its engine running.

"There they are," Maggie said, gasping for breath and pointing down the street.

When they got to waiting car, Juliet jumped out. She immediately took Joey by the hand, but the child resisted. Maggie knelt down next to Joey.

"Juliet and Ron are going to take care of you for a couple of days. Just until I can come and get you. But we have to hurry," Maggie said.

Joey's eyes filled with tears. "How do I know you'll come for me?"

"Because I told you I will. Now go with the Freys. They're going to keep you safe," Maggie commanded. Then she gave Joey a quick hug, stood, and planted a kiss on Juliet's cheek. "Guard her with your life," Maggie said.

"We will," Juliet responded.

A minute later, the Freys were driving toward their mansion in New Jersey. Joey was in the backseat of the car. She was shaking from all that had just happened and worried that something awful would happen to Maggie and Juju and she'd never see them again.

Chapter One Hundred Thirty-Nine

B y the time Maggie and Juju got into downtown Kensington, it looked like a war zone. Police cars and SWAT vans littered the streets. Some of the young prostitutes were crying and called out to Maggie as she passed, but Maggie kept walking, just as Colby had instructed. *Stop for no one. Get back to your apartment*, he'd said.

Maggie and Juju paused for a brief moment when they saw Rock pushed up against a police car as an officer handcuffed him. Feeling their eyes on him, Rock looked over at the two girls. Juju gave him the finger; Maggie held his gaze.

"You fuckin' no-good whore," Rock screamed at Maggie.

Maggie did a curtsy and walked on.

Rock watched as she strutted down the street. His rage boiled as he realized that his own bitch had set him up. Maggie had outsmarted him. She'd help to take down everything he'd built. Rock felt like a complete fool, and his anger grew stronger. He felt as though he had the strength to break out of the metal cuffs, run down the street, and rip Maggie's limbs from her body. Instead, the police officer shoved him with force into the backseat of the cruiser.

Then the officer pushed him over on the seat. "You fucking, low-life scum. Don't worry. Where you're going, there will be plenty of time for you to be angry. So for now, keep your shit together, or we'll make it harder on you."

It wasn't until three o'clock the next morning that Colby rapped on the apartment door.

Maggie opened it cautiously. She and Juju had been unable to sleep. They felt wired. Maggie threw her arms around Colby's neck, and he held her close.

"It's done," Colby said.

Stepping inside the apartment, he closed the door behind him.

Maggie and Juju watched him, their eyes like hungry animals' as they craved information.

"It all happened pretty smoothly. Two officers were shot in one of the houses they raided. One of the officers died, and the other is in critical condition," Colby recited.

Maggie's eyes grew sad. "What about Rock? He'll go to prison?" she asked, wanting confirmation.

"He sure will. Rock's going to prison for a very long time, thanks to you," Colby said, knowing that she'd worry if she thought Rock would be set free.

"Fuckin' A," Juju rejoiced. "And they arrested Thelma?"

Colby smiled and nodded. "Someone—I can't imagine who—put quite a hurting on her."

Juju beamed victoriously. "That chick had it comin' to her."

Then he grew serious. "There is one thing," Colby said, looking right at Maggie.

"What?" Maggie shrieked.

"This was the biggest bust in Kensington in the last twenty years. My police chief and the lead detective I work for would like to meet you and personally thank you for all that you've done," Colby said, beaming.

Maggie slapped his arm. "You're such a troublemaker."

"No, I'm serious. They really do want to meet you. I told them I'd ask. It's completely up to you. If you're not comfortable, they'll understand," Colby said.

"I guess it's fine," Maggie said, looking at Juju, who nodded. "Are they going to come here?"

"No, we'll drive down to the police station and meet them there," Colby explained.

"When?" Maggie asked.

"We'll meet them in the morning. I'll pick you up around eleven, OK?" Colby said.

Then Maggie turned to Juju. "Will you come with me?"

"Hell, yeah!" Juju shouted.

As the girls lay on the mattress together after Colby had left, they giggled about the damage Juju had done to Thelma.

"Juju, I'm not sure what I'm going to do now. I mean, we have to get Joey from the Freys, but we're going to have to get real jobs," Maggie said.

Suddenly, the new freedom was liberating and paralyzing. Being free of Rock and his guys had only seemed like a fantasy. With it all behind her, Maggie slowly began to panic. What would she do now? How was she supposed to start her life over? Then it dawned on Maggie that there was hard work ahead.

At the station the next morning, Maggie and Juju held hands as they followed Colby into a large, well-lit room with lots of tables and chairs. There were police officers drinking coffee and eating junk food from the vending machines against the wall. Still following Colby, they walked through the room as the officers watched them closely. Colby led them into a cozy office that had a large, mahogany desk and a long, leather sofa.

Several men turned to greet Colby. Finally, he stepped aside as he introduced Maggie and Juju to each of the very official looking men in suits. The last man to be introduced had been leaning over the desk with his back to them, writing in a small notepad. He finally put the pad away, looked up, and strode toward the girls.

"Hey," Colby said. He seemed happier to see this man than he was to greet the other suits in the room. "Maggie, this is Detective Harker."

As Maggie extended her hand, Detective Harker seemed to be in a trance. He looked into her soulful blue eyes. There was no doubt in his mind. He'd looked at her picture a million times over the last nine years. He took her hand in his and held onto it tightly.

"Maggie, it's a pleasure to meet you," Detective Harker said with sincerity.

"Nice to meet you, too," Maggie responded, trying to pull her hand from his. But the Harker guy wasn't letting go. He just kept looking into her eyes and smiling. Maggie thought he was a little odd, but then his name jumped out at her. *Rae Harker was the detective who worked with my parents when I went missing*, she remembered.

Maggie turned to her friend. "This is Juju," she said, hoping Harker would let go of her hand.

Coming to his wits, he let go and addressed Juju. "So you're the little girl who put the hurting on that big woman?" he asked, beaming with pride.

Juju puffed her chest out, feeling for the first time in her life like she had a reason to be proud. "Yep, that's me. I hope that bitch rots in hell," she added.

Detective Harker nodded and returned his gaze to Maggie.

"What?" Maggie asked, growing antsy from the attention Harker kept giving her.

"I know you," Harker stated. "We've never met, but I know you."

Harker could see by the strain on Maggie's face that he was freaking her out.

"What I mean is, I know your parents," Harker clarified.

Maggie's heart seized. She looked at Colby, who seemed just as confused. "Yes, I read about you in the newspaper," Maggie countered.

Detective Harker looked surprised.

"Well, it was good to meet you," Maggie sputtered abruptly. "We're gonna get going now."

Detective Harker raised his hand, and Maggie stopped immediately. "I need you to stay," he said. "I have some things I want to talk to you about. Important things that you'll definitely want to hear."

Chapter One Hundred Forty

————————◼————————

etective Harker escorted Maggie over to the sofa and asked everyone to leave the office.

"I want Juju and Colby to stay," Maggie said.

After the other officers left, Detective Harker turned to Maggie. "Your parents have been looking for you since the day you went missing. Given that you're over eighteen, you can decide on your own now. But I really think you should consider being reunited with them. Your mother and father are terrific people. They've dedicated the last nine years to helping other missing children."

The four of them were silent as Maggie looked down at her hands. Finally, she found the courage to speak. "I'm not the eleven-year-old girl they lost," she shamefully explained.

"They won't care. Your parents deserve to know you are alive. There's nothing stopping you now. All the bad guys are locked up. This is your chance, Maggie," Harker stated in a hopeful voice.

"Maggie," Colby interjected, "you have to make this decision. I know that you've always wanted to see them again," he reminded her.

Maggie looked at Juju.

"Hey, don't look at me," Juju said. "What the fuck do I know about parents? But 'member how happy the Freys were when they realized Seth was their son? It's worth a shot. If they don't like who you are, ya can just walk away."

"OK, but Colby and Juju go with me," Maggie told Detective Harker.

Harker slapped his hands together and jumped to his feet. "Maggie, you have no idea how happy your parents are going to be."

"I hope so," Maggie mumbled, embarrassed to think about all the things she'd done in her life.

Harker saw the remorse in her eyes. "What happened to you was not your fault. All the things you did were a matter of survival. Trust me, they'll understand. You don't have to tell them anything that you don't want them to know. The ball is in your court, Maggie."

Maggie nodded. "When?"

"I have a habit of just dropping in on them unexpectedly. Would you be willing to go see them now?" Harker asked excitedly.

Maggie looked down at the clothes she was wearing. Her old, torn jeans and faded T-shirt made her look poor, but at least she didn't look like a hooker, except for the five-inch platform pumps she was wearing. Besides, it wasn't like she owned anything that was decent enough for the occasion.

"Sure. Let's go," Maggie said, apprehensively.

Maggie sat in the passenger seat while Colby and Juju sat together in the back of the car. Detective Harker chatted about nothing as he tried to contain his own excitement. As they drove toward Maggie's old home, she didn't recognize much until Harker turned onto her street. She looked at the houses and had vague memories of the neighborhood where she'd lived more than eleven years ago. Finally, Harker pulled into the Clarkes' driveway. Maggie stared at the front door and then took in the rest of the house. It hadn't changed much.

"Ready?" Harker asked.

Maggie's heart was pattering in her chest. "I'm scared."

"I know you're scared. This is a lot all at one time. Just relax. I'll bring them out to meet you."

Maggie sat in the car and watched through the open window as Harker made his way to the front door of the Clarkes' house.

Harker rapped on the door. In less than thirty seconds, a young girl opened the door. "Hi Detective Harker," Mara said.

"Hi, Mara. Are your mom and dad home?" Harker asked.

Before Mara could yell for them, Lorraine came walking toward the front door with a big smile at the sight of Detective Harker.

Harker was beaming.

"You look happy today, Harker. What's going on?" Lorraine asked.

Harker kept smiling at Lorraine, and then he whispered to Mara, "Go find your dad."

Mara ran back into the house as Lorraine stood at the doorway.

When Rob appeared in the entryway, Harker said, "I need you to come outside."

"Now what, Harker? You have a stray animal you need our help with?" Lorraine joked.

As they walked toward Harker's car, Maggie opened the door and stepped onto the driveway. The Clarkes stopped in midstride.

"Who is that?" Lorraine asked mindlessly, as she approached the girl.

She stared at Maggie; she saw her eyes and her features. It was her beloved child. "Oh my God."

Mother and daughter stood looking into each other's eyes for a few short seconds. Then Lorraine opened her arms, and Maggie slid into them like the missing piece of a puzzle.

Lorraine cried, "Oh my God. My Maggie...my Maggie...my Maggie."

Lorraine hugged Maggie so tightly that it startled her. Then the reality hit her like a ton of bricks. "Mom? Mommy? Oh, Mom, I missed you."

The two held each other and sobbed. Even Detective Harker couldn't stop his emotions from flowing.

"Maggie? Baby, is it really you?" Rob cried.

Maggie nodded, and Rob threw his arms around his wife and daughter. Several minutes passed before they began to unfold from each other. Lorraine took Maggie's hand in her own as they stood staring at one another.

Rob leaned over and shook Harker's hand. "Thanks, Rae. I don't know how you found her, but thank you."

"Well, that's a long story. But let's just say your girl here is a real hero and leave it at that," Harker said, not wanting to reveal any information that belonged to Maggie.

"Come inside," Lorraine said, pulling Maggie along.

"Wait!" Maggie turned to Colby and Juju and waved them over.

"These are my best friends, Colby and Juju," Maggie said.

Lorraine and Rob exchanged quick hellos, still in a state of shock that their daughter was back with them. Once inside the house, Lorraine found Mara sitting at the kitchen table, her knees pulled up to her chin. When she saw all the adults enter the room, she rushed over to Lorraine and took her hand.

Lorraine bent down. "Mara, this is our daughter, Maggie," she stated with glee. She leaned over and gave Maggie a hug. "Remember we told you about her?"

Mara nodded. Her head hung, and her hair covered her face.

Lorraine and Rob were so happy that they were practically dizzy and didn't notice the change in Mara, but Maggie noticed it quickly. She'd seen that look on Seth's face when he thought Colby was going to take her away from him.

Maggie bent down and pulled Mara's chin up with her index finger. "Hi, Mara. Everything's going to be fine, and now it looks like I have a little sister," she said.

Mara's head jolted up, and her face lit up with excitement. "Wow, that's so cool," she said, relieved that Maggie wasn't going to make her leave.

Hours passed as they all sat in the Clarkes' kitchen talking about how the Clarkes came to find Mara, what Maggie's brother, Keith, had been doing, and anything else they could think of to avoid talking about what had happened to Maggie in all the years she had been gone. Lorraine could see that her innocent daughter was no longer there. She had grown into a beautiful, loving woman, but the hard edge came through loud and clear. Lorraine and Rob both knew their daughter had been through hell.

It was early evening when Rae Harker announced that he needed to head back to the precinct. As Maggie got to her feet, Lorraine grabbed her hand. "Won't you stay? You can sleep with Mara in your old room."

Maggie sadly shook her head. "No. It would be better if I go back to my place."

Maggie had no intention of staying at her parents' home. In an odd way, there was almost no connection between the daughter she had been and the person whom she had become. Maggie felt detached from Lorraine and Rob. She was just getting a taste of freedom and she wasn't willing to give it up. Maggie loved her parents, but the bottom line was that she didn't know them anymore. As such, Maggie came off as oddly distant to the Clarkes. Maggie's homecoming had been much less than the three of them had dreamed it would be, and each of them wished it could have been more.

Lorraine's shoulders dropped. "Where do you live?"

"Kensington," Maggie admitted.

Lorraine visibly shivered and then immediately regretted it. She didn't want to make Maggie feel uncomfortable about anything.

"When can we see you again?" Lorraine asked, still holding onto Maggie's hand.

"I'm not sure. I...I..." Maggie looked to Colby.

"I can drive you here whenever you want," Colby offered.

Maggie smiled, reminding Lorraine and Rob of the magnificence that remained in her.

"How about if you come for lunch tomorrow?" Lorraine asked.

Maggie nodded. "OK. That would be OK."

"Terrific!" Rob exclaimed. "Maggie, we want to talk to you about what happened. We never stopped searching for you. We want you to know that not a day has passed that we didn't talk about you."

"Thanks," Maggie muttered, feeling guilty that she hadn't thought about them in a while. "Maybe someday we can talk about everything. I'm not ready to do that now, though."

"Fair enough," Rob stated. "Lunch tomorrow, then?" he asked, hoping he hadn't scared her off.

"Sure. We'll be here," Maggie said.

Sitting in Rae Harker's car as they drove back to the police station, Maggie stared out the window.

"Maggie, I know this has been really hard on you. But at some point in the very near future, we'll need to talk about what happened to you. We have to do our best to make sure it doesn't happen to others. OK?" Detective Harker said.

"I know. I figured as much," Maggie mumbled.

For the remainder of the ride, Maggie was flooded with emotions. She was happy for her freedom and to have seen her parents again. But it wasn't the same. It wasn't how she'd imagined their reunion. Her parents looked much older. But what was really nagging her was the feeling that Lorraine and Rob needed something from her that she wasn't certain she could give to them.

Chapter One Hundred Forty-One

Two weeks later, Maggie and Colby drove to New Jersey to pick up Joey at the Freys' house. Joey started jumping up and down as soon as she laid eyes on Maggie.

"You came for me!" Joey yelled, wrapping her arms around Maggie.

"I told you I would," Maggie said. "Are you ready to go?"

Joey had packed a small suitcase that the Freys had bought for the occasion. Inside were new clothes they also provided for her. Joey walked over to the Freys and gave each of them a good-bye hug.

Juliet was wringing her hands together. "We're really going to miss you, Joey. If you ever want to stay with us or come for a visit, you're always welcome."

Maggie reached out and took Juliet's hands in her own.

"You haven't seen the last of us. We're going to be around, and I'm sure Joey will want to come and stay with you for a few weeks in the summer," Maggie said.

Joey nodded. "Yeah, I'm gonna come back. You promised we'd go to the beach, 'member?"

Juliet's eyes filled with tears. "Of course I remember, Joey. We're going to have so much fun."

Colby, sensing that the Freys needed to talk to Maggie privately, pulled Joey along. "Let's go, lady. Your chariot awaits," he teased, taking Joey's hand and leading her outside to the car.

Ron moved closer to his wife and draped his arm around her shoulder to give her support. Then he looked at Juliet and nodded.

"Maggie, this is hard for us. You and Joey and Juju are all we have left of Seth. I'm afraid..." she looked at Ron. "We're both afraid you'll move on, and we won't see any of you again."

Maggie could feel Juliet's deep anguish. Seth looked so much like his father that it was as if Ron was a grownup version of the boy she'd always loved. Her heart ached for the couple who were trying desperately to hang onto the only link to their son they had left.

"Juliet, we're family now. We aren't going anywhere. Seth wanted us all to be together. He told you that himself. I don't want you to worry, OK?" Maggie soothed.

"OK," Juliet stated sadly.

"In fact, I was thinking you two could come back to Philly for a weekend this month," Maggie offered.

Juliet perked up. "That would be wonderful. We'll rent a suite at The Four Seasons that has a couple of bedrooms. You all can come and stay there. It'll be so much fun," she gushed.

"That'll be great. Let's plan on it," Maggie replied.

Over the next six months, Maggie continued to work at Double Visions. She'd passed her GED and had applied to local colleges. Juju, Maggie, and Joey still lived in the rundown apartment in Kensington. Maggie and her parents had managed to develop a healthy relationship, and she had even told them about some of the things that happened over the past eleven years.

Maggie realized, through her parents' insight that being an unwilling participant in anything is nothing at all like being a willing participant. Lorraine and Rob had learned over the years that victims of abuse often felt like everything that had happened to them was their fault because, in some way, they'd participated. The only people to blame were the brutal savages who forced her to participate.

Once she was able to wrap her mind around this enlightening concept, Maggie opened up to her parents about her past. For the first time since her kidnapping, Maggie felt free of shame.

A few months later, Juju announced that she was moving in with her girlfriend, Rory. With this news, Maggie thought about taking Joey and moving out of Kensington. One night, as Maggie and Colby were going to dinner, she mentioned the idea of moving closer to her parents.

"It's funny you should bring that up," Colby began. "I was thinking I'd like to move out to the suburbs soon. Maybe we can get an apartment together. You know, as roommates."

Maggie and Colby had remained close. While they each had a heavy crush on the other, there had been too much turmoil as Maggie tried to settle in with Joey and reestablish a bond with her parents. They got together as friends, but nothing more.

"Roommates, huh? Well, that's an idea," Maggie responded giddily.

"Yeah. You, Joey, and me. I think we could make it work. Besides, you two have grown on me, sort of like mold that you can't get rid of," Colby teased.

Maggie threw her head back and laughed, her silky black hair flying behind her. Colby's groin stirred as he watched her in awe.

"So? What do you think?" Colby asked.

"I think it's something I have to give some serious thought. I also have to talk to Joey. I want to make sure she'd be comfortable moving away from her school and moving in with the likes of you," Maggie joked.

In the weeks that followed, Maggie and Joey agreed that it would be a good idea to move in with Colby. Lorraine and Rob were thrilled to have their daughter closer and offered to help get them started. Then they gave Maggie the greatest news.

"We want you to know that we still have your college fund," Lorraine stated, giddy to have her daughter back.

"My college fund?" Maggie asked with scrunched brows.

"Yes. Your college fund. We set one up for you and Keith when you were born. We never stopped putting money into yours. We hoped that one day you'd come back to us. There's enough money in there for you to go to a good college," Lorraine explained.

Maggie squealed, "Wow! Thank you so much. I never expected anything from you."

Lorraine and Rob watched as she happily told Mara what great parents they had. Mara giggled and joined in on Maggie's excitement. "Do I have a college fund too?" Mara asked.

"Of course you do," Rob lied.

He and Lorraine had discussed it, and when the time was right, they'd take out a loan for Mara's education. They'd originally planned to use the money they'd saved for Maggie, but once she returned, that idea was dead.

As days turned into weeks, Maggie, Colby, and Joey prepared to move into their new apartment. They had found an affordable two-bedroom apartment in Whitemarsh, the town next to her parents'. As the time to move crept closer, Maggie and Joey became more excited. For starters, they were happy to move to the suburbs, where there was less congestion. But they were most excited about having a real bathroom in their new rental. Colby was also excited, but not for the same reasons. He was excited at the prospect of becoming more than just a good friend to Maggie.

On the day they moved, Maggie and Joey walked to a small deli in the early afternoon to pick up sandwiches and to say good-bye to the many people they knew in the area. Several of the young prostitutes came to see them one last time and wish them luck. Most planned to continue with prostitution, but they were grateful to be free of Rock.

Juju and Rory showed up at the apartment in Kensington and helped them load their meager belongings into Colby's car. As they stood at the curb, Maggie grabbed hold of Juju. They squeezed each other tightly for several minutes. When they parted, they were both choked up.

"We're going to see each other all the time," Maggie reassured Juju.

"I know, but it just ain't the same anymore. I moved out, and now you're movin' outta Kensington," Juju yammered. Juju didn't want to mention that Seth was no longer with them. The memories and the loss were just too painful.

"I guess we're getting old," Maggie joked unsuccessfully, trying to lighten the mood.

Colby came up behind them. "Are you ready to go, Maggie?"

Maggie nodded and looked at Juju. "I'll never forget how you saved my life and rescued me from the snow."

Juju grimaced at the thought. "I'll never forget how you moved in and took over like a bossy beotch."

They laughed and hugged once more before Maggie turned and got into Colby's car. As he pulled away from the curb, Joey looked out the back window and waved until Juju and Rory faded from sight.

Chapter One Hundred Forty-Two

———————————————————■———————————————————

"Well, ladies, this is it. We all get to start over again," Colby said with enthusiasm.

Maggie was leaning against the car window and didn't respond to his attempt to pick up the mood. Colby knew there had been many changes in Maggie and Joey's lives over the past nine months. Losing Seth, leaving Kensington and everyone they knew, freedom from Rock, and finally, saying good-bye to Juju—at least temporarily—had taken its toll.

"All right, now look. Juju will come and visit, and it's not like we aren't ever going back to Kensington to see her. This isn't an end to things; it's a new beginning. The three of us are off on an adventure. We're all *roomies* now, and we're going to have lots of fun and make new memories. So cheer up, you two. You're bringing me down," Colby lectured.

When neither Maggie nor Joey responded, Colby added, "OK, then. I guess I'll just be talking to myself from now on. Maybe that won't be so bad; at least I know I'll always agree with myself. Wow, Colby. You're right. We are going to have a lot of fun together. By the way, did I tell you that you're the most handsome man on the planet? Yeah, and you have a great personality, too. Everyone wants to be around you," Colby rambled.

Maggie and Joey couldn't help but laugh at his performance.

"You're such an odd man," Maggie said, chuckling.

"Yeah, Colby. You're weird," Joey chimed in from the backseat.

"Oh, I see. So you two only say stuff when it's to mock me. I get it. You're both just lucky to be with a cool dude like me," Colby told them.

The two girls laughed harder. "Oh, right. You don't have a cool bone in your body. I mean, seriously, Colby, you're cool through Joey and me. You're only cool by association," Maggie teased.

Joey was energized by the banter. "Hey, can we get pizza for dinner tonight?"

Maggie looked over at Colby. "I don't know. What do you think, Colby? Should we get the brat in the back pizza for dinner?"

"I'm not so sure, Maggie. I mean, she has been good today, and if she gives us hugs when we get to our new apartment, then *maybe* we could think about it," Colby teased.

"You two are nasty; and Colby, your breath stinks; and Maggie, your hair has knots in the back," Joey fired back, giggling.

The three continued to chatter and joke until they pulled up in front of their new apartment. Colby had managed to break through the gloom that had filled the car and gave them a reason to be excited.

As they entered their new apartment, Maggie and Joey looked around in surprise. The apartment was completely set up. The two girls stood motionless with their mouths hanging open. After a couple of seconds, they rushed around to look at everything. There was living room furniture and a dining room set. The kitchen had been fully stocked with appliances and all of the other essentials. Even the refrigerator and cabinets were filled with food. As they walked into the bedroom that Maggie and Joey would share, they found a king-sized bed, two large dressers, and night tables on either side of the bed. The entire room had been done in hot pink and white with random splashes of bold colors on the walls.

"Did my mom and dad do all of this?" Maggie finally asked Colby.

He shook his head. "They did buy all of your bedding. Your mom actually picked out the colors to use in your bedroom. They wanted to buy a lot more stuff, but I told them we had it covered."

"We have it covered? Are you kidding? Where am I going to get the money to pay for all of this fancy stuff?" Maggie asked.

"You're not. You're going to concentrate on going to college and getting a part-time job, remember? That's what we agreed. Then, after you're making a billion dollars a year, I get to sit back and sponge off of you," Colby said, toying with her.

Maggie was immature when it came to finances and what things cost. Working for Rock, she wasn't given enough money for anything but essentials. She had no idea how much money Colby had spent to set up the apartment with all of the new and beautiful things. Just as she didn't realize that the one hundred dollars a month in rent she was going to pay Colby would only cover the monthly electric bill. It didn't matter to Colby, though; he would have let them live there rent-free. But Maggie had insisted on pulling her weight. If only she knew that the monthly lease alone was two thousand dollars. With that price tag, however, came one of the best school districts for Joey and a five-minute drive for Maggie to see her parents.

On their first night in the new apartment, and after Joey was sleeping, Maggie and Colby sat on the soft, plush sofa in the airy living room. Colby had brought them each a cold beer, and they were sipping on the fizzy liquid as Maggie rambled on about how much she appreciated everything he'd done for her.

"I'm not an idiot, Colby. Not many men would want to take on an ex-hooker and the kid she found as roommates. You know that Joey and I come with our unique set of problems. But it doesn't seem to bother you. Why is that?" Maggie asked.

"My parents raised me to be open. They taught me how to find the good in people. Just because someone had a horrible life doesn't make them bad. Just because you and Joey were sold for sex as kids doesn't make you unworthy of great things in life. In fact, I think it makes you even more deserving of the things that bring you joy. My mom and dad always wanted me to accept people for who they are, that's all. I'm not saying they want me hanging out with serial killers or child molesters, but they would never pass judgment on someone who has been through the things you've been through," Colby explained.

Maggie nodded as she began to understand that Colby viewed her as a human being worthy of happiness. She smiled and leaned into him. Colby leaned forward, and in the next moment, their lips brushed. Maggie's blue eyes were ablaze, and Colby could feel the blood pumping through his veins. The two had waited a long time for intimacy. They'd both always wanted it from each other, but under the circumstances, they had avoided that type of relationship. But now everything was different. Maggie was no longer obligated to sell her body to survive, and suddenly their newfound freedom turned the heat up on the passion they'd suffocated over the past few years.

Colby leaned in again, but this time he wrapped his thick arms around her small waist and pulled her into him. His light-brown, almost hazel eyes bored into hers as he slowly placed his mouth on top of hers. The passion and fire that sparked between them made it impossible for either to stop or pull away. They lay together on the sofa, kissing and running their hands over each other's bodies. Colby rose from the sofa, pulled Maggie gently to her feet, and guided her into his bedroom.

Inside Colby's room, Maggie unbuttoned his shirt and ran her soft fingers over his wide chest and rock-hard biceps. Their mouths touched every wonderful place on each other's bodies as they undressed each other, one piece of clothing at a time. Then they stood naked in the middle of Colby's bedroom. Colby slowly ran his tongue over Maggie's collarbone and gradually downward. He stopped to take her breasts into his mouth, lingering for just a moment as his tongue danced around her nipples. His plump lips kissed her belly and hips. Moving toward his destination, he slid his tongue down her navel until he was finally between her legs.

The moans Maggie released surprised her. She'd never felt anything so good in her life. Maggie pulled on Colby's hand, and he rose, following her over to the bed. She lay on her back and pulled him to her. She grabbed onto his firm ass as he entered her, and her heart soared with an exhilaration and pulse-pounding elation she'd never known. When they were finished, Maggie lay next to Colby. Their legs and arms were intertwined.

"I love you, Maggie. I don't want to freak you out. We've known each other for a long time, and I want you to know that I love you," Colby admitted.

Maggie smiled, but still didn't look at him. "Thanks."

"Thanks? Really?" Colby said in a hurt voice.

"Yeah, thanks," Maggie said with a giggle.

"Wow," Colby gasped. "You're a harder nut to crack than I'd thought you'd be."

Maggie propped herself up on one elbow. "Well, I never indicated that loving me was going to be easy," she said and put on a pouty face.

"No, you didn't. But *thanks*? That's all I get?" Colby said with a smile.

"Oh, all right. I love you, too. There. Now are you happy?" Maggie joked.

Colby started tickling her under the arms. "Oh yeah, I'm real happy. I've been following you around like a lapdog for a couple of years and after I finally make love to you, you toss me aside like a dirty rag."

Maggie laughed and rolled on top of Colby's naked body. "You're a very tasty dirty rag. So given this information, I may not toss you aside just yet," Maggie said, and gently sucked his earlobe.

"Enough talking," Colby said, as he embraced Maggie and began to respond to her sexual advances.

They made love a second time that night. Afterward, they lay in each other's arms, and for the first time since Maggie could remember, she slept in peace.

Chapter One Hundred Forty-Three

The next morning, Joey sauntered into Colby's bedroom, still rubbing sleep from her eyes.

"Why are you sleeping in here?" Joey mumbled incoherently.

Maggie lifted her head slightly off the pillow. "Well, I figured you wanted your own room."

As Colby stirred next her, Maggie put her finger over her lips to tell Joey to be quiet. She slipped from under the covers, grabbed Colby's large T-shirt, and put it over her head. Then she led Joey out into the kitchen.

"Colby and I like each other, Joey. So, we slept together last night," Maggie explained.

Joey scrunched up her nose. "Why would ya wanna do that? I hated doin' those things they made me do when I lived in that place where you found me."

"Well, that's a good question. When you do those things, have sex, with someone you really, really like, it's a lot different. It makes you feel good instead of bad," Maggie tried to explain.

"So Colby didn't hurt you last night?" Joey asked. The young girl knew sex to be ugly, painful, and dirty.

"No, he didn't hurt me. He would never hurt either of us. So, the thing is, I'm probably going to share Colby's room with him. That will leave you a room all to yourself," Maggie said.

"OK, that's fine. As long as you're happy, I'm happy," Joey said sincerely.

***

Maggie's life shifted significantly once she moved in with Colby. Although she was happier than she'd ever been, she had a nagging fear that something would go wrong and take away everything she now had. Over the first six months of living together, they had fallen deeply in love. It was almost hard for Maggie to imagine life without him. He was warm and loving to her and Joey. Maggie couldn't believe how much her life had changed.

Since leaving Kensington, Maggie made regular visits to see the young prostitutes who had been left to fend for themselves. Some of the girls were still on the streets, selling their bodies without pimps, while others had found shelters and other forms of government help to get them back on their feet. A few of the girls had been reunited with their families and no longer lived in the rectum of the city. More often than not, the Clarkes traveled into Kensington with Maggie. It was important to the Clarkes to understand the life Maggie had lived during the long years she was away from them, but even more important was their urge to keep Maggie safe from further harm. The work Lorraine and Rob had done with other missing children and their families during Maggie's agonizing absence had helped prepare them for the harsh world their daughter had inhabited.

It wasn't until late fall the following year that, while visiting Shiver at Double Visions, Maggie had the urge to contact Tony and Vincent. She had kept their phone number in a safe place, and since she had no way of contacting Emma, she decided to reach out to them and find out what had become of her friend.

"Yeah?" Tony huffed into the phone when he answered.

"Tony? This is Maggie." There was a long pause. "Maggie from Double Visions. Emma's friend."

"Ohhhh yeah, little Maggie. How the hell ya been? Vincent and me were just talkin' 'bout ya da other day. We's been wondering what happened to ya. We heard all about that big bust in that shit hole where ya live," Tony said.

"I'm doing really well now, Tony. I moved in with my boyfriend. We live in Whitemarsh, and things are going great," Maggie explained.

"That's real good. Have ya seen your parents?" Tony wondered aloud.

"Yep. I live five minutes from them, so I get to see them all the time," Maggie said.

"Well, me and Vincent are real happy for ya. How's everythin' else?" Tony asked, wondering what the real reason was for Maggie's call.

"Everything is fine. I just thought maybe you'd like to meet me and Joey for lunch someday. I was actually wondering how Emma was doing. I don't know how to reach her," Maggie said.

"Well, Emma's been away for a while. Not sure when she's comin' back to town. Who's this Joey guy ya want us to have lunch wit'?" Tony asked.

Maggie giggled. "Joey is a girl. She was Seth's best friend. Her mom sold her when she was little to some asshole, so now she lives with Colby and me."

"Her own mudder sold her when she was little? She's a fuckin' sorry excuse for a woman," Tony commented in an angry voice. "Listen, why don't you and Joey meet us at the Melrose tomorra afternoon? How's that sound? It'll be good to see ya."

It wasn't normal for Tony and Vincent to meet people outside of the mob for lunch or any other meal. But for Maggie, they'd make an exception. She was a good kid, and when she lost her boy, the two men had felt badly that they couldn't do anything to help her. A good meal at the Melrose seemed the perfect opportunity to do something nice for her. Besides, Tony was curious about the big bust that took place in Kensington. It was always good to know how things went down on other criminals...there was always something to learn about the police.

The next afternoon, Maggie and Joey got off the bus and walked a few short blocks to the Melrose Diner. The restaurant was bustling with loud chatter and high-pitched laughter. Maggie led Joey to the back of the diner, where she'd spotted Tony and Vincent. Before she reached their table, a man working at the diner approached. "Nah, you can't go back there," he said, trying to keep everyone away from Tony and Vincent.

"Jimmy," Vincent yelled. "She's OK. She came to see us."

Jimmy nodded and stepped aside to let Maggie and Joey pass.

The two large men stood, and each took a turn giving Maggie a hug.

"Sit down, sit down," Vincent said with enthusiasm, gesturing to the two seats across from them.

"This is Joey," Maggie said once they were seated. "Joey, this is Tony and Vincent."

Joey immediately felt intimidated by the two men. For starters, they were tall and wide. But what really made her nervous were the holstered guns she noticed on each of them when they hugged Maggie.

"Hi, Joey," Tony said, "it's nice to meet ya."

Joey nodded but remained silent, watching both of them carefully.

Tony, Vincent, and Maggie chatted about Double Visions, and then she filled them in on her life after Kensington. They had just finished eating when Maggie rose from the table.

"I have to go to the bathroom. I'll be right back," Maggie announced.

She stood and turned to walk toward the bathroom when suddenly she stopped and sat down again.

Tony took a long gulp of his coffee. "What? Ya changed your mind?" he teased.

But Vincent didn't play into it; he was too busy watching Maggie. The color had drained from her face, and her hands were shaking. Maggie's eyes bulged, and for several seconds, Vincent could tell she was holding her breath. Tony was still digging into his apple pie when Vincent nudged him under the table. He looked up at Maggie and put his fork on the pie plate.

"What's wrong, Maggie?" Vincent asked in a dark voice.

Tears filled Maggie's eyes, and she shook her head ever so slightly.

Joey immediately grabbed onto Maggie's forearm, sensing her fear.

"Maggie?" Tony said. "Tell us what's wrong."

Maggie cleared her throat, and in a shaky voice, she whispered, "The man in the orange shirt, sitting behind us."

Tony strained his neck until his eyes landed upon a large, lanky-looking white man. His greasy hair hung around his baggy, puffy eyes. He was hunched over his meal with his arms on the table, guarding his plate like hungry dog.

"Yeah, I see him. He looks like a fuckin' pig," Tony commented. "What about him?"

Maggie closed her eyes and shook her head slowly. "Joey and I have to go. We have to get out of here."

Tony and Vincent were confused. "Did that loser mess wit' cha on the bus ride here or somethin'?" Vincent guessed.

"No," Maggie said quietly, "that's the man who kidnapped me. That's John William."

Chapter One Hundred Forty-Four

———————————◼———————————

Tony was the first to react. He reached into his pocket, pulled out a pair of sunglasses, and handed them to Maggie.

"Put these on and get outta here," Tony instructed.

Maggie's body felt like it was made of stone, but she willed her legs to lift her body from the chair. Joey was standing next to her and grabbed Maggie under the arm to hoist her up. One step at a time, Maggie headed toward the door with Joey beside her. As they approached the table where John William was sitting, Maggie paused and stared at him. Feeling an unwanted presence, John William looked up from his bowl of clam chowder and sneered at them. His eyes washed over Maggie and then Joey with perverted lust. Maggie remembered the look well, and her fear began to subside as rage pushed away any feelings of nervousness. Maggie looked over her shoulder. Tony pushed his chin toward the door to indicate that she had to keep moving.

As the two girls passed, John William gawked at Joey, and they heard him say, "Mmmmmm." He was too stupid to look at their faces. Had he looked up, John William might have recognized Maggie. Even after all those years, Maggie looked like an older version of herself from childhood.

Once outside the diner, the fall air hit Maggie in the face, and she drew in a deep breath. She and Joey walked quickly toward the bus stop. Maggie looked back several times to see if Tony and Vincent had emerged from the diner, but they remained inside, and so did John William. She didn't know what they had planned, but Maggie knew that whatever it was, the two men did not want Joey and her hanging around the diner to find out. As reality set in, Maggie's anger grew until she could literally chew on the hate she felt for John William.

Maggie held onto Joey tightly as they sat in the very first seat on the bus, heading back to Whitemarsh. Maggie's insides were churning just as they had when she was a little girl. She was thinking about her life inside the prison with Cali, Max, and the others. Her thoughts landed on Seth, the child whom John William had murdered.

"Maggie, that man looked really mean. He's the one who stole you," Joey stated.

Maggie nodded. "Yes, he's the one who took me and Seth."

"Do you hate him?" Joey asked.

"Yes, I hate him. I hate him a lot," Maggie confirmed.

"Well, I hope he dies," Joey said.

"So do I," Maggie agreed. "I hope he dies a prolonged, painful death."

"Prolonged?" Joey asked.

Maggie looked down at Joey. "Yes, prolonged…it means I hope he has pain for a long time before he dies."

Joey squinted. "Just like we had a lot of pain when they had sex with us when we were kids, right?"

"Yes. Nothing could be as painful as what we went through. Oh, and by the way, you're still a kid," Maggie reminded her.

"Yeah, I know," Joey said. "I remember when I first came to Kensington, and the kids at school used to tell Seth he was damaged goods. You know, I think we're all a little damaged. What do you think?"

Maggie put her arm over Joey's shoulder. "I don't think we're damaged, Joey. I think our experiences make us who we are, but that doesn't mean there's anything wrong with us."

Joey pondered what she'd been told. "I don't get it."

Maggie leaned closer. "There are lots of people who go through bad things, but that doesn't mean there's anything wrong with those people. Look at us, for example. We went through bad things, but it doesn't mean we aren't really cool chicks."

Joey smiled. "Yeah, you're right."

The two fell silent, and then Joey spoke again. "Maggie? I'm glad you picked me that day…from that place where they were keeping me, I mean."

"Me too, Joey, but I wish I could've taken all the other little girls away from that place too," Maggie admitted.

Joey nodded. She had been frightened by seeing John William in the flesh at the diner. She was scared that the man who'd stolen Maggie would take both of them back to the dreary place where men touched her in places that made her skin crawl and made her guts twist into tight little knots. But nothing bad had happened, she told herself over and over again as she rested her head in the crook of Maggie's arm and let the sound of the bus tires lull her into a sense of numbness.

Maggie gave thanks as the bus left the city limits, and she wondered what, exactly, Tony and Vincent were going to do about John William. Their reaction had startled her. Even though she was initially scared when she saw John William, the look on Tony and Vincent's faces made her feel exhilarated, even powerful. She imagined them telling John William what a piece of shit he was and scaring the hell out him with their sheer size and malicious demeanor. She basked in the thought of John William being scared and looking over his shoulder the whole way home.

Chapter One Hundred Forty-Five

Over the next six months, Maggie began taking college courses to become a social worker. She had an undeniable urge to help people in need. At first, she joined her parents with the work they did with Rae Harker. But as time went on, Maggie felt she had an opportunity to help the children who were still on the streets and prostituting to stay alive.

Maggie began by spending more time on the streets of Kensington. Of course, there was still organized prostitution and drug dealing. Once Rock and his gang were arrested, it wasn't long before others took over the various territories. Maggie sought out some of the underage prostitutes first and tried to convince them to return to their families, to get off the streets. Some actually listened, and with Colby's help, they were placed back with their families. But others, who had no one in the world who cared about them, drew Maggie to Kensington day after day.

Maggie's most satisfying moments were when she met with Max and Cali's parents. She had made a pact with Max and Cali that one day, their parents would know everything, and she intended to fulfill her promise to them. Maggie took Ron and Juliet Frey with her to meet the two sets of parents. The only gift Maggie had to give them was information. It was a sad meeting, but at the parents' request, she described the lives and deaths of Max, Cali, and later, Seth. Max and Cali's parents had finally found closure, even though it was painful. Both couples were grateful to Maggie and the Freys for contacting them, and they vowed to stay in touch with Maggie.

Lorraine and Rob had bought Maggie a used car, and Colby had taught her how to drive so she could get back and forth to Kensington. Colby tagged along with Maggie two or three days a week "to help," but it was really because he was concerned for her safety. It was no secret that Maggie had helped to bring Rock to his knees, and Colby feared that Rock would have someone on the outside harm her.

After almost nine months of school, working a part-time job, and talking to the people of Kensington, Maggie felt exhausted. She and Colby were sitting in the living room after Joey had fallen asleep one evening. Colby rubbed his hand down her leg. "You're looking very beautiful tonight," he said.

"Oh, I'm sure my T-shirt and baggy sweat pants are a real turn-on," Maggie teased.

"I like my women dirty," Colby said, brushing her ear with his tongue.

Maggie giggled. "I'm really tired. How about if we call it a night?"

Colby stood, gently grabbed Maggie's hand, and led her into their bedroom. Maggie went into the adjoining bathroom to brush her teeth. She came back into the room, stretched her long arms, and growled out a loud yawn. Colby looked up from the bed, where he was sitting.

He stood and walked over to her. He put his muscular arms around her waist and pushed his groin toward her groin.

"I love you, Maggie," he whispered in her ear.

Maggie guided him over to the bed and removed his boxers. She kissed his chest and slowly moved down his body until her plump lips caressed his penis, ever so softly and gently.

Colby reached down and pulled Maggie up until they were eye to eye. He put his lips on hers. Instinctively, they opened their mouths, and their tongues tangoed. Colby lay Maggie back on the bed and put his mouth over her right breast, and then he slowly bathed her body with his lips and tongue until they were both unable to hold out any longer. As Colby entered her, they were filled with a yearning and love for each other that was so intense it felt like the world had ended, and they were the only two people left.

When they finished making love, Colby went out into the kitchen and brought back a bottle of champagne and two glasses.

"Well, this is a little fancy. Don't you think?" Maggie questioned, wondering why he'd decided on the expensive bottle of champagne that his parents had sent them when they moved in together.

Pretending to talk like a caveman, Colby grunted, "Nothing is too fancy for my woman."

Before Maggie could come back with a funny comment of her own, Colby dropped to one knee and held a diamond ring out in one hand. He took her hand in his. "Maggie, will you marry me?"

Stunned into silence, Maggie sat and stared at Colby. She hadn't thought about them getting married. *He couldn't want to make a wife out of a whore*, she thought. Almost a minute had passed as Maggie sat silently, staring at Colby in disbelief.

"Um, you want to cut a brother a break, here? You're making me really nervous," Colby said.

Maggie's eyes met his. "I love you, Colby…"

"But?" Colby pressed.

"But you come from a good family. A nice background, and I, well, you know where I come from, and believe me, you don't know half the things I did with other men over the years. I'm just confused, and I want you to really think about this before you get into something you'll regret," Maggie explained.

"I will never regret loving you. Your past is something that was dealt to you, not something you did by choice. There's a difference. You did what was required to stay alive so I could find you," he said. "I'm not an idiot, Maggie. I know what I'm doing."

Maggie smiled sweetly, and her eyes looked intensely blue in the warm lighting of the bedroom. "Are you really sure you know what you're doing? Have you talked to your parents?"

"I'm a grown man, and I don't need my parents' permission. However, I did tell them I was going to ask you tonight," Colby replied.

"And?"

"And they know all about you, even some of your past," he said to put her at ease. "All they care about is that I'm happy. They trust me to make good decisions. They're great people, and you're going to love them."

Maggie relaxed a little knowing that Colby's parents were OK with him getting married. Then Colby gave her the rest of the information.

"I've already asked your father if I could marry you…he said yes. Your mom was pretty happy about it too, I might add. I mean, I am the most handsome, charming, remarkable man *ever*," Colby sang.

"Yeah, and humble. You forgot to mention how humble you are," Maggie teased.

"OK, let's try this again," Colby said.

He stood up, grabbed the glasses and champagne bottle, and walked out of the bedroom to the hallway. He turned on his heel and came back into the room. He dropped to one knee, holding out the diamond ring, and took her hand in his.

"Maggie, I love you. I don't care what happened in your past because I'm marrying you to go with me into the future. Nothing you can say would change the love and admiration that I have for you. So...please, stop being a nudge and tell me, will you marry me?"

Maggie intentionally delayed answering. Then she ran her fingers through his thick hair. "Yes, I'll marry you, but don't say I didn't warn you."

They shared a prolonged kiss, and then Colby slid the diamond ring onto her finger. Maggie looked down at the ring. "This is beautiful. It's so big. Does Joey know?" she asked.

"Who do you think helped me pick out the ring?" Colby said with a grin.

"That sneaky little rat," Maggie sang.

Maggie cast her gaze down to the brilliant stone on her finger. Her life had changed so much over the last couple of years. So much happiness and an equal amount of sorrow, she thought. Then, like someone had slapped her across the face, she looked at Colby with urgency.

"What's wrong?" Colby asked.

"Nothing...I've got to call Juju. She's going to freak the hell out when I tell her this one," Maggie sang as she skipped toward the phone.

Chapter One Hundred Forty-Six

The two months that followed were the most invigorating of Maggie's life. She and Colby made wedding plans. Lorraine and Rob insisted on paying for the wedding, despite Colby's insistence that he had it covered. Juju was to be Maggie's maid of honor, and Joey and Mara were to be her bridesmaids. Keith, Maggie's brother, would stand as Colby's best man.

Two days before Maggie and Colby were to get married, Edward and Penny Derby, Colby's parents, arrived. It was the first time they'd met Maggie in person. The morning of the day they were to arrive, Maggie's nerves got the better of her. She had tried on and tossed aside every dress in her closet. Finally, she called Lorraine.

"Mom?" Maggie said in a desperate voice when Lorraine answered the phone.

"What is it, honey? What's wrong?" Lorraine asked, instantly panicked.

"I don't know what to wear, and what if Colby's parents hate me?" Maggie cried.

"Oh for goodness sake, Maggie. First of all, no one could ever hate you...you're a very unique and special woman. Second, you have plenty of dresses you can wear. Why don't you wear the black dress with the light purple stripes we just bought?" Lorraine suggested.

"Do you really think so?" Maggie asked.

"Yes, I think it's perfect," Lorraine stated in a comforting tone. There was a long, awkward pause, and Lorraine knew there was more that Maggie was worried about. "What is it, Maggie? What's bothering you?"

"What if...what if they think I'm not good enough for Colby? Oh, Mom, you know some of what I've done. Would you want Keith to marry a girl who was a hooker?" Maggie whined.

"Maggie Clarke, that's all behind you now. If Colby's parents are anything like him, they won't give a rat's ass about any of that stuff. Stop putting yourself down and quit judging yourself. Everyone loves you and admires you for all that you've coped with in life," Lorraine lectured, annoyed at the thought that someone would ever judge her daughter.

As it turned out, Lorraine was right. Edward and Penny were warm and charming. Their love for their son was palpable. Colby had filled his parents in on some of Maggie's past, and to their credit, they viewed her as a strong and powerful force to have survived such a horrid childhood. Besides, Maggie and Joey were irresistible with their fun-loving ways and quick wit.

On the morning of the wedding, Maggie woke up and turned on her side. She looked at Joey and Juju, who had slept with her the night before.

"Morning, girls. Time to wake up," Maggie said gleefully.

Both girls opened their eyes and smiled. Then they slowly climbed out of bed and began the process of getting ready. Maggie had selected a simple, off-white satin gown with tiny pearls sewn around the bust. She had insisted on something a bit more demure than Lorraine had wanted her to wear.

Maggie and Colby were married in the church where Maggie had been baptized. The reception for sixty close friends and family members took place in a restored barn at the Terrain at Styer's in Glen Mills. The day was perfect, right down to the toast that Juju gave as the maid of honor.

Juju stood from her seat next to Maggie. "Tonight, we're here to celebrate two people who got hitched. I always knew Maggie would get married someday, and I always knew she'd marry somebody great." Juju turned to face Colby. "Colby is a really cool guy and has been great for all of us." Then she took Maggie's hand in her own. "I know Seth is looking down from heaven and is really pissed off he ain't here, but he'd be really happy that ya picked Colby to marry."

Finally, Juju looked out over the wedding attendees. "Maggie is the first person in my life who really understood me. She's always loved me for who I am. That's just how she loves. So here's to a hundred years of happiness." Juju lifted her glass and turned back to the newlyweds. "Now, Colby and Maggie, go on your honeymoon and make me an aunt. I love ya both."

The wedding had been simple and perfect, as far as Maggie and Colby were concerned. It wasn't until after they returned from their honeymoon that Colby gave her the news he'd been keeping from her.

"Maggie, I know you're still in school. But I was thinking that instead of walking the streets of Kensington a couple of times a week, we should open a place where kids and teenagers can go," Colby said.

"What does that mean? Like a shelter?" Maggie asked, intrigued.

"Well, it means we can open a place where kids can get help. I don't know. A hot meal, counseling, clothes…we can figure it out," Colby explained.

"That sounds great, but where are we going to get the money to do all of this?" Maggie asked.

"You know, for a girl who always has her nose buried in a book, you're not all that resourceful, are you?" Colby mocked.

"What do you mean?" she asked, her curiosity piqued.

"What's your last name?" Colby asked.

"Clarke. I mean Derby," Maggie said, playing along.

"Right." Colby exhaled in an exaggerated fashion. "I'm a descendant of Elias Hasket Derby," Colby said.

Maggie cocked her head to one side and gave him a confused look.

"My father is the only surviving heir of Elias Hasket Derby. He was a very wealthy merchant who died in the late seventeen hundreds and left a large fortune. The generations after Elias continued to grow that fortune. My father is a very rich man." Colby sat quietly and let the information sink in.

"Does that mean you're rich?" Maggie finally asked, catching on.

"Well, yes, it does, Mrs. Derby," Colby said.

Silence followed.

"So, that means I have money we can work with to open a place in the city. The kind of place you dreamed about having, Maggie," Colby explained.

Maggie studied him. "Why didn't you tell me before now?"

"Well, you never asked," Colby countered.

"Oh, right. Like it's perfectly normal to ask a man living in Kensington who is helping break up a prostitution ring if he is filthy rich," she chided.

"I think it's a perfectly reasonable question to ask," he said.

Maggie considered the information she'd just learned.

"Why didn't you ask me to sign a prenuptial agreement?" Maggie wondered.

"Because I plan on being married to you until we're shriveled up, old prunes," Colby remarked.

Maggie embraced him. "Listen, you might shrivel up, but I'm not. I intend to keep my girlish figure, bub."

"I've given some thought to what we should call this place," Colby began. "I think it's important that the name represents you and the people who you've loved and lost."

"So, what do you think we should call this place?" Maggie asked.

"Seth's Fortress," he said with certainty.

"I love it, Colby. Seth would have loved it too," Maggie said with a heavy heart.

A few months later, Maggie and Colby opened Seth's Fortress in Philadelphia. The organization focused on homeless teens and prostitutes. It provided food, counseling, safety, and shelter to those in need. It was a place where kids found solace. There was a difference between prostitutes who were willing to sell their bodies and those who were unwilling. The signs were subtle to most, but not to Maggie. She could pick out the kids who had been forced into the business. Often, the police punished these young girls and boys for doing what they were being forced to do. News of the place spread quickly. Within three weeks, they were helping at least a dozen kids a day.

On Maggie's days off, she often took Joey to a movie or to the local bowling alley after school. Joey had a knack for all things athletic, and she'd grown fond of bowling after one of the girls in her class had a birthday party at Facenda Whitaker Bowling Lanes. Maggie and Joey enjoyed the time together; bowling was their "special" thing to do.

Maggie was returning to her seat after throwing a strike when she saw the long, narrow face and black eyes staring at them. His hair was still shoulder length and greasy. His hunched posture looked demented, and his large hands hung at his sides like dead weights.

Maggie stood, frozen in time, and her body was unwilling to take commands from her mind. She wanted to take Joey by the hand and run. Her breathing was labored and she felt lightheaded. It was too much for her to see him again. Maggie feared that the end of her life was soon.

A yellowish-brown, toothy smile spread across John William's gruesome face. Her fear and shock was evident, and her reaction brought sheer pleasure to the hideous creature. John William thumped down the two steps and into the pits where the bowlers sat. He continued to walk toward her, and she managed to make her right foot move and then her left. She made it back to Joey right before John William entered the area where they were sitting.

Chapter One Hundred Forty-Seven

———————————

"Well, if it isn't Maggie. Look at you, all grown up and trying to act like you're not a filthy whore," he ridiculed.

"What do you want?" Maggie asked.

"Oh, I just wanna catch up. See how you've been. Find out who this gorgeous little creature is here with you. I could get a pretty penny for that one," he said.

"You need to get out of here before I call the police," Maggie threatened.

John William started to laugh. "You won't call the police. Because if you do, then Myles would surely kill you and that little bitch of yours," he said, gesturing toward Joey. "I'm pretty sure she's gonna be my bitch soon."

Joey was standing behind Maggie. Her face drained of all color as she grabbed onto Maggie's hips.

"Leave us alone," Maggie said in a weak voice.

"Nah, the fun is just startin', bitch. Myles has been looking for a new girl, and it looks like you got the kid he wants."

Maggie's mind was whirling as she frantically tried to come up with a way to get away from John William. Suddenly, she realized that there were many people around them, and she wasn't a helpless eleven-year-old anymore. She straightened her back and took a step closer to him.

"I suggest you leave us the fuck alone, John William." Maggie yelled his name. "Otherwise, I'm going to make such a scene that you'll wish you never knew me. Who the hell do you think you are? I'll tell you who you are; you're a fucking low-life, maggot-eating swine," Maggie spat.

John William was an imbecile, but he wasn't stupid. He knew Maggie would do exactly what she'd just described. So instead of standing there, he gave them a sinister grin, turned, and headed to the bar inside the bowling alley.

"Maggie, let's leave," Joey said.

"No. If we leave now, he'll just follow us home. It's too dangerous," Maggie warned.

Maggie took Joey by the hand and rushed over to the counter where the cashier stood.

"Can I use your phone?" Maggie pleaded.

The old man behind the counter gave her a searching look. Satisfied that she wasn't trouble, he handed her the phone. "I'll dial. No long distance calls."

Maggie pulled the piece of paper from her purse and read off the numbers as the old man dialed. It rang four times, and at the thought of no one answering, panic rose and fell in waves causing her stomach to clench into a tight knot. After the fifth ring, a voice sang in her ear.

"Yeah?"

"Tony?"

"Who the hell is this?"

"This is Maggie. I need your help," she begged.

"Where are ya, Maggie?"

"Facenda Whitaker Bowling Alley," Maggie stated. "I'm here with Joey, and the nice man at the shoe counter is letting me use the phone."

"I see. What exactly is the da issue?" Tony asked.

"John William," Maggie said.

"He's dare now?" Tony asked.

"Yes."

"He botherin' you?"

"Yeah. He said he liked Joey," Maggie said. The old man at the shoe counter was listening to every word. She hoped Tony would pick up on what she was trying to say.

"Is that right?" Tony asked rhetorically.

"Yep," Maggie said, grateful that Tony and Vincent had met Joey at the Melrose.

"OK, here's what you're gonna do. Stay put. When ya see me and Vincent come in, pretend like ya don't know us. Then get in your car and go home," Tony instructed.

"OK, but…" Maggie hesitated, worried that John William would find out where they lived.

"You just do what I'm tellin' ya. Everything will be fine," Tony assured her.

It took Tony and Vincent forty-five minutes to get from South Philly to the bowling alley in the suburbs. Maggie saw them before they saw her. In fact, she wasn't sure they saw her at all because they didn't acknowledge her. She watched them enter the bar. Then she told Joey it was time to leave.

"But that asshole is still in the bar," Joey argued. "What if he follows us home?"

Maggie could see John William sitting on the barstool closest to the door. He gave her a menacing wave.

"We have to go, Joey. We can't stay at the bowling alley forever. It'll be OK. Trust me," Maggie assured her.

Maggie and Joey went up to the counter, paid for their lane, and then proceeded out to their car. Sure enough, John William was starting his date-rape, child-stealing, murder van when Maggie backed out of the parking space. As she drove slowly back to her apartment, she watched him following in the rearview mirror. She didn't know what kind of car Tony and Vincent drove. She began to worry that they hadn't recognized him in the bar, and John William had managed to get away from them. Maggie pulled into a space at her complex and led Joey up to their apartment.

She watched John William from the window until finally he drove off.

Maggie didn't dare call Tony again to confirm they had followed John William. She only hoped they had, and they would threaten him enough that he would never think about going near her or Joey again. Maggie could not conceive of what Tony and Vincent had planned for John William to keep him away from her.

Chapter One Hundred Forty-Eight

T ony called his boss, Salvatore, from the bowling alley. Tony and Vincent had told Salvatore all about Maggie and her trauma as a young child. Salvatore also knew that Maggie was Emma's only good friend from Double Visions, and Salvatore adored Emma.

"Sal, 'member that girl we talked about? Emma's friend, Maggie, from Doubles? She's the one who lost her little boy not too long ago to AIDS," Tony explained.

"Yeah, Tony, I remember. Why? What's going on?" Salvatore asked.

"Well, Maggie called us. She and her kid were bowling and that mother-fuckin', child-stealing ass-wipe shows up. This is the same guy who kidnapped her. Now the bastard is lurking around and threatenin' her. The girl was real scared, so Vincent and me drove here to the bowling alley. Now, we're sittin' here, watchin' the douche bag drink a beer at the bar. You know what we talked about if it ever came to this. We're gonna move on it this time," Tony said.

"Yeah, do what you have to do. But stick to the plan. Keep things clean and simple. Are you bringing in soldiers to take care of this?" Salvatore asked.

"Nah, me and Vincent are gonna enjoy takin' care of this one on our own. I'm gonna call a couple of the guys to help with the heavy liftin', though."

Tony and Vincent sat in the bar and waited for John William to finish his beer. As he stood to leave, the two mobsters followed. They saw him get into his van and follow Maggie back to her apartment. They watched as he scowled at Maggie and Joey as they got out of their car and rushed into their apartment. When John William drove off fifteen minutes later, Tony and Vincent followed him.

Tony and Vincent already knew where John William lived. They had followed him home from the Melrose. But today, they trailed him to be sure he didn't go somewhere other than his home.

John William parked in front of a row home on Erie Avenue in Philadelphia. The two men sat and watched as John William heaved his lanky body up the broken cement steps to his equally broken-down home.

The front porch was littered with broken chairs and large, warped, cardboard boxes filled with old car parts and rusty appliances.

"Let's give him ten minutes, then we'll move," Vincent said.

Tony looked in his rearview mirror at the men who came to help them. The men watched the house as dim lights illuminated the first floor and then the second floor.

"That must be the dipshit's bedroom," Vincent commented, pointing to the second floor.

Tony nodded. "It's time to move."

Tony, Vincent, and two of their meanest soldiers crossed the street. The front door was easy for one of the soldiers to unlock. Inside the house, there were pictures of naked children strewn across the ripped, busted-up sofa. It wasn't lost on Tony or Vincent that the pictures of the innocent young children were actual photographs.

"Sick fuck," Vincent whispered.

The four men quietly made their way up to the second floor and to the room at the front of the house. All of the lights were off by now, and the creeper lay sleeping in bed. The men followed the sound of snoring in the dark.

They moved swiftly to the four corners of the bed. Once they were all in position, Tony bent over John William and grasped him around the throat. John William drew in a quick breath as his eyes snapped open.

"What do you want?" John William managed.

"We wanna talk about a girl named Maggie and a little boy, who just died of AIDS, mind you, named Seth. You remember 'em, don't cha?" Vincent said.

John William began to struggle. But the four men had him pinned to the bed.

"Yeah, we thought you'd remember 'em, since ya was at the bowling alley today watchin' Maggie," Tony remarked.

"So ya see, we understand ya took them when they was just little. Ya remember doin' that, right?" Vincent said.

John William remained still. He began breathing deeply through his nostrils, and then he broke into grotesque laughter. Without knowing who Tony and Vincent were or that they were high on the Philadelphia mafia food chain, his thoughts gravitated to the creatures he worked for and their ability to get even. John William smoldered with defiance, and his eyes narrowed with evil amusement.

"You don't know who you're fucking with," John William stated.

The lines around Tony's mouth tightened. Then he lifted his chin slowly and took a long, exaggerated breath in through his nose.

"See, now, you probably shouldn't have said that," Tony said, "'cause now you're just instigatin' us to make things even more painful for ya." Tony rubbed his chin with his free hand. "Although, I ain't so sure that what you have comin' to ya could be any more painful."

Tony looked to Vincent and the other two mobsters, who all returned his contagious smile. John William struggled against the men who held him to the bed, and in an instant, Vincent snapped a cuff around John William's wrist, pushed him up on his side, yanked his other arm behind his back, and cuffed the other wrist. John William kicked at the men until Tony pulled a jagged twelve-inch blade from the holster at the back of his belt and jammed it into John William's thigh.

"You stop kickin', or I'll cut your fuckin' legs off," Tony threatened.

Finally, John William realized that he was in deep shit. Fear replaced the arrogance on his face. His wide eyes and the downward turn of his sloppy lips were telltale signs that he was scared. The four men quickly moved John William from the house into Tony and Vincent's car.

"Try not to leave any pig scum on my seats," Tony remarked to John William.

"Fuck you!" John William yelled.

With the car still in park, Vincent leaned over the backseat and clobbered John William in the face with a nose-splattering punch.

"Keep your fuckin' mouth shut," Vincent warned.

"You didn't get any of that Chester-the-molester blood on my seat, did you, Vin?" Tony mocked.

"Nah, but I got some on my hand," Vincent responded. He pulled a towel from under the front seat and wiped off his fist.

"Ya think we should cover his eyes, Vin? Or should we let him see where he's goin'?" Tony asked, tormenting John William.

"Nah, I think we oughta keep the sick prick guessin'. I'll cover his eyes. That way, it'll be a big surprise." Vincent laughed.

Vincent leaned over the front seat again, cut John William's dirty undershirt from his chest with a knife, and tied it around his head, over his eyes.

"You like this whole blindfold thing, don't ya, scumbag? You're into kinky shit, right?" Vincent taunted.

John William remained motionless in the backseat of Tony's car; blood oozed from his nose and dripped over his fleshy, misshapen, swollen lips. His mind whirled as the car drove at a high rate of speed. Then they began to turn—left, left again, right, left...*Where are they taking me?* John William wondered.

Then gravel crunched under the tires as the car inched its way toward Tony and Vincent's destination. Tony stopped the car and turned off the engine. John William focused on getting through whatever torture they had in store for him and then getting back home to let Myles know he'd need help to get even with these thugs.

"Let's go, you dimwit," Vincent snarled. He roughly pulled John William from the backseat of the car.

John William's ankles had been tied together, and he hobbled to keep his balance. Vincent, Tony, and the other two mobsters lifted John William and carried him feet first into an old, deserted house in Bucks County that was owned by the mob family.

"Take him downstairs," Tony barked. "We got everything waitin' for him."

Down in the basement, Vincent removed the shirt that covered John William's eyes, and Tony switched on the flashlight.

"Nice place, ain't it?" Tony growled. "Probably a step up from that prison where you were taking those kids."

John William followed the beam of light along the splintered ceiling rafters to the cinder block walls. Then the light went to the dirt floor, which was dotted with puddles of stale water where rain leaked in through eroded cinder blocks. He breathed a small sigh of relief; it was a nasty, rotten place, but no worse than the prison where Maggie and Seth had lived.

John William looked up at Tony. "What do you want from me?"

Tony smiled wickedly. "Well, now that's a good question. We want to know who your boss is, that's all."

John William returned an evil smile. "You don't have a chance in hell of getting me to tell you anything."

"Oh, I see," Tony said calmly. Then Tony lifted his arm and shone the flashlight at a chair ten feet from where they stood. "Move him closer," Tony said.

Tony and Vincent could feel the fear in the air as John William gawked at his future.

"Yeah, you ain't such a smartass now, are ya?" Vincent said.

"This here is called the Judas chair—some medieval contraption we like to use on special people like you," Tony said in an icy voice.

As John William got a better look at the chair, his body began to shake. Over a thousand sharp, metal spikes covered the back, armrests, seat, leg rests, and footrests. John William had seen a lot of sick shit in his business, but this was altogether different. The chair screamed pain and agony.

Then, John William reverted to the nine-year-old boy tied by his parents to the chair under the stairs. His phobia of being in tight spaces, tied up, or confined, came crashing down on him. He suddenly felt as though he was being choked. His legs began to tremble.

"So, here's what's gonna happen...you're gonna tell us who the boss of your kiddy ring is. 'Cause if you don't, guess where you're goin'?" Tony said. "Right. You're gonna sit in that chair, and all those sharp, spikey things are gonna rip through your rotted flesh."

Through the thick fog of his anxiety attack, John William considered his options. If he told them what they wanted to know, Myles's organization would surely kill him—they'd probably shoot him in the head. However, if he didn't, these guys were going to strap him in the chair and make sure his death was long and excruciatingly painful. He decided quickly that he'd rather be shot in the head. He might even have a chance to run before Myles and the other sex traffickers could find him.

"Speak fucker!" Tony yelled, his patience wearing thin. "You want to remain silent, huh?"

"If I tell you, then you'll let me go, right?" John William asked, eyeing the chair with pure fear.

"Like I said, ya tell us who the head guy is or you're gonna have a seat in dat chair."

"His name is Myles Cabello," John William admitted.

"Oh yeah?" Vincent said. "And where does this asshole, Myles Cabello, live?"

"In New York City," John William confessed.

"Is this Myles guy the same guy who made Maggie his girl?" Tony asked.

John William nodded.

"Let's just review here for a minute. This Myles guy, dis grown fucker, took Maggie, an eleven-year-old kid, as his girlfriend, right?" Tony asked, his voice becoming low and steady.

John William looked at him. "Yeah, that's him."

"I see. So then let me get somethin' else straight. You're the lick-ass that took Maggie away from her family, and then you brought her to this guy, Myles, who had sex wit' her all da time. Do I have dat right?" Tony said.

John William nodded.

"Oh, I'm sorry. I didn't hear ya," Tony said with rage.

"Yes...yes. I took her because Myles was the boss, and he told me what to do," John William said, trying to deflect the blame.

"Hmmm, that's interesting. So, are ya sayin' that when ya forced Maggie to have sex down in the basement of some house where ya kept kids in dog kennels, this shithead, Myles, made ya do that too?" Vincent asked.

John William shook his head. "That was a mistake, and I'm sorry I ever did that to her. I'll apologize to her, I swear I will."

"You know what cha are? You're a filthy little weasel who hurts little kids. Do ya think you're foolin' us? Ya think we're stupid?" Vincent said, clutching John William's chin in his large hand.

Vincent released his grip and turned to Tony. "What do ya think we oughta do with him, Tone?"

Tony pulled a fat cigar from his pocket, bit off the tip, spit it on the dirt floor, and worked on lighting it. After several minutes had passed, he finally spoke. "Well, he told us what we wanted to know. But he's a real fuckin' menace to society, and well, little Seth died 'cause of what he did and all. And, well, Maggie told us a couple of other kids under *his care* died, too, when they lived in dat house. So I say we do what we said we were gonna do," he stated.

"Get all of his clothes off," Tony told the two mobsters, who were there to help.

Chapter One Hundred Forty-Nine

John William's clothes were cut from his body, and he stood in the damp, dark basement naked and scared. The four men stood around him in a circle, each of them watching him, provoking the same fear that he'd made so many children feel. They knew it would never be possible to match the fear of a helpless child who had been taken from her family, but they wanted him to get as close to that breaking point as possible.

One of the mobsters pushed John William toward the chair. Then the other gangster gave him a hard nudge.

"Please, I told you everything I know," John William begged. "You said you would let me go if I told you."

Tony cocked his head to the side and looked at Vincent. "Did we say dat? We never said we'd let him go, did we?"

"Nope, I didn't hear nobody say nuttin'. Did you two fellas hear me or Tony say we'd let this good-for-nuttin' little bitch go?" Vincent asked the two mobsters.

They both shook their heads. Their pinched expressions looked set in concrete. They were serious about the work that had to be done.

Tony grabbed John William by the cuffs around his wrists and dragged him close enough to the chair that his knees were touching the edges of the spiked leg rests.

"Now, ya see these spikes? What happens is when ya sit on the chair, those sharp, metal spikes go into your skin. And when dat happens, you'll start to bleed real slow, 'cause ya see, if you're strapped down real tight to the chair, which ya will be, those spikes will stick in ya, and it won't let the blood drain outta ya real fast. Eventually, you'll bleed to death, but nice and slow, see? And when you move around, or we move ya ourselves, those spikes dat are already stuck in your skin—did I mention that?—they'll hurt like hell. In fact, I'm sure it'll feel like you're actually in hell," Tony taunted to prolong John William's anxiety.

Even in the cold basement with its dirt floor and cinder block walls, the sweat was pouring down John William's face, chest, and back. As he stood with his knees touching the formidable chair, he understood his fate. Tony and Vincent couldn't know that they had picked the one form of death that John William feared most. His memories of when he was a small boy returned, and he could vividly recall his parents tying him to the metal chair naked and leaving him in the small closet under the stairs for hours. John William was finally feeling the fear and panic that the children he had kidnapped felt when they awakened in the back of his van.

Tony stepped closer to John William, who felt Tony's hot breath on his face as he said, "It's time, John William. By the way, who da fuck in their right mind calls themselves by their first and middle name? The only people I can think of who do dat are serial killers. Did ya ever notice that, Vin? Those serial killer motherfuckers use their first and middle names so they always got three fuckin' names. Probably 'cause they're all crazy bitches like this sorry-ass slob."

"You know, Tone, I never thought about dat. You're right, though... they always got three names," Vincent said, playing along to extend John William's discomfort.

Tony took a step away from John William. The two mobsters stepped forward and removed his handcuffs. Then they turned John William so his back was facing the chair. They slammed him down into the staked chair. Screams of terror erupted from John William's very core. He squirmed, attempting to get off the chair, but that only drove the metal stakes farther into his flesh. Then Tony fastened one of the leather armrest straps as tightly as he could; Vincent did the honors on the other side. They bent down and strapped John William's ankles as tightly as possible to the legs of the chair, embedding spikes into his calves and thighs. Finally, they fastened the strap around his neck. John William was transported into hell, a hell on earth, as he waited for death.

Tony and Vincent stepped back from the chair and looked at him.

"Holy shit," Tony bellowed, "that's gotta really hurt your balls."

Tony leaned down and put his nose to John William's nose. "It does hurt your balls, doesn't it? And uffa, ya probably got one of dose spikes stuck up your ass, too. My suggestion is ya try and stay as still as ya can 'til ya just fuckin' die."

Over the next two days, Tony and Vincent stayed with John William. When they leaned down to talk to him, they'd press on his arm or leg, driving the spikes deeper into his body. At one point, Tony took a wooden box filled with old, heavy tools and threw it onto John William's lap. They didn't let him sleep; they slapped him in the face or threw water in his face if his eyes closed. Their goal was to make sure he stayed awake to feel every moment of his horrible circumstances.

At the end of the second day, John William died when Vincent grabbed him by the ears and repeatedly slammed his head into the spikes of the headrest. It was an appropriate and torturous death for John William. Tony and Vincent felt as though they had given the rodent a proper send-off into eternal hell.

As they left the property in the middle of the night and dumped John William's naked body on the side of the road, with his own driver's license shoved into his mouth, they felt victorious. They left the ogre in a place where they knew his body would be found, and they rejoiced in the work they'd done. There was no greater feeling than punishing those who deserved it the most.

"We did real good, Vincent," Tony commented as he drove back to Philadelphia.

"I know, Tony. I think it's one of our best kills yet," Vincent answered, reflecting back on all the pain associated with the method they'd used to kill John William.

"Now we need to see about this Myles guy," Tony said thoughtfully.

"Yeah, I already have one of our soldiers on it," Vincent said.

"Good. One down, one to go."

The Final Hours

———————————— ■ ————————————

After seeing John William, a day didn't go by that Maggie didn't look over her shoulder, waiting for him to reappear. Lorraine was driving Joey to and from school to be sure no one got near her. Colby was on guard, as well. Lorraine told Detective Harker what happened at the bowling alley, and he made sure the police watched Maggie's apartment and Joey's school. Maggie never uttered a word to anyone about her phone call to Tony and Vincent.

Maggie couldn't believe she was reliving her nightmare. She had a constant, gnawing fear in the pit of her stomach. Her thoughts wandered to the things they'd do to Joey if John William got his hands on her. She could barely think about it without becoming edgy and short-tempered.

Three weeks after seeing John William at the bowling alley, an envelope arrived in the mail. There was no return address. She turned it over in her hands as if expecting something terrible to happen. Sitting in her living room, Maggie ripped open the envelope. Inside were two clippings from two different newspapers.

MAN FOUND DEAD ON SIDE OF ROAD IN BUCKS COUNTY

A local man was found dead on Swamp Road in Doylestown on Tuesday. The body, discovered by motorists, was naked and covered with what appeared to be multiple stab wounds. The victim was identified as John William McCloud, 32.

The coroner's report said that over a thousand puncture wounds were found on McCloud's head, back, legs, and arms. The report indicates that the victim bled to death. The Bucks County District Attorney's Office is investigating. Anyone who has information related to the crime is encouraged to call the local police department.

McCloud was the son of the late Daren McCloud of Philadelphia, the last caretaker of a former prison on Fairmont Avenue in Philadelphia.

Maggie sat back on her sofa and tried to absorb what she'd just read. She thought back to the day at the bowling alley when she'd called Tony to report that John William was following her. As the story of his horrifying and painful death began to sink in, Maggie felt a sense of liberation. John William had ruined her young life. His actions had caused Seth, Cali, and Max to die. A feeling of joy and freedom began to form, and stress poured out of her body as if someone had opened a faucet in the center of her soul. John William had finally gotten what he deserved, even though no amount of torture could make up for the pain and suffering he'd caused so many children. She rose from the sofa and, although it was only noon, went to the kitchen and grabbed a bottle of beer from the refrigerator. She settled back down on the sofa and looked at the second article in the envelope:

PROMINENT NEW YORK BUSINESSMAN FOUND DEAD

City real estate developer Myles Cabello was found dead on Monday in a Dumpster near his apartment on the Upper East Side of Manhattan.

Cabello, a native of Brooklyn, was 46. Police said Cabello was found hog-tied with his throat crushed and his genitals mutilated with what the coroner believes was a razor blade. The cause of death was suffocation, according to the coroner's report. A police spokesman told reporters, "Whoever killed Mr. Cabello really wanted him to suffer. The way in which he died indicates that this was not a random killing, but a calculated homicide to insure that the victim's death was painful and prolonged." According to police, Cabello was last seen leaving a bar two blocks from his apartment at around 10:00 p.m. the night he died.

Cabello's wife, Harriet, told a Channel 7 Eyewitness News reporter, "Myles was a man of honor. He always put his children and his family first. He was a good man who never harmed anyone in his life." Mrs. Cabello went on to explain that her husband had no enemies, and she and her three children were shocked and deeply saddened by their loss. "Our family hopes the person responsible for killing Myles is found and put to justice."

Police continue to pursue all leads in the case. The Cabello family has posted a $25,000 reward for any information that leads to the arrest of the person responsible for his murder.

When Maggie finished reading the second article, tears were dribbling down her chin. These were not tears of sadness, but tears of retribution. She felt euphoric. Many others were involved in the sex-trafficking cartel; she knew that. But it gave her peace to know that the two men who had obliterated her childhood and killed the people she loved were now dead.

Maggie didn't share the articles with anyone. Instead, she lit them on fire and let them burn to ash in the kitchen sink. As they burned, she thought about Cali, Max, and Seth. In the end, they had all won. Tony and Vincent had killed John William and Myles. She felt no guilt and had no sense of wrongdoing because the two barbarians got exactly what they deserved. Maggie would never mention a word to anyone about what she knew. It was a dirty little secret that she intended to take to her grave.

"Hello?"

"Tony, it's Maggie. I just wanted to say…I just wanted to say hello. I'm doing really well now. Will you tell Vincent that Joey and I are doing really good?" Maggie asked.

"Yeah, I'll tell him," Tony said, feeling good about killing the two grimy cockroaches.

"You're good men," Maggie stated.

"You take care, now," Tony said, his voice thick, and then he hung up the phone.

"Who was that?" Joey asked as she walked into the kitchen.

"Oh, nobody. Wrong number," Maggie said.

But as Maggie turned away from Joey, she felt breathless. She flipped her long blonde hair over her shoulder. Then Maggie closed her eyes and took long, even breaths in through her nose, suddenly aware of all the delicious aromas in her kitchen. The eleven-year-old who still lived inside of Maggie Clarke-Derby had finally witnessed true justice.

Maggie could finally put the scared and abused child to rest.

Continue Reading...

Find out what happened to Maggie's friend, Emma. Continue reading…

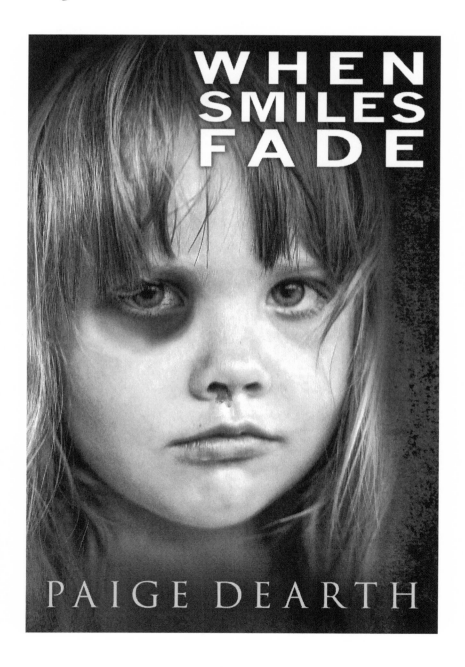

The Seed Is Planted

——————————————■■■——————————————

"**E**mma! Get your ass down here, you stupid little bitch! What the fuck did I tell you about not living like a pig?" Pepper screamed.

Panic-stricken at the thought of what would happen next, Emma rushed her younger sister, Gracie, over to the bedroom closet and pushed the tiny child inside. Before shutting the door she said, "Don't move or make any noise." Then in a softer whisper she warned her younger sister, "You have to be really, really quiet. I'll be right back. I promise."

That was code for "be invisible." Gracie obeyed her older sister, tears of fright silently dribbling down her cheeks.

Emma rushed into the hallway and stopped to look at her mother, who was standing just inside her own bedroom. "What the hell did you do now?" she accused. "How many times do I have to tell you to do what you're told? You brainless idiot!"

Gracie listened from the closet to the rapid patter of eight-year-old Emma's feet as she ran down the stairs. There was an eerie silence during which she unconsciously held her breath. Then the first blow was struck. Followed by others. Gracie cringed at her older sister's muffled shrieks of torment as she imagined the scene downstairs with telling accuracy. Emma, she knew from past experience, had once again been transformed into her father's punching bag. She wondered why their mother didn't go and help Emma. Resisting the urge to run downstairs, Gracie stayed hidden upstairs in the bedroom closet as she was instructed, waiting for the beating to end, scared that her father would come for her after he was finished with her older sister.

Down in the kitchen, Pepper Murphy lurched around, unsteady on his feet. He towered over his young daughter, contemplating her stricken face for several minutes and deriving a sickening enthusiasm and fresh energy from her growing terror. She stood before him, whimpering from the fear that was planted in her heart, wishing, as always, that her father's love for her would overpower his fury. That never happened. When she had worked herself up into a frenzy of fear, Pepper punched her in the eye. Emma lost her footing and hurtled back into the doorframe. Almost immediately, her face began to swell at the site of impact.

Snatching her up by the collar of her shirt, Pepper slapped Emma across the face with such force that he split her lip open. Blood gushing into her mouth and down her chin, she watched as her father walked over to the stove and turned on the burner. When the cold black coil began to glow a scorching orange, he shut the burner off and stood glaring at his daughter. Her body involuntarily shook as she wondered what he was going to do to her. Huddled in the corner of the kitchen, Emma wished the walls would open so that she could crawl inside of them and find the needed protection from her father's wrath. "Please, Daddy. Please don't hurt me. I'm sorry," the child begged.

His eyes bored into hers, undeterred by her fear and pain. Emma watched in terror as the corners of his mouth curled up, until he was smiling like a sadistic monster. She trembled visibly in anticipation of what was to come. Her father suddenly pounced on her. Grasping her by the arm, he dragged her, kicking and screaming, over to the hot burner. Then he seized her left hand and ordered her to unclench her teeny fist. After she opened her hand, Pepper slapped her palm down on the hot burner in one swift movement, holding it in place for a couple of seconds and letting the young, tender skin boil and blister from the intense heat that still remained. Then he bent down, his face close to his daughter's, and snorted, "Oink! Oink! Oink!" into her ear.

All through the ordeal, Emma's shrills of agony sliced through the silence of the house. Valerie lay on her bed upstairs. Her mind filled with raw horror as she imagined what would happen to her if Pepper killed the child and was sent to prison. She prayed that he wouldn't take it too far this time. She didn't give a thought to the suffering that her older daughter was enduring at the hands of her husband. It was as if she had ice water running through her veins in place of blood.

As Emma collapsed on the floor, Pepper stood over her threateningly. Speaking in a tight, cold voice, he said through clenched teeth,

"You are a worthless piece of shit. I don't know why I just don't kill you right now. I'm giving you another chance to act like a human being. You can forget about eating dinner tonight. I don't see why a little pig like you should be fed. Consider yourself lucky that I don't beat you to death." He began to leave the kitchen, but turned back at the doorway and bellowed, "You better have this place cleaned up before I get home from the bar!" With that final warning, Pepper grabbed a beer from the refrigerator then stormed out of the kitchen and left the house.

Emma remained sprawled on the floor, paralyzed by the depth of her own despair, her eight-year-old mind trying to recover from what her father had just done to her. Then she scolded herself for failing to wash that one dirty fork that Valerie had left in the sink when she had gotten home from school. Maybe if she had washed it, none of this would have happened, she tried to rationalize, looking for some reason why she deserved such harsh punishment. She sat staring at her blistered, deformed palm. The pain the burn caused was only secondary to her overwhelming despair at being unloved.

This year of her life was when Emma became acutely aware of the possibility that Pepper might actually kill her. The years prior had been hard for her, but now that she was getting older her thoughts and senses were on high alert and she could no longer deny them. She grappled with finding different ways to behave that would stop the abuse, not because she was afraid of dying, but because she was afraid to leave Gracie alone with her parents.

After Pepper had burned her hand on the stove, she did everything in her power to fly below his radar. She made sure to clean the house after school every day and took special care in making his meals. But nothing lightened his fury. It was a Wednesday night and Emma was sitting at the kitchen table doing her homework after she had finished cleaning up from dinner. Her father staggered back into the kitchen to get himself another beer. He opened the can and took a long, hard swig. His head hung as if it were too heavy for his neck to hold as he eyed her with disgust. "I don't know why you bother with dat school shit; you're never gonna 'mount to nuttin' no matter how hard you try," he babbled through his drunken daze.

Emma looked up at him, her heart pounding in her chest. "My math teacher thinks I'm really smart. She told me that if I wanted to,

I could be an accountant someday," Emma said, hoping to make him feel proud of her.

Pepper stomped over to the table and picked up one of her pencils and thrust the point into her forearm. The pencil stood at attention as she looked on in shock. She quickly yanked the pencil out of her arm and ran to the sink to wash off the blood with soap and water. "See dat! Now you're not so worried 'bout pretending like you understand anything in those books of yours. Let that be a lesson not to leave your stuff all over my kitchen table. Now get this shit out of here!" he bellowed.

Pepper was tireless in his violent treatment of Emma. To her, the slaps, punches, and kicks came from a bottomless pit of hate that burrowed deep in her father's soul. The endless bruises he left on her made Emma feel hopeless and ashamed. Alone in the bathroom, Emma would study the wounds and scars that Pepper gave her. She was consumed by her sense of loneliness and lack of power to change her circumstances. She was completely at his mercy and knew he could do whatever he wanted to her, regardless of how broken she became.

It was a warm morning in August and the two girls were jumping rope in the backyard. Pepper got annoyed because they were making too much noise while he was nursing a burning hangover with vodka. He flung open the back door and stood holding his aching head. "You two shut the fuck up. You hear?"

They immediately went silent and stood perfectly still. He turned and went back into the house, and Emma was lulled into a false sense of security as they began running through the yard, playing tag. Moments later, the rotted screen door burst open and Pepper barrelled down the cement steps into the yard. He grabbed Emma under her arm and pulled her into the house. She began to plead with him, knowing she was in for something terrible. "I'm sorry, Daddy," she cried, "I swear, we'll be quiet. OK, Daddy? Please don't hurt me," she cried.

Pepper grabbed the soft flesh under her upper arm and pinched as hard as he could. Emma went to her knees as she tried to get him to release his hold. He dragged her into the living room where there was an old wooden trunk. "You want to disobey me? Well then, there is a price for that," he said calmly.

Pepper pushed the glass vase filled with dusty plastic flowers off the chest. It slammed to the floor and shattered into a million pieces.

Emma's eyes bulged as she frantically wondered what he was going to do to her. As her father lifted the lid to the trunk, she shrunk away from him trying to run and escape. He lifted her around the waist, her feet flailing as she tried to break away from his tight grip. Her movements made it impossible for him to get her legs into the trunk. Growing more irrational by the moment, he clamped his teeth on her shoulder until he could taste her blood in his mouth. Then he twisted her arm behind her back until he heard the pop as it dislocated at the shoulder. With excruciating pain in both shoulders she stopped fighting and sank into the trunk. After he slammed the lid shut and locked it, he left her and went to find Gracie. Ignoring her own painful injuries, Emma's gut twisted as she heard her father slapping Gracie around the living room. I wish I were a superhero, she thought, so that I can break out of here and help my sister.

Inside the trunk her body was twisted in an unnatural position. Her legs were folded at the knees behind her and her torso was bent at the waist so that her nose touched her knees. There was not enough room in the small space for her to reposition herself, and after a couple of hours her limbs went numb.

After the first twenty-four hours had passed and he hadn't let her out, all she wanted was to die. She reveled in the idea of leaving her measly existence and finally being free of her tormentor, believing that death was a much more appealing option than her current living conditions.

During her imprisonment, every so often her father would flip the trunk on different sides, smashing her dislocated shoulder and twisted body against the walls of the wooden box. Two days later, when he finally opened the lid and let her out, Emma could barely walk.

She literally crawled, with Gracie's help, over to the sofa where she lay for another four hours. Finally she managed to get to her feet. As she headed toward the foot of the stairs to go up to her room, Pepper put his foot in front of her. Unsteady on her feet, she crashed down onto the floor. She broke her fall with her hands before her face hit the floor and she scurried like a wounded animal to get away from her father. He stood over her and began to laugh. He laughed so hard that tears streamed down his face as his daughter watched him, humiliated and defeated.

Then, without warning, her stomach twisted into a tight knot as disgust for her father overcame her anguish. She felt a surge of hatred so profound that no one could stop it from taking complete control of her. It shook her entire being. Emma grappled with an idea so horrifying that it took her a while to accept it: she now believed that her father was the devil himself in a man's body. This conviction would mark a new beginning for her, eventually determining who she would become. The seed had been planted.

Chapter One

————————————■————————————

It was a cold November night a little more than a year later and the temperature had dipped into the low thirties. The family was having dinner in the small, dimly lit kitchen. Valerie's eyes were fixed on her plate as Pepper grumbled about his boss and how much he despised the man. That evening, like most others, his drinking had started before he even got home and only ramped up the moment he walked through the front door.

Emma had just spooned some peas onto Gracie's plate. The six-year-old reached for her glass of water and accidentally caught her father's freshly opened can of beer with her small arm. Pepper erupted. His face looked like a twisted mass of bumpy, pulsating flesh as the veins in his temples stood out and he turned bright red. Clenching his fists, he put them up against Gracie's dainty face and yelled, "You fucking little whore! You spilled my beer! You're an idiot, just like your sister!"

Without warning, he yanked the terrified child out of her chair and flung her down on the floor. Before she could recover from the shock, he bent down and slapped her in the face, sending her flying across the kitchen floor. Her body seemed weightless, like a rag doll, as she tumbled head over heels and landed on the other side of the room. Pepper trudged over to her, buried his fingers in her hair, and closed his fist over a handful of strands. Then he pulled her upright until she was standing. Gracie's face twisted with pain as she let out a blood-curdling shriek.

Her father ground his nose against hers. "You fucking maggot!" he yelled. "I never wanted you! You belong to that stupid bitch over there!" He gestured toward Valerie. As Pepper released his daughter's hair, she fell back to the floor.

Stunned by what had happened, Emma ran to her little sister. She desperately hoped her mother would protect them, even though Valerie had proven time and again that she wouldn't. She now snapped at her father. "Why don't you leave her alone? You bully!" she screamed.

Outraged by what he considered to be the ultimate form of disrespect, Pepper snatched a frying pan from the top of the stove and whacked the side of her face with it, knocking her unconscious. When Emma woke up, she found herself lying on the cement steps that led from the back of the house into their small yard. Dressed only in the jeans and sweater she had worn to school that day, she felt the cold seeping into her bones, clearing the cobwebs of confusion that had clouded her mind. Emma picked herself up and knocked softly on the back door.

Pepper, who had been waiting for her to wake up, immediately flung open the door, startling her. "You think you're smart?" he snapped. "You think you can talk to me like that? Nobody tells me what to do in my house! Tonight, you'll sleep outside and learn never to talk back to me, girl!"

After he had slammed the door in her face, Emma huddled into herself, trying to keep warm. The wind slashed through her worn clothing, increasing her desperation to find shelter. Afraid to go too far, she decided to seek refuge on their front porch. There, she remembered, was a broken down sofa that had never made its way to the trash.

Mrs. Tisdale, her elderly neighbor who lived across the street, was looking out her window as Emma made her way to the front of their row home. The old woman watched the child move slowly up the front porch, trying to step as lightly as possible so that the creaky boards wouldn't betray her presence. Then her eyes widened in alarm as the little girl crawled under the worn cushions on the sofa and completely vanished from sight.

Mrs. Tisdale kept her eyes glued to the sofa for more than fifteen minutes before she put on her coat and went across the street to find out what the hell was going on. She approached Emma with great care, so as not to startle her, and gently lifted the cushion covering her face. "Child," she murmured, "why you out here in the cold? Where's your mama?"

Her eyes red from crying, Emma replied, "My father is making me sleep outside tonight. He was hitting my little sister and I yelled at him to stop. So he hit me with a pan and put me outside. This is my punishment."

"Well, I'll be dipped in shit if a little child like you is gonna sleep out here in the cold!" the elderly neighbor said in a huff. "Come on, baby, you sleepin' at my house tonight."

Emma's body stiffened with resistance. "No, Mrs. Tisdale," she protested, "I have to stay here so I can get up in the morning and get out back before my father goes to work. If he finds out I didn't stay on the back steps during the night, I don't know what he'll do to me."

Mrs. Tisdale gave her concern due consideration. "Okay then," she conceded, "you'll come sleep at my house and we'll set an alarm so that you can get up before he does. That way, you can go back on those steps before that bastard goes off to work. okay, baby?"

Comfortable with Mrs. Tisdale's proposition, Emma dug herself out from beneath the cushions and followed her across the street. Once inside her own house, Mrs. Tisdale wrapped Emma in a warm blanket and made her a steaming cup of cocoa. The chocolaty milk warmed her insides, filling her with a sense of security. Emma was grateful for Mrs. Tisdale's kindness as she lay, warm and cozy, on her neighbor's sofa waiting for sleep to provide a temporary release from her life.

This was the first real encounter that Emma had with Mrs. Tisdale. From here on the relationship grew, and over time, the girl came to rely on her for the support she needed to make it through each treacherous day. Mrs. Tisdale was well aware of how Pepper treated his two daughters. As a result, she tried to compensate by showering the children with the love their parents couldn't seem to find for them. Mrs. Tisdale failed to understand how Valerie could allow her husband to beat their own children. If it were her husband, the old lady told herself, she would surely have set things right. Hell, she thought, I'm gonna try my best to set things right and I ain't even married to that no-good dirty, rotten bastard.

Chapter Two

———————— ■ ————————

A voluptuous black woman, Mrs. Tisdale had short salt-and-pepper hair that fell about her head in large curls. Her eyes were such a light brown that people mistook her eye color for hazel. Her bright smile lit up her jolly face, and her hands, although extremely large, gave Emma tender comfort when she needed it most. Mrs. Tisdale's loving ways filled the girl with joy, and when the old woman laughed, a rumbling sound rose from deep within her belly, making the child's heart soar and offering her a temporary reprieve from the darkness that enveloped her life.

From the time she had gotten to know Emma, Mrs. Tisdale often brought up the issue of Child Protective Services, explaining to the girl that they offered a way out of her predicament. The old lady wanted to alert them so they could take Emma and Gracie away from their brutal father, but the child had pleaded with her to keep the secret. Not understanding how the system worked, Emma feared that they would take her away and leave Gracie at home to become the new target of Pepper's abuse.

"Mrs. Tisdale," Emma had sobbed, "it won't be any use. My mother will just stick up for my dad and tell them I'm lying."

Against her better judgment, Mrs. Tisdale had let it go. Instead, she had turned to prayer, asking for peace and love to be bestowed upon Emma.

At home, Emma lived in fear, but with Mrs. Tisdale, she always felt safe and secure. Life was sweet with her elderly neighbor, regardless of how short-lived those moments of happiness were. When Pepper was at work or drowning himself in booze at the bar, the child helped Mrs. Tisdale fold clothes and do small chores, listening intently to the stories the lady shared of her own youth. Emma would pretend that her neighbor was her real mother, knowing that if she were, her life would be very different.

In the neighborhood, Mrs. Tisdale was regarded as a tough old black woman. Nobody in Norristown fucked with her. She had three grown sons. They were big and they were mean. When it came to protecting their mama, they were ruthless. Her sons were always nice to Emma, because their mama had explained to them, "The poor child has to put up with brutal beatings from her papa. He's a sorry excuse for a father. We need to give her as much lovin' as we can, so she knows people care for her. Otherwise, she's likely to turn out just like him. Children become what they know. You hear me now?"

Rather quickly, Emma secretly began to wish that Mrs. Tisdale's sons would stop Pepper from hurting her. But just like Valerie, they never came to her rescue. Emma had no choice but to carry the burden of her sickening youth alone.

Chapter Three

———————■———————

Pepper Murphy's mother had died in childbirth, leaving his alcoholic father to raise the boy. The man often beat his small son, berating him time and again for killing his mother. The boy's destructive temper evolved over time, fueled by his anger and helplessness as he endured daily rounds of abuse from his father. When he was still a young boy, Pepper had taken to hiding behind bushes and cars and either throwing large stones at other children as they walked by or whacking them on the back with thick tree branches. He did these things in an attempt to release his own anger.

In middle school, he acquired quite a reputation as the class bully; he would hit and verbally abuse his classmates for no good reason, leaving them defenseless and humiliated. As a young teen, Pepper's explosive anger at his peers escalated to intolerable levels, often leaving his weaker prey with scars and bruises from his boiling rage.

By the time he reached high school he was drinking and smoking and had only a couple of close friends. However, when he entered eleventh grade, Pepper's shop teacher took a liking to him. The teacher realized that with some encouragement the boy could be saved from the fate that he was heading toward. He thought Pepper could someday be a talented home builder, a dream of Pepper's from the time he was small and had used his homemade wood blocks to build houses.

Pepper's whole attitude changed with the positive attention he received from his shop teacher. He made the teenager believe that he could actually do something good so that he would become a man that others respected. For the first time in his life, Pepper was filled with optimism. He quickly became likeable to many of his peers. He enjoyed the last two years of high school—making new friends, going to parties, and becoming the guy that all the girls wanted as their boyfriend.

When he graduated from high school, he had big plans of setting up his own construction business with his closest friend. They talked with excitement about getting contracts for building houses for a large company. The two friends mapped out how they would start out with smaller construction jobs before branching out to build homes on their own. They agreed to save a portion of their earnings from each job to purchase their first company truck.

Only four months after they graduated high school, the two young men signed their first contract. They believed that all of their dreams were coming true. "We need to celebrate! We're on our way to the big time," Pepper boasted. "Let's go to the bar and have a few beers."

They had only been at the bar for an hour when Pepper raised his beer. "Here's to building houses, buddy!"

As they banged glasses and chugged their beers, a beautiful woman named Valerie walked in front of them. Pepper and his friend stared at her, along with every other man in the bar, as she made her way over to a table of friends. That was the night Pepper and Valerie first met.

Pepper and Valerie were almost immediately infatuated with each other. Her beauty stirred a sexual hunger in him that he couldn't control and she was smitten by his apparently strong, protective nature. The two made an attractive couple. Pepper was tall and full-bodied and his intimidating stature matched his burly character. Pepper's jet-black hair and thick, dark eyelashes set off his blazing green eyes. His full lips complemented his long, slender nose, and his rugged features and square jaw made him appear fearless.

Valerie was equally attractive, but what she possessed in physical beauty she lacked in brains. She had long, straight blond hair that fell to her shoulders like strands of golden silk. Her eyes were stunning, almost royal blue, and her pale pink pouty lips were plump and inviting. She was tall and thin with full breasts, a tiny waist, and curved hips.

Valerie's parents had died suddenly when their car slid off of a bridge on an icy winter night two days before Christmas. She was just thirteen-years-old with no other family, and spent the next five years of her life being raised in various foster homes. She carried an unrelenting resentment towards her parents who died and left her alone. Moving all the time annoyed the shit out of her and she hated having to adjust to new families and different rules.

By the time she was fourteen-years-old the other foster girls had taught her how to use her body to get men to do whatever she wanted. These girls influenced her into being manipulative and self-absorbed. Her mannerisms and good looks often created tension between each of her foster parents. The men took her side while the women resented that she stole all of the attention that rightfully belonged to them. Valerie lied and cheated to her foster parents, teachers and anyone else who stood in her way. The once sweet child had grown into a despicable young woman. Finally, when Valerie turned eighteen, she and another girl who she knew from foster care moved into a cheap, run-down apartment over a pizza shop in Pottstown.

Pepper and Valerie were inseparable at first. He took her to the movies where they sat in the very back row, kissing and groping each other. When the weather turned warmer, Valerie made picnics with egg salad sandwiches, potato chips, and homemade blueberry pie. They would spread a blanket out in Valley Forge State Park where they ate their lunch and talked about how much they liked being together. Since their conversations lacked substance, they spent most of their time together kissing and sexually teasing one another.

They had been dating for six months when, after Pepper had one too many shots of whiskey, he forced himself on Valerie against her will during one of their usual make-out sessions. Valerie was devastated that he had stolen her virginity. When she found out she was pregnant with Emma, she threatened to tell the police that she had been raped by him if he left her.

When Pepper turned to his old high school shop teacher for advice, he told him in no uncertain terms, "Good men take care of things when they make mistakes. If it's true that what you did was a mistake then your only choice is to marry her and raise the child together."

Pepper's attraction to Valerie had always been a physical one and he had never planned on spending his whole life with her. But between his shop teacher's advice and her threat of lying to the police, he grudgingly agreed to stay with her. Pepper, for his part, was forced to work on an assembly line at the local auto factory in order to feed his new and unwanted family. Abandoning his friend and the dream of his own business made his heart heavy and filled him with bitterness.

By the time Emma was born, Pepper already resented the baby who, he firmly believed, had destroyed his dream and stolen his life. It was inevitable that she would never know a father's love. She only knew the man as a large and frightening creature she had to please at any cost. But no matter how hard she tried, she was never successful. She clung to the only option available to keep his violent temper at bay—obedience. It might, she hoped, help to lessen the intensity of the physical and emotional pain he caused her.

Despite her dismal circumstances, Emma was still a sweet-natured child, respectful toward everyone she met. People took to her easily, and those who knew her well sensed a deep sadness about her. They couldn't help being moved to pity. A beautiful girl, she seemed to have the perfect combination of her parents' good looks. Blessed with her mother's blond hair and her father's piercing green eyes, she was taller than most nine-year-olds, her height alone leading people to believe that she was older than she actually was. She worked hard every day to keep her spirit intact in the unhealthy, dysfunctional place she knew as "home." While her father abused her physically and emotionally, her mother constantly blamed her for Pepper's rotten temper. "The two of us were doing fine," Valerie would explain as if it were really true, "until you came along and ruined everything we had."

Three years younger than Emma, Gracie was an average-looking girl with curly black hair and deep-set brown eyes. Her nose, a bit too large for her long face, merely accentuated the thinness of her lips. Although far less attractive and more timid than her sister, Gracie was equally sweet-natured. The child's only asset in life was her sister, who acted as her protector and was the only one to stand between her and their heathen father. As Emma grew older, she often spared her younger sister from their father's beatings by pushing herself forward as a buffer. When Gracie was old enough to understand her sister's sacrifice, her emotions were set in turmoil between guilt and love.

The so-called Murphy family lived in a small home on Chain Street in Norristown, Pennsylvania. They lived largely on bare essentials; sometimes even those were lacking. Their row home was a run-down shack that appeared on the verge of collapse. The wood porch had rotted and its roof was supported by four-by-fours sloppily nailed in place to prevent it from crashing down. The floorboards creaked when walked on, their mushiness giving a bit beneath their feet.

Inside, the once white walls were yellowed from Pepper's chain-smoking. The long shag rugs were old and so matted down with over-use that their fibers felt perpetually soggy under their bare feet. The furniture was secondhand with pieces of foam peeking out from the ripped upholstery in several places. The absence of adequate lighting made their home feel like the inside of a cave; but for the glare of the small television that stood on a battered table, there was almost no light at all.

Valerie and Pepper earned so little money that putting food on the table took great effort. The family rarely owned anything new and relied on handouts that were offered at local churches. Of the little that the couple earned, a major chunk went toward supporting Pepper's addiction to booze. The financial strain that the couple lived under only brought more tension into the home. Pepper knew they were des-tined to be poor white trash and for this he despised his family.

Emma and Gracie were submerged in dreariness day after day. They didn't enjoy the small gestures of affection like most other children that didn't cost anything to give, like a hug or a tender pat on the back. With no relief from their dismal circumstances in sight, they clung to each other to save themselves from the misery that threatened to swal-low them alive.

Made in the USA
Monee, IL
23 May 2021